ASCENSION

VICTOR DIXEN

Translated by Daniel Hahn

HOT
KEY
BOOKS

First published in French by Éditions Robert Laffont, S.A. Paris, in 2015

First published in Great Britain in 2018 by
HOT KEY BOOKS
80–81 Wimpole St, London W1G 9RE
www.hotkeybooks.com

This book is supported by the Institut français (Royaume-Uni)
as part of the Burgess programme.

ROYAUME-UNI

A CIP catalogue record for this book is available from the British Library.

ISBN: 978-1-4714-0684-3
also available as an ebook

1

This book is typeset using Atomik ePublisher
Printed and bound by Clays Ltd, St Ives Plc

Hot Key Books is an imprint of Bonnier Zaffre Ltd,
a Bonnier Publishing company
www.bonnierpublishing.com

For E.,
For my parents,
And for Ulysse, who,
whether on earth or in space,
will surely go on a very fine journey.

Dream as if you'll live forever,
Live as if you'll die today.
James Dean (1931-1955)

GENESIS PROGRAM

CALL FOR CANDIDATES
Six girls on one side. Six boys on the other.
Six minutes to meet. An eternity to love . . .

Make History with a Capital H!

After the multinational investment fund Atlas Capital bought NASA with all its equipment from a heavily indebted US government, they decided to accelerate the advances in space conquest. How? Thanks to advertising revenue . . . and you! Genesis is both a unique space project and an entertainment program the likes of which has never been seen before: our first attempt to colonise Mars, and also the greatest TV show in history. And you can be a part of it!

Find Love with a Capital L!

All young people at peak fertility who are living on Earth are invited to apply to the Genesis program. The twelve chosen contestants – six boys and six girls – will get to know one another during their one-way trip to the red planet, where they will eventually start their families. They will have five months to attempt to win one another over and choose the partner with whom to procreate. In exchange for their participation in this unique adventure, the on-board cameras will broadcast their speed-dating sessions in space, and every other moment of the rest of their lives on Mars, every hour of every day.

GENESIS PROGRAM
Are you aged between 16 and 19?
Do you want to be a part of the genesis of a new world?
Submit your application today,
and write the most beautiful love story of all time: yours!

ACT I

1. Shot

D -55 mins.

'Léonor, how does it feel to be leaving the Earth for ever?'

'Léonor, are you looking forward to it?'

'Léonor, are you scared?'

'Léonor!'

'Léonor!!'

'Léonor!!!'

Hundreds of arms stretching out with cameras and microphone booms reach towards me like tentacles, over the uniformed shoulders that are trying to hold them back.

One journalist manages to force his way through the cordon of security guards to shove his microphone under my nose, fixing me with his rapacious, piercing blue eyes.

'Any last words, Léonor?' he asks with a predatory smile. 'Any regrets, perhaps?'

'None, how about you?' I reply, flipping him my middle finger in a gesture I just manage to correct into a V for Victory.

What the hell was that about, asking me if I have any regrets right before leaving – was he just trying to provoke me? What's the vulture after? Tears? Fistfights? Well, he won't be getting

5

either. Serena's given us plenty of warning that the journalists are going to try to corner us, hoping to get themselves a scoop. They must be ravenous: they've been waiting a full year for the chosen candidates to be revealed, as our whole training took place in complete secrecy. Today's the first time they've seen us in the flesh, and it'll be the last too: in a few moments, we're going to be taking off and never coming back. So of course they want to get something huge from it. Everybody knows a photo of a distraught face always sells better. No way am I going to let myself be manipulated by some paparazzo who wants to sell my tears at the price of gold; so I unleash my very loveliest smile, the one I've been practising in the mirror every morning since I signed with my sponsor, the high-end fashion house Rosier & Merceaugnac.

Then I tear myself away from the pack that's yelling my name and dash for the staircase leading to the launch platform, my long red hair lifted by the breeze that's coming in from the sea at the edge of the Cape Canaveral air base. I climb the last three steps, repeating my mantra to myself: *You're a Rosier model now, Léo. Do try and stay classy.*

If I'm honest, if I did have to be in fashion, I would have imagined myself more a designer than a model, given my passion for drawing and my approximately zero comfort at being in the public eye. And these astronaut boots and this space suit don't exactly give me gazelle-like grace. The aluminium platform that's serving as my catwalk gives out a metallic moan under my soles. I look up: there it is, the launcher, a rocket as tall as a fifteen-storey building, vaster, more overwhelming . . . more *real* than anything I've dreamed of till now. All round the platform, four giant screens are showing a diagram that explains the protocol of the Genesis programme to the onlookers, doubtless for the hundredth time.

'. . . as we welcome our intrepid pioneers, our great conquerors of space!' says a voice through the monumental speakers. 'There are twelve of them: twelve young people chosen out of millions of candidates, following an international selection process that has been utterly unprecedented. An extraordinary journey awaits them, the most magnificent journey in human history! They will travel further than Yuri Gagarin, further than Neil Armstrong, further than any human has ever travelled before. Their amazing voyage will unfold in six stages which will be transmitted directly back for broadcast on the Genesis channel, twenty-four / seven, thanks to our interplanetary laser communications system.

'*One*, the simultaneous launch of the twin capsules, girls in one and boys in the other, towards the *Cupido* spacecraft that is currently awaiting them in orbit around the Earth;

'*Two*, connecting the two capsules to either side of the *Cupido*, in two separate compartments;

'*Three*, activating the nuclear booster and sending the *Cupido* on a trajectory towards Mars, for an interplanetary transit of one hundred and sixty-one days;

'*Four*, aligning the *Cupido* with the Martian orbit, in the wake of the red planet's moon Phobos – ideal positioning for targeting the landing site;

'*Five*, the final casting-off of the two capsules, as the lucky candidates are welcomed into Mars's gravity well;

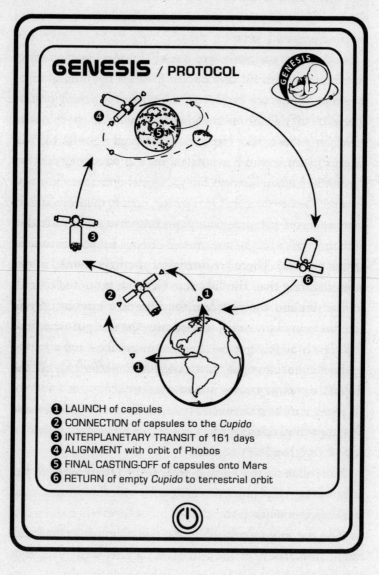

GENESIS / PROTOCOL

1. **LAUNCH** of capsules
2. **CONNECTION** of capsules to the *Cupido*
3. **INTERPLANETARY TRANSIT** of 161 days
4. **ALIGNMENT** with orbit of Phobos
5. **FINAL CASTING-OFF** of capsules onto Mars
6. **RETURN** of empty *Cupido* to terrestrial orbit

'*Six*, the *Cupido* returns empty to the terrestrial orbit, ready for the next cohort of astronauts to be sent off two years from now.'

I join the other girls, who are already lined up at the foot of the launcher, in front of a curtain that's a rainbow of logos in every colour and every size – big logos for the *platinum* sponsors (they're the ones who've shelled out a whole load to buy themselves a passenger); medium-sized logos for the *gold* sponsors (those who have placed their products in the ship that's waiting for us up there in space, just hoping they'll appear on screen as often as possible); small logos for those small-fry *silver* sponsors (though even these have had to sacrifice half of their year's ad spend for the right to one square centimetre of that curtain). There are dozens of spotlights aimed at me, more dazzling than the July sun. Cameras mounted on rails spin all around the platform, buzzing like insects. I try to give them my best smile, to play the part of a girl who finds this all completely normal, though the reality is I'm about as comfortable as a fish out of water. I'm feeling so hot it's like the thermal regulator on my undersuit is broken. I can't wait for the ceremony to be over and to be up there in space, headed out towards my destiny!

Kris puts her hand on mine.

'You're the reason we're here, Léo the Determinator!' her crystal-clear voice slips into my ear.

The Determinator is the nickname Kris uses when she wants to tease me about my stubborn side. But she's entitled to call me whatever she likes: she's practically a sister to me, ever since the morning when we first met on the single runway of a tiny airport, lost in the furnace that is California's Death Valley. That was a year ago. I was straight off the plane from France, she had flown in from Germany the night before; of the six girls selected for the Genesis programme, we were the first to arrive at the training camp that recreated the conditions on Mars. We were delirious with happiness. We were dying of fear. I confided in her like I'd never done in anyone before, the words coming naturally to me in English, the official language of the Genesis programme. I told her about my life as an abandoned child, the welfare services, the waltz of foster families – it did me a world of good. It was friendship at first sight, a friendship that never failed. Kris lit up my days all through the training programme with her cheerfulness, and I supported her with my famous certainties – things like *We'll get there, soldier Kris, no question about it*.

Kris told me that she came from an industrial area in Germany that had been devastated, eroded by unemployment like so many parts of Europe. Her father had died in an accident on the assembly line just days before the town's last factory was automated, and her mother had followed him a few years later, carried off by grief and untreated pneumonia. Kris at the time had just turned seventeen. She had decided to set off for Berlin in search of a new life, and there she had ended up as a cook in an all-night restaurant (she claims confidently that she cooks like a real expert, and that her crème brûlée with lemon zest is to die for!). The fact that we were both orphans brought us close; such a coincidence, I told myself, out of a population of several thousand candidates! Except it was no coincidence, as we soon realised. The other four girls who joined us that evening were, each in her own way, completely without any ties, with nothing and nobody to keep them back on Earth: that was one of the selection criteria for the Genesis programme.

'On the left of this curtain, you will see our six female contestants. On the right, our six male contestants. Pretty girls and handsome boys, brought together on Cape Canaveral peninsula in Florida!'

A rostrum has been set up at right angles to the curtain, topped by a lectern behind which perches a bald, well-built man in a grey suit. It's him, the voice in the speakers: Director Lock, our Mr Mars, in person. He used to be one of NASA's top execs, before the new Ultra-liberal government in the US put his space agency up for sale along with a whole heap of things like the postal service, the highways and the whole set of national museums . . . A huge garage sale, the great electoral promise of President Green, all to try to wipe out the country's enormous debt. *'Take America out of the red with President Green!'* – that was his campaign slogan.

A private company acquired NASA two years ago, for an undisclosed sum. Atlas Capital: an investment fund, the kind that buys up companies in trouble with the sole aim of gutting them and maximising how much cash they can extract. With NASA, it all went according to plan. Atlas immediately booted out half the staff; roughly speaking, all those who weren't working directly on the conquest of Mars, a project that was quite advanced at the time of the purchase but which had never been brought to completion owing to the lack of public funds. The Atlas people salvaged everything: the launch base

11

at Cape Canaveral, the control centre at Houston, the craft waiting in orbit around Earth, the equipment already left on Mars by earlier unmanned missions – everything! They decided to relaunch the project, and more: to make it the greatest reality TV show of all time, thanks to which they were confident about recouping their investment, recovering their costs and filling their pockets. And so the Genesis programme was born, with Gordon Lock as its technical director.

'Today you are meeting the fortunate chosen ones for the first time,' he went on. 'After all these months of waiting and speculation since the announcement of the Genesis programme, after millions of volunteers applied, you are seeing them right now just as I see them, on the two parts of your screen . . .'

From up on his perch, Director Lock is able to see both sides of the curtain. Behind him hangs the huge logo of the Genesis programme: a planet Mars in which the silhouette of a foetus is curled up. The same logo is sewn onto the pocket of his waistcoat, and onto the helmet of each of the security guards. A womb-planet – it's actually quite daring; I bet the publicity team worked day and night to come up with that. It's pretty in-your-face as a logo, but at the same time it's memorable, it hits the nail precisely on the head, and it isn't lying about the programme's ultimate goal: establishing a fertile human colony on Mars. If I'd been given a brief like that, I can't imagine I would have done any better.

'. . . but the boys and girls, however, have never met. They have lived through their training year in two separate camps, at the heart of Death Valley, the girls on one side and the boys on the other. They have received, in parallel, robust instruction to make them experts in their respective domains. They have never met . . . until today!'

Director Lock pauses and then looks at us, his pupils shining with excitement, glancing once to the right, once to the left. All around the platform, the four giant screens convey his image increased in size a hundred-fold. I can't help thinking about how I'd sketch his portrait if I dared. That's my way of seeing the world, through my artist's eye. It allows me to position things at a bit of a distance, as someone who all too often reacts instantly in the moment. It helps me to get a bit more perspective on people who impress me, as someone who has so often been looked down on myself. In this case, for example, the director's bare forehead made me think of a bald planet. His sun-reddened skin, seeded with pores, conjured up the surface of Mars, blasted with craters. They say people often resemble their dogs; Gordon Lock, however, resembles his planet: it would make a cool caricature, something not too mean and which no doubt would have made him smile himself. No sooner do I imagine it, than I feel the muscles of my face unclench, my diaphragm relax.

I breathe.

I cast my eyes over Mr Mars, who is after all the genius behind the whole programme. They come to rest on the large digital clock suspended in the air above the launch platform. It displays the countdown in sparkling numbers: D -52 mins . . .

'Man has already gone to space. He has already eaten, slept, worked there. But he has never fallen in love. That, then, is the essential ingredient for the success of the Genesis programme. It's the prerequisite for the pioneers to be able to procreate, establish their families, put down the foundations of a lasting colony on Mars, making History with a capital H. Let me now call upon somebody who can explain it better than anyone, the executive producer of the Genesis programme: the distinguished Professor Serena McBee herself . . . !'

Make History with a capital H, just like they'd written on the call for applications . . . That's why I'd sent in my details without a single second's hesitation, as soon as I'd seen the ad in a free newspaper on the Paris metro: because I had no *history*, even with a small *h*, of my own. Love and all that crap isn't really my cup of tea. When you're abandoned unconscious at the age of three in a trash can, you're pretty well placed to understand that love doesn't count for much. Because that's it, that's my history, nuts as it may seem: thrown away like an old tissue, rescued in extremis by paramedics, revived in hospital, thrown out to social services. Love has never been a part of my life, and it's not going to be making a surprise entrance now.

What I want is something more solid, more durable. What I want is glory, and I know that I'm not going to get it here on Earth, not since I had to quit school and my drawing classes to go and work at the Eden Food France factory just to get by. I swore to myself that I wouldn't give up my dreams a second time, that I'd be the first girl to plant my easel on Mars. It was this hope that gave me the fight to get through ten rounds of interviews with the Genesis programme recruiters, until I met Serena McBee in person. It was this hope that propelled me all the way through my year's preparation in the desert of Death Valley, despite the fifteen-hour training days and the nights too filled with adrenaline to sleep. Straight ahead,

Léonor! Don't turn around, there's nothing for you here. No family, no bonds. Earth has nothing to offer outcasts like you. But Mars! Look at the stars, they're calling you – and most important of all, never look back.

And I hadn't looked back, ever since I posted my application form to the Genesis programme. It was in the postbox at the entrance of the hostel for young workers where I lived, not far from the factory – in other words, a different life. But this morning, as we wait for the person to whom we owe our place on the launch platform, I can't help looking over my shoulder.

I'm taking a look back at last.

And what I see sends a nasty pang to my stomach, something vicious I hadn't expected.

The journalists seem terribly far away, as though they're at the bottom of a dizzying abyss. The shadow cast by the launcher is too dark for me to make out their expressions. I don't know these people who are blaring out my name as though I were a thing they owned. They're nothing to me. And yet, from this day forth, they will never stop peering at me via the cameras, commenting on my tiniest gesture, dissecting my every insignificant word. The thought makes my belly clench until I feel sick. I hate this feeling of senseless hesitation, this unbearable doubt that pours into my veins like a poison, that transforms the normal anxiety of my departure into something more profound, more dangerous . . .

(*Could Léo, the Determinator, have broken down?* hisses a little voice in my head. *Or has she only just realised the incredibly stupid thing she's doing?*)

Serena McBee appears all of a sudden on the rostrum, tall and slender in her grey suit in the Genesis colours, at the neckline of which swish the frills of an elegant white silk blouse that is as dazzling as her smile. Gossiping tongues say this smile is frozen on by now, because Serena is so botoxed that she can't manage very much expression; but I know that's not true, that under the bob of impeccably cut silvery hair, Serena's smooth face is simply the reflection of a deep inner tranquillity. Every time I see those huge water-green eyes, calm like the surface of a lake, the magic works. I feel the knot in my stomach relax. I seem to hear Serena's peaceful, level voice: *What doesn't kill us makes us stronger.* That's what she's always said to us, right the way through our preparation, to help us whenever we were a bit down.

'Good morning, my dear Gordon; good morning, ladies and gentlemen of the media; good morning to all of you who at this moment are watching us from the four corners of the globe,' she announces, gracefully straightening the collar of her suit, adorned with a delicate silver brooch in the shape of a bee. 'And finally good morning to you, my very dear contestants! Seeing you now looking so wonderful, so radiant, I can't help thinking back to what you were barely a year ago . . . Unpolished gems. And today you are perfectly shaped to suit the mission that awaits you. If only you knew how proud I am of you!'

In the eyes of the general public, Serena McBee is the undisputed queen of male–female relations, a Stanford-trained psychiatrist who for twenty years has produced and fronted one of the most watched talk shows in the United States, *The Professor Serena McBee Consultation*, onto which she invites celebrities and their partners – a kind of couples therapy with live hypnosis session, her speciality. Atlas has given her carte blanche to stage the Martian mission; while Director Lock supervises the technical aspects, the show itself is in her charge, start to finish.

But to me and the other girls standing up against the curtain, Serena McBee is much more than the executive producer of the Genesis programme. She is the fairy godmother who has chosen us to go to Mars. She is the lucky star without whom our dream would never be realised. She is the good stepmother who saw I could do something with my life other than preparing dog-food at the Eden Food France factory: Serena managed to achieve the magic trick of transforming this Winalot Cinderella into an outer-space princess.

'*Six girls on one side. Six boys on the other. Six minutes to meet. An eternity to love,*' she reminds the spectators. 'We received more than eighty million applications for this mission, and that alone would make it a huge success! Today I must say thank you from the bottom of my heart to all those who sent in their application forms. I would like to tell them that they shouldn't have any regrets if they haven't been accepted on this occasion; they might be a part of the next rocket in two years' time. And I'd like to explain to them how we reached our final selection. You see, for a long time, those in charge of preserving the NASA flame and the other space programmes were making a mistake. They thought what they needed to do was send robust couples to space, couples whose relationships had been tested over years of living together. They were wrong. Already-formed couples have less chance of surviving the isolation of space and the prospect of never again returning to the planet where they have their memories, their lives, their families. With this in mind, the preparatory psychological studies we carried out during the selection process led us to select young men and women with the fewest attachments possible: orphans and those with no families. It is because their love *will be born* in space that it will be able to survive in their new world! It is because they have nothing to regret on Earth that they have everything to hope for on Mars! Our fortunate volunteers, all of them young adults or emancipated minors, will go through the interplanetary transfer side by side, the *Cupido* split into two hermetic sections. Each day of the week, for a little over five months, one participant will be able to invite a passenger of the opposite sex of his or her choosing for six minutes of one-on-one speed-dating in the *Visiting Room* located where the boys' compartment meets the girls' –'

'With no touching allowed,' interrupts Director Lock, waving his index finger at the cameras. 'The Genesis programme is also an entertainment programme, and it's rated U for a family audience!'

'You needn't worry, my dear Gordon. A reinforced glass screen separates the *Visiting Room* into two sections: our lovebirds will only be able to touch each other with their eyes. Every Sunday, they will draw up their *Heart List*, a ranking that you will be able to follow in real time on the Genesis channel, dear viewers, until the craft comes into alignment with the orbit of Phobos, on Sunday 10 December, by which time each will have chosen his or her partner. That very day, the couples will come down to land on Mars, where they will

18

be officially married. Don't forget! Throughout the journey you will be able to pledge gifts by dialling the number that's up on your screen right now, to increase your favourite participant's *Dowry*. The money collected will allow them to acquire by auction the equipment that NASA has been leaving on Mars over these past years. Since the base was purchased, we have baptised it *New Eden*, as it will welcome these Adams and Eves to a new paradise!

'And might I remind you, my dear viewers, that the more credits a participant has in their Dowry, the more comfortable the life they'll be able to live with their future spouse: they will live in a larger habitat among the six available *Love Nests*, with the seventh Nest acting as an emergency back-up module; they will have more food to consume; they will benefit from a more complete survival kit. And of course, it isn't impossible that your gifts might have an effect on the rankings . . . Somebody wealthier is always more seductive, as money goes hand in hand with love, as it always has done. And so we're counting on you . . . or rather, our twelve contestants are counting on you!'

Serena pauses.

She puts her hands with their polished nails onto the rim of the lectern and inhales deeply, sweeping the audience with her water-green eyes.

'And now, the big moment has arrived! Right now they are still strangers, but they are destined to be the most legendary lovers of all time . . . They won't see each other until they are in space, but now is the moment they will hear one another's voices for the first time . . . I'm so excited for them, and I'm sure you are too. Director Lock, over to you!'

The jingle of the Genesis programme rings out from the speakers. It's the chorus of '*Cosmic Love*', the duet performed at the organisers' request by two great international stars, the Canadian Jimmy Giant and the American Stella Magnifica. For a few moments, the bass makes the whole height of the curtain tremble. I know it's a stupid thing to say, especially as the lyrics are pretty dumb, but I do get chills when I hear this song that's been specially composed for us – and partly for me. I imagine this is what football players feel when the national anthem comes on; except that I'm not a stadium goddess, just a little orphan who can't believe where she's standing. I've practically got tears in my eyes from these emotional rollercoasters – first going pale with nerves, then feeling like I'll burst from doubt, and now practically crying out from sheer delight.

Him: *You sky-rocketed my life*
Her: *You taught me how to fly*
Him: *Higher than the clouds*
Her: *Higher than the stars*
Both: *Nothing can stop our cosmic love*
    Our cosmic love
    Our co-o-osmic lo-o-o-ove!

The music stops abruptly to give way to a pre-recorded drum-roll.

I feel my heart leap in my chest, echoing the last *boom!* – this is it, the final stretch!

2. Reverse Shot

The enormous backs of Gordon Lock and Serena McBee rise up opposite the six young women and young men holding their breath on either side of the curtain, tiny silhouettes buttoned into their white suits, carefully lined up like tin cans in a bowling alley.

There is a monitor set into the base of the lectern, which is visible only to the speakers.

The words of the speech scroll up the prompter as Gordon Lock utters them.

'It now falls to me to ask each participant to reaffirm their commitment, solemnly, one final time.'

Gordon Lock's hands are clutching the edge of the lectern.

A drop of sweat runs down his brow and splashes onto the screen, obscuring the words 'one final time'.

21

3. Shot

D -30 mins.

I've always told myself that I would never have any reason to care, no interest in knowing who might be behind the curtain. I've always told myself that this whole 'perfect couple' story is just a bit of sentimentality to give the masses something to dream about, that Mars was the only thing that mattered. And most of all, I've always sworn that I wouldn't allow myself to get carried away by the hysteria of the game, that I'd go through it at as much distance as I could, sticking to my own rules. But now that the moment has come, I can't take my eyes off the stupid piece of fabric hanging between me and my future.

And what if there isn't a boy I like?

(And what if there isn't one who likes you, what then?)

And yet I'll have to end up with one of them. Sleep with him. Carry his children. This dizzying sequence of thoughts makes my head spin like it did my first time in the centrifuge.

At that moment I feel Kris's hand tighten around mine.

Is she really expecting to meet the man of her life? She's

spent every evening of our year in training with her nose in the romantic novels she so loves – it's her little weakness – imagining which of the heroes the boy she'd end up marrying would look like.

I keep my eyes riveted on the curtain.

I don't dare look at Kris for fear that she'll read the concern on my face, me who's supposed to be She-Who-Never-Doubts.

Director Lock turns towards the side of the curtain that remains invisible to us and leans into his microphone.

'Tao, eighteen years old, a citizen of the People's Republic of China, sponsored by the Huoma automobile construction company, Engineering Officer: do you agree to represent humanity on Mars from this day forth until the last day of your life?'

A booming 'I accept' resounds from behind the curtain. At once my brain gets carried away, trying to envisage the person who could have given out such a war cry.

Tall . . . deep voice . . . no hesitation . . . no regret . . .

But Director Lock is already turning to the first girl in our line-up.

'Fangfang, twenty years old, a citizen of the Republic of Singapore, sponsored by the Croesus Business Bank, Planetology Officer: do you agree to represent humanity on Mars from this day forth until the last day of your life?'

'I accept!' cries Fangfang, straightening her square glasses over her perfectly plucked eyebrows.

She puffs out her chest, as if better to exhibit the Croesus logo on her suit, sewn in Latin letters paired with Chinese ideograms. Always at her best, Fangfang, the eldest of us, the voice of reason whose steadfastness and seriousness I so admire.

I'd really like to be calm like her right now, but my heart is still racing in my chest.

'Alexei, eighteen years old, a citizen of the Russian Federation, sponsored by the Ural Gas Company, Medical Officer: do you agree to represent humanity on Mars from this day forth until the last day of your life?'

'I accept!'

The dumbest thoughts, worthy of a twelve-year-old kid, burst from my mind like meteors: Does he like vodka? Does he wear a fur hat? Russia has often been an ally of France, if I remember right from my distant history lessons; might that perhaps be an excuse for some bilateral reconciliation?

'Kirsten, eighteen years old, a citizen of the Federal Republic of Germany, sponsored by Apotech Laboratories, Biology Officer: do you agree to represent humanity on Mars from this day forth until the last day of your life?'

Kris's 'I accept!' wakes me like a rifle shot – distinct, powerful, with no reservations and no echo but the crackling of the flashes and the trembling of the red roses in the large vases arranged at the foot of the rostrum.

The director pivots once again, like an unstoppable metronome. He addresses the most junior members of the team: Kenji, representing Japan, financed by Dojo Video Games, and then Safia, the Indian ward supported by Karmaphone telephone manufacturer. She speaks her vow with the same sweetness she brings to everything. I stare at the serene expression on her face, searching in vain for a reflection of my own agitation. My eyes come to rest on the red dot that decorates her forehead, a third eye in accordance with her religion – this morning it can't help but make me think of the planet Mars, the un-lidded eye watching me from the depths of space, waiting for my turn to come.

(You shouldn't be going, Léonor . . . rustles the little voice, like a breath of air under a poorly sealed door. *It'll be the worst decision of your whole existence; you already have your suspicions as to why . . .)*

I barely hear the director calling on the fourth boy, Mozart from Brazil, eighteen years old, sponsored by the Brazimo construction company; now there's only this voice inside me, speaking ever louder.

(The scent of roses in your nostrils, that's the last time you're ever going to breathe that . . . the caress of the warm wind on your forehead, that's the last time you're going to feel that . . .)

'Elizabeth, eighteen years old, citizen of the United Kingdom, sponsored by Walter and Seel insurance, Engineering Officer . . .'

Liz, in turn, accepts, revealing a row of dazzling teeth worthy of a toothpaste ad, just as perfect as her straight nose, her high cheekbones, her endless neck emphasised by the ballerina bun on her head. Such class, seriously, and never an ounce of doubt.

During all this time, that infernal tune never stops sounding in my head, like a scratched record.

(The sparkle of the sea, down there at the bottom of Cape Canaveral, that's the last time you're going to see that . . . But the people on Earth, they're going to be seeing you from every possible angle until the last day of your life!)

25

I chew the inside of my cheeks to silence this voice that is filling me with doubt just when I'm supposed to be a rock of certainty – the voice that the psychological tests were never able to detect or I never would have been selected. It comes from somewhere far away, from my past . . . It comes from somewhere so close, right behind me . . . It's always been there, crouched at the back of my neck, waiting till it's too late – because it is too late, isn't it, too late to go back . . . ?

D -24 mins.

'Samson, eighteen years old, a citizen of the Federal Republic of Nigeria, sponsored by the Petrolus oil company, Biology Officer . . .'

The pain of my teeth chewing into my cheeks muffles everything.

D -23 mins.

'Kelly, nineteen years old, a citizen of Canada, sponsored by Croiseur, the producers of transportation equipment, Navigation Officer . . .'

The warm blood runs onto my tongue. I know that the metallic taste of haemoglobin comes from the iron it contains; after all, I'm the head nurse on the girls' team. But at the same time, I can't get the sticky idea out of my head that it's also the taste of the iron-rich surface of Mars, that screwed-up dead world where nothing grows and nothing lives.

D -22 mins.

'Marcus, nineteen years old, a citizen of the United States of America, sponsored by the Eden Food International food processing group, Planetology Officer . . .'

At the mention of Eden Food, memories of the factory flash instantly back to me, especially of my few friends there, who I'm never going to see again – just think, if somebody had ever told me that the name of my old employer would make me nostalgic!

D -21 mins.

'Léonor, eighteen years old, a citizen of the French Republic, sponsored by Rosier & Merceaugnac luxury house of cosmetics, liqueurs, fashion and jewellery, Medical Officer: do you agree to represent humanity on Mars from this day forth until the last day of your life?'

At the exact moment Director Lock speaks this last word, *life*, I feel something go click inside me.

It *isn't* too late.

There's still time to refuse. It's my choice, my final freedom, and nothing and no one can take it away from me – not the year of training, not the dozens of contracts I've signed, not the legions of viewers lurking in wait like so many moray eels behind their screens for the twenty-three weeks ahead.

(Refuse . . . hisses the little voice sweetly into my ear. *You know you're not made for this mission, with what you've got to hide. You know if you take off with the others, you'll suffer as nobody has ever suffered before. Refuse now . . .)*

It is as sweet as a caress.

Sugared like a promise.

Almost friendly.

(They'll bring you down off the platform. You'll lose the limelight, the glory, the infinity of space, to return to the shadows, to anonymity, to the tins of mass-produced dog-food, to that narrow little world of Earth without adventure, without cameras . . . without pain.)

I can still say 'no'.

It would be crazy, the furthest extreme of sheer madness, but it's possible, it's entirely possible!

I just need an insane burst of courage to get it out, that nothing little word, that tiny syllable, when the whole world is waiting for me to say 'yes'. As for Serena who believed in me so strongly, who was ready to bet on an orphan girl nobody wanted . . . She'll understand. She has always understood me and stayed with me, right from the start, whatever my choices.

'Well then, Léonor,' crackles the voice of Director Lock, 'I'm waiting for your answer. The boys are waiting for your answer. The whole of Earth is hanging on your lips . . .'

I raise my head slightly.

Every camera is trained on me.

On the two giant screens standing above our side of the platform, my face is reproduced twice, two mutinous faces riddled with freckles, framed by untameable curls the colour of flames. In that close-up I can see every speck of the Rosier powder the make-up women have covered me with to try to mask the freckles that consume my skin, in vain.

'I refuse,' I breathe out.

'Léo!'

Kris's hand, which has been in mine this whole time, clenches like a vice.

I look towards her. Her face, with skin so perfect it doesn't need any make-up, has lost its angelic beauty. Under her delicately curled blonde hair, which we both spent hours preparing for the launch ceremony, there's the devastation of a battlefield, trembling in agitation.

'You can't do this to me,' she whispers, her eyes shining with tears. 'You can't abandon me, not now!'

All the way up on the rostrum, Director Lock gives a little cough into his mic.

'Young ladies, this is not the moment for whispering. May I remind you that the launcher takes off in exactly twenty minutes?'

'They didn't hear you!' Kris continues to beg in a thin voice taut with emotion. 'Nobody heard you but me. Don't throw it all away; you've always said you were going to be the first person to draw the Martian landscapes! Tell them you accept. Oh, tell them, Léo, I'm begging you. Tell them for yourself . . . for me.'

I gulp.

There is no longer a little voice behind my head, no more knees quaking like jelly.

The moment when I could have changed my destiny has passed. The Determinator has had a small temporary misfire, but it's now fully functional once again.

Because if there's one thing I'm certain of, it's that, for me, Kris is the closest thing I've got to a family. Not the one who threw me away as though I were a piece of trash, not them, but the one who welcomed me with open arms the very first day we met.

'I accept, of course . . . !' I shout, spitting bloodily in front of the entire world. 'I said I accept!'

4. Reverse Shot

Launch platform, Cape Canaveral Air Base
Sunday 2 July, 1:05pm

'The transit phase of the Genesis programme may now officially begin!' Gordon Lock declares.

No sooner has he spoken these words than some of the spectators race towards the stairs, launching themselves at the platform.

The Genesis programme jingle starts to play in a loop in the speakers and mixes with the throat-grazing yells of the journalists calling out the astronauts' names. While the security guards escort the participants at a run towards the launcher, the director's hand closes around the sleeve of the psychiatrist's suit, below the lectern.

Discreetly.

Firmly.

'She hesitated,' he whispers in her ear in a voice that no longer has any warmth in it. 'The last girl. She hesitated, right there on the launch platform, I'm sure of it. I had a sense that she was going to do an about-turn . . . or worse. I'm warning you, Serena: if that girl ever suspects anything . . .'

'She doesn't suspect a thing,' replies Serena McBee drily, pulling her arm free. 'They have no idea what awaits them, none of them, any more than the dozens of journalists bombarding them, the hundreds of engineers surrounding them or the millions of viewers watching them. They have no idea at all.'

5. Shot

D -19 mins.

'This way, ladies,' shout the security guards.

The music is deafening.

Confusion.

Crushing.

A chaos of limbs and heads, above which beam the numbers on the clock, imperturbable: D -19 minutes.

I feel myself being rushed towards the vast bulk of the launcher, a metal cathedral flanked by the booster towers, at the peak of which gleam the two tiny cone shapes of the twin capsules: girls to the left, boys to the right.

'Kris!'

I try to grab hold of Kris's arm, as I'm sucked in by the bustle in front of me – she's quite clumsy and I worry that she's going to stumble without somebody to support her. But there are hands grabbing onto my suit, trying to hold me back to ask me one final question, to capture one final cliché.

I turn around, ready to dispatch the journo who is holding me back, by throwing punches if I need to. He's a large dark Latino man dressed in a blue Hawaiian shirt with a sea-bed print, his face ravaged by a three-day beard, his eyes dark and shining. A pretty handsome guy, actually, if you like thirty-year-olds. His shabby bearing, his surfer shirt covered in swordfish and dolphins, his shock of unkempt hair: all of it is in sharp contrast to the designer suits and impeccable blow-dries of the other journalists. A shark's tooth on a thin leather strap is hanging around his neck over his open collar, quite different from the interchangeable neckties of his colleagues. I reckon he's a second-rate journalist who doesn't belong to one of the leading outlets of the international press, maybe even a freelance hack just trying his luck. To judge by the bags under his eyes, he must have slept right outside the launch zone, and not very well, to be sure of a place at the press conference. That almost makes me want to answer his questions out of solidarity. And also because of that little pirate thing he's got going on which I'll admit I don't dislike – Captain Shark's-Tooth, of the High Seas!

But the way he grabs hold of my wrist, as though he wanted to unscrew it, quickly dissuades me: I realise he's as much of a vulture as all the rest, maybe even more famished than they are.

'Wait . . . !' he commands in a hoarse voice, which struggles to be heard above the shouts of his colleagues all around him. 'You mustn't –'

Shark's-Tooth doesn't get the chance to say any more. Two security guards built like tanks lay hands on his shirt, and drag him away with them so violently that they make a button pop open. But the guy clings to me like a shipwrecked man to his life raft, like a hawk to its prey!

34

I feel myself thrown violently forward.

My feet get tangled up.

My fingers slip.

They find Shark's-Tooth's belt.

They close on the object that's clipped on to it.

Instinctively I bring my hand towards me, and look down: in my palm is a cellphone, the kind of thing we've been forbidden from possessing since we first signed up for the Genesis programme, all our communications with the Earth being handled exclusively by the production team. I look up again: the security guards have finally managed to yank this cretin off me, dragging him into the throng. Shark's-Tooth calls one last word back to me that I don't understand, then the pale shape of his face disappears, snatched up by the sea of bodies that closes around him.

I straighten myself up, instinctively slipping the phone into the all-purpose pocket of my suit, which is designed to take tools and samples of Martian ores.

A movement of the crowd propels me back against Kris.

'Thanks, Léo,' she pants. 'Thank you for saying yes. Thank you, thank you, thank you! I promise you won't regret it. And besides, I'm sure you're going to have all the boys at your feet, my lovely leopard.'

I force a smile. Leopard, that's my other nickname, along with Determinator. A bit of wordplay that Serena came up with, in reference to my prominent freckles. She's so kind, is Serena. She's really got this amazing knack for transforming each of our defects into an asset.

We are all pushed into the elevator that is positioned against the right flank of the launcher, which is to take us up to the girls' capsule. It's only a simple aluminium platform, set on top of a crane that will collapse on lift-off; here, too, a camera is lying in wait for us, a fat black ball hanging from the guardrail.

'Wipe your eyes,' I tell Kris reluctantly, tying my thick red mane in an elastic. 'The audience are watching us. And besides, the other girls needn't know I hesitated, right?'

These girls who have been at our side since the start of the training, with whom we've stuck together over the last twelve months, are no longer just friends: they are also participants in the programme, simultaneously indispensable teammates and direct competitors. Each of them has gone through the apprenticeship necessary for the successful progress of the mission. All four of the others are leaning on the guardrail. The competition on the programme is going to be tough: Fangfang the Singaporean, a walking encyclopaedia who's always so well turned-out, our Planetology expert; Kelly the Canadian, the pilot, who's sexy in a space-adventurer kind of way, our Navigation expert; Liz from England, supermodel mechanic, Engineering Officer; and doll-like Safia from India, her fiery eyes ringed with kohl, our Communications Officer. Do they already know which boy they will head for just based on the voices we heard behind the curtain . . . ? Personally, I've no idea. A black hole. And so I focus on Kris, who's all real.

She wipes her cheeks with the back of her hand. Then she squats down to bury her face in the curly white coat of Louve, the dog she's responsible for as our Biology expert, destined to represent the animal kingdom on Mars. She's a mongrel I'd guess is somewhere close to a royal poodle, according to what I picked up from studying the breeds on the Eden dog-food tins. The boys are boarding their side with a male dog I haven't yet had the honour of being introduced to, by the name of Warden. The Genesis programme is playing matchmaker all the way.

D -18 mins.

The aluminium platform begins to move.

The journalists and the security guards shrink from view as we rise up along the smooth surface of the launcher. They are transformed into insects, even Serena whose magnificent silver hair glows like the metal carapace of a beetle.

'Look over there!' cries Safia in her reedy voice. 'All these people are here . . . for us!'

She's pointing at the edges of the base, the tall wire fences that are barring access. A real human tide is pressing against these barriers, hundreds of thousands of people who have come to watch the blaze of the take-off from a safe distance, just to be able to say, 'I was there!' Some of them are perched on stepladders to get a better view, others on the roofs of their cars, as far as the eye can see, which is all the way to the end of the Cape Canaveral peninsula. Seriously impressive; all the more so after our year of isolation in Death Valley.

'It's magical,' sighs Kris, her eyes quite dry now, dazzled.

D -17 mins.

'It's chilly up here.' Liz shivers as we pass the tips of the boosters. 'I should have put on two undersuits.'

37

She really feels the cold, Liz, constantly bundled up in pale jumpers and scarves right up to her bun. Under the massive suit that makes her look like an American football player, her supermodel body doesn't have an ounce of fat to keep her warm.

'You can say that again,' says Kelly. 'It's blowing a gale like on Mars!'

The Canadian's long bleached hair is flying all over the place.

Is this being done for stylistic effect, aimed at the camera hanging from the guardrail of the elevator?

Is she trying out her seduction techniques on the audience, in anticipation of the sessions in the Visiting Room with the boys?

So long as she isn't already on course to collect a load of money in her Dowry, and buy the best set-up in New Eden!

'You're wrong,' Fangfang corrects her, straightening her square glasses the way she does whenever she speaks, teacher-like. 'On Mars the atmospheric density is actually so thin that the wind has to blow a hundred times faster than on Earth just to move the tiniest speck.'

Fangfang seems to be talking too loud, as though her explanation wasn't just for Kelly's benefit but also for the public currently listening to us via the camera.

'So it would take a real hurricane to straighten your hair,' the Singaporean goes on. 'And what's more, Kelly, may I remind you that protocol forbids us from wearing our hair loose during manoeuvres.'

Kelly blows out her bubble-gum, menthol blue like her lip-gloss, till it pops.

'That's something protocol doesn't allow either, I know,' she says before Fangfang is able to say a word.

She spits her gum over the guardrail. Then she covers her hair with a headband and puts her earphones in to listen to her music, throwing a complicit wink at the cameras, as if to say, 'I'd rather be deaf than have to listen to a bore like her.'

D -16 mins.

The elevator stabilises about a hundred metres above ground, opposite the black hole of the airlock, open like the mouth of a dead fish in the side of the conical capsule.

I let the others get past – Fangfang, Kelly, Safia, Liz and Kris, followed by Louve who sticks to her like glue.

I stay behind for a moment.

Up here nobody can ask me another mean question to try to make me crack, or cling on to me like I belong to them.

Up here you can no longer hear the shouts of the journalists or the violins from the jingle. There's nothing but the blowing of the wind. For one last time I look at the twin blues of sky and sea; the reflection of the sun on the cabin of the launcher; the clock, tiny now, announcing very seriously:

D -15 mins.

I've been waiting for this moment for months – or rather, no, my whole life. And now that I'm here, it's all going too quickly. So I'm granting myself just a few stolen seconds off the precision-choreography timing, just to savour the calm. I want it. I need it.

The camera stares at me in silence.

It's like a single eye. The eye of a Cyclops with neither cornea nor iris, just a huge, black pupil. I stare back, imagining the hordes of viewers hiding behind it. *I warn you: don't expect any circus tricks from me*, I tell them in my mind. *Don't expect my hair loose, teasing winks, lessons recited by heart. I don't know how to do any of that. But I promise you'll get all my passion when I arrive on Mars, with or without a fiancé!*

6. Reverse Shot

Launch platform, Cape Canaveral Air Base
Sunday 2 July, 1:10pm

'Her again! What the hell's she up to now? Why hasn't she gone into the capsule?'

Gordon Lock is clinging with both hands to the edge of the lectern, as though he wants to rip out the monitor embedded in it. He's sweating more and more profusely. Fat drops are beading on his brow. They splash onto the surface of the screen, where Léonor's face is displayed in close-up – luxuriant hair that the elastic can barely contain; a perfect oval face flecked with freckles; sumptuous bronze eyes, glowing like a smouldering fire: a leopard right down to her eyelashes.

'She . . . she . . . she seems to be looking at me,' stammers Gordon Lock. 'It's like the brat can see me and she knows everything, like she knows all about the Noah Report –'

'Pull yourself together,' retorts Serena McBee coldly. 'She's the one being filmed, not you. And you destroyed the file with the Noah Report yourself – no traces remain.'

'Tell her to get into the capsule. Talk to her through the speakers! You're the executive producer, you're the one who

41

chose the candidates, you're in charge of keeping them under control!'

'Talk to her yourself, if you care so much. And risk ruining everything.'

Gordon Lock angrily seizes the microphone, and presses a button in the lectern.

At once, the blaring of the jingle stops, to be replaced by his furious breathing that makes the loudspeakers roar like the noise of an approaching storm.

On the monitor, Léonor shifts her gaze. She looks at the blue sky all around her, eyebrows raised, in search of a cloud she can't see anywhere.

Unable to find the words, frightened by the noise of his own breathing, Gordon Lock takes his finger off the transmission button as quickly as if he'd been burned. His face is white as a sheet, and bathed in sweat.

All of a sudden, a muffled sound comes out of the monitor, from the airlock behind Léonor: 'Léo, hurry up! We're going to take off!' – it's the other passengers calling out to the straggler.

'That's it, go on . . . Listen to them . . .' mutters Gordon Lock through his teeth, in a tiny voice that nobody else can hear, not even Serena McBee.

But the monitor is still showing pictures of the girl on the elevator platform. She looks back towards the craft, then her eyes dive back into the camera.

'Go in,' Gordon Lock begs again. 'Please . . .'

Finally Léonor turns on her heel, and disappears into the mouth of the capsule.

* * *

42

At the precise moment when the airlock closes, the speakers fall silent for good.

All the projectors switch off.

The livid face of an immense digital Director Lock disappears from the four public screens. They turn black, the colour of space.

Standing behind his lectern, the flesh and bone Director Lock wipes the sweat from his forehead. He once again presses the transmission button, this time without a moment's hesitation. A second ago he was a man consumed with doubt about everything, not least about himself, but now he's the technical director of the Genesis programme once again.

'Clear the platform,' he orders through the speakers. 'All engineers to your posts in the control room. Ten minutes to lift-off!'

Before taking the stairs that lead down from the rostrum, with all the microphones now switched off, Serena McBee whispers a few words into her colleague's ear.

'You're making me think I ought perhaps to show you a couple of relaxation techniques one of these days, Gordon,' she says calmly. 'They'd stop you from panicky reactions like that. After all, it's the contestants who are going to die in a few months, not you!'

7. Shot

'Pressurisation?' asks Kelly.

'A hundred per cent,' answers Liz, carefully recording the figure in the flight log.

Kelly, Liz and Safia are all sitting in the first row of the narrow capsule – or rather, they're lying back horizontally, in seats moulded to help us to cope with the acceleration on lift-off. It makes sense that they should be side by side, as the Navigation, Engineering and Communications Officers have to work together during the critical parts of the flight. Who was it carrying out these roles in the boys' capsule again? I no longer remember the names – I need faces; I have a visual memory – I owe my drawing skills, my one talent, to that . . . Admittedly not the most obvious one to highlight in a seduction competition.

'Ambient oxygen levels?'

'Optimal.'

'Ventilation?'

'Activated.'

Kelly turns round sharply in her seat, towards the second row, where Fangfang, Kris and I are lying.

'As someone who knows the protocol so well, Fangfang, could you stop that dog from gnawing on the transmission cables? Let me remind you that it's forbidden to let animals roam about during manoeuvres.'

Fangfang hesitates for a moment, no more than a second – a second in which I wait to hear her rebuffing Kelly, as I certainly would have done in her place. But she settles for touching her glasses the way she does whenever something bothers her, before passing the muzzle to Kris so she can fasten it over Louve's mouth. There's always been some tension between Kelly and Fangfang, ever since the first day of training in Death Valley; but up till now, the Singaporean has taken it personally. I guess the relaxation sessions under hypnosis have really helped her to form her nerves of steel, like the other girls – once a week, for a year, Serena saw each of us in her study for a one-to-one session from which the others emerged entirely freed from tension, perfectly calmed, ready for a restorative night's sleep. I was the only girl on whom it didn't work. Completely unable to let myself go under. 'You're so highly strung, un-hypnotisable!' Serena would say to me, laughing. 'My therapeutic talents can do nothing for you, I'm sorry to say. I can, on the other hand, prepare you a nice cup of chamomile tea with honey harvested from my own estate: the supreme remedy to help you sleep!'

I smile at the thought of all the litres of chamomile I swallowed over the months. It was delicious, but it never stopped me waking up at 4 a.m. almost every night, after one of the fire-filled nightmares I've been having ever since I was little.

'All set?' Kris asks me, dragging me from my thoughts.

Her face is radiant. Her braided hair looks like a princess's crown. She's living out her dream – our dream.

I take a deep breath.

The air that enters my chest is already no longer terrestrial air. It's a skilfully concocted composition, which will be constantly renewed over the twenty-three weeks of the journey. The launcher hasn't lifted off yet, but in a sense we've already left. I feel my excitement rising from each second to the next.

'All set,' I say, before clamping my helmet onto my head.

'Do you read me, ladies and gentlemen?'

'Perfectly on the girls' side, Serena,' replies Safia in her childlike voice, turning a knob on the dashboard.

The executive producer's face appears on the transmission monitor. Her silver bob stands out clearly against the padded backrest of a black leather armchair. At the foot of the screen, the final seconds before lift-off tick away: D -30 secs . . . D -29 secs . . . D -28 secs . . .

'Well, girls – I can still call you girls now, can't I, since you aren't married women yet!' says Serena into the microphone she's holding. 'You won't be until you arrive on the surface of Mars. It's so romantic, nowadays, the waiting. It's quite lovely, the whole courtship thing. I'm sure you'll inspire thousands of young people right across the world.'

Serena has always put us on a pedestal, since after all she was the one to choose us – *you girls are the best, the most beautiful, the most wonderful*. I suppose she must have done the same with the boys, over the last twelve months, till they were raring to go, making them feel like space heroes.

'I'm also making the most of the fact that I can still talk to you without a lag, since the further you get from Earth the longer the transmission time will be. You remember why?'

'Because the *Cupido*'s laser transmitter can't send information faster than the speed of light, which is three hundred thousand kilometres per second,' Safia reminds us, demonstrating that she has the whole Communications dossier at her fingertips. 'So, there are fifty-five million kilometres between us and Mars's position when the *Cupido* reaches it. Which means that once we're there it'll take three minutes for our signal to reach Earth, and three minutes to receive the return signal. It's what's called communication latency.'

'A perfect explanation!' Serena congratulates her. 'The Genesis programme depends on optic transmission by laser, much more effective than electromagnetic transmission by radio, which previous space missions have had to settle for – but the speed of light remains an unsurpassable physical frontier. Every day of travel will take you one light second further away – a second and fourteen centiseconds, to be exact – until reaching three light minutes at your destination. So it will just require some patience during our exchanges, waiting for the answer to each question before asking the next, breathing from your belly like I've taught you. You do remember, don't you? Here, let's do a little relaxation session, right now before lift-off.'

Serena's voice gets deeper, incantatory.

'One, I empty my lungs all the way down and I close my eyes . . .

'Two, I sink into my belly and I see a great calm ocean where dolphins are swimming . . .

47

'Three . . .'

I disconnect myself mentally from the screen, and through the visor of my helmet I focus on the dozens of LEDs lit up on the dashboard. Best leave the hypnosis to those people lucky enough to be receptive to it. The best way for me to centre myself is by drawing. And when I haven't got a pencil or a stylus in my hand, I draw with my eyes, I focus on what's in front of me – looking at reality in its smallest details helps me slow my thoughts.

I focus on the LEDs and I begin to count them, comparing their sizes and their colours, storing up a whole load of information in my head so as not to think about everything else.

'Nine . . . !'

'Eight . . . !'

'Seven . . . !'

A voice chants the countdown in my helmet.

On the transmission monitor, Serena is still gazing lovingly at us, but her encouragements are swallowed up by the countdown; just above her, sheltered under a glass dome, the on-board camera is watching us too, and through it the millions of viewers.

'Six . . . !'

'Five . . . !'

'Four . . . !'

A seismic shaking comes from the rocket's innermost depths. The engines are powering up. Down there, beneath my feet, I know it is hell: the tank stuffed full of propellant has ignited. Best not think about it.

At last I close my eyes.

'Three . . . !'

'Two . . . !'

'One . . . !'

Behind my closed eyelids, there is no ocean, there are no dolphins.

There is just a black, cosmic night.

'Go . . . !'

D +05 secs.

Strapped to the front of a train whose brakes have failed.

That's the demented image that comes to mind: the vibrations propelled deep into my bones; the roaring of steel crushing my ears; the acceleration that flattens my stomach against my spine.

This is different from our simulation sessions in the centrifuge.

This is more freaky.

This is more magic.

This is more real.

Through the narrow reinforced windshield, the sky erupts at top speed. On the altimeter on the dashboard, the numbers tick over even faster.

Somewhere in the distance, Serena's voice continues to sound haltingly, half eaten by the exertions of the engines at work.

'One, I empty my lu-lu-lungs . . .

'Two, I sink into my be-be-belly . . .

'Three, I fill back up with air starting from my nave-nave-navel . . .'

The seats, the metal wall, the instruments on the dashboard are all shuddering as though the whole capsule has been overcome by a terrible epilepsy; only the dome of the camera remains fixed, trained on us.

The rocket continues to accelerate as we rise further into the atmosphere. In one minute the speed has increased ten-fold – I know this because I've learned it, but this is the first time my body really understands what that means.

Two thousand kilometres an hour . . . This figure means nothing if you've never been lying on the seat of a rocket, crushed by a gravitational force that's doing everything it can to try and keep you on Earth.

I feel a pressure on the back of my glove that's different from the acceleration.

I look down: it's Kris's hand, clamped to mine.

D +02 mins.

The altimeter announces *forty-five kilometres*, the height of five Mount Everests stacked one on top of another.

The roaring of the engines seems less deafening now. The boosters are already spent, five hundred tonnes of propellant gone up in smoke in a few minutes.

'First phase of ascent completed!' crackles Kelly's voice inside my helmet.

I hear the boosters detaching from the rocket with a great metallic tearing sound: they fall back down to Earth, vast empty shells ready to sink into the waters of the Atlantic Ocean.

But not us – we keep on going, towards Mars.

With each second that passes, my body feels heavier.

I try to see if Kris is OK.

There's no way.

I can't move.

My head is concrete, my neck cast-iron.

The rocket continues to pick up speed in its final effort to tear itself free from the pull of the Earth.

'Acceleration?' asks Kelly, her voice trembling.

'Just passed 2.5 g,' Liz struggles to reply.

If there's any trouble at all with the launcher's main engine, the protocol predicts that we should come back down to Dakar, on the other side of the Atlantic. All breakdowns and failures have been meticulously predicted for the first minutes of lift-off, the scientists relying on the long history of space conquest. But the further we get from Earth, into interplanetary regions where mankind has never ventured before, the less precise the protocol will be.

The altimeter reaches its round number: one hundred kilometres above sea level.

'Acceleration?'

'We've . . . we've . . . just . . . reached . . . 3 g . . .'

Three times Earth's gravity.

At 3 g the back of your seat digs into your sides and your back until you and it become one.

At 3 g, each intake of breath is painfully difficult, the air is a viscous fluid sticking in your lungs.

At 3 g, the rays of the sun become as heavy as liquid gold,

flowing slowly from the black hole of the sky onto the dashboard.

At 3 g, your brain itself is transformed into treacle.

At 3 g, you no longer think.

D +10 mins.

All at once, the invisible hand crushing my body relaxes.

All at once, the straps clinging to my suit fly off, at the same time as all the sheets from the flight log that had been resting on Safia's knees.

There is a great trembling, down there, under my feet, then total silence. Behind the darkened windshield, space is sprinkled with stars.

'Lower tank released!' announces Kelly's voice. 'Final ascent completed! You can open the hatches, girls!'

Kris's hand is still clamped to my glove.

'I think you can let go of me,' I say, raising my visor. 'It's not like I'm about to fly away, you know.'

Yet it does feel as though I'm about to do just that. After having felt several tonnes heavier, my arms now seem to weigh almost nothing, like the weightlessness sessions in parabolic flight. But it's not just my arms threatening to take flight – it's my heart too, beating in my chest as strongly as the wings of a bird about to take to the air: *This is it, Léo! You've done it! You're there! You're in space!*

'The two capsules are in orbit!' announces Serena. 'All good on your side, girls?'

She's still there, smiling in the small window of the transmission monitor, which the chaos of the lift-off hasn't shaken. Only her eyes move, alternating left and right, following the two screens bringing her images of the two capsules launched into the emptiness of space.

'All ace on our side!' says Kelly, putting her headphones back on.

The first notes of *Rebel without a Cause*, the latest album from Jimmy Giant, Kelly's compatriot and idol, introduced by the press as 'the new James Dean', burst through the speakers and fill the capsule.

'All set for orbital dock with the *Cupido* in exactly seven hours and twenty-five minutes!'

8. Out of Frame

The Cape Canaveral road
Sunday 2 July, 7:45pm

A small black campervan with tinted windows and chrome-plated rims is driving along the road that crosses Cape Canaveral, flanked on either side by low vegetation the summer has turned brown. The van's heading east, towards the sea that looks fiery in the late afternoon light. A few cars are moving in the opposite direction, heading west – the last spectators retuning to the mainland after the lift-off, the tune of 'Cosmic Love' coming through their open windows. The black campervan passes them and soon there are no more vehicles on the asphalt strip. The only witnesses to the vast crowd that only a few hours earlier was gathered here are the beer cans strewn over the verge and the disembowelled crisp packets that the evening wind is carrying from bush to bush. Here and there, loudspeakers mounted on metal pylons broadcast a woman's voice in a loop, courteous but firm: 'We would like to inform all our visitors that access to the Cape Canaveral peninsula closes at eight o'clock. Please return to your vehicles and make your way towards the exit.'

But the black campervan rushes along the line of pylons without slowing down.

It doesn't stop till the very end of the road, at the foot of the tall fence spiked with barbed wire that prevents access to the launch zone. Notes carrying the good wishes of thousands of people are stuck to the bars, brief words sending good luck to those who have flown off, confiding their hopes and prayers to take with them into the sky. There are even bunches of flowers, soft toys, and various other gifts left there by those who have remained behind on Earth. Between all these offerings, you can see the launch zone, two hundred metres beyond the bars: a metal platform topped with cranes and flanked by large cubic hangars ringed with brightly lit roads. The place is completely deserted.

The door of the campervan opens.

An elegant young man, preppy-looking, gets out: beige chinos, a navy blazer impeccably cut, a red polo shirt. His brown hair is carefully combed, a side parting, his face crossed by a pair of black-framed glasses. He's holding a small black plastic case, which he presses with a movement of his thumb – *click!* – before bringing it to his mouth: it's a dictaphone.

'*Letter to my father.* Sunday 2 July, Cape Canaveral air base,' he records.

He looks at his watch.

'It's seven forty-five p.m. I'm standing at the fence that is said to be one of the best-guarded places in the United States. I'm about to prove the contrary. I hope you'll like the demonstration, Father. In any case, when you receive this recording, it will be too late to stop me.'

He releases the button, brings the dictaphone back to his trouser pocket. Then he approaches the fence, his foot pushing aside a huge red synthetic velvet cushion in the shape of a heart. Finally he opens his hand – in his palm is a fat beetle reflecting a silvery gleam.

'You're up, little bug,' murmurs the young man, examining the insect one last time.

Looking at it close up, it isn't really a beetle. Its silvery elytra are made of aluminium, its legs of metallic fibres, and its bulging eyes look like two tiny camera lenses.

The young man squats down, puts his hand through the bars and places the fake insect on the other side, on the pebbly ground of the base.

'Hey! What are you doing here?'

The young man stands up as a guard bursts out of the small shelter where he's been hiding, wearing the uniform of the Genesis programme – matching grey short-sleeved shirt and trousers, cap printed with a planet enclosing a foetus.

'You're not allowed to be here, sir, you're –' he begins.

He breaks off to size up the visitor from head to foot. He notices that, behind the blazer and the black-framed glasses, he's younger than he'd first thought, eighteen, twenty at most, so he really didn't deserve that 'sir'.

'Didn't you hear the announcements, kid?' he says now, bringing his hand to the revolver clipped to his belt. 'The peninsula closes at eight, same as every evening. Cape Canaveral is private property since Atlas bought it, not a public park. Go on, scram, or I'm taking down your plate number!'

The young man in the black-framed glasses slips his hand into the inside pocket of his jacket and takes out what looks like an early-generation cellphone, a kind of chunky remote control with a short antenna.

'Oh, damn!' he says with a glance at the screen. 'You mean I'm too late for the launch?'

He sniffs noisily. The smell of kerosene is still in the air, mixed with the heather close by.

The guard blinks under the visor of his cap; the setting sun is blinding him slightly.

'Of course you're too late!' he replies, exasperated. 'Haven't you seen the TV, heard the radio, read the newspapers, checked the news on your phone?'

'Well, no . . . And besides, I can't seem to get –'

'That's normal; phone signals are jammed on the whole peninsula, a question of secrecy. Only Genesis walkie-talkies work on here. There's no chance of getting a signal, specially not with a phone that looks like it's come from the Ark. Even my ten-year-old daughter has a more advanced model! You and technology don't exactly get along, do you?'

The young man shrugs. The breeze from the ocean swells his jacket, ruffles his hair.

'If I'd known, I would have come earlier to watch the lift-off. Such bad luck, coming all the way from Beverly Hills . . . Not only for this though, you understand: Dad bought me this campervan so I could do a tour of our beautiful country over the summer vacation, before starting at Berkeley next fall. Hey, you think you could arrange a little private tour of the base, something to really remember?'

The guard is taken aback for a second, brow furrowed and mouth half open.

'Hold on a minute,' he says, finally, in a sugary voice. 'I'm going to ask the management –'

Doing just as he said, he unclips his walkie-talkie with one hand, and walks a few steps off, the other hand still resting on the grip of his revolver.

The young man takes advantage of the moment to tap away on his enormous telephone. A message in digital letters appears on the screen:

SATELLITE CONNECTION IN PROGRESS . . .

But the guard sees none of this. He's too busy speaking into his walkie-talkie, his back turned so the visitor can't hear his conversation.

'Hey, Bob? Derek here. There's a real greenhorn kid who's shown up at the launch zone in spite of the curfew, you know the sort, proper daddy's boy, real cocky. Car's got California plates. Send me over the security fellas, yeah?'

The guard put his walkie-talkie back in its holster, a smile on his lips.

'Sorry, no can do, kid,' he says, turning round. 'I'm afraid your little private tour's going to be taking you to the secur—'

A roar of the engine swallows up the end of his sentence, the tyres kicking up a great ochre cloud that rains back down onto his uniform. By the time the dust clears, the campervan is a long way down the road towards the mainland.

9. Shot

'Target minus one hundred metres,' crackles Kelly's voice.

We've been moulded into the hollows of our seats for more than seven hours, helmets firmly on our heads, chests crushed by the safety-belts.

But I don't feel the aches and I don't feel the cramp. I'm too focused for that, busy reproducing on the screen of my small sketching tablet the fascinating sight of the craft that's passing in front of the capsule's windshield.

The *Cupido*.

I've seen pictures of it many times, I've dreamt about it often, and there was even a scale model in the entrance hall of the training camp. But the reality exceeds anything I've imagined, and I so want to etch it onto the memory of my tablet, to remember it for ever.

This gem is the last word in space technology, the project which under NASA swallowed up hundreds of millions of dollars over more than twenty years under the name *Vasco da Gama*. And the very moment this Rolls-Royce of space was up

59

in orbit, finally ready to be used for Mars exploration, *bam!*, the new American president decides to melt down the crown jewels and sell them off . . . Such bad luck for the engineers who had devoted their entire existences to the project. Such bad luck, too, for the highly qualified astronauts who had trained for years in the hope of being the first to travel to the red planet. Most of those guys are unemployed now. To create more of a spectacle and make as much money as possible, Atlas chose to open the programme up to amateurs, unknowns who anybody could identify with. They changed the name of the craft – and they chose *Cupido*, after the god of love, the angel Cupid tasked with unleashing his arrows at us during the programme . . . It's pretty well perfect. Seen from up close, the *Cupido* really does look like an angel. But a dreadful angel, an angel almost thirty metres tall, floating silently in the gloom of space and on the screen of my sketching tablet.

With the end of my stylus nicely wedged into my astronaut's glove, I've reproduced the four parts of the vessel, fitted into one another over the course of the launches that have gone before us, as there isn't a launcher powerful enough to put a vessel like it in space all in one go (likewise, this giant is far too large to enter the Martian atmosphere without crashing, which is why we'll land in our light capsules). The propulsion unit is the largest of the modules, a vast cylinder housing the miniaturised nuclear plant that will propel us to Mars – that's the body of the angel. The two tubes that make up the living compartments are connected perpendicularly above the trunk like the two arms of a T – these are the angel's wings. At the place where the wings meet, at the top of the craft, is the smallest module, a dark glass sphere haloed with a circular satellite dish that's giving off a luminous beam – that's the head of the angel, the Holy of Holies, that holds the mysterious *Visiting Room* . . .

'Target minus forty metres . . .'

I look up from my tablet. On the transmission monitor, Serena has been replaced by Roberto Salvatore, the Navigation instructor who trained Kelly. Roberto is wearing the grey uniform of the Genesis programme. His branded cap, on his chubby head, makes him look like a fast-food server who's overdone it on his own merchandise. You wouldn't know it, but he's one of the NASA old guard, almost as high-ranking as Director Lock, one of those who found favour in the eyes of Atlas; he's undoubtedly one of the best pilots anywhere in the cosmos – respect!

'*A little to the right* . . .' he guides us, his double chin trembling each time he gives an instruction. '*Straighten the angle of approach by two degrees . . . Now step on the gas and give it some good acceleration. The boys' capsule is close behind you, I'm counting on you to reach the Cupido first, girls!*'

At the mention of the boys, my eyes drop to the rear-view screen that is filming space behind us. There's a tiny cone, there behind us, lost among the stars. It's the second capsule. It doesn't look like it's moving, but in reality it's circling the planet at the same speed as us, eight kilometres per second. It's so funny to think that inside that metal tip no bigger than the head of a pin is the person I'm going to spend the rest of my life with.

* * *

'Target minus twenty metres . . .'

All of a sudden the capsule lights up, all my attention on the windshield again. A dazzling spotlight bursts onto the *Cupido*. The white ceramic tiles that cover it are suddenly aflame like plumes of light.

It's the sun rising on Earth.

The fifth sunrise we've witnessed since our departure.

We've already done five complete circuits of the planet, once every hour and a half, each time coming a little closer to the orbit of the craft.

This time, it's the one. We're just at the axis of the left wing, the living compartment for the girls. A few more strokes of the stylus, to capture the reflection of the sun on the *Cupido*'s head . . .

'Target minus ten metres . . .'

The docking bay at the end of the left wing is coming closer . . .

and closer . . .

and closer . . .

and closer . . .

'Target minus two metres . . . prepare for docking!'

The capsule shudders.

The light for the pressurisation system flashes up on the dashboard.

Roberto's double chin stops trembling on the transmission monitor:

'Docking successful!'

'Hmph,' says Kelly, boastfully. 'Child's play for a curling pro

62

like me . . . I'll just try and do as well in five months when we have to land our capsule right on the nose at New Eden, once we've reached the orbit of Phobos.'

'I'll leave you now. I've got to guide the boys for their own docking onto the right wing. If they get theirs wrong, they're off on a merry-go-round ride around the Earth for another ninety minutes.'

Safia is the first to release her seatbelt. She immediately starts floating, and tries to retrieve the pages of the flight log that are spread over the whole ceiling like clouds.

'I don't believe we have been given authorisation to unbuckle,' says Fangfang the killjoy, true to form.

'Authorisation granted, my dear Fangfang!' says Serena, who has just replaced Roberto on the screen.

The safety belts come off, one by one.

The girls rise into the air laughing the way children must laugh on Christmas Day, though I've never experienced such a thing myself. What a relief to be able to take off the elastic that has been imprisoning my hair and let my long fiery curls spread all around me. It feels like I'm coming back to life!

'Come on, Léo!' calls Kris.

She takes me by the arms and lifts me from my seat as easily as if I were a rag doll.

The pressurisation light turns green.

The airlock of the capsule docked with the craft opens with a resonant click. Behind it we see a narrow tunnel. It sucks all six of us into the depths of the *Cupido*, the first humans inside since it was assembled in orbit.

* * *

'Welcome home, girls!'

Serena's voice is so clear I almost expect to find the real flesh and blood Serena waiting for us as the end of the tunnel, in the living compartment.

She isn't there of course, but what I find takes my breath away just as much.

'Cool!' cries Kelly. 'It's like we're in a Canadian woodcutter's cabin – but the billionaire's version!'

And she's right. The tunnel comes through the floor of a circular room of some forty square metres, entirely panelled in natural pine – so unlike the white plastic of the confinement cell where we spent our last month of training, in Death Valley. Three pairs of bunk beds in brushed metal are bolted to the floor, all around the trapdoor through which we've arrived. Blankets made of fine warm cashmere are attached to the sheets with velcro strips, to combat the weightlessness. Each bed is topped with the dome shape of a camera, and a high-resolution screen showing a variety of terrestrial scenes: sunset on a snowy mountain . . . herds of deer grazing in a daisy-sprinkled clearing . . . and, of course, a calm sea in the moonlight where dolphins are swimming. It's not hard to guess who programmed the images on the screens!

'NASA conceived the interior décor of the craft with very Earth-like materials so as give the astronauts as little feeling of dislocation as possible, to let them have a gentle transition to their Martian lives.'

Serena's face is smiling at us through a fourth screen, set into the side of the ladder that goes up to the second level of the compartment. The Dolby Stereo system transmits her voice with a crystalline clarity.

'So, girls, do you like your room?'

A roar of happiness answers her.

We extricate ourselves from our cumbersome white suits, keeping only the skin-tight black undersuits, which are much more comfortable and much more becoming. Once they have been freed, some girls fly quite gracefully, like Liz and Safia, others more laboriously, such as Kris who has never been completely at ease with the weightlessness. Even Louve is yapping like a young puppy, her feet kicking at the air like a windmill.

'Léo and I will take this one!' cries Kris, contorting herself to reach the bed with the deer. 'Hey, Léo, will you let me have the top bunk?'

I nod.

'No problem, Kris,' I say. 'Even if right now concepts of "top" and "bottom" don't really mean much!'

As though she were really taking part in our conversation inside the room, while in fact she's thousands of kilometres away, Serena takes up my passing comment.

'Good point, Léo. As long as you're weightless, there's no up and no down. You'll have to wait for the *Cupido* to be launched on its Earth–Mars trajectory for its two wings to go into rotation around the central pivot, using the centrifugal force to create an artificial gravity during the twenty-three weeks of your journey, as all your viewers can see now on their screens.'

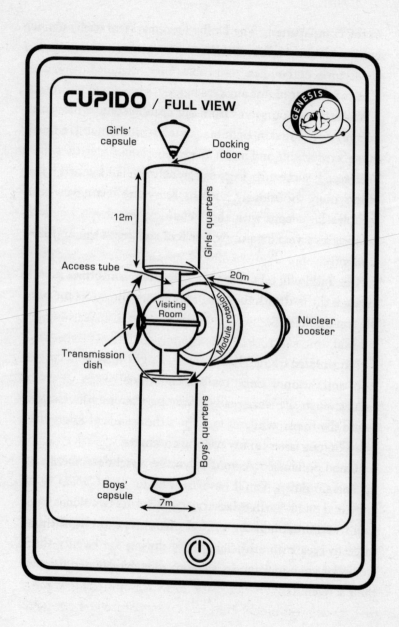

Serena's face is replaced by a 3D sectional view of the *Cupido* against the background of a starry sky. Its twin wings turn slowly around the head that is haloed by the transmission dish, which combines a good old-fashioned radio-electric antenna with a latest-generation laser terminal.

But we're all too excited to sit through a lesson on astrophysics.

Kris is already dragging me towards the ladder at the end of the room; she pushes the trapdoor over the bars, so we can fly up to the second level.

'And this is your living room!' announces Serena triumphantly.

Her face appears on a wide-screen, just below a camera that has been skilfully camouflaged in the surface of a digital clock displaying the time in Tokyo, Beijing, Singapore, New Delhi, Moscow, Abuja, Berlin, Paris, London, Ottawa, Washington, Brasilia: from east to west, the capitals of all the countries the passengers hail from.

'A relaxation corner for reading!' cries Safia, doing a headstand on a black leather sofa, decorated with cushions velcro'd into place.

'A kitchen area for cooking up a storm!' says Kris next, running her hands delightedly over the magnetic utensils on the sparkling ceramic work surface.

'Awesome! We can power up!' says Kelly. 'That'll go down well – I was running low on my tunes and I can't do without my daily dose of Jimmy Giant!'

She puts her small music player on the table under the digital clock – from its shiny black appearance, I immediately guess that it's a latest-model charging table, onto which we only have to place our games consoles, readers and other gadgets for them to be recharged in just a few minutes. Six digital tablets are awaiting us there already, held in place on the magnetised surface – one for each of us, marked with our names.

'These revision tablets contain all of the lessons for studying during the journey, to keep your instructors' teaching fresh in your mind,' says Serena. 'A kind of holiday homework, if you like. We've tried to make everything as attractive as possible, and you can revise wherever you choose: stretched out on your bed, running on a treadmill, or settled nice and comfortably in the lounge.'

'My revision's going to be happening right here, where it's lovely and warm!' says Liz, gliding towards the designer fireplace, set into the wall facing the wide-screen.

A fireplace.

Where there's a nice fire blazing.

On a spaceship!

'Umm,' Fangfang brings her hand nervously to her glasses, 'isn't that a bit dangerous? I mean, not just because of setting fire to the compartment, but isn't there also a risk it'll use up all the breathable oxygen?'

'None at all,' replies Serena. The fire's just a holographic projection, with integrated heating and pre-recorded crackling sounds. Pretty realistic, isn't it?'

Another burst of delight.

And an understanding at last of what it means to be 'at home', after a whole lifetime of feeling like an outsider!

'You have two other floors I'll leave you to explore for yourselves,' Serena goes on. 'The bathroom on the third – which is also the storeroom and laundry room – and the gym on the fourth. The whole thing makes up a charming quadruplex, a hundred and fifty square metres of living space.'

'What about this?' I ask, launching myself towards a nook embedded beside the kitchen area, protected by a pane of glass.

'That's the goods lift that draws on the stores of food stocked up in containers on the third floor – enough for the five months of travelling, don't you worry. You won't be short of water either, so long as you use it with some restraint, and you will contribute to feeding the source: your urine will be recycled all the way through the journey with a state-of-the-art filtration system! But enough of these technical considerations, which are hardly the most glamorous part: I do believe there's a delivery just arriving in the lift now ...'

At these words a rumbling comes up from the depths of the living compartment, allowing us to guess at the sophisticated machinery hidden behind the apparent simplicity of the wooden walls. A bottle appears behind the glass, which slides open.

I lift it out, while 'oh!'s and 'ah!'s ring out all around me.

It's chilled, a plastic valve in its neck with a built-in straw. Elegant writing is displayed on the beautiful golden label: *Champagne Merceaugnac, Cuvée Impériale, Grand Cru millésimé 1969 – Année de la Lune.*

'You can all thank Léonor – it's a gift from her platinum sponsor!' says Serena, raising her voice to be heard above the girls' shrieks. 'Unfortunately you couldn't pop the cork for safety reasons because of the weightlessness, but I can assure you it tastes the same through the straw. The vintage is from the year man first walked on the Moon: I thought it would bring you luck. I hope you like it, because there are another six bottles waiting for you, for uncorking in celebration of your six marriages once you've arrived on Mars.

'For now, while we await the imminent docking of the boys' capsule, I invite you to share a drink with your fans, girls. You've brought out the crowds!'

Serena's face disappears, giving way to a live video stream showing a sunny park where thousands of people have gathered, so packed together you can't even see the green of the grass. At the end of the park a giant screen has been set up which shows the six of us sitting around the dining table, the cameras from the *Cupido* filming us at this very moment.

'A hundred thousand people have spent the night watching you in Singapore where it's nine in the morning, from the Hong Lim park, the place in this city-state dedicated to public demonstrations,' Serena's voice explains. 'The Singaporean authorities assure me it has never held this many people since it was first created!'

At these words, a roar comes from the park, seeming to rise all the way up to us through space: 'Fangfang! Fangfang! Fangfang!'

Blushing all the way to her ears, the Singaporean gestures two V's for victory with her hands, which are immediately reproduced on the giant screen in Hong Lim Park.

The video feed from Singapore disappears, to be replaced by a large river set ablaze by the rising sun, temples and homes with very long shadows on both sides. A vast crowd of pilgrims in white trousers and saris hastening to the bank chanting prayers which include the same two syllables over and over: 'Sa-fia'.

'The sacred city of Varanasi, on the bank of the Ganges, 6:30 in the morning,' Serena tells us. 'Countless Indians have come to send good wishes to the one who wears their colours, dedicating offerings to her in the shades of Mars.'

And each pilgrim does indeed put a small craft of palm leaves down in the river, carrying red carnations, that sails off amid a constellation of others.

This mystical vision that seems to have come straight out of the mists of time fades like a dream, replaced by its counterpoint: a hypermodern highway, with buildings on either side bearing vast illuminated advertising hoardings. The traffic has been cut off, helicopters patrol the night sky, a multicoloured crowd waves Canadian flags printed with the red maple leaf.

'Dundas Square in Toronto, nine p.m.,' says Serena. 'It's evening in North America. We estimate that nearly two million Canadians have taken over this most famous place in the city and the surrounding streets for a party that's going to last all night . . . in your honour, Kelly!' At that moment, all the screens in Dundas Square stop broadcasting their respective advertisements to display Kelly's face, reproduced hundreds of times, over a declaration of love in maple-red letters: *Canada loves you, Kelly!*

In the craft where we are watching the scene, dumbfounded, Kelly lets out a few words that summarise what we're all feeling.

'I . . . I'm blown away . . .'

But the wide-screen has already passed on to another city. After the big buildings of glass and steel, these are elegant old facades on the embankments of a black river. A huge monumental wheel is turning slowly, lit up with thousands of bulbs flickering happily. In each pod, big groups of people are waving the Union Jack and singing at the tops of their lungs.

'In Europe the party has been in full swing for some time already,' says Serena. 'In London, for example, on the banks of the Thames, where it's two o'clock in the morning . . .'

The bulbs stop flickering to light up all at once, drawing a gigantic name in luminous letters that go right across the wheel: *Elizabeth*.

'. . . as in Berlin, at the foot of the Brandenburg Gate . . .' Serena continues, while the picture shows a monumental six-legged arch topped by statues of horses drawing a chariot.

Impressive speakers are blaring out a techno remix of '*Cosmic Love*', while projectors in all colours sweep across a sea of wildly gyrating dancers. The camera zooms in on a group of girls having a wild time, jiggling about on a podium in the middle of the square – they've all done their hair in a crown of braids just like Kris's, and it's to Kris that they're addressing the heart shapes they're making with their hands while miming kisses.

'. . . or finally in Paris, on the Champs-Élysées.'

The six-legged gate gives way to another arch I know well: the Arc de Triomphe! Below it, the most beautiful avenue in the world is swamped with a whole river of partygoers who are spilling down into the Place de la Concorde. My heart gives a big *boom!* in my chest, though it isn't only my heart, it's also the French air squadron that pierces the wall of sound in the dark sky, writing my name in letters of smoke lit up by the projectors. The chords of *The Marseillaise* fill the space, while a huge banner unfolds under the Arc de Triomphe. It's a picture of me in an astronaut suit, taken no doubt during the press conference, hair radiating around my face like a sun, eyes looking towards the stars that fill the Paris sky.

I don't have time to recover my breath, or to wipe away the tears in the corners of my eyes.

Serena is already back on the screen, champagne glass in hand.

'And we in turn wish you a good trip too, girls,' she said. 'Allow me to raise a glass in your honour, in the name of all the inhabitants of Earth who are watching you at this moment. We drink to your success – and above all, to your loves!'

The wide-screen zooms out abruptly to show us a group shot of the programme's whole training team gathered together in the Cape Canaveral control room. They're all there, in the Genesis uniform: the men and women who have trained us for a year, who in some ways have replaced our absent parents to make us the young women we are today. Serena McBee, Director Gordon Lock and Roberto Salvatore, of course, but also:

Geronimo Blackbull, the funky Engineering instructor, with his long ponytail dyed crow's-wing black and his skin as wrinkled as an iguana's, somewhere between Native American chief and rocker granddad;

Odette Stuart-Smith, Planetology instructor, full of common sense and good principles, sporting her famous tri-focal glasses that look like two telescopes set on stalks;

Archibald Dragovic, Biology instructor as brilliant as he is eccentric, utterly devoted to science, who stubbornly refuses to take his lab coat off from over his Genesis uniform and whose shock of greyish hair full of static electricity looks like it's suffered from the mysterious experiments on radiation he conducts night and day in his laboratory;

and my own instructor, my own personal hero, Dr Arthur Montgomery, impeccable as ever with his tie, his thin white moustache neatly trimmed and his sharp side parting with not a hair out of place (not that he has much of it).

The only person missing is Sherman Fisher, the Communications instructor – Serena told us he was absent for the ceremony, presumably sick. But all the rest are there: the cream of NASA, the veterans kept back by Atlas to serve as our mentors, for us kids who just a year ago didn't know the first thing about Mars. They're properly good people, great examples of generosity who have devoted their lives to space and who have passed on their knowledge to allow us to make the flight, we who don't have a hundredth of their experience. Each of them is holding a champagne glass out towards us. And each of them in chorus takes up Serena's toast, in a single voice that sends waves of pride and gratitude into the very core of my bones.

'To your loves!'

10. Reverse Shot

Control room, Cape Canaveral Air Base
Sunday 2 July, 9:15pm

'Merceaugnac Cuvée Impériale?' splutters Roberto Salvatore, spitting his mouthful of wine back into his glass. 'And meanwhile you serve us common sparkling wine!'

'Calm yourself, my dear Roberto,' murmurs Serena McBee. 'We all know you're a classy gourmet, but do try to grin and bear it. There will be plenty of time for the rest of us to celebrate with champagne, when the profits from the broadcast start coming into the coffers. We've already confirmed more than a billion viewers for the lift-off, and that's just live at prime time, not counting the re-broadcasts that will at least double the stakes.'

She puts her glass down without having even moistened her lips, and gestures to the technical director and the five instructors to approach so as to avoid the attention of the engineers who are still in a carnival atmosphere, clinking glasses in the control room.

'The participants have only got sparkling wine too,' she whispers complicitly. 'How could they tell the difference, nobodies like them who've never tasted champagne before in their lives? I just had the vintage labels unstuck and put onto any old bottle – the real vintage wines are at this moment in the cellar of my home in Long Island, just outside New York City. We can empty them together, when Atlas pay us our bonuses at the end of the journey.'

'You're heartless,' says Director Gordon. 'When I think those young people have only a few months to live . . . You could at least have offered them real champagne.'

'I'm just a pragmatist. I won't have you judging me, talking as if butter wouldn't melt, Gordon Lock; you're just as mixed up in this business yourself, right up to your neck. All seven of us stand to gain from this. And to lose too. So pull yourself together, drink your sparkling wine, and smile. Actually, I think the moment might have come for you to give your little speech for the benefit of your team – it's vital that they suspect nothing, all the people who don't know about the Noah Report. We need them to fulfil their tasks obediently right up to the end. My production assistant will escort you to the rostrum.'

Without waiting for an answer, Serena McBee presses a manicured finger onto the silver brooch adorning the collar of her suit – it contains a disguised microphone. She murmurs a few words.

'*Serena to Samantha*. Come here.'

A few seconds later, a young woman in a grey jacket appears, with the Genesis logo on her chest, a badge saying *Samantha* pinned below it, a silver earpiece attached to her temple.

'Yes, madam? You called?'

'The technical director would like to say a few words. Do go with him, please.'

Gordon Lock parts his lips to reply, but no words come out. Then he turns on his heel, furious. He follows the assistant towards the rostrum, down the path bordered by screens behind which stand the ex-NASA men and women, decked out in the grey uniform of the Genesis programme. Everywhere there are pats on the back, congratulations, happy laughter: 'We've done it!'; 'We've put our passengers in orbit!'; 'It was long, it was difficult, but it was all worth it: Mars is finally within humanity's grasp!'

When Gordon Lock steps onto the rostrum, he is welcomed by thunderous applause, which he tries to sweep away with the back of his hand as though it were a cloud of midges. But in vain. The staff are too happy to notice how uncomfortable the director is; they can only see their hero, who knew how to negotiate with Atlas, who saved the NASA Mars programme.

The young woman with the earpiece presses a microphone into his hands. He takes it and makes an effort to recompose the smile he was wearing several hours earlier when he was standing in front of the cameras on the launch platform.

'Ladies and gentlemen, my dear colleagues,' he begins in a voice that is artificially cheerful. 'Today will go down in history. In less than an hour, the *Cupido* will be propelled towards Mars, fulfilling the launch phase of the Genesis programme –'

He doesn't have time to finish his sentence because he is once again buried under the applause. He has to wait a long minute before he can continue with his speech.

'The launch phase of the Genesis programme has been

successful,' he goes on, 'but our work continues. Our new employers, Atlas Capital, have closed the historic control centre in Houston to reassemble it all here, at Cape Canaveral. In the coming months, we will all be living in this very base, keeping watch night and day to be sure that all goes well aboard the craft, until the alignment with the orbit of Phobos. Our colleagues from McBee Productions will also be living in this building, to assemble the pictures from the on-board cameras in real time, so that they can be broadcast twenty-four hours a day on the Genesis channel. Atlas Capital is counting on us all, scientists and media professionals alike, to make this programme a huge success. I know you have all chosen your profession not for the money – this programme will hardly enrich any of us – but out of passion, the conviction that you are serving a noble cause. I also know that some of you were not altogether comfortable with the idea of a spectacle, with the seduction game, with the prospect of sending young people into space instead of duly qualified astronauts. But today, with the success of the lift-off and the new planetary craze, I think I can state that everybody's doubts have been swept away. Long live Mars! Long live space!'

The crowd takes up Gordon Lock's final words in a unanimous, thunderous cry: 'Long live Mars! Long live space!'

'Through our collaboration with McBee Productions, the population of Earth, who for too long have lost interest in space exploration, are once again fascinated just as they were back in the days when the first man walked on the Moon,' Director Lock adds. 'It required a little bit of production work to revive the general interest, but that in no way damages the programme's scientific ambitions, quite the contrary. The rights to broadcast worldwide, the contributions from the sponsors and the advertisers, the gifts pledged by the audiences: all this will generate revenue that allows Atlas to pay for the cost of the *Cupido* and the New Eden base that has already been left on Mars, and, what's more, to continue to finance the colonisation of the red planet in the years to come. That future has never looked so bright for all those of us who are such fervent defenders of space. This is the dawn of a new age of great human adventure, the start of a Martian civilisation. Our dream is coming true, my friends, and thanks to Atlas – what am I saying, thanks to you! – this dream of ours has become the dream of all humanity!'

This time it has reached its peak: cheers, bravos, whistling, the control room echoing like a theatre auditorium during a curtain call. Director Lock's rictus grin is so fixed that it looks sewn onto his face. He is sweating so copiously rings are forming in the armpits of his jacket.

Abruptly he undoes the collar of his shirt.

A button comes off and falls onto the rostrum, where it starts to roll.

Samantha, the assistant with the earpiece, brings her shoe down onto the button to still it. She holds a glass out to the speaker, who sucks down the contents in long draughts as though he hasn't drunk in days, as though his life depended on it. Then he steps down off the rostrum, to be welcomed like the messiah. People raise glasses to him, bring him bouquets of flowers, surround him with gazes that shine with admiration. Somehow or other, he manages to tear himself away from the tormenting congratulations and rejoins the small group of instructors assembled around Serena at the back of the control room.

'You knew just the right words, my dear,' says the executive producer. 'But it's not all over yet. We've still got our little debrief meeting, just for us, you remember . . . ?'

'Oh, I'd forgotten that,' murmurs Gordon Lock, visibly exhausted and in a hurry to get this damn day over with. 'It can't wait till tomorrow?'

'I'm afraid not. You see, Dr Montgomery received a message from the security services during your speech . . .'

'A message? What message?'

Serena McBee smiles, as usual. Beside her stands Arthur Montgomery, very upright in his Genesis jacket; he, however, is not smiling, true to form as the austere man he is.

'Ruben Rodriguez is waiting for us in the bunker,' he says, drily. 'He's cracked.'

11. Shot

'They're not messing us around, are they, Léonor?'

'I'd guess not, Kelly. But you know, I'm hardly a connoisseur.'

'You aren't a connoisseur? I thought in France you drank champagne in your baby bottles?'

'Really? And when you're bottle-feeding in Canada they give you beer, right?'

Kelly bursts out laughing.

'I wish!'

All six of us are floating in our undersuits, in the middle of the living room, holding hands to keep ourselves stable in the air. Only Kris and Liz have kept their hair tied, a crown of braids for one and a bun for the other. Fangfang's and Safia's burst out around their faces like corollas of black flowers. Kelly's make me think of a sun, the rays of blonde locks pointing in every direction. I tell myself that would create an amazing result with the 'watercolour' function of my big digital drawing tablet – I can't help it, I was born with digital paintbrushes instead of eyes. I'm in a hurry for the artificial gravity to come into force, so I can unpack my materials at last and get to work!

'It just doesn't seem like very much,' says Kelly, taking a small mouthful through the straw, before passing the bottle on to Kris for a second round. 'One bottle for six, that's not a lot. And when I think there were meant to be seven of us . . .'

'Seven?' asks Kris, taking the bottle carefully.

'Sure. There are seven Love Nests, in that base of theirs, in New Eden.'

Fangfang gives one of her usual little coughs, to indicate that she has a correction to make.

'I should remind you that the seventh habitat is only for use in emergencies, in case of technical failure of one of the other six. If all goes well, we'll never set foot in it.'

But Kelly is too busy watching the level of champagne in the bottle to pay too much attention to the Singaporean.

'Hey, go easy on the fizz!' she calls out to Safia. 'You're not eighteen for another eight months. There's no point getting yourself wasted just so you can be sure to get the last mouthful. After all, we all know we're going to be married within the year, isn't that right, girls?'

Wild laughter.

Contentment.

Trust.

I don't know whether it's the champagne or the weightlessness, but I've never felt as close to my teammates as I do now.

'You're all amazing, so beautiful,' murmurs Liz when everyone has recovered their breath. 'Listen, we need to remember this, really engrave it in our memories. We're

82

incredibly, extraordinarily lucky. Whatever happens, whatever the challenges that lie ahead, we need to keep supporting one another the way we do now. Till the very end. Till the orbit of Phobos. Till we touch down on Mars.'

Liz has always been the biggest team player. As the solitary one myself, I admire her at-all-costs team spirit, which maybe she gets from her years of classical dance, when she was part of a company. Ever since the very first day of training, she has always smoothed off the rough edges and bonded the group. Today I sense that she's expressing out loud a hope that we're all feeling: that we will remain a tightly knit group despite the competition. And at this moment it does seem possible, yes, really possible if each of us pulls her weight.

'The boys, the game, that whole thing, in a way it's just there to divide us,' adds Liz without worrying about the cameras. 'But what unites us today is stronger than what will try to separate us tomorrow. It's not the individual dancers who determine the quality of the performance, it's how well the whole corps de ballet gels. We're sisters, Mars sisters. Never let's forget it. *One for all . . .*'

I hold on to Kris's hand to my right, Safia's hand to my left. Each of us is smiling, even Kelly and Fangfang. And each of us responds in chorus, all speaking in English but with the accents of six countries.

'*. . . and all for one!*'

At that moment the puffy face of Roberto Salvatore appears on the wide-screen.

'Announcement for all the girls and boys,' he says. 'The *Cupido* is lined up for propulsion towards Mars on automatic pilot. Return to your rooms immediately and put your suits back on.'

'Oh no, Robbie, don't be mean!' sighs Kelly. 'Don't make us put those horrors back on!'

'It's protocol, Kelly. They'll help you to handle the acceleration from the nuclear booster, lying down, for as long as it takes to attain cruising speed. Then you can forget all about your suits for five months – all the way till it's time for you to go back down into the capsule for the drop-off onto Mars.'

I'm just fine.

Lying here in my suit, kept in place in bed by strips of velcro.

The doubts, the stresses, the questions, I'm leaving it all behind me. The room has changed to night-time lighting, subdued. My hair is floating above the pillow, all around my face, like a red cloud protecting me. Beyond the undulating curls, I can barely make out the dome of the camera that is fixed to the ceiling of my bed, directly beneath the mattress where Kris is stretched out now. It doesn't bother me. It's part of the furniture, that's all. You just have to not think too much about what's behind it, the whirlwind of TV studios, the presenters, the adverts, the families of spectators, in all those countries, those whole continents – that amazing show that we'll be the only people in humanity not to watch, we twelve participants, because we're its stars.

I take a deep breath, and close my eyes.

The softness of the suit pressing slightly against my back is the only sign that we are gradually accelerating, much more pleasant here than in the launcher.

In space, there is no atmosphere to cause friction with the craft.

In space, there is no air to relay the vibrations of the nuclear booster.

And so I sink into the depths of the cosmos and of sleep,

discreetly,

silently,

under the delicious illusion that nobody, on Earth, can see me.

12. Reverse Shot

Fallout Bunker, Cape Canaveral Air Base
Sunday 2 July, 11:05pm

The man with the shark's tooth is sitting on a metal chair, against the concrete wall of a circular, windowless room, lit by halogen spotlights at maximum intensity. The light that falls on him, white and surgical, leaves shadows that seem to hollow out his unshaven cheeks; it glints on the metal cuffs that connect his hands, which rest on his knees, and attach his ankles to the legs of the chair.

In front of him is a large circular table around which seven people are sitting: the five instructors from the Genesis programme, and Gordon Lock, presided over by Serena McBee on a large black leather chair with a padded backrest. There is a digital wall facing them, a gigantic screen that stretches from floor to ceiling, divided into a grid of multiple windows showing images from the cameras on board the *Cupido*. At this moment, each room is still and silent, even including the two chambers where the girls and boys are dozing. Only the central window shows a different picture: the recording of the lift-off ceremony. It progresses in sequence – the speech by the technical director, the solemn confirmation of the twelve contestants, the indescribable bustle just before the firing off.

The central screen zooms in on this last sequence. Among the journalists attempting to hold the girls back to ask them one last question, a single silhouette stands out: there can be no doubt, it's the same blue Hawaiian shirt worn by the prisoner seated on the chair, collar gaping open, face distorted in a silent scream – there's no doubt it's his.

'Freeze it on his image!' says Serena McBee, pressing a button on the small command panel set into the round table just in front of her armchair.

The central window immediately freezes on the large open mouth of the man with the shark's tooth, two steps away from the last girl, the astronaut girl with the red hair.

'It's late, Ruben, it's been a long day and we're all tired,' says Serena, articulating each syllable carefully as though speaking to a child. 'We only want one thing: to get out of this damp bunker and go to bed. So for the last time, what did you say to that girl? Did you say anything to her about the Noah Report?'

'I didn't say anything, Serena, I swear it! The security guards took me away before I was able to get two words out. They must've taken me for a madman. I spent the day in a cell, until I was able to convince them to notify Dr Montgomery. I told them I needed some kind of pill to calm me down. And here I am in the bunker, on time for our debrief meeting. Are you going to release me, finally?'

'Not so fast, my dear Ruben. I still can't understand what could have got into you. You were supposed to prepare the two mongrels, Louve and Warden, just giving them a sedative so they wouldn't be making a racket the whole lift-off, and then you were to stay behind obediently at your animal store to wait for events to proceed. You aren't made for the stage like we are, not you, you're supposed to stay in the wings. So can you explain what you were doing on the launch platform? You wanted an autograph perhaps? Just as well you didn't go up among the journalists with your Genesis jacket on!'

The prisoner is quivering on his chair. His eyes sweep across the floor of the room, trying not to catch the seven judges' eyes.

'I . . . I don't know what came over me . . .' he stammers. 'It was just when I saw the youngsters all ready to go up into the rocket, on my little telly in the animal store, it was such a shock. I needed to come see them in the flesh. And there it was even worse. They looked so happy to be leaving, not knowing they were heading off for death! They had such hope in their eyes, such expectations!'

Serena gives a long sigh.

She adjusts the small gold signet ring adorning the little finger of her left hand; a coat of arms engraved on the face; a hexagonal crest like a honeycomb, enclosing a bee.

'We have great expectations too, Ruben,' she says. 'We too have been nurturing great hopes. But you very nearly disappointed them. You very nearly ruined everything. And I really thought that we could trust you . . .'

'You can!' cries Ruben, looking up suddenly.

For the first time, he looks his interlocutor in the eye, a nervous tic making his eyelids tremble.

'It was just a moment of weakness. It won't happen again!' he promises. 'I haven't said anything about what I know to the security guards, nothing at all. I haven't talked to my wife about it, she doesn't know a thing, you're not at any risk from me.'

But Serena shakes her head sadly.

'I do wish I could believe you, my unfortunate friend. But my experience as a psychiatrist has taught me that men always commit the same mistakes, over and over. If you've cracked once, I fear you will crack again, like poor Sherman Fisher.'

At these words, Ruben literally collapses on his chair. He's no longer a strapping young man, but a little boy. A little rascal who's done something really stupid, and who's trying to avoid the punishment that he knows is inevitable.

'It's not fair,' he sobs. 'The only thing I wanted was to go on quietly doing my job . . . To keep looking after the animals . . . I never asked to be taken into your confidence . . .'

'None of us asked for that,' replies Serena calmly. 'But that's the way it is. Fortune has required that there be nine people sharing this secret: Gordon Lock, the technical director; myself, the executive producer; the instructors Roberto Salvatore, Geronimo Blackbull, Odette Stuart-Smith, Archibald Dragovic, Arthur Montgomery, Sherman Fisher; and finally you, Ruben Rodriguez, who dealt with NASA's animal store before the buyout and now works for Atlas like the rest of us. We are the only operatives aware of the Noah Report, the viability study demonstrating the flaws in the Martian habitats. Nobody but us in the whole Cape Canaveral air base knows that the six pairs of lizards, rats and cockroaches sent secretly to Mars by NASA in the seventh habitat, during the last transfer, all died suddenly after nine months. The Love Nests are really Death Nests, quite incapable of sustaining life. It's a fact that only we know, us and those in charge at Atlas who've decided to launch the programme anyway, bearing in mind the billions they'd already invested. Neither the engineers working under Director Lock nor the editorial team from my own production company suspect the truth. At this very moment, the former are working in the control room and the latter in the editing suite, never suspecting that the contestants are flying towards certain death.

'Of course, there's no question of leaving them to agonise in faulty equipment for days, possibly for months, under the eyes of the cameras – that would be bad for the morale of our audiences, and some of them might even get the idea of asking Atlas to return the money to invest it in some cause or other; no, we'll be staging a *tragic event*, nice and clean, absolving Atlas of any responsibility, to eliminate the twelve participants in one go shortly after their landing on Mars. The money collected over the course of the journey will allow Atlas easily to recover costs and present an excellent profit for the shareholders. Not to mention the very nice bonus our employer has promised us: half on arrival on Mars, in exchange for our discretion; the other half after the *tragic event*, in exchange for our crocodile tears. Remember the oath that we took, we allies of silence, right here in this bunker more than a year ago: words are silver . . .'

'. . . but silence is golden!' The five instructors take up her words in chorus, like a mantra.

Serena McBee brings her hands together on the table, a worried expression on her face, which in her case translates into a minuscule crease on her botoxed forehead.

'And that silence, Ruben, you have broken – or at least you've attempted to, like Sherman Fisher did before you. Just imagine what would happen if the world learned that Atlas had launched a mission to Mars in the certainty that all its passengers would die on arrival! An accident, yes, those things can happen, the history of space conquest is punctuated with them and no one will hold it against Atlas: NASA did survive the *Challenger* space shuttle explosion in 1986, then the *Columbia* in 2003. But a premeditated murder . . . Public opinion would never forgive that. Just imagine the media scandal, the trial for murder, the rest of our lives spent behind bars! Come, come, you've really disappointed us, my friend. You've really disappointed *me*. When I think that I personally vouched for you to Atlas, that I told them you'd be able to cope even though you were younger and less battle-hardened than the other allies of silence . . . Today your very existence puts us all in danger.'

Ruben starts to tremble all over; his handcuffs clink against each other, like castanets.

'I never wanted to break the oath,' he groans. 'I've worn it against my skin for months. Look!'

He puffs his chest up towards the spotlights. Through his half-torn collar, under the thin black leather strap holding the shark's tooth, there shines a chain that comes down to between his pecs, where a golden pendant is hanging, shaped like a military ID tag. Seven capital letters are engraved on the metal surface, making up the word SILENCE.

'I made this tag to remind myself of my promise whenever I'm shaving in the morning, in the bathroom mirror,' he says. 'To remind me that *silence is golden*. For over a year, it's been

91

my sole obsession: *keeping quiet*. Does a single brief second of weakness erase all those efforts? Don't make me suffer the same fate as Sherman, I beg you . . . I'm the father of a little girl . . . And who'll take care of the residents of the animal store if I'm not there to keep that going?'

Sweat is pouring down Ruben's cheeks, droplets forming at the end of the hair on his chin, sliding down the shark's tooth and the military tag. His moist eyes blink frantically in the spotlights that are half blinding him.

'Tsk, enough of this childish behaviour,' Serena scolds him. 'Your bugs, your guinea pigs and your lab rats will all get along just fine without you, you can be sure of that. Your wife and her kid too. As for your flashy trinkets, which I do find of rather doubtful taste, you can put the hardware away. We do try to discourage that kind of thing in responsible adults. You've brought harm to all seven of us. It seems right to me that all seven of us should vote to decide your fate. For me, I think I've already been quite clear what I think. You could have changed your destiny as a poor second-generation Cuban immigrant, Ruben Rodriguez. You could have become immensely rich, instead of wasting away in your pathetic animal store. You could have brought happiness to your family with the wave of a magic wand, if only you'd kept to your place. But you weren't up to it. It's with the greatest sadness that I vote for your death. You must be in no doubt about that. You next, Roberto.'

The Navigation instructor clears his throat, sending a shockwave through his double chin.

'He has broken the oath. He's a traitor. He deserves to die.'

Ruben opens his mouth to reply, but it's already Geronimo Blackbull's turn to speak.

'Death.' The Engineering instructor strikes, his voice tobacco-coarsened and gravelly.

'Death,' adds Archibald Dragovic at once.

The Biology instructor's eyes seem to be moving in two different directions, his hair quivering under the waves of barely suppressed laughter that shake his white shirt, as though he were finding the whole thing thrilling.

'Just look at him,' he murmurs. 'It's like he's in the electric chair!'

Ruben is indeed trembling so hard that the vibrations of his body are being passed through the chair, whose legs are jolting about on the concrete floor. He turns desperately to look at Odette Stuart-Smith, the Planetology instructor, dressed in a beige polo-neck that comes right up to her chin, over which gleams a small silver crucifix.

'Odette!' he begs her. 'You were Sherman Fisher's neighbour and his friend. You're a real woman with a real heart, I know you are, a woman of faith! Not a cold robot like Serena, not a psychopath like old Dragovic who wiped out half my animal store with his radioactive experiments – save me, for the love of God!'

It's a waste of effort. Ruben struggles to meet Odette's eyes to discern a glimmer of compassion there, but he can't do it: the lenses of her glasses are too thick, submerging the iris and pupil under an impenetrable dull grey film.

'Do not take the Lord's name in vain, it's not right,' she says in her high-pitched voice. 'And besides, one must take responsibility for one's actions. I vote for death. But you can be sure I'll pray for you, Ruben, just like I prayed for Sherman.'

Trying to ignore Dragovic's sniggering, the unfortunate Ruben addresses Dr Montgomery in a heartrending cry.

'Have pity, doctor! You take care of men, I take care of animals – we both know the value of life, you and I!'

Arthur Montgomery looks at him without blinking, his steely blue gaze betraying no hint of emotion. His snowy moustache barely rises when he speaks the sentence.

'Death.'

Ruben cracks.

He starts yelling at the top of his lungs, tearing his throat.

'Help! Help me! Help me!'

Her hands placed delicately over her ears to protect herself from the shouts without messing up her bob, Serena contents herself with waiting for the prisoner to wear himself out.

'You can spare our eardrums and your vocal chords,' she says at last. 'The allies of silence have chosen the most silent place in Cape Canaveral for their HQ. You know as well as I do that here in this fallout bunker, buried twelve metres below the launch base, nobody will hear your screaming.'

She rubs her long, manicured hands, making her bracelets jangle.

'Well. It seems that an absolute majority has emerged quite clearly. But at the risk of disappointing the big kid that Archibald has somehow managed to remain, I fear the electric chair is not an option. We will need to choose some less spectacular method. Dr Montgomery could for instance force on you the dose of sedative you demanded, Ruben. He could give you a little injection – you know, like the ones you give your sickly animals at the end of their lives, it's not too bad at all. But for such an important decision, we do require unanimity, do we not?'

By way of an answer, the prisoner gives out a pitiful wail – his voice cracking, he cannot articulate a single word.

Serena now turns to Gordon Lock, glistening with sweat more than ever.

'Well then, my dear, you are the last one to vote. What is your verdict? Didn't you call me heartless just a few hours ago? The time has come for you to show your nobility of spirit. It's entirely up to you to let our friend Ruben here go. If you're ready to take the risk, of course.'

Gordon Lock tenses the muscles of his square jaw, as though he were trying to crush his own teeth. Finally, a barely audible wheeze escapes his lips.

'Excuse me?' said Serena, beaming as usual. 'We couldn't quite catch that.'

'Death,' repeats Gordon Lock, grimacing.

13. Shot

D +18 h 05 mins.
[1st week]

Total silence.

I'm floating.

In space.

I'm curled in on myself like the foetus in the Genesis logo, with no helmet and no suit, dressed only in the black undersuit as thin as a second skin.

There's no longer a capsule or a spacecraft, there's no more game or programme.

There's just the stars that turn slowly about me.

Or to be more precise, I am the one turning about myself, seeming to be inhaled by all of space. In front of me a small blue ball is hiding the sun. Is that Earth? I squint my eyes behind my hair, which is given a life of its own by the weightlessness, trying to make out the outlines of the continents, the shapes of the oceans.

It's too far . . .

It's too brief . . .

Already my feet are tipping over my head and I find myself facing the opposite way, facing a second ball diametrically opposite the first, just as small and isolated in the midst of the void.

A red ball.

Mars.

No continents here, no oceans. Just the red flats of the plains, the red shadows of the mountains, the red fault-lines of the canyons that tear across the planet like badly healed scars.

I turn.

The Earth. Slightly smaller. Slightly more distant.

I turn.

Mars. Slightly larger. Slightly closer.

I turn.

The Earth.

I turn.

Mars.

I turn.

An ocean of fire! There, behind the Earth, the sun has risen. Its rays burst like arrows through the void, piercing right through me. My undersuit catches fire as readily as a cigarette paper. The smoke gets into my nostrils and my lungs, suffocating me. I can feel my skin baking, covering in blisters that pop one after another, sizzling . . .

I open my eyelids abruptly, but I can see nothing . . .

– the blaze of the sun is still in my eyes!

I feel my chest rising, but I'm unable to move . . .

– the smell of burning is still in my nostrils!

It was just a nightmare, another one: a nightmare of smoke and flames no different from the ones I used to have every night on Earth . . .

– the sizzling of the blisters is still on my skin!

I sit bolt upright.

The outlines of our space room appear suddenly in the gloom; the smell of recycled air, vaguely resembling the smell of plastic in a new car, swallows up the smoke; the feeling of my long hair weighing heavily on my shoulders tells me that gravity has been restored to the craft; but my skin is still crackling beneath my undersuit. In a panic, I start ripping off the velcro strips that are holding me in bed, unzipping my suit, before realising that the crackling isn't coming from my skin, but from one specific point on my right thigh.

What is that?

I slide my hand into the all-purpose pocket in the suit. My fingers find an object that is vibrating intermittently, transmitting silent waves through my whole body.

It's the phone belonging to Shark's-Tooth, the shameless journalist who collared me on the launch platform just before lift-off. It's buzzing obstinately, in silent mode, otherwise it would have woken the other girls who are still sleeping soundly in their bunks.

I begin to move to take it out of my suit.

But I stop at the last moment, hand still in my pocket, elbow drawn back – my eyes fixed on the camera above my bunk, filming twenty-four / seven.

I don't want the whole world to think I'm a thief, even if it's true. It doesn't fit the space heroine image I want them to have of me. And besides, personal communication equipment is strictly forbidden by the regulations.

I stretch back out slowly, I yawn to loosen my jaw and manage to pull the cover over my head with a grunt, pretending to go back to sleep.

Nicely curled up under the cover, I finally remove the phone from the all-purpose pocket. It's a Karmaphone, classic model. The screen lights up my little cashmere cave. *Bzzz!* A message appears in digital letters:

IT'S TIME! REPEAT ALARM IN 2 MINUTES OR CANCEL?

It's morning in America, 7:35 a.m. according to the little clock at the top of the phone screen. The beginning of a new day. I'm seized by a vague sense of guilt. Is poor Shark's-Tooth going to have an unexpected lie-in thanks to me? Is he going to get an earful from his boss for showing up late to the newsroom? But he must already have realised he's lost the phone he uses as an alarm clock . . . And besides, he's a pirate, he isn't answerable to anyone!

I press cancel.

The telephone stops vibrating. The alarm message disappears, to be replaced by the telephone's welcome screen.

Mechanically I run my finger over the *unlock* icon.

Password? the phone asks me.

With my fingertips I type: *WALK THE PLANK*.

Bzzz! – the screen goes red and announces: *Incorrect password*. Three attempts left before the device will be locked.

Let's see.

I type out another password, just for a laugh: *PIECES OF EIGHT*.

Bzzz! Incorrect password. Two attempts left before the device will be locked.

Well, Shark's-Tooth, what could you have chosen as your password? I turn the phone around in my hands. On the back, it's protected by a plastic casing with a picture of a huge white shark with its great mouth open, rising up towards the surface of the sea where a tiny bather is swimming oblivious to the danger. I recognise the poster from *Jaws*, an old movie I watched at the hostel for young workers and which scared the crap out of me.

Matching pendant and cellphone case: you might say my corsair has something of an obsession with sharks . . .

So I give it a try: *SHARK*.

Bzzz! Incorrect password. Final attempt before the device will be locked.

I'm now completely taken by this game.

It's like a treasure hunt – me, the fearsome buccaneer Léo the Red, who lives hidden away in her marine grotto, whose silhouette in leopard-skin makes sailors of the seven seas tremble, I *must* find the booty that Shark's-Tooth and his gang of ruffians have buried on a mysterious island.

I *must* find the password!

Excited by this outlandish scenario, I close my eyes and focus on all the facts I have stored in my brain.

The scene of our departure is reassembled in my mind, the way things do when I start to draw. It all comes back to me: the horde of journalists, the sound booms bristling like spears, the mics held out like fists – and in the middle of it all, that man who threw himself at me.

I force myself to zoom further into my memories. I see the guy's tired face again, his eyes red like embers, the shark's tooth hanging at his neck, the completely crumpled Hawaiian shirt. What was it he yelled in my ears just at the moment he threw himself at me? '*Wait . . . !*' – yes, that was it, that's all he had time to say, no doubt to try and extract a last-minute confession from me before the security guards pulled him off me, tearing his shirt.

Close-up of the button popping off, of the collar open over his chest.

There was something that glinted in the hollow of his breastbone, between his pecs – something gold . . . a fake military ID tag . . . a dog-tag like some men wear to try to make themselves seem adventurous. I hadn't registered the kind of tacky trinket till just now, there were so many other things taking up all my attention; but I can see it again perfectly, in the calm deep down in my heart: a gold tag, engraved with seven letters that spell out the word SILENCE. That's just how my memory works, like a camera that captures everything about a moment, even if I don't remember the details till later.

SILENCE . . . Funny word for a dog-tag; they're normally used for putting your name and blood type, stuff like that. But it's kind of poetic, now I think about it. That's going to add something substantial to the film I'm making about Shark's-Tooth, the lone adventurer who has taken a vow of silence, whose fearsome silhouette splits the oceans at the bow of his ship that sails under the black flag. I've always been keen on silence myself, the faithful friend that accompanies my thoughts when I wake up before dawn, the shadow that follows the stealthy tip of my stylus when I'm drawing alone on my big drawing tablet (an old model I bought on sale with my wages from the factory; the most precious thing I own). Silence doesn't lie, it's purer and truer than most words. *And what if that's it, the password?* It would be ironic, requiring silence to make a voice-carrying device speak!

I use up my final chance, with the tips of my fingers: SILENCE. The screen turns green with a little *beep* of approval.

Nicely done! Between Captain Shark's-Tooth and Léo the Red there's got to be some kind of telepathy going on! Who knows, maybe he's my soulmate, not one of the six landlubbers currently sleeping soundly in the *Cupido*'s other wing.

As expected, the network gauge is on zero.

The icons line up on the screen: weather, music, gallery . . .

Weather – no, I don't need this app to tell me it's not a good idea to leave the craft without a pressurisation suit . . .

Music – no, not yet time to be waking the girls up; even if there's no day or night in space, wake-up time on board is set to the east coast, to begin at eight a.m., the time of high ratings when Americans are watching TV while gulping down a coffee before heading out to work . . .

Gallery – well, why not? I'm curious to see what my soulmate's life looks like. *May I, captain? After all, if the dreadful Léo the Red and the no less dreadful Shark's-Tooth are made to be together, they should have no secrets from each other, right . . . ?*

I touch the gallery icon.

A mosaic of miniature photos unspools onto the screen. I touch the first.

The man who appears in the photo is quite different from the one I met on the launch platform, who yanked my wrist while trying to keep me back: close-shaven, smiling, relaxed, tanned arms under the same lagoon-blue Hawaiian shirt, but this time ironed. *If you'd smiled at me like that instead of unscrewing my arm, maybe I would have listened to you, Shark's-Tooth! Maybe I would even have answered!*

I slide my finger across the screen to move on to the next photo.

The handsome Shark's-Tooth is now seated at a seafront restaurant, with a winning smile, beside a young curvy blonde woman. Behind them, a stunning sunset is turning the beach pink. *So who might that be, Shark's-Tooth? Just an acquaintance? You've not mentioned her before . . . They do say pirates have a woman in every port . . . !*

Next photo: Shark's-Tooth and his 'acquaintance' again, but they're no longer at the restaurant. She is holding a bottle and he has a baby in his arms. A very rosy baby. A baby good enough to eat. Not the kind of baby you dump in the first trash can you find. They look so happy, all three of them, it's sickening. *Shark's-Tooth, you pirate! You've made your very own little cabin-boy behind my back! It's all over between us!*

I turn off the phone. All this may be just a game, but I'd rather remember Shark's-Tooth as a fearsome pirate, not a contented father. The sight of that blossoming family makes me a little queasy. Why? Because it's the opposite of my own experience on Earth? Or because I'm not sure that I'll even know happiness like that on Mars?

A piece of classical music suddenly bursts into the room. Taken by surprise, I quickly slip the phone under my mattress, vowing not to take it out again for a long time, and I pull the blanket down over my suit. The volume of the music coming out of the speakers in the ceiling increases, while the lighting gradually comes up. All around me, the girls are stretching with a sigh.

The screens inset above each bed all come on simultaneously to reveal Serena, leaning back in her black leather padded armchair. Today she's wearing a mauve blouse under her grey Genesis tailored jacket, with matching amethyst earrings – and her silver brooch in the shape of a bee, as always, her trademark.

'Good morning, dear contestants; good morning, viewers who are joining us once again on the Genesis channel!' she says into her microphone. 'I hope you've slept well!'

'Like princesses!' says Fangfang with her usual enthusiasm, from the upper bunk of the second bed.

With her velvet mask on her forehead and her hair carefully smoothed back in a night-time headband, she really does look like a waking princess. Practically the opposite of Kelly, who is struggling to sit up, weighed down by the space suit, groaning like a grumpy bear, her hair in a mess and chewing-gum on her lips – there's no way of knowing whether she fell asleep with last night's gum or if it's a new piece.

'So can we finally take off these instruments of torture?' she grumbles, looking down disgustedly at her outfit. 'I've had it with this constant aching!'

'Yes, Kelly,' answers Serena. 'The *Cupido* has been launched on its Earth–Mars trajectory at cruising speed. You will be able to remove your suits again and change into something more elegant, without the risk of your clothes flying up to the ceiling. From now on, and for the twenty-five weeks to come, the centrifuge will make the ship's wings turn at two rotations per minute, recreating an artificial gravity that is equivalent to the one awaiting you on Mars – that is to say, just over a third of terrestrial gravity.'

I undo my velcro strips, which are pointless now, and remove my suit. Even if my body does feel far lighter than it did on Earth, there is at least an up and a down, a floor and a ceiling.

'It's so amazing, this feeling!' cries Liz as she puts her foot onto the floor, from the lower bunk of the bed she shares with Fangfang. 'It's like I've lost all my extra kilos!'

'Stop kidding around,' yawns Kelly, as she feels around for her music player in order to wake up to the voice of Jimmy Giant. 'You don't *have* any extra kilos.'

'I do, right here, look . . .' says Liz, as she in turn extricates herself from her suit.

She contorts herself to try and pinch a little fat beneath her undersuit, without managing to, of course, as there's nothing there to pinch.

'That's enough chat, girls!' says Serena. 'I've been told your breakfast is awaiting you on the second floor. And in a few hours the first round of speed-dating will begin. This week, it's the girls who are issuing the invitations – ladies first. You will all have to get yourselves ready, as we will only be drawing lots at the last minute to see which lucky girl will have the honour of starting the game, in the privacy of the Visiting Room!'

'Do you know who you'll invite, if it's your name that gets chosen?'

It's Safia, our youngest, who asks the question that's on all of our lips, before sticking her nose back into her bowl of coffee decorated with the Coffeo logo. She won't turn eighteen till the night before we land on Mars and enter into matrimony – barely a grown-up and already married, with long years ahead of her to people her new world. But that's what lies in store for all six of us, isn't it?

We're gathered around the brushed-steel dining table, perched on tall stools screwed to the floor. The breakfast rations, all supplied by Eden Food, are spread out on the bar, each in its vacuum packaging stamped with the logo of one of the food processing group's brands: Happy Bear muesli, Krunchy Bit crackers, Mama's Secret spread. There are two jugs of water for diluting the powdered drinks, one hot one for the Daisy Farm milk and one cold one for the Liquid Sunshine orange juice. At the foot of the bar, Louve has her muzzle stuck into her own metal bowl painted in the Best Friend Forever dog-food colours. *Grandma's Recipe 'blanquette de veau'* flavour, one of the varieties in the French gastronomy range for luxury pooches, which I used to hand-ladle at the Eden Food France factory till it made me nauseous.

'Honestly, I don't know who I'll choose if I'm the one who has to go first,' says Fangfang, fiddling with the arm of her glasses. 'No idea at all.'

'Me neither,' admits Safia. 'That's why I asked.'

'The Russian Alexei's voice really did something to me,' says Kris, dreamily. 'He reminds me of the hero of a novel I once read, *The Prince of Ice*, set in the time of the tsars. It still gives me the shivers.'

'Don't get carried away,' smiles Liz. 'We haven't even seen

these boys' faces. But we could have been told a bit more about them. I don't know, a little descriptive card with a headshot, something like that. Right now we're flying blind, with nothing but their names.'

'And what names!' exclaims Kelly. There's seriously one called Mozart! *Mozart* – who'd give their kid a name like that! It actually makes me want to invite him, just to see if he's wearing a powdered wig and a beauty spot on his cheek. Also he's the one on the guys' side who's the Navigation Officer, who'll be steering their capsule down for the landing on Mars.'

She takes a bottle of Maple Gold syrup and drowns the cracker in a sticky flood, before turning to me.

'What about you, Léo? You're very quiet. Is there a particular one you'd be keen to see first?'

I put down my glass of orange juice. The painful image of Shark's-Tooth and his little family comes back to me. Whichever boy I choose, there'll never be dinner on the seashore, we'll never have a sunset over the ocean. The only beaches we'll look at will be those on Mars – dusty, reddish beaches, which haven't been caressed by a wave since the planet dried up millions of years ago.

I drive these pointless ideas out of my mind. Now isn't the moment to lose myself to nostalgia, but to unveil to my teammates and the viewers how I intend to conduct the game, rather than letting myself be led by it. A strategy I've been brewing for months.

'Serena said that the production team are going to draw lots for the first contestant, right?' I say. 'When my turn comes, I'm going to do the same thing: I'm going to draw lots for the name of the boy to invite. I'll do the same for my first six invitations, so as to avoid any kind of prejudice. And then I'll re-invite each participant in his turn, once every six goes. Until the end of the trip.'

'You've never told me about this,' says Kris, just a little reproachfully. 'And anyway, I don't really understand the principle. That means you'll invite each boy the exact same number of times?'

'That's right. No favouritism. The same time for each to talk, like candidates for a presidential election during a campaign. And at the end, when we line up with the orbit of Phobos before the final jump, I'll put together my final Heart List in full possession of the facts.'

'Are you kidding or what?' Kelly bursts out laughing. 'Is it just so the people watching think you're playing fair that you say that, or do you really believe in your system? The Determinator's led us to expect better. Even Fangfang couldn't have come up with something so *psychorigid*.'

'Not psychorigid: *rational*,' I correct her with a smile. 'We all have different ways of approaching the speed-dating. What I've just explained to you, that's my way. My way of keeping control: my own rules of the game.'

We spend the hours that follow taking possession of our little areas. We start off by sorting out the bedroom. On each side of each bunk bed there's a built-in wardrobe, divided in two: one side to store our huge white suit, the other for arranging the personal belongings we've brought with us from the Earth, in the hold of the capsule. Apart from my small sketching tablet and my big drawing tablet, mine consist of a few pairs of threadbare jeans and faded T-shirts from which I can still detect a faint odour of dog-food. It's a funny contrast with the brand-new Rosier clothes I've been handed in order to act as a living clothes-horse: wonders in silk, taffeta and satin in a whole range of blacks, and even a slit dress in red chiffon worthy of the Oscars, which the stylists dyed exactly the same colour as my hair – basically the kind of thing I'd never wear, not even if you put a gun to my head. I've also brought a complete make-up kit, with an even more sophisticated range of shades than I've got in the memory of my tablets – I'm sure you need some kind of PhD to know how to use them. And the highlight: a river of diamonds in a velvet case. No doubt the other girls would drool over it if they saw it, but since I never wear jewellery this intimidates me more than anything . . . I'm pretty sure the diamonds will be staying in their case, and it's just bad luck for the Rosier & Merceaugnac publicity team.

'The final touch!' says Kris on the other side of the bed.

Using a strip of velcro she attaches a pretty reproduction of an old painting to the back of her wardrobe door. It's a Virgin Mary with long blonde hair and light-coloured eyes, whose sweet and slightly dreamy expression isn't entirely unlike Kris's. On her knees she's holding a haloed child, who is smiling at her.

'She looks like you,' I say.

'Oh no, I don't think so,' says Kris modestly. 'I don't look anything like a Botticelli model. But I do like this picture a lot. It calms me. It inspires me.'

I nod. I'm not a believer like Kris is – I don't have firm ideas on the subject anyway – but I think I understand what she means. The painting is beautiful, full of meaning and hope for us, we who tomorrow will be Mars's first mothers.

Once we've put away our things, we take it in turns to use the bathroom, two at a time – one in the shower, the other sitting on the bench screwed to the floor facing the mirror. Fangfang and Liz go through first, and the other girls take advantage of the gym while we wait. It's completely fitted out with the most modern machines, arranged in a circle all around the room. Kris and I each mount one of the cycles screwed to the floor, while Safia sets about practising her yoga stretches on a mat.

'Hey, girls, take a look at this,' calls Kelly, earphones in her ears.

She's pulling on a cable attached to a hundred-kilo weight, as easily as if it weighed no more than a feather.

'Superwoman had better look out!'

'Not bad at all,' smiles Serena through the screen set above each fitness machine, and on the dashboard of each of the bikes. 'But I must remind our viewers that the weight labelled a hundred kilos only weighs ten in reality. In fact, the gravity generated by the centrifuge lessens each time we pass through a hatch to move up a level. The closer we get to the central pivot and the Visiting Room, the lighter we feel, as our viewers can see, as can you girls, in the diagram appearing on the screen . . .'

A cross-section of the *Cupido* appears on the screen, just as it did yesterday.

The image zooms in on one of the compartments, which pivots to ninety degrees to demonstrate to the viewers the effect of artificial gravity: the far end of the wing becomes the bottom, the place it connects to the rotor becomes the top.

'The layout of the rooms was planned to optimise your comfort,' comments Serena's voice, off-screen. 'Gravity reaches forty per cent in the room furthest from the axis of rotation, the bedroom on the first floor; that is the most pleasant place, the one closest to the terrestrial conditions you've just left. In the living room on the second floor, gravity is down to thirty per cent. On the third, in the bathroom, it falls to twenty per cent. Finally, on the fourth floor, in the gym room where you currently find yourselves, gravity is no more than ten per cent – an environment that is destabilising for you, no doubt, but perfect for training you to deal with the effects of weightlessness.'

The cross-sectional view continues up from the living quarters towards the central bubble, and pivots ninety degrees once again. Two small black silhouettes are floating in the bubble, a girl on the left and a boy on the right. You'd think they were a pair of fish in a fishbowl. A fishbowl split in two by a partition of impassable glass.

'Beyond the fourth floor of each of the compartments, you come into the bubble of the Visiting Room, where there is no gravity at all,' says Serena. 'Each interview with the boys will take place floating in the air. I should remind you that only your audience on Earth will have access to these amazing pictures, as with everything on the Genesis channel – you passengers will just have to try to imagine the words and looks being exchanged in the Visiting Room!'

The cross-sectional view vanishes from the screen, and Serena's beaming face reappears.

'Each day, one of you will fly up to meet a boy, like a pair of angels,' she says. 'Hard to imagine a more romantic encounter, isn't it?'

'Unless the angels get space sickness and puke up their Krunchy Bit biscuits and their Coffeo coffee and milk,' Kelly points out, popping her gum. 'At least with the partition it means we won't get our dates all disgusting . . .'

I'm the last of the girls to use the shower. I let Kris go ahead of me, then I help her do her complicated braids, then we're back in the bedroom. Honestly, I don't know how she does it, I'd never have the patience. A hurried shampoo, too much time with the dryer for my taste, that's all I've ever been able to do for my hair; it gets its revenge in its own way, with these rebellious curls that are impossible to straighten.

But today there's something different about them. Today, what little water we're entitled to is rolling down my thick red locks instead of soaking into them. The feeling on my skin is weird too. The drops are light as snowflakes and at the same time as hot as kisses – or at least the way I imagine them, as I've never let anybody kiss me. The explanation for this phenomenon is connected to the lack of weight, of course: at twenty per cent gravity, the water hardly weighs a thing, it tends to settle rather than flow. You need to brush it along to make it move towards the drain in the shower compartment, behind which it will be recycled throughout the whole flight.

While my hands are rubbing my body, I can't help think

112

of the hands of the boy who in December will be following the same route. It won't be a half-imaginary character like Shark's-Tooth, but a real boy of flesh and blood, with real desires and real revulsions.

(Won't your fiancé be disappointed by this body that he will have chosen without ever having been able to touch it, like one of those things people buy on the internet never having seen them in reality . . . ?)

I sponge down my legs, muscly from all the nights of running in the empty streets around the hostel for young workers, when I couldn't get back to sleep after my nth blazing nightmare.

(There's no after-sales service on Mars, no 'satisfaction or your money back' guarantee . . .)

I scrub my milk-white chest, the only part of my body where the freckles have forgotten to burst out.

(On Mars, there's no possibility of returning your purchase, even if the article you have chosen proves to have some hidden flaw . . .)

I shudder at the fateful moment when my fingers make it past my right shoulder. All at once, without warning, the sweetness gives way to utter horror. One centimetre earlier: skin as smooth as a polished pebble; one centimetre later: a wrinkly, misshapen texture, from the top of my shoulder blades down to the slope of my butt. My skin remembers the fire of which I have no memory myself, and yet which changed my life for ever. If I hadn't received third-degree burns, maybe my parents wouldn't have left me for dead in that trash can . . . Maybe I would have lived through my childhood and adolescence with them . . . Maybe I would even have loved them . . . I would never have sent in my application for the Genesis programme, and I would have . . .

(It's too late to rewrite the past now, Léonor.)

I'm suddenly aware of the small voice that's been hissing in my ear since I got into the shower – the same voice that shook me on the launch platform, that almost made me give up on the mission, that lies in wait for the briefest moment of doubt to try to get the upper hand.

It comes from that place on my back where I put my fingers. I seem to feel its forked tongue caressing my ear lobe.

(It's too late to think about who your parents were: you'll never meet them.)

(It's too late to weigh up the consequences of your application to the programme: you'll never be able to turn around.)

(You chose to leave, Léonor, and now it's too late for regrets.)

(It's too late!)

(It's too late!)

(It's too late!)

I give the shower door a kick and burst into the bathroom, the only room in all the living quarters spared by the cameras and the eyes of the viewers.

But not by the mirrors.

My reflection appears to me brutally in the circular glass that goes right around the room. Impossible to escape the image of my back, captured by the part of the mirror covering the store cupboard behind me and reflected in the one facing me above the sink.

The Salamander.

That's what I call the burn that almost killed me when I

was three years old, taking my epidermis, dermis and nerve endings. A whole part of my body that's become foreign to me. A parasite. It's shaped like a long scaly lizard made up of successive courses of skin grafts, bursting out over the right side of my backbone, the claws clinging on to my shoulder and my side. Its slightly purplish colour seems artificial, supernatural. Like the salamander of legend, it can live in fire without being killed by it. It's inexhaustible, it will never leave me, it will keep on hissing away at on the back of my neck until I draw my last breath, it . . .

'Léo! Léo! They've just announced the results of the draw, they've –'

The hatch in the floor of the bathroom comes up quickly to reveal Kris's head, the golden locks I helped to braid myself.

'– chosen Fangfang.'

Kris's face is frozen in a mask of astonishment, as a look of shock widens her beautiful blue eyes. I see myself reflected more cruelly there than in any mirror, as what I really am: an abomination.

Kris should never have seen me naked.

She had no right.

She's betrayed me.

'Léonor, your – your back . . .'

But I'm no longer Léonor. I'm the other me I've created within my inner world: Léo the Red, the savage, the bloodthirsty. Unable to control herself, she leaps onto the hatch while the words spew from her mouth like vomit.

'Get out! If you mention this to anyone, I'll kill you, I swear!'

14. Reverse Shot

'Have you seen that thing on her back? A real shame, for one who's such a looker!'

Roberto Salvatore gives a grimace of disgust.

He's sitting at the round table in the gloom, beside the programme instructors and Director Lock. The bunker's halogen spotlights are off. The only source of light is the digital wall at the back of the room, and its grid of images captured by the cameras on each level of the *Cupido*: on the left, the girls; on the right, the boys; in the middle, in the main window, is the Genesis channel as it appears to viewers, the only slight difference relating to the editing time – for now it's showing a static shot of the living room where the girls are gathered.

But in the bunker, it's the screen showing the bathroom that has everybody's attention.

The two-way mirror is filming everything that happens.

It is filming Léonor's nakedness.

It is filming the burn that stretches down her back.

118

It is filming her panicked reaction when she leaps onto the hatch and stamps it down over Kris's head.

Finally it films her collapsing onto the closed hatch, broken.

'Ugh!' goes Odette Stuart-Smith, pursing her lips. 'Just as well the Genesis channel doesn't show the pictures from the bathroom, so it remains suitable family viewing!'

'I think that would actually be a good idea – an uncensored adult version available with a subscription,' says Roberto sleazily, his large face lit up by the light from the digital screen. 'I'm sure there are plenty of people who'd be happy to pay to look at that!'

Gordon Lock cuts the conversation short before Odette Stuart-Smith has the chance to become more indignant, and turns toward Dr Montgomery.

'What does that girl have on her back?' he asks. 'A kind of leprosy? A vast birthmark?'

'I don't know . . .' answers the doctor, smoothing his thin moustache.

'What do you mean, you don't know? You're a doctor, and this girl was your pupil!'

'Indeed. I was charged with instilling the basics of medicine in her, not checking her vitals. I'm not the person who made the selection for the programme.'

The heavy reinforced door at the back of the room opens, letting in a burst of white, electric light.

'Serena McBee?' Gordon Lock calls out, blinking, dazzled. 'Is that you?'

'Of course it's me,' answers the psychiatrist. 'Along with the rest of you, I'm the only person with access to this NASA-era fallout bunker. I've given my editing team upstairs all the instructions they need. In any case, most of the camera movements are programmed in advance, taking account of the communication latency that will be growing over the course of the journey: thanks to a facial recognition software, our machines can zoom in automatically on faces to capture the participants' emotions in close-up. So I can join you here no problem, to watch the first speed-dating session, which will begin in a few minutes. I'll be providing a voiceover commentary for the young lovebirds from here in the bunker.'

She closes the door and sits down in her large padded leather armchair, facing the small control panel located alongside her mic.

'What I mean is, you're the person behind this, aren't you?' Director Lock continues. 'You're the one who confirmed the final selection of the girls? You must have seen them all naked, you can't deny it! You planned the presence of this girl with the monstrous scar in the spacecraft, and you knew exactly what you were doing!'

Serena McBee looks up at the screen showing the girls' bathroom, where Léonor's hurled-down body lies. The girl's magnificent red hair, still damp, is snaking over the tiling like algae. Her face is out of view, flattened against the floor. Her body is no longer a body, it's a rock bearing down with all its weight on the hatch. The curves of her hip crushing her leg, of her shoulder crushing her arm, both dotted with freckles. As for the burn itself, it looks like a patch of purple lichen, like the ones often seen colonising rocks on the seashore.

'Monstrous?' says Serena McBee pensively. 'Monstrosity is in the eye of the beholder.'

'Spare us your psychological gobbledegook,' Gordon Lock interrupts her. 'I'm ready to bet that a hell of a lot of monstrosity will be in the eyes of the boys when they discover what's hidden beneath this girl's dress. Are you really such a sadist? I feel sorry for this girl, and I feel sorry for the poor boy who chooses her. The passengers are destined to die soon enough – I know it, you know it, we all know it – but why insist on ruining what little life they have left? It's inhuman. It's counter-productive. You're going to sicken the viewers, and when they stop watching the programme, oh, you'll be a real winner then, won't you?'

'Yet again you have failed to understand, my poor Gordon.'

'Excuse me?' splutters Director Lock.

'What's going to happen will be just the opposite. The viewers aren't going to be disgusted. On the contrary, they're going to be touched to the very heart. You see, humans are gregarious animals, compassion is built into their genetic code. It's a fundamental psychological gift – I call it the herd instinct. Though of course they do not hesitate to sacrifice their fellow man when their own interests are at stake. Our unfortunate Sherman and Ruben have paid the price, those who stood between us and our fortunes, those who threatened to get us put in prison. The herd instinct didn't save them.'

Archibald Dragovic can't help smiling, while Roberto Salvatore recoils into his fat, Geronimo Blackbull fidgets nervously with his cigarette lighter, his nails yellowed by tobacco, and Odette Stuart-Smith squeezes the small crucifix hanging around her neck. As for Arthur Montgomery, he merely

121

fixes his blue-eyed stare on the middle of the table, and says nothing.

'Chin up!' says Serena now, clapping her hands like a schoolmistress trying to reawaken her class. 'There's really no reason to worry ourselves sick. I can confirm that most people, if they were in our situation, would indeed have reacted as we did. But in the comfort of their own living rooms or bedrooms, behind the screen? They can't help being moved by the ill luck of these poor deprived souls who are not in competition with them, who are no threat to them. And they can't help but send even more money for the Dowries, from which Atlas will of course be passing on a tidy percentage to us in our end-of-journey bonus.'

This thought relaxes the atmosphere at once. Geronimo Blackbull puts away his lighter and Odette Stuart-Smith lets her crucifix fall back onto her turtleneck.

'You're quite right, Serena,' she says. 'Just because someone defends himself when attacked, doesn't make him a bad person. If all people of goodwill turned the right cheek each time they were slapped on the left, how far would the world get then?'

'Nowhere, my dear Odette!' replies Serena. 'It wouldn't get anywhere! We're endowed with an instinct for self-preservation, which is a powerful counterbalance to the herd instinct. There's no shame in having it.'

'And as for us, even we can be touched by the passengers on the *Cupido*,' adds Roberto Salvatore. 'Now I think about it, we've actually done these nobodies a favour by sending them into space. It will be a brief experience, certainly, but so remarkable compared to the pathetic, dull existences they would have had on Earth.'

'Bravo, Roberto!' says Serena, encouragingly. 'You at least have understood me immediately, I'm pleased to see! Ever since we've known about the Noah Report, I've deliberately guided my choices towards these nobodies, as you say. For three reasons:

'The first is the one I have just explained to you: I'm counting on prompting sentimental tears like no one's ever cried before, so much that we'll need to instigate a disaster contingency plan to avoid a flood. Every one of the candidates I've chosen has a secret like Léonor's. A painful secret, which they'll do anything to hide from the others, but for which the viewers will pity them.

'The second reason is that with social misfits without any attachments, we won't have to worry about any legal proceedings from the families or any such nonsense when they disappear at the end of the journey – and so we won't have any compensation to shell out.

'And finally the third reason, well, you know this already . . . The *tragic event* that will put an end to the programme will look all the more natural for being caused by an unstable dropout. The relaxation sessions I carried out under hypnosis in Death Valley allowed me to identify which one of the twelve selected candidates had the most malleable mind. I used the opportunity to programme that one candidate mentally, so that they would depressurise the Love Nests once on Mars. It will be much more elegant than suffering agonies in defective habitats! All it will take will be a word from me and my creature will fall into a sonambular state, and carry out quite unconsciously what has been planned with mechanical

123

precision. In the eyes of the viewers, their act will look like an attack of sheer madness, like those school killings that so regularly make the headlines. Nobody will know that it was all painstakingly rehearsed during the training year, not even the future murderer who has retained no memory of this conditioning they received entirely under hypnosis!'

15. Shot

D +21 h 20 mins.
[1st week]

I get up slowly.

I do always get up eventually.

Each time I fall.

Each time somebody hurts me.

Each time the Salamander is just about to do away with me.

I pull on my knickers, my jeans, my T-shirt.

The girl in the mirror does the same.

This isn't the morning she's going to straighten her hair, put make-up around her eyes, play the seductress that she is not. She isn't the one fate has chosen today. But she can't stay where she is, in the bathroom. In a few moments, Fangfang will have to come through here to reach the Visiting Room. Best take the initiative.

I take a deep breath, and raise the hatch.

'There she is!'

I put my feet onto the rungs of the ladder, one after another, feeling all eyes trained on me, even Louve's.

All the girls are ready, dressed, made-up. I feel even more pathetic than ever in my shapeless old T-shirt.

'Girl, are you totally nuts or what?' splutters Kelly without bothering to spit out her chewing-gum.

She's wrapped in a pair of jeans so figure-hugging it looks like they've been sewn directly onto her long legs; a tiny red-checked short-sleeved blouse is knotted over her belly; a piercing glints in her stomach, and gigantic golden hoop earrings, matching her new lipstick, tremble on either side of her face each time she says a word.

'Have you seen what you did to Kris when you closed the hatch on her head? Have you? You've really got to be careful!'

My eyes wander towards the sofa.

Kris is lying there, supported by Safia and Liz. Under her beautiful braided locks, her pale forehead is studded with a bump, gleaming, swollen with violet blood. *An egg* . . . That's the first thought that comes to mind, though I know it's ludicrous: *the Salamander has laid an egg.*

A groan escapes my lips.

'Oh, Kris, Kris . . . !'

'She's been given some aspirin, an anti-inflammatory, whatever we could find in the pharmacy cabinet,' says Safia, who is enveloped in a saffron-coloured sari that makes her look even more like a precious doll than ever. 'She can barely stand up. We knocked on the hatch at least a hundred times to call you, but you didn't answer. You're the Medical Officer, Léonor. What are we supposed to do?'

Darling Safia, the only one not looking at me like I've got the plague, asking my advice.

What should I tell her?

Dr Montgomery's first aid course races through my mind, but in no logical order. *Electrocution, cardiac arrest, haemorrhaging . . .* and I remember all of it except what needs to be done in the event of a blow to the head. It takes years to train a doctor, and I thought I'd get through it in twelve short months, all because I swotted over the textbooks night and day, all because I was given the grand title of *Medical Officer* that I don't in the least deserve . . . In reality what counts isn't textbooks or titles. It's practice, experience, all those things I don't have, and which are the only way you can remember all the right things to do when you're faced with an unexpected emergency.

Perhaps if I touch Kris it'll come back to me?

I move towards the bed.

'Don't come near me!'

Kris looks daggers at me. I've never seen her eyes this colour. The sky-blue has turned to night-time. The pupils are dilated like an owl's.

'I swear I didn't mean to,' I breathe. 'If you knew how bad I feel . . .'

Kris bends her knees, raising her legs to block the way between me and her. The light blue silk dress that she put on in case she was chosen for the Visiting Room slips over her calves.

'I said don't come near me – what the hell is wrong with you? I don't need your help. You're sick! Just imagine if it's my turn tomorrow and Alexei sees me like this.'

These words in Kris's mouth tear at my heart. *Sick.* Is that what she thinks, that I'm sick, contagious? Is that what she's told the other girls and, through the cameras, the billions of viewers watching us at this moment? 'Don't get too close to Léonor, she's carrying the most dreadful sickness on her back, something really repulsive'?

A commotion shakes the whole cabin of the spacecraft.

It makes me think of thunder, but it's only a drum-roll. Serena's voice comes out of the speakers.

'What are you still doing in the living room, Fangfang? The speed-dating begins in five minutes!'

Fangfang is blinking, perhaps from nerves, perhaps because she sees less well having taken off her glasses to reveal the fake lashes she's stuck on specially for the occasion, along with a dark green bandage dress.

'But I've been ready here for hours!' she cries. 'It's just that Léonor was blocking access to the upper floors!'

'Now, now, we'll have no squabbling! Hurry up to the Visiting Room, unless you want to risk missing out on precious minutes of speed-dating. The viewers won't wait. The title sequence is about to begin: one, two, three – *go!*'

Just as Fangfang hurls herself onto the ladder, the wide-screen in the living room goes black.

Outer space. The cosmos sown with stars, with no beginning and no end, dizzying.

An instrumental version of '*Cosmic Love*' strikes up, violins and synths at top volume against a backdrop of swirling Milky Way. A pre-recorded voice, hoarse and portentous like on a trailer for a Hollywood movie, comes over the music: '*Six girls on one side . . .*'

The screen closes in on a computer-generated image representing the Cupido launched full-speed through the middle of the void. The camera passes through the metal wall and reveals a view of the girls' compartment – our compartment. It's peopled with two-dimensional silhouettes – our silhouettes – like paper characters cut out and stuck straight onto the décor. I recognise the photos that were taken of us during our training in Death Valley. I didn't know they would be used for the title sequence, which we haven't been shown till now. The name of each girl appears briefly in the titles over the images on the screen.

    Title: Fangfang, Singapore (Planetology)
    Title: Kelly, Canada (Navigation)
    Title: Safia, India (Communications)
    Title: Elizabeth, United Kingdom (Engineering)
    Title: Kirsten, Germany (Biology)
    Title: Léonor, France (Medicine)

The other girls seem hypnotised at the sight of their images on the screen. Their eyes are shining. Even Kris's. It sends a shiver down my spine, all those flattened silhouettes, frozen in their Genesis outfits. It's like we're ghosts. It's like we're dead.

Unable to stay in the living room a second longer, I raise the hatch in the floor, without anyone paying me the least bit of attention. Anyway Kris is so livid there's no way I could approach her. I jump onto the ladder that goes down to the bedroom. I need to huddle under my blanket. To curl up into a ball, far away from all this.

But at the bottom of the ladder the speakers are broadcasting the same deafening music.

Above the three beds, there are no more deer, no more dolphins, no more mountains: the screens are showing the same computer-generated image.

Impossible to escape the title sequence.

Impossible to look away at the moment when they're finally going to show the faces of the boys.

Voice off: 'Six boys on the other.'

A quick zoom out. The camera pulls out of the craft, circles round it, and re-enters the boys' chamber, which is identical to ours. There, too, the camera pans across six motionless silhouettes while the overlaid titles introduce their names.

Title: Tao, China (Engineering) – square-jawed; a thick neck with prominent muscles; powerful as a minotaur, all the way to the tips of his black hair that sticks up in a short crew cut.

Title: Alexei, Russia (Medicine) – a pair of blue eyes, the kind that turn heads; his hair is smooth, aristocratic blond; a Prince Charming smile, dazzling, full of self-control and confidence.

Title: Kenji, Japan (Communications) – hair sculpted with gel, across his forehead, and exploding in every direction like on a manga hero; behind the lattice of sharp locks, which fall down across his forehead like a mask, he looks lost.

Title: Mozart, Brazil (Navigation) – tanned cheeks and full lips; his black hair, lustrous and curled, moves in a way that is incredibly romantic; but beneath it, his eyes are hard as bullets.

Title: Samson, Nigeria (Biology) – his shaven head looks like a sculpture carved out of obsidian, the head of a sphinx or a pharaoh whose green eyes have something supernatural about them.

Title: Marcus, United States (Planetology) – brown hair, slightly tousled; *a line of ink snakes its way under his neck and disappears into the collar of his black T-shirt, immediately inflaming my artist's imagination*: what does that tattoo represent? an animal? a face? a word?; *and light grey eyes, silvery under his thick eyebrows, which plunge deep into my own and seem to challenge me*: 'It's just up to you to find out.'

And that's it, it's over.

No way to pause on one of the faces.

No way to rewind to see them again.

They've already gone, and the title sequence continues.

Voice (off): 'Six minutes to meet . . .'

Fade to black. The Visiting Room appears in static shot: a perfectly spherical room, with transparent walls, separated down the middle by a reinforced glass screen that stretches from floor to ceiling.

Voice (off): 'An eternity to love . . . !'

Zoom in towards the stars through the glass walls. The planet Mars appears from the depths of space, gradually growing.

I throw myself onto my bed, terrorised by this red, palpitating thing that's racing towards me through the three screens in the three corners of the room.

I want to close my eyes.

I can't do it.

The music gets dramatically louder, now overlaid with words.

Him: You sky-rocketed my life

Her: You taught me how to fly

131

Him: Higher than the clouds
Her: Higher than the stars
Both: Nothing can stop our cosmic love
Our cosmic love
Our co-o-osmic lo-o-o-ove!

Voice (off): 'The Genesis programme. When the most ambitious scientific programme meets the most thrilling speed-dating game . . .'

Morphing: three foetuses emerge at the heart of three Mars planets, forming three Genesis logos.

Instrumental climax.

Voice (off): '. . . you get to be the live witnesses to the most beautiful love story of all time!'

Fade to black.

But Serena did remind us: only the viewers on Earth can see the images that will follow. So the next six minutes belong to Fangfang, to the boy she has invited – and to all humanity, with the exception of the other ten passengers on the *Cupido*, the only human beings with no access to the Genesis channel.

All the screens go off at once.

ACT II

16. Genesis Channel

Monday 3 July, 11:00am

Fade in from black.

Static shot of the inside of a huge glass bubble, seven metres in diameter; beyond the spherical walls, the stars drift silently; at the top of the bubble, you can see the halo of the transmission dish, and its laser beam that sends information back towards Earth.

Title: *First session in the Visiting Room. Hostess: Fangfang, 19, Singapore, Planetology Officer (communication latency: 2 seconds)*

The left-hand hatch opens to the sound of a drum-roll.

Fangfang raises herself into the Visiting Room. In order to contain her hair in the zero gravity, she has tied it into an elegant bun brightened with a silver clip. She blinks – she's wearing contact lenses, which she isn't used to.

Suddenly the sound of a voice: *'Fangfang, welcome to the Visiting Room!'*

Fangfang gives a start. She looks around her, trying to identify where the voice is coming from.

Serena (off): *'It's me – Serena – speaking to you. You have the honour of starting the game, Fangfang. Be sure to close the hatch well behind you, so there aren't any indiscreet ears listening to what's said in the Visiting Room over the next six minutes.'*

Fangfang does as she's told. She turns the lever that seals the hatch from inside.

Then she flies up slowly, swimming over towards the transparent partition that divides the Visiting Room into two hemispheres.

Eventually her fingers find the smooth glass wall. She brings her two hands to rest on it. Delicately, as if afraid to break it.

Serena (off): *'You know almost nothing about the boys. And yet today you must invite the boy of your choice into the Visiting Room. So tell us, Fangfang, whom would you like to invite?'*

Fangfang: 'I would like to invite Tao.'

Serena answers with a slight two-second delay.

'A definite decision, no hesitation at all! Can you explain to us, to the viewers and to me, why you're so sure of yourself, and how you came to make your choice?'

Fangfang: 'China is the country that is culturally closest to Singapore. Cultural proximity is one of the most important predictive factors for a couple to succeed. I speak Chinese fluently, I can cook Chinese food, I have all the assets to make a Chinese man happy. Statistically, Tao is the one with whom there's the best chance of it working out.'

Serena (off): *'Bravo, Fangfang! I see you've studied the question very carefully! It's a very well thought-out choice. But in love, is it really possible to think everything out? Watch this space to find out, right away, with Tao!'*

Drum-roll.

The right-hand hatch now opens. Tao's crew cut appears first, then his head and his American football-player's shoulders. The pecs that stretch his white shirt, the neck that is too muscular for him to do up his top button, the endless legs in their black trousers: the body that emerges from the hatch is nearly two metres tall.

Close-up on Tao's broad face, which lights up with a smile when he sees Fangfang. Suddenly he seems younger, softer, full of innocence behind that impressive athletic build.

Serena (off): '*Fangfang, Planetology Officer; Tao, Engineering Officer; you have six minutes to introduce yourselves to each other, and at the same time to the viewers watching you, live, and who are burning with curiosity to hear your stories. Now I shall stop talking – it's your turn. Start the clock!*'

The dial of a stopwatch appears on the screen, marked from one to six. The countdown begins, the hand starting to make its way around the dial.

Tao rises into the air, his huge body gliding with the strange grace of a sperm whale across the sea bed.

'Hello,' he murmurs – his voice is surprisingly soft for his physique, almost shy. His English is marked by a heavy Chinese accent.

Fangfang: 'Hello.'

Tao: 'Thank you for inviting me.'

Fangfang: 'Not at all.'

Silence.

Alternating close-ups on the smiles of Fangfang and Tao, each as visibly embarrassed as the other.

Fangfang briskly takes the initiative with the conversation, suddenly launching into a speech that is clearly not improvised:

137

'I chose you because I'm the girl most able to make you happy. I speak Chinese. And I know how to cook Chinese food too.'

Tao: 'That's great!' He's delighted. 'But you know, we aren't allowed to speak any language but English during the whole programme, so the viewers can follow everything we say to each other. And I'm not sure we'll find the ingredients for Chinese food here, or on Mars.'

Fangfang replies quick as a flash, evidently ready to meet any objection. 'That's a merely material detail. The most important thing isn't that I can *actually* speak and cook Chinese, it's that I *potentially* speak and cook Chinese.'

Close-up on Tao's baffled face: 'Uh . . . Sorry, I'm not sure I've understood what you mean.'

Fangfang: 'What matters is cultural proximity, isn't it? It's the cultural baggage we carry with us, everything the two of us share without needing to express it.'

Tao: 'Um, really . . . ?'

Fangfang: 'Yes. It's statistical.'

Tao: 'Statistical . . . ?'

Fangfang: 'It's been proven, if you'd rather put it like that. And also . . . I like you.'

The Singaporean emphasises these final words with a skilfully rehearsed batting of her fake eyelashes. It seems to hit the target as Tao's cheeks flush slightly.

Fangfang: 'We're made to be together, us two. Actually, how many kids do you want? I think eight's a good number. It's a lucky number for you Chinese, isn't it? Eight, isn't that the number for prosperity?'

Tao opens his mouth, then closes it again. He folds and

unfolds his arms, as though suddenly embarrassed by his body. Only his legs don't move: they float beneath him, quite still.

Fangfang makes the most of the silence to throw him another flirtatious glance, doing her seductress number: 'You have an amazing physique, if you don't mind my saying. How did you end up with muscles like that?'

Tao: 'I used to work in a travelling circus. The circus where my parents left me when I was a little boy, because they didn't have any way to feed me or to raise me out in the village. I became an acrobat. I was the one who balanced on one hand at the top of the ladders. I was the one who carried the weight of the whole human pyramid on his shoulders. Yes, I was all that and much more, before . . .'

Fangfang: 'Before the Genesis programme, you mean?'

Tao doesn't answer, but Fangfang is too over-excited to notice. She just keeps going.

'I grew up without my parents too. They died in a plane crash when I was really small. I was raised by Singapore as a ward of the state. They immediately spotted my intellectual potential, and placed me in a school for the gifted. Just before enrolling for the Genesis programme, I was doing a PhD in pure mathematics. Four years ahead of the other students, as I skipped four years . . . So anyway, with your physical genes and my mental ones, we're going to produce remarkable babies, the most beautiful babies on Mars!'

Fangfang seems to be on a roll, but all of a sudden the bell announces the end of the interview.

Serena (off): '*Time's up! Fangfang, Tao, have you been seduced by the charms of your interlocutor? Sssshh! Don't say anything for now! It's time to return to your respective compartments. I would like to remind viewers that as of now they can send their gifts to stock up the dowries of these two splendid young people, and so allow them to obtain the very best of New Eden.'*

Fangfang and Tao draw back from either side of the screen, reopen their respective hatches and disappear through the access tubes that lead to their compartments.

Fade to black.

Credits.

17. Reverse Shot

Fallout Bunker, Cape Canaveral Air Base
Monday 3 July, 11:10am

The halogen spotlights of the bunker come back on abruptly, while the end titles of the Genesis programme continue to roll on the central screen of the digital wall.

Sitting at the round table with the other instructors, Roberto Salvatore lets out a whistle between his fleshy lips.

'Mamma mia! The gifted one might have done a doctorate in pure maths, but she's about as skilled as an amoeba where seduction is concerned! She blew it with the Chinese kid, and I'd bet the viewers won't be sending her a cent!'

On the opposite side of the table, Serena McBee puts down the microphone she had been using to make her commentary right the way through the speed-dating.

'We will see what Tao and the viewers thought,' she says, relaxing comfortably into her armchair. 'We may be surprised. You see, Roberto, matters of love are every bit as complex as your business with rockets and launchers and space ballistics.'

'But you must admit, talking to him about making babies at their first interview, that's a sure way to make any man run

141

a mile, even a common street performer!'

Geronimo Blackbull nods vigorously, his long loose hair shaking like vines either side of his lizard face.

'I can't help wondering why she was selected,' adds Gordon Lock, with a challenging look at Serena McBee. 'Let's just hope the viewers don't switch off!'

Archibald Dragovic, in his usual way, merely chuckles unnervingly, his exotropic eyes as round as saucers, his hair more electric than ever.

'Come now, that's enough!' Odette Stuart-Smith cuts them off sharply.

She glares at her male colleagues through her tri-focal glasses.

'You're practising scientists, not barflies sitting in front of the TV set at your local. Follow Arthur Montgomery's example – he at least is a gentleman who knows how to behave.'

Roberto Salvatore shrugs his stooping shoulders.

'A gentleman, my foot! I'm sure the doc is thinking exactly the same things we are. He's a man, like us.'

Dr Arthur Montgomery stops smoothing his moustache for the first time since the start of the viewing.

'Yes,' he says, 'I am a man. But first and foremost I am a doctor. And this doctor was too focused on the way the boy moved in zero-gravity to examine the girl too closely. The contraction of the abdominal muscles to control the dead weight of the lower part of his body . . . The way his arms stand in for his legs in keeping balance . . . All tremendously interesting. And the strangest bit of it was that the girl seemed to have no idea at all that she was talking to a paralytic.'

18. Shot

All around me the screens have been quiet for several long minutes.

The violins and the voices have stopped, giving way to the silence of the cameras that are still spying and still filming.

They chuck us the title sequence just to excite us, to get us going, but then they keep what's said in the Visiting Room secret along with all the other images from the Genesis channel. We're supposed to be the performers in the programme, not its viewers. That's how the game works. *Secrets. Competition.* At this moment, in the Visiting Room, Fangfang must be doing all she can to seduce the contestant of her choice. At this moment, in the living room, the other girls must be in a heated discussion as they try to imagine the boy in question. Unless they're still discussing me, revealing to viewers across the world the monstrosity I bear on my spine . . . Through the closed hatch it's impossible to make out their conversation, even pricking up my ears. I can only imagine what they're saying, imagine all the people who were cheering me out on

143

the Champs-Élysées yesterday now grimacing to hear these revelations, smiles changing into looks of disgust. I can hear them from here: 'What? They lied to us? That's how it goes. Léonor: lovely face, but a nightmare round the back!'

The thought fills me with terror and makes me want to cry.

Instead I get up and feverishly snatch my sketching tablet from my wardrobe.

Draw.

That's always been my solution, whenever everything goes wrong. Run away from the real world that does so much harm, to take refuge in my own world, the one where I feel like I can control everything.

The tip of the stylus starts to slide over the smooth glass surface, trembling slightly at first, but then more and more assured as I disconnect myself from the spacecraft to focus on the small white rectangle of the screen – my window onto elsewhere, my escape route. A girl looking like me begins to appear. Her ragged skirt shows the curve of her hips. A leopard-skin bodice is laced up across her chest. A black headband ties her thick hair. In her fist she is gripping a flintlock pistol, which is pointed towards me.

Beneath my fingers, Léo the Red has just been born.

19. Out of Frame

A beach thirty miles from Cape Canaveral
Monday 3 July, 4:30pm

The car park just up from the small beach is deserted, apart from one single vehicle.

It's the campervan with the tinted windows.

The young man in the black-framed glasses has taken off his blazer. The back of his red polo shirt is damp with sweat, the muscles straining through the fabric as he contorts himself to install a parabolic antenna onto the roof of the campervan. He checks the connections, redirects the dish, gives one final glance towards the Cape Canaveral peninsula whose shape he can just make out in the distance. From this far away, from the mainland, the cubic hangars in the launch zone look like tiny Lego bricks.

The young man takes the dictaphone out of his pocket – *click!*

'*Letter to my father.* Monday 3 July, four thirty pm. Following a night of adjustments, my installation appears to be up and running. In just a few seconds it will be the moment of truth. The point of no return. I wish I could have avoided all this, Father, but you left me no choice.'

Click! – he puts the dictaphone away and returns to the campervan.

Behind the tinted windows, the dashboard looks more like that of an airplane cockpit than a simple camper: dozens of LEDs, buttons and dials have been patched on alongside the traditional gauges for speed and fuel. The young man settles into the driver's seat and picks up a keyboard on which he starts typing feverishly. The passenger seat, meanwhile, is filled with a central processing unit connected to the strange telephone resembling an oversized remote control, and a monitor filled with the lines of code the young man is in the process of typing. A laptop with its screen off is sitting beside it.

The young man presses enter with a sigh.

For a few seconds the monitor turns white, then five reception bars appear on the screen one after another, along with a message of success:

SATELLITE CONNECTION ESTABLISHED
MINI-DRONE OPERATIONAL
IMAGES RETURNED IN 5 SECONDS
4 SECONDS
3 SECONDS
2 SECONDS
1 SECOND

The screen blinks, it is streaked with stripes of light . . . then stabilises on an unchanging image: the launch base, seen from ground height, with the GPS coordinates of Cape Canaveral in

146

one corner: 28° 29' 20" N 80° 34' 40" W. It's the exact spot where the young man placed his strange beetle the previous evening.

'Yessss!' he shouts, throwing his whole weight against the backrest of his seat.

He catches sight of his own image reflected in the rear-view mirror: his face under his brown hair is crumpled by tiredness and his cheeks are hollow after an all-nighter spent setting up the connection, but his intelligent brown eyes are sparkling with excitement behind his black-framed glasses.

He grabs hold of his dictaphone – *click!*

'*Letter to my father.* It's done, I've managed to get round Genesis's jamming system. My mini-drone is operational, ready to stroll into the base, to film the underside of this appalling money-printing machine that's been organised by an investment fund who don't know the first thing about space. I'm going to prove to the world that the Genesis protection system can be hacked, that the whole scheme is amateurish, that Atlas Capital are clowns who don't know what they're doing. The public are always keen to learn what's going on behind the curtain, to dig around in the faults in the system, to discover who's secretly pulling the strings.'

The young man takes a deep breath, before continuing.

'I'm picturing you listening to this recording, Father, and I seem to see you turning pale. Are you wondering why I'm doing this? Are you wondering why I'm taking so many risks, why I'm jeopardising my future and your career? You know very well. Mars has always been my dream, ever since I was small. Even in primary school I was already spending all my school vacations in space simulation camps, I was spending all my pocket money to collect the stickers for the *Space Heroes* albums – I had at least three of each! I should have been chosen for this mission. On paper, I was the ideal candidate: top of the class in high school, captain of the rowing club, medal for best young scientist in California at age sixteen, son of a high-ranking executive at NASA working on Genesis. You remember the state I was in when I discovered a year ago that I wasn't one of the twelve candidates selected to head off to Death Valley? But I pulled myself together. I told myself that you surely *had* to have good reasons, you and your colleagues. I convinced myself that the ones you'd chosen must have been even more over-trained than me. And then yesterday, on TV, along with the rest of the planet I learned the identity of the astronauts you'd never wanted to reveal to me, your own son, on some pretext of confidentiality. I couldn't get over it. Those good-for-nothings, those social misfits with no experience of space, those were the ones who had stolen my place and all my childhood dreams? It looked more like a tacky Saturday-night talk show! I tried contacting you to demand an explanation. You didn't answer. You dropped me. Why? Why! Well, you're really going to have to respond to this recording. When you receive it, the whole world will have witnessed the hacking of Genesis, but you alone will know it was your son Andrew who was behind it. Imagine the scandal, if I were to reveal who I am in public! Imagine how your employers at Atlas Capital would react, if they learned I've managed to infiltrate the programme thanks to a satellite phone and everything you've taught me! I'll only keep quiet in exchange for a promise that you'll have to respect this time around: that I'll be part of the *Cupido*'s next voyage to Mars in two years' time.'

Click! – Andrew puts down the dictaphone.

With the back of his hand he pushes away his hair and wipes the sweat from his forehead.

Then he presses a few keys on his keyboard and picks up a joystick that looks like the kind used for video games. The image on the monitor begins to shake slightly; it isn't a loose connection, but the mini-drone setting off, out there on the pebbly ground of the base.

A slight humming comes from the monitor's speakers, as the little metal elytra start to vibrate and the mini-drone takes to the air, gradually picking up altitude over Cape Canaveral.

With a movement of his thumb, Andrew pushes the joystick upwards.

The ground recedes quickly. The fence cluttered with teddy bears and well-wishers' cards disappears from view, as does the cap of the guard who is still on lookout at the end of the road, without suspecting what's going on right above his head.

The mini-drone cuts through the air in the direction of the largest of the hangars, marked with a huge planet logo, its roof bristling with parabolic antennae pointed skywards. It travels along the huge white concrete wall, dives down towards a half-open door a few steps from the one where some officers in grey Genesis uniforms are taking a cigarette break and chatting.

Unseen, unnoticed, the mini-drone barely bigger than an insect slips in through the doorway. The monitor screen goes dark for a moment, just enough time for the on-board camera to adjust to the artificial illumination after the broad daylight. Soon the picture of a long white neon-lit corridor appears. The mini-drone flies past several closed doors, all of them identical.

Suddenly a door on the right-hand side opens and a woman hurries out, her arms filled with files.

'Careful!' says Andrew, pulling on the joystick to straighten out the mini-drone, which has been destabilised by the current of air. The image on the monitor skims dangerously close to the left-hand wall, but the mini-drone just dodges a collision and sets off faster than ever back towards the end of the corridor, following the hurrying woman. A lit-up sign is shining above the double doors that block its view: *Control room*.

The woman in a hurry grabs the badge she's wearing round her neck and holds it up to the electromagnetic box that controls access to the room.

There is a resonant beep, and the red light on the box turns green.

The doors part with a light hiss, revealing a huge circular room, in half-darkness pierced by dozens of computer screens. Behind them, the programme's engineers are busying themselves.

'And here we are!' says Andrew, jubilantly. 'Now, let the show begin!'

Keeping the mini-drone hovering on the spot with the joystick, he types a code into his keyboard with his free hand, then turns on the laptop computer beside the monitor.

An internet site appears on the screen, showing its heading in thick, red, aggressive letters:

Genesis Hacking
Behind the scenes at the Genesis programme
like you've never seen it before!

'Go!'

Andrew presses one final key, and the footage being captured by the mini-drone is streamed onto the Genesis Hacking site, in sync with the monitor.

Then he takes the joystick back into his two hands, and sends his spy flying over the ranks of engineers. Sometimes he dives down behind one of them and captures an image of a computer screen, showing both the ballistic trajectory of the *Cupido* through space and the craft's fuel and oxygen levels, or other pieces of technical information that the public are not supposed to know.

Each time an engineer stretches in their chair or turns around, Andrew flicks the joystick to make the mini-drone rise up, its slight humming masked by the noise of the ventilators that cool the control-room machinery.

From time to time, Andrew glances at the laptop. A counter scrolls very quickly under the streaming footage, tracking the number of web users visiting the Genesis Hacking site.

12,039 . . .

12,082 . . .

12,141 . . .

The smile on Andrew's lips is getting wider every second.

He pushes the joystick forward, towards the platform at the back of the control room, where a bald, broad-shouldered man is standing and giving instructions to various members of staff.

'Director Lock!' murmurs Andrew.

The mini-drone stabilises, hovering stationary above Gordon Lock's gleaming scalp.

Andrew turns a thumb-wheel on the edge of his joystick to

adjust the sound input, until the voice of the technical director of the Genesis programme is sounding loud and clear through the monitor's speakers . . . and in the video being streamed to the entire world.

'. . . *print me out the full report with vital statistics in both compartments of the* Cupido, *for the routine daily check.*'

'*Right away, Director.*'

'*Don't forget to include the radiation levels.*'

'*Understood, Director.*'

All at once a digital ringtone sounds in the campervan. It's 'The Imperial March' from *The Empire Strikes Back.*

'Now really isn't the time!' says Andrew.

Without letting go of the joystick, he rummages around the jumble of electrical cables strewn over the floor of the vehicle and ends up finding his phone – a regular model, compact, not a massive satellite phone like the one he uses to control the mini-drone.

The name of the person calling appears on the screen, accompanied by a picture showing the grim black helmet of Darth Vader.

Incoming call: Mother ship.

Andrew sighs. He puts the joystick down reluctantly, moving the mini-drone far from Director Lock and sending it to rest on top of a wall in the control room. He presses a key, and the video pauses on standby on the two monitors.

Only then does he put down the joystick and pick up the telephone.

'Hello, Mother? If you're calling to ask me for news, I can tell you everything's fine, I'm currently . . . um . . . in Louisiana.

It's so cool doing this tour of the country before Berkeley, I'll almost forget my disappointment at not being a part of the voyage to Mars. *Almost.* But the thing is, I'm driving at the moment, so can we please talk later, OK?'

Andrew is about to hang up, but the voice in the phone immediately dissuades him.

'Andrew Ethan Fisher! Pull over at once.'

The young man freezes. A wrinkle passes over his smooth forehead – is it possible that his mother has guessed that he isn't in Louisiana, but in Florida, in the process of infiltrating – altogether illegally – one of the best-guarded places in the country?

'Right, OK, fine,' he mumbles. 'I'll pull over. There. I'm parked. What's up?'

'Your father . . .'

'Ah, so the communications expert has finally decided to give some sign of life, after three weeks without news? He's suddenly remembered he has a family and a son? If I were on Mars, I can assure you I'd be in more regular contact with him from my habitat there.'

'Andrew, please shut up. Stop it with this obsession of yours about Mars! Your father . . . Sherman is dead. They've just found his body in Death Valley.'

20. Shot

'You've got a real gift, Léo.'

I look up from the sketching tablet that's resting on my knees. I've been taking refuge in my bed with my breakfast and my stylus ever since the wake-up symphony sounded, at the start of our second day en route to Mars. There was no way I was going to face the looks of the other girls, still less experience their insults. I'd rather wallow in my Krunchy Bit biscuit crumbs – even if they scratch at me furiously, between my mattress and my pyjamas.

All the same, there's no way I can escape now: Safia's kohl-rimmed eyes are staring at me from less than a metre away. She is impeccable as always, already dolled up from head to foot. She has replaced the red dot on her forehead with a small blue spot, matching her new sari.

'It's amazing!' she says, leaning over my shoulder for a better view. 'It's you, isn't it?'

I look at the picture I was in the middle of drawing, the one I started yesterday: Léo the Red and her threatening pistol. A

154

galleon has appeared, at whose prow she is standing. In the place of an ocean, it's sailing through a sea of stars.

'It's Léo the Red, setting off to invade Mars,' I say. 'Best not to trust her though – they say she's pretty trigger-happy.'

Safia smiles knowingly.

'Got it, I'll be careful. May I?'

She takes the tablet delicately and slides her finger across the screen to move on to another picture. A man appears, his trouser legs rolled up over his bare ankles, with a leather waistcoat worn directly on his skin, his chest covered in necklaces of sharp teeth. He wouldn't look out of place on the cover of one of Kris's romance novels.

'What about him?' asks Safia. 'Who's this handsome terror? He doesn't look like he can be one of our boys.'

'That's Captain Shark's-Tooth, the man who fights sharks with his bare hands,' I say. 'He's both Léo the Red's sworn enemy and her star-crossed lover. He's taken a vow of silence, swearing he won't speak another word till he's reunited with her. Only then, when he is face to face with her, will he speak again. To challenge her to a duel, or to ask for her hand.'

'Your imagination! Where do you find all this stuff?'

I just take the tablet back from her and switch it off. There's no chance I'm going to tell her Shark's-Tooth is based on a real guy who's already married off with a real wife and a real baby. I'd prefer to forget all that. The character I've created is far more mysterious.

'Is Kris doing better?' I say.

'Much better. Her bump is half the size it was yesterday. A good night's sleep has done her a world of good.'

Safia sits down on the edge of my bed.

'You know,' she says, 'they're soon going to draw lots for the second time, for the girl who'll get to do today's speed-dating. Imagine if it's you! You ought to go upstairs and get ready with the others.'

'To be insulted and called a psycho? No, thanks – no way.'

'Don't beat yourself up. I'm sure it was an accident, what happened to Kris with the hatch.'

'Well, you're wrong. It wasn't an accident. I slammed that hatch down by jumping on it with both feet!'

I'm immediately cross with myself for being so brusque. I bite my tongue, thinking that if I were to just cut it off once and for all it'd probably be for the best. Why do I always have to be so provocative? Why am I trying to send Safia packing when all the evidence suggests she just wants to be nice?

'Sorry,' I murmur. 'I'm just a bit . . . on edge.'

'We all are,' says Safia, taking my hand gently. 'And that's normal. The stress of leaving, the thrill at this extraordinary adventure we're all going through, the idea of the millions of kilometres of emptiness surrounding us . . . not to mention the pressures of the game! Fangfang is in seventh heaven. She told us Tao was fabulous, a physique to die for, and that she was sure she'd scored some points with him.'

The pressures of the game! If Safia only knew . . . The real pressure I'm feeling is the idea that Kris might have told the other girls what she saw in the bathroom, and that Fangfang then rushed off to pass the information on to Tao. Of course I'll have to reveal my secret to the boys sooner or later, or at least to one of them. But not so quickly. Not like this. Maybe

156

at this very moment the boys all see me as a monster, and nobody will ever invite me into the Visiting Room.

This stress level is transforming me into a living pressure cooker. I'd give anything to blow the lid, even if it's just for five seconds, to talk to someone about it. Safia, who is looking at me with her big doe eyes full of understanding, is undoubtedly the most suitable person.

'I need to ask you something,' I say. 'But this is for you, Safia, and only you.'

I emphasise these last words, *only you*, with a pointed look up at the camera above the bed, and I formulate a few words of apology for the benefit of the viewers.

'I'm sorry, ladies and gentlemen, but it's a rather intimate matter . . .'

Then I pull the blanket over my head.

'Come under here,' I whisper to Safia.

'Under the blanket? You think we're allowed to hide ourselves from the cameras?'

'Well, of course, otherwise they'd have put them in the bathroom too. We could go up there, but I just don't fancy walking past the other girls right now . . .'

Safia slips her head and shoulders under the thin piece of cashmere, where I'm already buried. I arrange it so there's just a little opening that allows enough light to see each other.

'Welcome to the marine grotto that serves as a den for Léo the Red. Just ignore the crumbs, I've been having a picnic, I'll shake it all out in a moment.'

'It's so funny!' cries Safia. 'Under here it really does feel like you're somewhere different!'

She lowers her voice instinctively.

'So, Léo, what did you want to ask me?'

'Did . . . did Kris tell you what she saw in the bathroom, when she came up yesterday to get me?'

'What she saw? No, she didn't mention anything special, what could she have seen . . . other than you?'

'Exactly.'

'I'm sorry, I don't think I understand.'

I feel a knot coming undone in the depths of my being.

Kris didn't say anything!

I feel like I'm starting to breathe again.

Kris didn't say anything!

'It's nothing,' I say, smiling. 'It's just that I have a little . . . birthmark that's slightly conspicuous on my lower back.'

I don't like lying to Safia, who is so kind to me. But my whole life is summed up in this lie: make out that I'm a normal girl, hide the Salamander. I don't think I have the strength to reveal it to Safia, not just now.

'Yes, I know, I'm being ridiculous,' I add, just to put an end to the subject for good. 'It's such a silly complex. But what do you expect? We've all got them, haven't we?'

Safia nods.

'I understand,' she says. 'As you say, we all have our little defects and we deal with them as best we can. I'm sure your birthmark is nothing at all. But I understand your wanting to hide it. That's your choice. If it helps you feel a bit better about yourself, I've got far worse . . .'

With these words, she lifts the blanket a bit more over her head and pulls aside her thick black hair, smooth and gleaming

158

like silk, to half open the neckline of her sari and show me the skin below her neck. Even in the half-light I can distinctly see sections of skin that are puffy and slightly darker, on the right side between her breastbone and where her breasts begin. These parts are no bigger than the marks left by droplets, nothing like the Salamander that stretches halfway down my back. But I recognise the rough look of skin that is burned, tormented, dead.

'A fire,' I murmur, my throat clenched with emotion.

'Not a fire, no. It was a man who did this to me.'

Safia is so close to me now that I can feel her breath on my face with each word she speaks.

'A man?' I say.

'The one my parents had chosen for me and who I refused to marry. I was sixteen, he was thirty-five. He couldn't handle my refusal. He tried to disfigure me by throwing acid at me, the way rejected lovers sometimes do in my country.'

'But that's appalling!'

'It's not as bad as the face of my attacker when I turned the liquid back on him. Just a few drops fell on my chest. Imagine what *his* face looks like, after three-quarters of the acid that was meant for me.'

Safia's story stuns me. She tells me all this without a quaver in her voice, without any emotion disturbing the beautiful smooth face just a few centimetres from mine – though it would have made more sense for her to be a total wreck. And to think I considered her a fragile little girl, much too fragile to travel to Mars! She had the courage to show me her skin, while I would never have the guts to show her mine. I'm a little ashamed.

159

'The most ironic thing of all is that this man took me to court,' she goes on. 'I just barely escaped prison. But I didn't escape the wrath of my family, who felt that I'd dishonoured them and nobody was ever going to want to marry me now. The day after my parents disowned me, I submitted my application to go to Mars. Serena selected me in spite of the shame that was being heaped upon me. Thanks to her, thanks to the game, I'm going to be able to have the life my people denied me: I'm going to be able to choose my husband.'

Safia pulls the neck of her sari closed again, and lets the black curtain of her hair drop back down.

'So you see, I don't think you should worry about your little birthmark,' she concludes gently. 'Now, better go upstairs and get ready. If it's your turn, you really won't want to go to the Visiting Room in your pyjamas!'

I nod, lightly shaking the blanket that's resting on my red curls like a veil.

'Thanks, Safia. I'm touched. Really. You can count on me not to mention your injury to anyone.'

'Same for your birthmark.'

My birthmark . . . A nice euphemism. And a nice feeling of shame. But Safia doesn't notice.

'Let's go?' she asks.

'Let's.'

21. Reverse Shot

'We're screwed!'

Roberto Salvatore bursts into the bunker, his bulky silhouette obscuring the digital wall where the contestants are busily getting ready for the day's speed-dating.

He throws a newspaper into the middle of the table, which is cluttered with coffee cups and the remains of breakfast, around which the other six allies of silence are seated. The first page carries a photo of a round, white, glowing ball.

'What's that thing?' yawns Geronimo Blackbull, the Engineering instructor.

He lifts his cowboy boots off the table where they'd been resting and leans his wrinkled face over the newspaper. His long, coarse black hair sweeps the donut crumbs lying on the table the way a trawling net sweeps the depths of the sea.

'Is it a new exoplanet discovered outside the solar system?'

'Don't talk nonsense,' says Odette Stuart-Smith, the Planetology instructor, sharply. 'You should realise that if that were the case, I'd have been the first to know.'

'Short-sighted as you are, I find it hard to imagine you could see beyond the solar system. You have enough trouble seeing past the end of your nose.'

Gordon Lock cuts their exchange short.

'That's enough! This isn't the time for such childish behaviour. For your information, this photo shows my own head, as seen from above.'

The technical director picks up the paper and reads the headline on the front page with fury.

'GENESIS PROGRAM HACKED! – the clandestine dissemination of images from the control room receives as many visitors as the official Genesis site itself.'

Gordon Lock shakes the newspaper as though merely touching it disgusts him.

'Ever since we spotted the Genesis Hacking site yesterday evening, we've known there's a bug within these walls,' he says. 'But that's no reason to lose our cool. We've already asked the US government to block the genesis-hacking.com URL. And for now the bug has only had access to the control room, where nobody knows our secret. This is not a red alert.'

'You mean it's not a red alert *yet*,' Roberto Salvatore butts in, his cheeks trembling, still emotional. 'Who can say what this damned bug really knows, and what revelations it's getting ready to make? And what if it learns about the Noah Report? And if it reveals to the whole world that the unpleasant little creatures secretly sent into the seventh Love Nest all snuffed it? The whole thing is your fault, Gordon. There's a spy that you weren't able to detect among your team of engineers. Good God, the guy filmed you from less than two metres away and you didn't even notice!'

Gordon Lock bangs his fist down on the table with all the strength of his wrestler's arms, upending a cup of coffee onto Archibald Dragovic's white shirt.

'These insinuations of yours are inexcusable! There's no way the staff in the control room has any suspicions about our little agreement, do you understand? *None!* And what's more, nobody working here has any interest in broadcasting confidential images just for fun when it means risking their job. Given the perspective of the shot, it's clear the camera wasn't being handled by a human.'

'Who, then?' says Geronimo Blackbull, rolling his black locks around the tips of his skull-ringed fingers, doubtfully. 'The ghost of a passenger from the *Challenger* craft or the victim of some other space disaster, come back to Earth to get revenge on the evil organisers who sent young astronauts to the slaughter?'

Odette Stuart-Smith turns pale.

'Shut up, you heathen, you satanic old hippy! Matters of the afterlife are not to be joked about.'

Instinctively she touches the small crucifix hanging over her turtleneck.

'Well, I don't believe in ghosts,' says Director Lock. 'I do, however, believe in technology. I think we're dealing with an airborne robot. A remote-controlled drone.'

'Impossible!' says Geronimo Blackbull. 'This place is a total electromagnetic fortress. Terrestrial communications are jammed across the whole of the Cape Canaveral site, except for the secured internal network, which only functions with wired surveillance cameras, the staff walkie-talkies, and Serena's brooch-mic. As for the outside world, there are only three possible signals, and we control them all. The first comes into the base: that's the data flow coming down from the *Cupido*, captured by our receivers. The two other signals are outgoing: the data returning towards the craft, allowing Serena to interact with the passengers, and the Genesis channel itself, once the footage has been edited, for broadcasting across the world. That's all. Not to upset our little church mouse here, but this so-called drone can only be running under the control of the Holy Spirit!'

Unable to take it any more, Odette Stuart-Smith crosses herself and babbles the first words of a prayer.

'May the Lord protect us –'

'We'd best not count on God to protect us. We should do it ourselves.'

All eyes turn towards the voice that has just spoken. It's Serena McBee, settled in her large black leather padded armchair, from which she's been silently listening to the whole conversation. She straightens herself up, her silver bob catching the beams from the spotlights.

'For once, Gordon Lock is right, there's no use panicking,' she goes on. 'Atlas expects a minimum of cool-headedness on our part, my friends. That's why they trust us, the allies of silence. We just need to redouble our caution. As for the Noah Report, I don't know how many times I need to say this: the encrypted electronic file has been deleted, and to the eyes of the viewers of the Genesis channel the seventh Love Nest is as empty as the others.

'This bunker, our HQ, has been gone over with a fine-tooth

comb to ensure that it doesn't contain bugging devices or hidden cameras. Furthermore, it's impossible to enter without the retina identification scan that's set to recognise only the eyes of the seven of us. In this place, we have nothing to fear. I've also had the editing suite secured: anyone going in there needs to pass through a controlled airlock. There's no way a drone could slip in there unnoticed. It's just a matter of finding out where it's hiding now. Is it still in the control room? We don't know what shape it is, how big, or the true intentions of whoever's controlling it. They certainly aren't doing it for the money, as the Genesis-Hacking site doesn't contain any advertising that could help us track them down. I'm sure the hacker will give himself away before too long. Next time he acts, I'll be lying in wait. Human psychology has no secrets from someone like me who holds the keys.'

No sooner has Serena McBee finished talking than another window opens in the digital wall at the back of the bunker, shrinking all the others.

The face of Serena's young assistant appears live from the editing suite, connected to the silver earpiece that's practically a part of her.

'What is it, Samantha?' the executive producer asks.

'I just wanted to notify you that the independently monitored drawing of lots has chosen Elizabeth, the British girl, for today's speed-dating. The session will begin in ten minutes.'

'Very good. I must admit, I do like this girl. She knows what she wants, and she won't let anything stand in her way to stop her getting it. All this while remaining beautifully alert to the rest of the girls, at least on the surface. This child will go far, not like those others who collapse in tears at the slightest bump, or sulk in their beds at the smallest setback. I'll do the voiceover from here in the bunker, same as yesterday. You may leave, Samantha.'

22. Genesis Channel

Tuesday 4 July, 11:00am

Open to black.

Static shot of the Visiting Room bubble, empty, swarming with stars.

Title: *Second session in the Visiting Room. Hostess: Elizabeth, 18, United Kingdom, Engineering Officer (communication latency: 5 seconds)*

Drum-roll.

Zoom in on the bun in Elizabeth's hair, emerging into the left-hand side of the screen through the hatch, from the access tube that leads to the girls' living quarters. Elizabeth is dressed soberly, as usual, in beige trousers that float around her ankles, a small off-white jumper with long sleeves and a collar that comes sensibly right up to her neck, hair trapped in the high dancer's bun.

Serena (off): '*Hello, Elizabeth! Sweet, calm Elizabeth, whose modesty and sense of fair play have, I'm sure, already persuaded our viewers . . . But will they persuade the boys too? My dear Elizabeth, how do you feel at this moment? Not too many nerves?*'

Elizabeth, with a mysterious smile: 'Thanks, Serena, all good.

I think I'm ready.' She carefully shuts the soundproof hatch behind her, before adding, 'And I hope our little arrangement still stands?'

Serena, five seconds later: '*Of course it does! You just need to gesture to the cameras. But let's not reveal any more to the viewers just yet, to keep it a surprise . . . Instead, tell us – which boy would you like to invite today?*'

Elizabeth: 'I'm going to choose Alexei, the Medical Officer.'

Serena (off): '*Aha, Russia! The great land of ballet! I'm sure that played some part in your choice. We will notify the lucky chosen one. We will be back shortly, Elizabeth.*'

The voiceover falls silent.

Elizabeth immediately unbuttons her trousers, which float off behind her like a dead leaf carried by the wind, revealing legs sheathed in black fishnet stockings. Then she removes her off-white jumper. Beneath it, her shoulders are bare and she wears a sumptuous corset in embroidered black velvet, decorated with tassels that glimmer like the stars beyond the bubble. She undoes the elastic holding back her hair, which spreads in a silky black banner all around her. The final touch: she takes a lipstick out of her bodice, and with an expert hand applies a deep red layer to her mouth, transforming her into a femme fatale.

Drum-roll.

Wide shot.

The stopwatch for keeping track of the interview appears superimposed on the screen, while Alexei's blond head emerges into the right side of the Visiting Room.

The camera zooms in: platinum blond hair with a haircut

straight out of a Hollywood movie, steel-blue eyes, a well-defined jaw, today's contestant looks every bit a photo from a fashion shoot, right down to his white suit with a collar lined with an elegant grey seam, emphasising the contours of his perfectly proportioned body.

Alexei, sighting Elizabeth: 'Whoa!'

Elizabeth, smiling: 'I could say the same about you: whoa! Good choice!'

Alexei, in a deep voice touched by a slight Slavic accent: 'You're absolutely . . . sublime! The other girls aren't all hot like you, right?'

Elizabeth winks: 'You've nothing to worry about so long as you can make it through this interview. The other girls are cute enough, in their way, but that's about it – if you know what I mean. This game is a competition, and I'm not sure they're cut out for it. There's no accounting for taste though, and I certainly wouldn't want to sound like I'm boasting.'

Alexei: 'Well, you've got plenty to boast about.'

He smiles with all his teeth, dazzling and perfectly straight. Little dimples appear in the hollows of his cheeks, which the camera doesn't miss.

Elizabeth, lowering her voice: 'Your smile's just too charming.'

Alexei, his voice lowered now too: 'You're the one who's charming me right now.'

Elizabeth: 'How about we tell each other a bit about our lives?' She looks at her watch. 'We've only got four minutes left – two each?'

Alexei: 'OK, I'll start. But if you don't mind, I'm going to

169

take off my jacket, because you're making me hot all of a sudden . . .' In a flash he takes off his jacket, undoes his tie, unbuttons the collar of his shirt and rolls his sleeves back over his forearms. '. . . and I'm going to close my eyes too, because you're dazzling me. If I keep looking at you I'm worried I won't be able to string two words together, and I don't want to seem like a moron in front of a girl like you!'

The two of them are overtaken by a fit of the giggles.

Close-up on Alexei's eyelids as they shut. Small tears form at the corners of his eyes, before detaching themselves like pearls and floating off across the Visiting Room.

Alexei, letting his blind body drift in space: 'I was born in a town on the outskirts of Moscow, to an unremarkable middle-class family. We weren't rich, but my parents got by thanks to their little grocery store. My father expected me to take on the business when he retired. But I wanted something different. Something higher, loftier, nobler. Ever since I was small I've dreamed of chivalry, of exploits beyond normal men, of the eternal Russia – the Russia of legend, which no longer exists. I stopped going to high school, to hang out with other young people who, like me, thirsted for something ideal.'

His eyes still closed, Alexei allows himself to turn slowly in the air, unfurling his long, lithe body.

The hand on the stopwatch superimposed on the screen reaches a semicircle: half the time has expired.

'I lived with my new friends for two years. I had great discussions, I did things I never could have imagined myself doing, I faced the urban jungle bravely, like an adventurer of old. And then one day I realised that even this was not enough for me. I needed even more. I applied for the Genesis programme.'

Alexei reopens his blue eyes abruptly: 'So, that's my story. Here I am today, following my childhood dream, trying from now on to be a knight of outer space.'

Elizabeth: 'That's a lovely story. Like in a novel. But aren't knights always supposed to die of love for a fair lady, to whom they offer their hearts? At least, that's how it is in operas and ballets.'

Alexei puts his hands on the glass wall that separates him from the girl: 'You were a dancer on Earth, weren't you, Elizabeth?'

By way of response, Elizabeth looks at her watch to see how much time she has left – more than two minutes – then gives a signal to the camera, thumbs-up.

At once a piece of orchestral music, incredibly beautiful, fills the chamber. All the stars in the sky seem to start waltzing.

Alexei opens his eyes wide, moved: 'I . . . I know this tune! It's a Russian ballet, isn't it? Tchaikovsky? *Swan Lake!*'

Elizabeth spreads her arms gracefully, miming the flight of a large black swan, wider and wider as the music swells. She rises up slightly before a submissive Alexei.

Elizabeth: 'I was a dancer, I still am, and I always will be, because it's something you are for ever. Like you, I've always aspired to rise higher than the banality of everyday life. My parents never understood; it was just a waste of time to them, not a real profession. They wanted to forbid me from dancing so I would concentrate on my studies. But I spent all my time practising, with one dream, just one: to join the Royal Ballet, the most prestigious company in England.'

The music surges dramatically.

Perfectly synchronised with the violins, mastering the zero gravity as though it were her natural element, Elizabeth spins across the bubble, a whirlwind of hair that looks like a whirlwind of black feathers. An elegant raising of arms to glance once more at her watch: more than a minute.

Elizabeth, speaking very quickly now: 'Repeated runaways. Endless conflict. Emancipation aged sixteen. I also joined a little company. Then another, slightly larger one. With a single aim: to compete for a place in the Royal Ballet. I worked day and night. No let-up. Until I could no longer feel my suffering. Until I had transformed my body into a work of art.'

The music darkens.

The hand of the stopwatch has almost completed its circuit: there are only a handful of seconds left. Elizabeth carries out an *entrechat* that is transformed into a leap of several metres. Her body cuts up through the Milky Way towards the transmission dish that sits atop the Visiting Room, the tassels sewn on her corset catching the starlight. She comes to rest against the glass partition, at the exact spot where Alexei is leaning. There, with disarming ease, she does the splits, and gazes into the eyes of the spellbound young man.

Elizabeth, without a pause, without catching her breath.

'That work of art could be yours, my gallant knight, as the Royal Ballet didn't want it. They didn't accept me. That very evening I submitted my application to the programme. I decided to be a dancer among the stars, even against all opposition. And you, Alexei, you can be my prince.'

Elizabeth brushes against the glass partition with her painted lips, leaving the imprint of a kiss a few centimetres from Alexei's face. At that moment, the bell sounds, bringing the music of *Swan Lake* to an abrupt end.

The interview is over.

Elizabeth presses against the partition to propel herself to the back of the Visiting Room, where she delicately retrieves her trousers and jumper and pulls them on again.

Serena (off): *'Brava! Bravissima! What a show! And especially what a surprise from the quiet Elizabeth, a white swan hiding a black swan beneath her plumage. But will Alexei call her back? We'll find out next week, when it's the boys' turn to invite the girls.'*

A re-clothed Elizabeth takes a handkerchief from her pocket to wipe off her lipstick, ties back her hair quickly with a new elastic. Then she takes a bow as if on stage, before reopening the hatch and being swallowed into the access tube.

Fade to black.

Credits.

23. Shot

D +1 day 21 h 45 mins.
[1st week]

Liz reappears in the living room, a slight smile on her pale lips – she never wears make-up, or only very little.

Her jumper is a bit crumpled, a few locks of hair have come loose from her bun, which looks less impeccable than usual – no doubt thanks to the zero gravity in the Visiting Room.

The other girls hurry over to her and flood her with questions, while Louve circles around and around, contributing to the conversation with yapping. I stay on the sofa, defensive – although my presence does seem to be permitted again, ever since Safia brought me back from my room none of the other girls has yet spoken a word to me. They're really making me feel like I'm in quarantine.

'Tell us!' cries Kris, who has always seemed taken with Alexei. 'Is he as cute as he is in the photo on the opening titles?'

'Er, mm-hmm . . .' answers Liz, jokingly, deliberately fanning the girls' excitement.

'Details!' demands Kris. 'We want details!'

Unable to contain herself any longer, Liz lets all her enthusiasm out.

'He is, he's magnificent! So natural, a smile like an angel! And romantic too, which doesn't hurt: a proper Prince Charming.'

'I knew it!' says Kris, triumphantly. 'Like *The Prince of Ice*!'

Then she adds at once, a little apprehensively:

'You think he liked you?'

'Me? Oh no! I'm just so . . . ordinary. He'll never want to see me again. Those are the only six minutes I'll ever spend with him.'

A concert of encouragement greets Liz's words. Hard to know if it's sincere, but that's the game, isn't it? The only one apart from me who doesn't seem to share in the general excitement is Louve. She is on the lookout beside her empty metal bowl, at the back of the kitchen area.

I move away from the group to stroke her head.

'Alexei's smile and Tao's muscles don't seem to interest you much, do they? All you're interested in is your lunch. Wait, I'll open a tin of Eden for you. *Couscous Royale* – how does that sound?'

I interpret Louve's brief barking as an enthusiastic *yes*.

A few moments later, she has her nose in a smelly yellowish mixture that reminds me of the delights of the Eden Food France factory.

'Léo . . . ?'

I jump back up.

Kris is standing there, behind me – not the hurtful Kris with the black eye I've recently met, no, the one I consider my sister – the Kris with the sky-blue eyes, nothing but sweetness and kindness.

'I want to offer you an apology, Léo . . .'

Her voice is trembling slightly. Her body too. She must be afraid I'll smash something else against her nose, my fist or the can-opener I'm still holding. The fact that she thinks I can still hurt her tears my heart.

'You're kidding, Kris!' I say, glancing over at the other girls, but they are too focused on Liz to pay us any attention. 'I'm the one who has to apologise, after what happened.'

Then I add, in a murmur, 'I guess I should have talked to you much earlier about my . . . *defect*, rather than letting you find it out that way. I was so afraid you'd be disgusted. Thank you for not saying anything to the others – I would have deserved it.'

Kris gives the beginnings of a shy smile.

'You don't disgust me,' she says. 'On the contrary, you're looking very pretty today.'

Very pretty? I notice my reflection in the little mirror hanging above the kitchen counter. While I had refused to take off my perpetual ripped jeans to put on a dress, I did venture to put on one of the Chez Rosier tops, the one I thought the most restrained: a small grey jersey top, that clings to my waist and my chest (I insisted that all my outfits cover my shoulders; the people at Rosier probably just assumed I was as susceptible to the cold as Liz). Quite a change from the shapeless T-shirts I usually wear. I exchanged my elastic – practical but dull – for a large black satin ribbon, deftly tied the way the Rosier people had taught me, keeping my mane of hair under control while giving it an undeniable touch of chic. Finally, I put on a little make-up – really not all that much, but given that I'm someone who never wears any at all, it was something of a revolution for me.

'Thank you,' I say.

Her face lights up.

The bump on her forehead has almost completely faded.

'I've managed to make a dessert with the ingredients we've got on board,' she says. 'Egg yolk out of a tube and powdered cream: I don't know how good it'll be. Also without very much gravity it isn't properly mixed. But I hope it's edible. I made a crème brûlée, leopard – your favourite.'

24. Reverse Shot

Fallout Bunker, Cape Canaveral Air Base
Tuesday 4 July, 11:55am

'There it is, the Sulky One has rejoined the gang of five!' says Serena McBee mockingly, gesturing towards one of the windows on the digital wall, on the girls' side. 'Look at them getting along again like a house on fire . . . up until the next crisis at least. Let's make the most of it.'

She presses her silver brooch-mic and quickly issues some instructions: '*Serena to the editing suite. Feed the channel from camera G2R – Girls, 2nd floor, right-hand view – and remain on there for at least a quarter of an hour, before returning to the boys' side. Beautiful reunions and great outpourings of the heart – the public always like that kind of thing.*'

The central window on the digital wall, the one showing the Genesis channel broadcast, is framed on a wide shot of the six girls sitting down for lunch. Kelly starts a round of applause to mark Léonor's return to the group. Kelly: 'So that's it, has the wildcat calmed down?'; Fangfang: 'Your new look suits you incredibly well, Léo!'; Liz: 'I'm so happy we're all together like before!'

But a few moments later, a new window opens on the digital wall to reveal the face of Samantha, Serena McBee's assistant.

'Ms McBee . . . ?'

'Yes, Samantha,' replies Serena, somewhat irritated. 'What's going on? I asked for a quarter of an hour on G2R, not two minutes. Am I going to have to pass over the control of the editing to the bunker, the way the protocol allows in times of crisis, to carry out my instructions myself?'

'No, ma'am, your instructions are very clear. But there are some gentlemen here from the police who would like to speak to you.'

The window zooms out slowly, to reveal two serious-looking men, in suits and ties. They are standing in the editing suite, beside the assistant.

'Can Serena McBee see us?' asks the older of the two.

'Yes,' replies Samantha. 'Ms McBee is currently in a meeting in the basement, but she can see you, hear you and answer you. Talk directly into the surveillance camera.'

'Ah, right . . . Umm . . . Hello, Professor McBee. This is Inspector Larry Garcia, FBI.'

'Good morning, Inspector,' Serena replies from the bunker. 'I'm sorry I can't come to see you right away. I'm just finishing an important meeting with my colleagues – you know how it is, the joys of live broadcasting.'

A pointed glance from Serena to the colleagues in question, seated at the round table, as if to indicate to them that everything is under control. The naked white lights from the halogen spots illuminate their worried expressions: Roberto Salvatore is tapping on the table-top nervously; Geronimo

Blackbull is examining the skull rings decorating his fingers; Odette Stuart-Smith grips her little crucifix; Archibald Dragovic and Dr Arthur Montgomery just clench their teeth; as for Gordon Lock, he's gleaming with sweat just as he always is whenever he's overcome by anxiety.

'The joys of . . . ?' echoes Inspector Garcia in the window of the digital wall '– ah, yes, of course . . . You must be very busy. My wife and I are big fans of your talk show, *The Professor Serena McBee Consultation*. The advice you provide in that most unique programme has been a great help to our marriage. The weekly bouquet of flowers – it works like magic!'

A smile passes across Inspector Garcia's face, a sign of small conjugal victories, of intimate joys.

'Thank you, Inspector,' says Serena. 'But I don't suppose you've come to Cape Canaveral to bring me flowers. What can I do for you? I can come upstairs in a few minutes, if you like?'

'No, do please finish your work, Ms McBee,' says the inspector, returning to his professional tone. 'It's nothing urgent. I just wanted to notify you . . . we've found your colleague, Sherman Fisher.'

'Sherman?' cries Serena, playing at surprise perfectly. 'Thank God – at last! I hope he's all right?'

'He was the victim of an accident on the road that crosses Death Valley. His car struck a rock. Most likely he died several weeks ago, but the amount of time it took to recover the body, and in such a desolate place . . . The burial will take place on Sunday, close to Beverly Hills. I'm sorry, Ms McBee.'

25. Shot

The symphony marking the start of our third day on board the *Cupido* sounds across the room. The screens above our beds light up to reveal Serena's face; today she's wearing earrings set with emeralds, perfectly matching her eyeshadow.

'Good morning, everyone! This is Wednesday, eight a.m. on the east coast of America! So, is everybody ready for a new day . . . and a new interview?'

A concert of agreements and yawns answers her.

We get up, one after another.

When my bare feet touch the floor, it feels so strange. My body feels too light. I'm still not used to forty per cent gravity. Nor is Kris, apparently, to judge by the way she tumbles from the upper bunk.

'Careful!' I say, just catching her.

'Oops! Thanks, Léo. I'm so clumsy. My head's spinning.'

'The bump?' I ask, concerned.

'No, I don't even feel it. But every time I move from the horizontal position to the vertical, ever since I've been on

181

board, I've been overcome by dizziness and nausea . . . Like those training sessions we had in the centrifuge, remember?'

'I'm sure it'll sort itself out in time, Kris. We've only just left; you have to give your body time to get used to it. If you want I'll give you an antihistamine jab to help; it's useful for space sickness.'

Serena interrupts our conversation – her face appears, replicated three-fold above the three bunks.

'Can I have your attention, please?' she asks.

There is a big, unanimous 'yes!' in response, but she remains immobile on the screen for a few moments, as though she hasn't heard. It's nearly three days since we lifted off, which means that we are three light-seconds away from Earth: it takes three seconds for our 'yes!' to reach Serena's ears, and another three seconds for us to hear her reaction.

'Very good!' she says at last, slightly out of sync. 'My dear girls, my dear boys, and all of you, my dear viewers, the moment has come for a first reviewing of the Dowries. Since the departure of the *Cupido*, the gifts haven't stopped flowing in from the four corners of the globe! Let's have a little look at where things stand.'

Serena's face disappears to give way to a chart with two columns: the girls on one side, the boys on the other, each with their headshot, ranked like horses at the races according to their winnings.

Dowry Funding Ladder

Female Contestants		Male Contestants	
Kirsten (DEU)	2,580,234 $	Alexei (RUS)	3,000,560 $
Elizabeth (GBR)	2,470,260 $	Tao (CHN)	1,905,345 $
Fangfang (SGP)	1,905,256 $	Mozart (BRA)	1,305,333 $
Kelly (CAN)	1,290,556 $	Marcus (USA)	1,103,510 $
Safia (IND)	845,567 $	Samson (NGA)	785,903 $
Léonor (FRA)	306,567 $	Kenji (JPN)	702,455 $

'*On the girls' side, Kirsten's charms have earned her some points. Maybe you've also wanted to make up for her little accident, my dear viewers?*'

I am the last in the ranking and by some distance – I would have been amazed if it had been otherwise. What is surprising is that there are still people who've shelled out three hundred thousand dollars for someone who knocks her friends out and spends three-quarters of her time drawing by herself on her bed.

'*On the boys' side, the big winner is unquestionably Alexei,*' Serena's voiceover continues. '*His smile is worth more than three million dollars already! But everything can still change, as we're only on day three of a journey that will take a hundred and sixty-one. So don't hesitate, dear viewers, keep sending in those donations! We'll review the table every Wednesday. And let me remind you that the money allocated to each candidate will allow them to buy at auction the equipment for New Eden that has been left on Mars, which we will be showing you at the halfway point in a special broadcast on your favourite channel: the Genesis channel, naturally!*'

The screen continues to show the table of Dowries for

several long minutes – which allows us time to get into a lather about the photo portraits of the boys, whom we have only so far glimpsed in the opening titles.

'Alexei really is *too* handsome,' sighs Kris. 'His eyes make me quite dizzy.'

'And they're even more dizzying in the flesh,' says Liz.

Kelly gives a whistle.

'Hang on, girls, if we're talking about eyes, have you seen Samson's? A green like that, *whoa*! He looks super buff – but so do Mozart and Marcus . . .'

'None of them's as buff as Tao,' says Fangfang decisively – she seems to have taken definite ownership of the Chinese boy. 'And besides, as for the colour of their eyes, we shouldn't care all that much about that – you may find some of these boys are wearing coloured contacts.'

A unanimous, reproachful *boo!* immediately shuts Fangfang up.

'Oh, please!' Kelly rebuffs her. 'That's like me saying Tao's biceps are silicone!'

'Alexei's eyes are obviously *real*!' adds Kris, ready to defend her Prince of Ice.

'And anyway, it's not just the muscles that count,' suggests Safia. 'I think Kenji is very cute in his way.'

'You're not wrong, there really is something in that wild, mysterious look of his,' agrees Liz. 'It's going to be a difficult choice, girls! Serena has done a really great job on the selection! I'm starting to wonder whether Léo wasn't right, with her rule of seeing a different boy each week. But not everybody has the discipline, or the patience.'

At that moment, the screen finally goes dark, leading to a wave of indignant protests that save me from having to say anything about my famous rule – I'm pleased about that.

'In any case, there's one thing that won't wait, girls,' says Kelly. 'The three crèmes brûlées left in the fridge yesterday. First come, first served!'

Hysterical yelling, a scramble towards the ladder that leads to the living room, and I'm not the last to hurry over there.

'I'm so glad we've made up,' says Kris, applying a coat of pastel-coloured polish onto her nails.

Standing behind the sofa, I'm finishing twisting her blonde braids into a crown around her head. I've adopted the black satin ribbon, whose ample bows 'blend in so harmoniously with my curls' (so says Kris).

'I'm very glad too,' I say. 'Not least because of the crème brûlée.'

Kris looks up at me, concerned.

'Not only because of that, I hope.'

'Of course not. Also because of the apple strudel, and the chocolate fondant. I only hope we have all the right ingredients on board.'

She bursts out laughing.

'You're impossible!'

'Maybe,' I say, and now it's my turn to smile, unable to keep a straight face a moment longer. 'But our friendship does have its practical advantages. If it weren't for me, your famous braided crown would be only a shadow of itself. Honestly, who was it that helped you to do it yesterday? It looked like it was made from ears of wheat.'

A shadow falls across Kris's face, a retrospective concern.

'Really? You're right, it's true that it wasn't the same as usual. Fangfang isn't as talented as you. Ears of wheat! Just as well it wasn't my turn in the Visiting Room yesterday!'

'Notice the beautiful rustic style, it's so adorable . . .'

'Léonor!'

'Oh yes, I assure you. Liz told us your Russian guy was a very natural type. Maybe he likes the countryside, peasant girls who smell agreeably of the harvest and tumbles in the hay.'

I assume the voice and mannerisms of a hairdresser at a classy salon.

'Now then, *madaaame*, am I tousling it to give it a bit of a sexy finish?'

Unable to restrain herself any longer, Kris leaps onto the sofa and jumps on top of me.

'Watch it, leopard – you're the one who's going to get tousled!'

A chase begins around the living room.

'Careful!' says Fangfang indignantly, raising her feet, whose toes are separated by cotton balls. 'You're such brats! Try and be a bit mature for a change. You're going to make me spoil my nails.'

But nothing can calm us down. We chase each other around like madwomen. We go down the rungs of the ladder four at a time, and so does Louve – it's well known that poodles are the best circus dogs! Barking, shouts of joy, more or less controlled slides, pillow fighting. Without catching our breath we burst back into the living room to a horrified look from Fangfang. She's right, we really are brats – and it can do you a world of good!

'Well, well!' a voice comes out of nowhere. 'Such excitement, girls, it's lovely to see.'

Serena has just reappeared on the wide-screen opposite the fireplace.

I finally stop, hands on my knees, out of breath from so much laughing and so much running, while Louve climbs the last rungs of the ladder, panting – she always finds it a little harder going up than going down.

'It's almost time for our daily interview,' announces Serena. 'Lots will be drawn for today's girl, just a few minutes after the session begins, as usual.'

The atmosphere in the living room seems to thicken all of a sudden, each of the girls holding her breath – apart from me and Kris, who are panting like animals. Who will be going up to the Visiting Room today? Perhaps Kelly, who is sporting a blow-dry worthy of a pop-star? . . . Or Safia, who has decorated her hands with henna motifs, like gloves of brown lace? . . .

'And the chosen one is . . . Léonor.'

26. Genesis Channel

Wednesday 5 July, 11:00am

Fade in from black.

Shot of the empty Visiting Room.

Title: *Third session in the Visiting Room. Hostess: Léonor, 18, France, Medical Officer (communication latency: 7 seconds)*
Drum-roll.

A flame appears at the left-hand side of the screen: it's Léonor's mane of hair, trapped in a ribbon. She's wearing the little grey jersey top from the day before, and her regular ripped jeans. The camera zooms gradually in on her face. Her cheeks are still red from running. Her large golden eyes, emphasised by a simple stroke of eyeliner that's black like the satin ribbon, reflect the stars that drift slowly across the infinity of space.

Serena (off): *'Now that's what you call a stunning view, isn't it, my dear Léonor? I'm sure you're busily recording everything you see in your artist's mind so as to produce a lovely piece of work for us later.'*

Léonor, enrapt: 'It's just . . . magnificent. More beautiful, vaster, more impressive than anything I could have imagined.

And the silence, Serena! I think I could stay here just listening to the emptiness for hours.'

The silence stretches out for seven seconds, enough time for Serena to hear Léonor's voice and then send hers back to the *Cupido*: '*For hours, you say? But let me remind you that you only have six minutes ahead of you! So tell us: whom have you decided to invite today? Are you curious to see Alexei and that smile that's worth its weight in gold? Or Tao with his Superman physique? Or would you rather try your luck with another contestant?*'

By way of response, Léonor slips her hand into the pocket of her jeans and takes out a handful of slips of paper.

Léonor: 'Serena, pick a number between one and six.'

A few seconds pass again, before Serena's disembodied voice sounds again: '*Excuse me . . . ? I'm not sure I've quite understood. Has the transmission come through correctly . . . ?*'

Zoom in on Léonor's open hand, in the palm of which the slips of paper are resting. Each of them is folded in four, with a number written on the back in black ink.

Léonor: 'Did you think I wasn't serious the other day, when I declared my rules for the game? I said that when my time came to go up to the Visiting Room I'd draw lots for the name of the boy. In real life, it's mere chance that determines who we meet. I'm just trying to keep my feet on the ground – in a manner of speaking.'

This time, Serena's laugh breaks through the silence.

'*I recognise that unbounded creativity of yours, Léonor! And your non-conformism too. Your own rules of the game, no less! You've got a lot of personality, and I like that.*'

Serena clears her throat: '*One. I choose the number one. Because*

I think in a mission like ours it's important for us all to remain united, the whole time: you, Léonor, and the passengers; me, Serena, and the organisers; and all of you, dear viewers, who are watching us at this moment. One irresistible surge of humanity all together bound for the planet Mars!'

Léonor puts five of the slips of paper away into her jeans pocket, keeping out only the sixth, which bears the number 1.

Close-up on her agile fingers as they unfold the paper, as delicately as if they were unwrapping a thin chocolate.

A name appears amid the folds: *MARCUS.*

Serena (off): *'Well, well! It seems we're going to be meeting a new contestant today, Marcus the American, Planetology Officer for the boys' team! Did I deal a winning hand? You'll see the answer to that for yourselves, in a few moments.'*

The voice disappears, abandoning Léonor to the silence of the Visiting Room. She allows her body to rise gently in the zero-gravity atmosphere. She lifts her hand to her hair, as though toying with whether to release it.

Before she is able to make a decision, a drum-roll – Marcus's head appears through the hatch on the right-hand edge of the bubble, followed by his whole body. He's dressed in black, a shirt and trousers that disappear against the background of space. His brown hair, thick and smooth, has been diligently combed, emphasising his regular features, the harmonious structure of his face. The light from the on-board spots make his grey eyes sparkle beneath his straight thick eyebrows, giving his stare an unusual intensity.

At the bottom of the screen the small dial of the stopwatch appears: the interview has begun.

Marcus: 'Hi. Thanks for inviting me.'

His voice is deep and warm. Slightly hoarse.

Léonor: 'Technically it was Serena who invited you. I just wrote six names on six bits of paper, and she chose one.'

The camera closes in on Marcus, framed around his shoulders. He gives a half-smile: the right corner of his mouth goes up, at the same time as the tip of his right eyebrow. The left side of his face remains immobile.

Marcus, a tad provocatively: 'I see. So, you're indecisive. The kind of girl who needs someone else to make decisions for her – a man, for instance.'

Léonor: 'For your information, I take full responsibility for the decision to let luck choose who to invite.'

Marcus: 'That makes sense.'

Léonor raises her chin, her golden eyes full of defiance. 'It wasn't as though I was suddenly going to fall in love at first sight with one of the six boys who I'd only seen in a photo for five seconds in the opening titles – not for you any more than one of the others, anyway.'

Marcus: 'It's interesting, really, your technique for chatting somebody up! Telling the guy you invite that he isn't your type.'

Léonor: 'That wasn't what I said . . .'

Marcus: 'Aha!'

Léonor: '. . . but maybe that's what I think.'

The bodies of the two young people are drifting slowly towards one another. They look each other up and down, carrying out a careful evaluation by eye.

Their hands come to rest on the glass wall at almost the same time.

Marcus's smile spreads to the left side of his mouth. 'You're kind of playful, aren't you, Léonor?'

Léonor can't help smiling in turn. However hard she tries to hide it, it's clear that she's touched. Intrigued. Or maybe more. Not least from the way she defends herself. 'And you, Marcus, you are presumptuous. *Indecisive* . . . *Playful* . . . So what's the next adjective you're going to come up with for me, given that you don't know me at all?'

Marcus: 'How about *charming*?'

His eyes are devouring the girl; the camera doesn't miss the tiniest thing either. It's so unusual to see Léonor smile.

So radiant.

So fleeting.

Léonor is already pressing against the glass to push her body back a little. She moves slowly away, across the bubble, elusive. But she can't take her eyes off Marcus's. 'I was wrong. *Presumptuous* is too subtle a word to describe such a crass pick-up technique.'

Marcus: 'So let me try something a little lighter.'

Without leaving Léonor time to answer, he runs his hands through his hair: a flesh-coloured rose bud appears between his fingers, out of nowhere.

He lets go of the stem, and the rose floats off into the stars. 'Hmm, too pale for you, that flower. Not enough personality.'

Marcus runs his hand through his hair again; this time, it's a fuchsia-coloured rose in full bloom that appears as if by magic between his thumb and his index finger.

He lets that one fly away too, sowing coloured petals across the Visiting Room. 'Too open, that one, too *Look-at-me!* It scatters to the four winds.'

192

For the third time his fingers plough through his hair, succeeding in dishevelling it; he takes out a perfectly proportioned red rose, whose striking, rich colour seems modelled exactly on Léonor's own red locks.

Marcus exclaims, in French: '*Voilà!*'

He bows his head slightly, his hair falling over his forehead, and holds the rose out toward Léonor, who looks at him amusedly from the middle of the bubble.

She smiles again. 'Let me guess . . . before applying to the Genesis programme, you were a florist?'

Marcus: 'I was a street artist. A beggar, if you'd rather, around Las Vegas, Phoenix, Los Angeles, well, lots of places, I guess. Having had to sleep under the stars, I know them all by heart and that made me want to go see them – the stars, that is. And what about you, you were a Rosier model, right?'

Léonor: 'Not exactly. I worked for your platinum sponsor, Eden Foods, and not as a receptionist either: I worked in their dog-food factory in Paris.'

Marcus: 'Well, even though I'm not a florist, I do know it's from manure that the most beautiful roses grow.'

Suddenly Léonor looks at her watch. To check the time? Or to escape from Marcus's gaze for just a moment, to hide her agitation and find the strength to take back control?

'Well, we've only got a minute left,' she says, eyes fixed on her wrist, 'I think it's time to drop the poetry and put our cards on the table.'

She looks up abruptly.

She's no longer smiling.

'If you'd seen me in the factory with my overall and my

hygiene cap, there was nothing rose-like about me. My scent was more like Winalot No. 5. And I'm sure you've brought a whole cargo of flowers to do your little number for each one of us – yellow roses for the blondes, violet for the brunettes, and these red roses for me, the resident redhead.'

Marcus: 'Ouch!'

He lets go of the last rose, which heads off to join the others on the ceiling of the Visiting Room.

Léonor: 'What's wrong?'

Marcus: 'This rose has thorns. It pricked me.'

Léonor: 'Well, maybe you need a smooth-stemmed flower that won't hurt you. I need a partner who doesn't make me lose my head. I've already told you: I don't want to fall in love instantly like a lightning strike. Lightning can . . . it can burn.'

The girl's voice trembles imperceptibly as she speaks this last word – but could the young man opposite her, and the viewers millions of kilometres away, have noticed?

Léonor: 'I don't want to be consumed like wildfire. What I want is to last. That's why I've drawn the name of my guest today by lots: to give each of you the same chance. I'll do the same for my next five invitations, for the next five fortnights: I'll draw lots. And then I'll re-invite each contestant in turn, the same one every twelve weeks. Finally, when we line up with the orbit of Phobos, I'll confirm my definitive Heart List, as rationally as possible.'

Marcus lets his arms float back down to his sides.

There are no more tricks to do, not today.

His own smile has faded too. His enthusiasm has plummeted. All that's left is a terrible disappointment.

'You mean you won't invite me back for another *twelve weeks*? Not till *September*? Even if you want to?'

Léonor nods gravely. 'Yes. And you're free to do the same, as far as I'm concerned. You can invite me once every six times. Any more than that won't do any good. I won't come. Not even if I want to. These are my conditions. My rules of the game.'

Marcus's thick eyebrows frown suddenly.

'And you call that *rational* behaviour?'

A shrill ringing sound answers his question.

The interview is over.

Serena (off): *'That's time! Not another word. Léonor, Marcus: time for you to return to your respective quarters.'*

But Léonor doesn't move.

Nor does Marcus.

He opens his mouth to shout something; no sound comes from his lips.

Serena (off): *'There's no point trying to talk. Communication between the two parts of the Visiting Room has now been cut off, to respect the equal time allocated to each speed-dating session.'*

Marcus falls silent, but his face is still twisted in rage.

He angrily lifts the collar of his shirt, revealing the start of the tattoo that appeared in the photo in the title sequence. The camera zooms in on the line of ink that is born at the base of his neck and dives down into the collar of his shirt.

Marcus undoes the top button. The line stretches further, bristling with thorns.

Marcus undoes the second button. Leaves with the most delicate of veins adorn the stem carved into his skin.

Marcus undoes the third button. A rose bursts onto his right pectoral muscle – a whirlwind of calligraphic petals making up a phrase that curls in on itself:

Seize the day.

Fade to black.

Credits.

27. Shot

'Well? How was it? Tell us!'

The moment I reappear in the living room, the other five girls leap on me as hungrily as Louve attacking her bowl in the morning.

They're all here, trembling with excitement.

'It was . . . weird.'

That's the only word I can come up with to describe what I've just experienced.

Because I really don't know what to think.

Because I'm torn between sweetness and bitterness, something I never would have thought possible.

From the very start of the interview, I felt the lava of my words burning inside my mouth, my famous irony gushing out like an eruption nobody could contain. But the expected conflagration never happened. There was something in Marcus's grey eyes that cooled my inner fire. A sort of calm. Seriousness. And perhaps – who'd have thought it, in this spacecraft in the grip of a round-the-clock competition, in this show that's

197

constantly looking for the wildest spectacle – yes, perhaps even a kind of sincerity. Hence the sweetness.

But the interview ended with a bitter taste that screws this recipe up completely, with Marcus's explosion of rage.

'You've got to tell us more than that, Léo!' begs Kris, hanging onto my arm. 'Just *weird* isn't enough! Ugh, it's such torture not being able to watch what happens in each other's speed-dating sessions! Did you really choose at random?'

'Well, yeah, like I said on the first day. Those are my rules of the game, don't forget.'

Yes, my *rules of the game*, but not Genesis's, who of course are betting on great flights of lyricism, devastating passions, romantic dramas and all that kind of stuff. I'd rather keep control of my own emotions. I want to protect myself. I want to choose whoever would be best able to accept us as we are, the Salamander and me. And above all – *above all!* – I don't want to fall in love with the wrong boy.

'Well, OK, so what was he like, this Marcus?' Kris presses me, yanking me from my thoughts.

'Soothing. Irritating. Predictable. Unpredictable. All of these at once. And so, like I said . . . *weird*.'

Kelly folds her arms over her little short-sleeved lumberjack's shirt and looks me up and down derisively, as she chews the gum of the day.

'Soothing *or* irritating? You've got to choose!'

I brush her insinuations away with the back of my hand.

'My head's on completely back to front, it must be because of the zero gravity.'

But the girls have no intention of letting me get off that

easily. All I've done is fan the flames of their curiosity. They need more details.

'Come on, Léo!' Liz begs. 'What did you say to each other?'

'We talked about horticulture.'

'Oh!' cries Fangfang. 'Did he tell you about enriching the soil on Mars with nitrogenous compounds, so that one day it might be possible to grow lettuces? That was a part of the Planetology training, which he must have gone through like me: a thrilling subject, but quite technical, and hard to fit into just six minutes.'

Blessed Fangfang, who can never help herself from bringing everything back to her books.

'No, he didn't talk to me about nitrogenous compounds or about lettuce,' I say, trying to smile. 'But maybe he did tell me about salads. Only time will tell. Now, I don't know about you, but I'm absolutely ravenous. Kris, can I give you a hand in the kitchen?'

Once lunch is over, the table cleared and the dishes cleaned with the electrostatic cloth (because we need to save on water, which is so precious on board), Liz suggests having coffee over a round of cards.

'I brought a French tarot set,' she says. 'It's a fun game a fellow ballet hopeful from Paris once taught me. I thought it would be a friendly way to kill time.'

'We'd be better off revising,' says Fangfang.

Kelly shrugs. 'Take a breath, nerd-girl! You're going to have five months for cramming!'

'I have a real subject I've got to master, not just the highway code of space,' says Fangfang, getting on her high horse. 'You've connected the capsule to the *Cupido*; it took you a few hours and now your little task is done. The craft is on the Earth–Mars trajectory and nothing and nobody can make it leave its course. But my job is only just beginning: Planetology is a complex science, that will allow us to locate our new world –'

'My *little task* is not done,' retorts the Canadian. 'Can I point out to you that we've not yet arrived on our new world. I'm the one who'll pilot the capsule from the orbit of Phobos, in five months' time. If I crash us somewhere or if I bring us down hundreds of kilometres from New Eden, what good will your Planetology lessons be then?'

Safia decides to try to stall them, before things get worse.

'We'll just play a few hands, before settling down to study, OK?' she suggests. 'Can anyone explain the rules to me?'

'Oh, it's not that complicated,' says Liz. 'Léo, can you lend me a hand to demonstrate? I'm sure you know how to play tarot, like all French people do, right?'

'I didn't often get the chance to play at the young workers' hostel. It was every girl for herself there. I may have forgotten some of the rules. I'm a bit rusty.'

'That's no excuse: there's a card to remind you on the back, with the points and everything! Come on, off we go!'

With some of us sitting on the sofa, others on the floor, we play in turn, five of us with the sixth as referee. I do my best to concentrate on the game while sipping my Coffeo instant coffee. But images from my six minutes in the Visiting Room keep scrolling through my photographic memory, superimposed onto the playing cards. As always, I feel as though I'm reliving what I've experienced, more precisely now it's a memory, frame by frame.

'I bid low!'

Marcus's eyes . . .

'Guard!'

Marcus's voice . . .

'The queen of hearts, a picture card for you!'

Marcus's roses . . .

I've never been a huge fan of flowers, not like most girls are. Flowers are too fragile for my taste. They fade and then they spoil, they're transient like a promise that isn't kept. Now, Marcus's roses, I reckon I could forget them easily enough. The first three he held out to me at least, the pink, yellow and red flowers. Only, the thing is, then there was a fourth: the tattooed black rose. That one will never fade – or rather, it will just wither as Marcus's skin, which is so smooth today, ages on Mars, next to the skin of whoever he spends his life with . . . That rose isn't made to deceive or to sweeten a false promise; what it says is no lie. It's a conviction that's so strong that a being of flesh and blood has engraved it into his body for ever. 'Seize the day!' Marcus and his rose say to me, in their slightly hoarse voice; and what do I reply? 'Not for another twelve weeks.'

After a dozen rounds of cards punctuated by bursts of laughter, an exclamation louder than all the rest pulls me out of my reverie.

'Where's the king of hearts got to?' asks Fangfang, who's so taken by the game she seems to have forgotten about her sacrosanct revision time. 'The round is over and nobody's played it. Kelly, you're the one who picked it up: did you put it in your kitty? You know that's not allowed in this game. Liz told us you can't discard a king!'

201

'Hey, easy!' the Canadian defends herself. 'I haven't touched your damn king of hearts.'

The conversation quickly gets heated.

'It's not *my* king of hearts, it's the game's. It's everybody's.'

'Right, that's right. Like Tao? You're going to share him too?'

Fangfang's cheeks flush behind her glasses.

'What exactly do you mean by that?' she asks.

'I mean that ever since your session in the Visiting Room you've acted like you're already married, you two. But I must remind you, nothing's happened yet. And if I also like Tao, for example, I won't be embarrassed to say so. Nor to invite him when it's my turn in the Visiting Room.'

'Don't argue!' says Liz. 'There are enough kings to go round for everybody on this spacecraft. We just need to use the rule card as the king of hearts until we find the real one, which must have slipped down somewhere. Come on – one more quick round?'

But no one is in the mood.

I feel my back itch.

You had your king of hearts in your hands, sniggers the Salamander. *But stupidly you lost him, and now the cards have all been reshuffled!*

28. Genesis Channel

Thursday 6 July, 11:00am

Fade in from black.

Shot of the empty Visiting Room.

Title: *Fourth session in the Visiting Room. Hostess: Kirsten, 18, Germany, Biology Officer (communication latency: 9 seconds)*

Drum-roll.

Kirsten rises slowly up the left side of the screen, trying to find her balance. But each movement seems to destabilise her a little more. Finally she resigns herself to holding her arms straight, down the sides of her blue silk dress, and smiling at the cameras as if to apologise for her clumsiness.

Close-up on her crown of braids, which glows as though it really were made of finely spun gold, subtle make-up illuminating her angelic face. Everything is pastel-coloured: a touch of mother-of-pearl on her lips, a hint of pink on her cheeks, a comma of white pencil at the corner of her eyes.

Serena (off): '*Welcome to Kirsten, our fourth girl! Is your head doing better now, my dear?*'

Kirsten hurriedly reassures her: 'I don't feel a thing.'

While the laser beam of the transmission dish broadcasts her reply to Earth, Kirsten dares to remove her arms from her sides in order to touch her forehead with her finger; there's only a very slight shadow to recall the existence of the bump, which has now almost completely gone down.

Serena (off): '*All the same, it was quite something! I'm sure your viewers would like to know what happened between you and Léonor in the bathroom.*'

Kirsten: 'It's nothing to do with Léo! I . . . I just slipped on the rungs of the ladder up to the third floor, that's all. I overreacted when I accused Léo, but I the truth is I ought to hold myself responsible. I'm so very clumsy.'

She gives an embarrassed smile, which makes her prettier still, while her words fly across space.

Serena (off): '*In this case, your clumsiness is a part of your charm, Kirsten. You've already conquered the hearts of millions of viewers, judging by the magnificent Dowry they're collecting for you. But I think today what you're after is one heart in particular, and those who have been watching our broadcast since the beginning can doubtless guess which it is to be. Kirsten, I'm asking you this just for form's sake: whom do you wish to invite?*'

Kirsten: 'I would like to invite Alexei.'

Nine seconds pass again in the bubble, during which time Alexei's name seems to echo around the room.

Serena (off): '*Splendid! While some of the girls seem to hesitate about which boy to invite, even allowing luck to choose for them, you have your ideas fully settled from the start. Can I ask you why, Kirsten? Is it his well-furnished Dowry? Is it the idea of combining your two fortunes, his being the best-supplied of the boys' and yours the largest of the girls'? Or is it, quite simply, the promise of a bit of Slavic charm?'*

Kirsten: 'It isn't the money, Serena. When I heard Alexei's voice behind the curtain, on the launch platform, it did something to me . . . When I saw his photo in the title sequence, that thing in me grew, and now it has come to occupy my whole being.'

Kirsten shrugs, a little embarrassed.

She adds a few words, lowering her gaze. 'I know I must seem very sentimental telling you this; people are going to take me for a silly girl who reads slushy novels. But I've always trusted my instincts.'

Drum-roll.

Close-up on the face of Kirsten, who bites her lower lip nervously.

Alexei emerges from the right-hand access tube, in his elegant and immaculate white suit with a grey seam, while the stopwatch timing the interview appears on the screen: 'Hello. Kirsten, right?'

He smiles generously, forming dimples.

Reverse shot – as though in a mirror, Kirsten's shy almost-smile also expands: 'That's right. My name's Kirsten. But you can call me Kris.'

Alexei: 'OK, Kris. So long as you call me Alex.'

Kirsten nods.

Her cheeks flush slightly. 'Alex, you're . . . just exactly how Liz described you . . . exactly how I imagined you.'

Alexei: 'And you're even more beautiful than I saw in the credits.'

Kirsten: 'You're kidding me.'

Alexei: 'I've never been so serious in my life.'

The young Russian allows his body to float up the bubble, his eyes never leaving Kris's, while she in turn tries as best she can to remain stationary.

Alexei: 'If Liz has talked to you about me, she must have told you a bit of my history – that I left my parents to go in search of adventure in Moscow, all that. But I don't know anything about you, Kris. Who are you? Or rather: who are you, besides an angel dropped down from heaven?'

Kirsten's cheeks flush a little more. 'I . . . there's nothing angel-like about me. Believe me. I'm just a girl like any other, with her good qualities and her failings.'

Alexei: 'Well, my eyes can see only good qualities, and zero failings.'

Kirsten: 'That's because you don't yet know me. And you're seeing me from too far away. You know the old saying: the devil's in the details.'

Alexei allows himself to float over towards the glass wall: 'Maybe I'm just short-sighted, as I still can't see anything. Help me out: what are your defects?'

Kirsten starts to count them out on her fingers. '*One*, I'm clumsy. It took me three times as many sessions in the centrifuge as the other girls to learn how to move in zero gravity without rolling over myself.

'*Two*, I'm scatterbrained. My instructor, Mr Dragovic, really tried hard to train me for a whole year, and I don't think I understood more than half of what he told me.

'*Three*, I'm really lacking in self-confidence. I still haven't gotten over being chosen for the mission, and I feel there must have been some mistake somewhere in the selection process. Without my friend Léo who supported me and motivated me throughout the training process in Death Valley, I wouldn't be here today.'

Alexei gives a big, genuine laugh.

He in turn starts counting off on his fingers.

'*One*, what matters in this mission isn't being able to float for six minutes in a glass bubble, it's keeping your feet on the ground – or rather, on Mars, where we will be spending the remainder of our lives.

'*Two*, old Dragovic is a completely insufferable mad scientist, according to what we heard from Samson, who's the Biology Officer on the boys' side.

'*Three*, you say *lacking in self-confidence*, I say *modest*. A virtue that seems cruelly absent from certain girls who are travelling on the *Cupido*.'

Kirsten raises an eyebrow: 'Certain girls? Who do you mean? No, I can assure you, none of us is at all big-headed, and we are a tightly knit team.'

Alexei just smiles mysteriously without giving away a name. 'I think if you do have a defect, just one, it's being naïve. But that isn't a disadvantage the way I see it. I'm an idealist, and I want the mother of my children to be one too.'

Alexei's blue eyes sparkle.

Kirsten lowers her voice instinctively. 'This ideal you're talking about . . . what is it, exactly?'

Alexei: 'It's the ideal of an indestructible couple. A love as strong as diamonds. A family forged out of steel.'

As Alexei is speaking these words, his voice sounds as hard as diamonds; his pupils glint like steel.

But a moment later, his irresistible smile warms his face and eyes once again.

Alexei: 'So, Kirsten, with your golden crown, are you ready to take up this challenge?'

The girl holds his gaze, without blinking or blushing this time: 'I've been waiting for it my whole life.'

The bell goes: the interview is over.

29. Reverse Shot

'A golden smile for him, a golden crown for her, golden dowries for them both – all I can say is, this is one golden couple, and that's something I know a bit about after twenty years doing my couples talk show! Thank you, dear Kirsten, thank you, dear Alexei, for these magical moments, and see you again soon.'

Serena McBee turns off the microphone through which she has been commenting on the day's speed-dating session, and puts it down on the table to await her next cue to speak.

On the digital wall opposite her, the central window fades to black.

The titles start to roll, scored by the music of '*Cosmic Love*'.

'And that makes four!' exclaims Serena, turning towards her colleagues, the other allies of silence seated around the table. 'I can tell you right now, those two are going to collect hundreds of thousands more dollars – and so will we, thanks to our bonus. Kirsten and Alexei are just what the under-fifty housewives dream of: they are young, gorgeous, and stupid. *An indestructible love* – what a gorgeous, high-flown phrase!

209

Nothing is indestructible down here. Sherman Fisher knows that better than anyone. Talking of which, Odette, I've had them buy you a plane ticket: you'll be going to his funeral tomorrow.'

Odette Stuart-Smith stands up sharply, trembling with indignation in her beige turtleneck.

'Why me?' she cries.

'Because you knew the deceased better than any of us, that's why,' Serena McBee answers calmly. 'Your house in Beverly Hills is right by Fisher's. The Genesis programme must send a representative to the ceremony, that's the least we can do. Anything less than that would be suspicious.'

'But what if the police suspect something?' protests the little bespectacled woman, shuddering at the very thought.

'The police suspect nothing,' Serena reassures her. 'I've talked to that inspector who showed up on Tuesday, that Larry Garcia guy: the investigators have concluded that it was a road accident, just as we anticipated when we staged it. Sherman's body was unrecognisable after two weeks in Death Valley alongside his overturned car, under a blazing sun, left to the mercy of the coyotes . . . As for the drug injected by Dr Montgomery, it would have dissipated long ago, undetectable in what's left of his veins. Come now, my dear Odette, don't make us beg! We're just asking you to show your charming little face at the burial. You'll do Miami–Los Angeles return within the day. Fulfil your responsibilities, which, if I might remind you, are nothing like as onerous as mine: as the selector of the programme, I'm the one who will have to justify it when one participant kills the other eleven, and you don't see me making a fuss about it!'

The Planetology instructor mutters a few unintelligible words, but she doesn't dare to protest more openly.

Gordon Lock takes advantage of the silence to pick up on the executive producer's last words.

'Quite so, Serena, now you mention it: you still don't want to tell us which of the twelve is the mysterious kamikaze? It would reassure us if we could know.'

'Uh-uh,' says Serena, shaking her head like a grown-up refusing a sweetie to an over-greedy child. 'I'd rather keep it a secret. If you instructors knew the identity of the astronaut I've hypnotised, there would be a risk of your behaviour changing unwittingly in your dealings with them . . . with potentially unpredictable consequences. I'd rather keep it a surprise for you. And in any case, if things go wrong, we've always got the back-up solution – the option of depressurising the habitats ourselves from here, thanks to the remote-control system Geronimo has cobbled together for us.'

Serena takes a small black box out of her python-skin handbag, shows it briefly in the manner of a shopping-channel presenter, then puts it carefully away again.

'But you needn't worry, I don't think such extreme measures will be necessary. I assure you the murderer will do their job properly, long before the technical faults in the habitats ever need to come to light. I will never need to use the depressurisation controls. The programme is running like clockwork now that it's all been launched. Each of us can even take some time away, while the production continues on its course. As you know, I'm planning to supervise operations from my house on Long Island, in New York State. The weather is delightful this time of year, and I need some air after these past few busy months. I'll keep monitoring the programme and I'll give my instructions from there. I won't be back in Cape Canaveral till December, for the end of the game, the happy landing, the joyful marriages – and the *tragic event*, naturally!'

Roberto Salvatore stands up, pale.

'Honestly, Serena, you just aren't thinking! Sure, that's what was planned in advance, but things have changed! Think about the drone that's within our walls, the threat of hacking hovering over our heads like the Sword of Damocles!'

The executive producer shakes her head, her expression indulgent, entirely composed.

'Calm down, Roberto. With your weight problem it's wisest – we wouldn't want you to have a stroke, and your heart isn't indestructible either. As I've already explained to you, the base has been secured, and there's nothing compromising that the drone can possibly discover or reveal. Besides, we've already taken supplementary precautions. Please explain, Geronimo.'

The Engineering instructor puts down the toothpick with which he's been busy cleaning his teeth. He clears his throat, shaking his long black hair, which looks more than ever like it has the consistency of boiled spinach.

Finally, retaining his perpetually bored expression, he speaks.

'We've put a special plan in place. The Rapax plan.'

'The Rapax plan?' says Roberto Salvatore. 'What's that?'

Geronimo Blackbull pulls out from under the table a black, shining, triangular object, a sort of manta ray about fifty centimetres long, furnished with two sets of propellers. He presses a button and the machine rises above the table in absolute silence.

'*This*,' he says, 'the fifth-generation Rapax. You see, drones work the same way birds do: there are prey and there are predators. This model here is the most compact and infallible drone-chaser ever created, equipped with hypersensitive frequency sensors and very precise laser shooters. Wonders of technology, these things, and totally inaudible – what could possibly be better for us, the allies of silence! We've positioned a hundred of these at every strategically significant point on the base. If the bug dares to take to the air just one more time, I assure you it'll be brought down in seconds.'

By way of a demonstration, Geronimo Blackbull hurls his toothpick towards the ceiling.

A luminous ray shoots instantly from the tip of the Rapax and strikes the little wooden stick in mid-flight, without emitting the slightest sound.

Grey ash falls to the table in a light shower.

Roberto Salvatore sits back down slowly, as though afraid an abrupt movement might unleash a new salvo from the Rapax.

Serena doesn't seem to share his concern – she gathers her personal belongings back into her handbag, gets up from her large padded armchair and heads towards the bunker door, which she activates by staring into the small box containing the retina ID scanner.

'I'm leaving you in the safe hands of Director Lock,' she says from the doorway. 'Over the next five months, you can contact me via my assistant Samantha. In the meantime, enjoy the show!'

* * *

Serena heads down a corridor with concrete walls, lit by neon tubes attached to the ceiling.

Her high heels click rhythmically against the floor, awakening muffled echoes.

She reaches an elevator, and the door opens for her without a sound.

She goes inside, presses the top button.

While a silent arrangement of cables and pulleys hoists her towards the surface, she examines herself in the elevator mirror. Her unwrinkled face betrays no emotion. Her permanent smile has disappeared for the first time, replaced by a smooth mask, a total absence of expression.

'Level Zero,' announces an automated voice.

Serena turns just at the moment the door slides open.

The smile has reappeared on her face, as though it had never left.

The loyal Samantha is there, waiting outside the elevator with her silver earpiece.

'Your jet is waiting for you on the tarmac, Ms McBee, ready for take-off.'

'Perfect, Samantha. This way I'll be home before evening. Have you informed Harmony?'

'Yes, Ms McBee. Your daughter is expecting you for the birthday dinner.'

30. Shot

D +4 days 08 h 30 mins.
[1st week]

'If you knew what it did to me, Léo! When he looked me straight in the eye . . . I've never felt anything like it in my whole life, not even in *The Prince of Ice*.'

Seated on the small stool in the bathroom, Kris still isn't done reliving her speed-dating session. She has been up on cloud nine all day. It's already ten p.m. in Cape Canaveral, and the lights of the *Cupido* have been subdued to recreate an artificial day–night cycle. But Kris seems far too excited to go to bed.

'I'm happy for you,' I say, untying the last of the braids – the others, already undone, are resting like a golden shawl over her shoulders. 'I just don't want you to get too carried away. After all, it's still the beginning of the journey and you've only met one boy.'

'But I don't *need* to meet any of the others, Léo!' cries Kris. 'I'm sure he's the right one: him, Alexei, no one else!'

I nod, without a word.

'And you'll know it yourself too, when you meet your soulmate,' adds Kris, without noticing my discomfort.

(Oh, you know already, don't you? murmurs the Salamander at the back of my neck. *Think back to what happened in the Visiting Room . . . Think back to how you felt . . .)*

Marcus's face flashes into my mind. I force myself to drive it away just as abruptly.

'Soulmate?' I manage to say, in a voice that is a little wobblier than I'd like. 'You really believe that? In the first place, I'm not even sure such a thing exists. And if it does, and each human being really does have one soulmate amid the billions of others, what's the likelihood of six of these perfect couples finding themselves on this spacecraft at the same time? None at all, if you ask me! Statistically, we're screwed.'

'Just wait a bit before jumping to conclusions, Léo,' says Kris with a smile. 'You've still got five boys to go, five chances to thumb your nose at those statistics. You just need to give them a chance to touch you . . . Stick the Determinator on pause for six minutes.'

'It's not that simple.'

'It really is, Léo. It's that simple. Six boys and six girls: it's actually the simplest thing in the world. Why don't you want to recognise that?'

Kris gets up from her stool to stand facing me. With her long blonde hair completely loose now, she looks more than ever like the picture that adorns the door of her wardrobe, Botticelli's Madonna.

She takes hold of my shoulders, brings her face up close to mine and looks me right in the eye.

'It's what I saw the other day in the bathroom, isn't it?' she murmurs hesitantly. 'It's that thing on your back?'

I take a deep breath. There's no sound beneath my feet, in the living room where three of the girls are glued to a comedy on the wide-screen; not a sound above me, in the gym where Kelly is burning off her excess energy on the treadmill before bed. Once closed, the hatches isolate the sound perfectly: here, in the silence of the bathroom, nobody can hear or see us.

'That thing has a name,' I say at last. 'It's the Salamander.'

'The Salamander?' asks Kris.

'When I was little, I came across a book in the orphanage library with pictures of imaginary animals: *The Fantastical Bestiary*, it was called. There was a page devoted to the Salamander, a black lizard with poisonous skin, that lives among flames without being consumed by them. I decided to give that name to the burn that nearly killed me when I was three. I'm sure it's the reason my parents abandoned me, and it has poisoned every day of my existence since.'

Kris quickly lets go of my shoulders – because she's afraid of being contaminated by contact with the Salamander through my jersey top?

'Does it hurt?' she asks.

'Depends. Sometimes the Salamander makes me itch to rip off my skin, and I imagine its claws tearing at me. Sometimes I feel nothing at all. But it's always there, hiding on my back, whispering into my ear. It's lying in wait for the day when I drop my guard, when it can finally win our hand-to-hand combat. It's already tried to bring me down four times – I've always got up again, so far.'

I feel my pulse racing in my temples.

What I'm about to tell Kris I haven't told anyone else other than Serena McBee, when I was going through the selection interview.

'The first time,' I tell her, 'was at the orphanage. I must have been five years old, six at the most. The Salamander was still young then, still moving, still burning. It wasn't violet-coloured, but pinkish; its texture wasn't wrinkled, but elastic. Every month, I had to report to the hospital to check on its development, receive skin grafts and treatment. The social services pretended it was just to check up on my freckles; they preferred to keep the real reason a secret from the other orphans, in case they bullied me. But one evening, when I arrived back from hospital, three little brats who took themselves for tough guys trapped me in a corner of the dormitory. They wanted to see if I had as many freckles on my body as on my face. I still remember the boy who tore off my shirt while the other two restrained me. "Toady-skin! Toady-skin!" he shouted. "Look at her toad skin!" His hand moved towards my tights, no doubt wanting to see if I was a toad down below too. I caught it mid-flight – between my teeth, since my arms were immobilised. And I bit him. Until I could taste the blood. His screaming did me a world of good; it was as though I were the one screaming through him, screaming out my shame.'

Kris's pupils dilate slightly in the scattered light of the bathroom. I seem to be pouring more than just memories into her – a tide of raw pain. But she tilts her head to encourage me to go on.

'By the second time the Salamander nearly killed me, the

scarring was almost complete. I was eight. It was the happiest day of my life. After years mouldering in the orphanage, a couple had finally agreed to take me. They were perfect. The woman had a very sweet smile, hair as light as a cloud and bracelets that sang happily around her arms each time she moved; the man was tall, strong, had a nice aftershave smell, and when he talked, his deep voice enveloped me in a feeling of well-being and safety. They signed the papers, took the medical files, received the compliments from the social workers for having had the courage to choose that particular orphan "despite her problem". Their courage didn't last long. That same evening, when it was time to apply the ointment that in those days I needed every night, the woman hesitated for a moment. Her hand hung in the air. Her bracelets suddenly stopped singing. When she touched me, I felt her fingers shudder with horror. The next day, the man drove me back to the orphanage without saying a word, as though he no longer wanted to share anything with me, not even his beautiful voice, for fear of sullying it. That same night, in the dormitory I'd thought I'd never see again, I took a vow – a vow never to give my trust to anyone. All the foster families that came after that were never more than just strangers to me.'

A few words escape Kris's lips. 'Léo . . . My poor Léo . . .'

She rests her hands on my shoulders, and suddenly I understand: when she pulled them back the first time it wasn't to keep herself away from me, but so as not to hurt me.

'When the Salamander attacked me for the third time, it was fully grown, set in position,' I say. 'I'd just started working at the Eden Food France factory. I'd been boarding at the young

219

workers' hostel for a few weeks. There was a laundry room with two washing machines in the basement. One Sunday when I'd taken down my basket of laundry, the director of the home came to see me. "The other girls have complained," she said. "They're afraid that your . . . peculiarity is contagious. From now on, for everybody's peace of mind, it would be better if you did your laundry by hand, in the sink in your bedroom. You do understand, don't you?" I took my laundry out of the machine without a word, even if inside me my belly was spinning like a tumble-dryer. "Yes, Madame Cochard." I waited till she'd turned on her heel before letting my tears flow. I haven't cried since, not even when the Salamander attacked me for the fourth time . . .'

'. . . three days ago, when I burst into the bathroom,' Kris guessed. 'Oh, Léo, if only I'd known. I feel so awful. And I do so understand now why you hesitated before taking the final step!'

'There's no reason you should feel bad. You aren't responsible, nor is Serena, the only other person in the Genesis programme who knows about the Salamander. I'm infinitely grateful – to her, for keeping me in the programme; to you, for staying my friend; and to both of you for keeping my secret.'

My heartbeat begins to slow.

I've got it off my chest. It's made me feel a whole lot better, but the wave of emotion has now passed and it's time I pulled myself back together.

'I'm the one who has to manage the Salamander,' I say. 'I know it'll attack me a fifth time, when my future husband learns of its existence. I just want it to happen as late as possible, and to prepare myself as much as I can first. Which is why I'm

220

also keeping this inflexible rule of inviting each of the boys in turn, just once every twelve weeks. Right before the final Heart List, I'll show the Salamander to the boy I've chosen, and who's chosen me, so that if he makes a commitment he does so knowing all the facts. The other girls think I'm stubborn as a mule, but now you know why I'm doing this: to protect myself. I will survive, you needn't worry. If there's one thing I've learned in my fifteen years stuck with the Salamander, it's that: how to survive.'

ACT III

31. Reverse Shot

The Villa McBee, Long Island, New York State
Thursday 6 July, 9:00pm

'You haven't even touched your plate, Harmony. We really can't go on like this. You must eat something. You have to get your strength back.'

Serena McBee is sitting at the end of a long ebony table overhung by a row of three magnificent chandeliers that shed a subdued light.

Facing her, six metres away at the foot of the table, at the end of a silk table-runner embroidered with honeycomb emblems, is a second chair. A stick-thin girl, dressed in a delicate grey lace dress with long sleeves, is hunched up in it. The porcelain plate positioned in front of her holds a pink half-lobster and a delicate bundle of green beans. The food is intact, not even touched.

'I'm not hungry,' says the girl.

Her voice is as fragile as glass. Her light-coloured eyes also look like glass marbles – indeed, her whole face has a curious transparency to it. Her skin is so pale and so fine that it's possible to make out the thin network of blue veins crossing it. Her long hair, of a diaphanous blonde, almost white, has the smooth, shiny consistency of gossamer. Despite her thinness, the girl's resemblance to the woman sitting opposite her is striking: these two are mother and daughter.

'It's not a question of whether you're hungry,' says Serena McBee sharply. 'People who obey their desires and their revulsions end up becoming enslaved. So easy to manipulate...'

Serena delicately takes hold of one of the many crystal glasses lined up behind her plate – a flute filled with champagne.

She brings it to her lips and savours it with pleasure.

'Mmm ... this Merceaugnac Cuvée Impériale 1969 really does live up to its reputation. The champagne from the year of the Moon landing, Harmony, just like the one we've given the participants – I've bankrupted myself but it's worth it! It goes marvellously with the lobster. Such a shame you don't want to try it. But maybe you're saving space for the birthday cake?'

Serena claps her hands, making her bracelets tinkle.

'The dessert!' she says.

Two young men in service waistcoats, who up till now have been totally silent and perfectly blended into the shadows by the wall, approach the table. They're so light on their feet that they seem to be levitating over the freshly waxed parquet floor. Each of them has a silver earpiece attached to his right temple.

The plates disappear without the slightest clink of crockery. They give way to two exquisite individual charlottes, real pieces of baker's craftsmanship made of sculpted meringue, scattered with bits of crystallised red berries that glow like rubies. The charlotte in front of Harmony is pierced by eighteen white candles, as thin as spillikins. Serena's, meanwhile, carries just one candle.

'Happy birthday to us both, darling!' says Serena, raising her champagne glass. 'The cook has used honey from the estate, that I collected myself. Come on, let's have a smile: you don't turn eighteen every day!'

'And what about you, Mom? How old are you today?'

Serena gives a silvery laugh.

'That, darling, is my little secret. There are some women who say that from a certain age they'd rather not count. I, on the contrary, keep a very careful count, even if I don't reveal it, and I consider each one of my birthdays a personal victory over time. You'll understand one day. For now, just blow out your candles.'

But Harmony hasn't yet finished.

'And my dad?'

'What do you mean, your dad?' asks Serena, putting her glass down abruptly onto the table. 'I've told you a hundred times that he died not long before you were born.'

'How old would he have been today?'

'That's a pointless and unimportant question. Now blow out your candles, my dearest.'

Serena's tone brooks no argument.

At the other end of the table, Harmony takes a deep breath. The pattern of veins on her temples and her forehead is accentuated as her lungs swell with air, as her body fills with newly oxygenated blood.

'Blow!' Serena demands.

From where she's sitting, in the half-light of the vast dining room, she cannot make out the little red droplet that has formed under Harmony's nose.

'Go on! All at once! Don't disappoint me!'

But the moment she breathes out, Harmony is seized by a violent coughing fit, which shakes her frail body. Two long threads of blood fall from each of her nostrils, mixing with the raspberry coulis in which the charlotte is soaking.

'Harmony!' cries Serena, rising from her chair. 'Not today, not on our birthday!'

But Harmony is no longer in a position to respond: overcome, she falls forward onto the table, smashing the crystal glasses whose shards mingle with her colourless hair.

32. Genesis Channel

Friday 7 July, 11:00am

Fade in from black.

Shot of the empty Visiting Room.

Title: *Fifth session in the Visiting Room. Hostess: Kelly, 19, Canada, Navigation Officer (communication latency: 11 seconds)*
Drum-roll.

Kelly emerges from the access tube connecting the Visiting Room to the girls' quarters, and shuts the hatch behind her. She has divided her abundant blonde hair into two braids that float on either side of her face; the two front pieces of her red-checked short-sleeved shirt, knotted over her navel, also rise, revealing a belly toned by time in the gym. The piercing shines like a star, among all those others scattered across the sky.

Serena (off): '*Hello, Kelly.*'

Kelly: 'Hello, Serena. You sound rather subdued today, if you don't mind my saying. Were you out partying last night?'

The silence that follows Kelly's question might suggest that the executive producer didn't take too kindly to Kelly's joke, but in reality it's nothing more than the communication latency between the spacecraft and Earth.

Serena (off): '*Out partying? Yes, you could say that. It was my birthday. I went to bed late. But enough about me – you're the heroine of the day, Kelly! Your first day in the Visiting Room! With whom are you going to share it? Are you also going to be tempted by Alexei?*'

Kelly twists her left braid around her fingers with their pink nail polish – matching her lipstick, naturally. 'Those Prince Charmings who look like they've stepped right out of the latest Disney movie aren't really my thing, to be honest. The only blond I like is Jimmy Giant, the new James Dean. I like rebels, hot-blooded types, not ice-men – I've been frozen enough for years back in Canada. Nigeria, Brazil, those appeal to me more than Russia. And besides, that Mozart intrigues me. I'm crazy about music and with that name maybe he's a musician – even though I'm sure he can't touch the hem of Jimmy, the god of country-rock.'

Drum-roll.

Kelly takes advantage of the brief pause to spit her chewing-gum into a handkerchief, which she puts away in the pocket of her jeans.

Then Mozart appears on the right-hand side of the screen. He too is wearing jeans, and a white V-neck T-shirt that shows off his muscles and his caramel-coloured skin.

Mozart, in a deep, languid voice: 'Hello.'

Close-up on his tanned face. His jet-black hair, smooth and shining, twists voluptuously down the back of his neck and over his temples, making him look like a young faun. His lips wear an irresistible smile, and his intense gaze is shaded by long black eyelashes.

Kelly: 'Hi, Mr Artist! Or should I say: *My greetings to you, Herr Mozart?*'

She gives a little bow in space, before looking back up abruptly, in a movement that flicks her braids behind her once again. 'Where's the white wig? Where's the face powder? The silk stockings? You weren't wearing them in the title sequence but I did think for the Visiting Room you'd at least have made the effort. I'm disappointed.'

Mozart: 'I've got the stockings on under my jeans. Shall I show you?'

He lifts his T-shirt, revealing perfectly outlined abs. The elastic of his boxers is visible over the waistband of his low-slung jeans.

Mozart: 'The boxers are fifty per cent silk, very tight fitting, super-comfortable. Shame you can't touch them to feel for yourself.'

Kelly gives a whistle. 'You do get straight to the point! Do you always show that chocolate-bar six-pack of yours on a first date?'

Mozart: 'Do you?'

Kelly: 'Me?'

Mozart: 'I really like your minimalist interpretation of the Canadian lumberjack shirt!'

Kelly slowly looks down at her own belly, at the knotted flaps of her shirt, before realising that she's baring every bit as much flesh as her guest and bursting out laughing.

Kelly: 'Touché! And I was expecting to meet a lisping marquis! I can tell we're going to get along! But your parents really called you Mozart? No kidding?'

The young Brazilian lets his T-shirt back down. 'My parents cleared off out of my life about five minutes after spitting me

231

out into the world, so I don't think they'd have had the time to give me my name.'

Kelly: 'Oh! So you were abandoned as a kid, like Léo!'

Mozart raises an eyebrow: 'Léo?'

Kelly: 'Another one of the girls on the *Cupido*. Forget it, you'll have plenty of time to get to know her. Right now, it's you and me. And you haven't yet answered me, about your name.'

Mozart: 'It was the girls in the Inferno favela who gave it to me – nice girls! But it's the only name I've got, so I like it well enough anyway.'

Kelly: 'The Inferno favela?'

Mozart: 'The foulest slum in Rio, where I come from. Well, even "slum" is too luxurious for that open-air dump, where the neighbouring favela ended up stretching out to try and fit everybody in. Can you picture it?'

Kelly, serious all of a sudden: 'I can imagine . . . well, I can try.'

Mozart: 'In the Inferno, it's kind of "every man for himself, and God for us all", though I can't say God ever helped me very much, if I'm honest. But I don't blame Him, the poor guy. I reckon He probably does what He can, and I'm not the vindictive type.'

As proof, he holds up the crucifix on a thick gold chain he has hanging round his neck.

'The folk in the favela, on the other hand, accepted me as one of their own. Petty crooks, two-bit forgers and thieves of all kinds: you'd think they were the rejects of humanity, but most of them were really big-hearted. It was a group of young women in the favela who brought me up, and I think of them as kind of my big sisters – well, when I say *brought me up* . . . They looked after me when they had time, because they kept themselves pretty busy picking up the tourists on the Copacabana and Ipanema beaches, or training in samba in the hope they might be the next carnival queens. I became as nimble as a monkey, and so small: I could sneak around Rio's chicest neighbourhoods and empty every pocket in the twinkling of an eye, for a bit of redistribution of wealth. You get it now, about my name? I was a young prodigy, a virtuoso, 'the Mozart of picking pockets'! Not that I'm boasting, oh, I've repented of all that – I've grown up; I couldn't do it any more; I wanted to turn the page and go back on the straight and narrow. So when the choppers came and sprinkled the favela with fliers for the Genesis programme, I decided to apply. You could say I was pretty lucky to be chosen, given my CV!'

Mozart looks Kelly up and down, with a kind of challenge in his eyes, a look that says, 'Bet that's shocked you!'

But far from taking offence, the Canadian smiles widely: 'Well, if you ask me, you've passed the first round of interviews with flying colours. First, you're an expert in Navigation, a real job that's properly in the thick of the action, not in one of those woolly subjects like Planetology. Second, I notice you're wearing the same brand of boxers that Jimmy Giant wears, so you have good taste. Thirdly, I'm totally compatible as far as personal experience goes, given how often I've been described as *trailer trash* – nice phrase, right? Just because I lived in a caravan with my mother and three brothers in a suburb of Toronto. Sure, it's true they were all unemployed, and the trailer was a bit small for five, which is why I decided to sign up for the Genesis programme, to get some air.'

Mozart jokes: 'So here we are, you and me: two pieces of trash chucked out into the emptiness of space . . .'

'Two *gorgeous* pieces of trash!' Kelly corrects him.

'My dream would be getting recycled together. Look, I'm starting already . . .'

With these words, the young man starts doing somersaults in the air with an unsettling ease, bringing tears of laughter to Kelly's eyes.

'Look! Cycling . . . re-cycling . . . re-re-cycling . . .'

All of a sudden Kelly stops laughing.

Mozart seems to notice, and instantly stabilises himself in the air. 'What's up?'

Kelly covers her mouth with her hand, an expression of horror on her face. 'Your . . . your neck . . .'

Quick as a flash, the camera zooms in on the back of Mozart's neck; as he spun around, his black hair lifted to reveal a small silvery metal marble catching the spotlights.

Mozart: 'What about my neck?' He brushes his hair down hurriedly. 'It's just a piercing, no worse than that. Like the one on your belly-button.'

But Kelly doesn't hear him.

She shouts: 'Stop! Stop the whole thing! Stop it right now!'

Mozart throws himself towards the wall, pressing his forehead against the glass.

He's shouting back: 'But what's gotten into you? What did I say? What have I done?'

Kelly: 'Get me out of here, goddammit! Get me out of here or I'm going to do something I'll regret!'

A shrill ringing suddenly drowns out her shouts – at the

bottom of the screen, the stopwatch has completed its circuit: it's over.

Serena (off): *'Come now, Kelly, why are you in such a state? Because of the mistakes of Mozart's youth? Are you really that shocked by his past?'*

But there's nobody to answer Serena's questions: by the time they reach the Visiting Room, Kelly has already unbolted the hatch and disappeared into the tube that leads down to the girls' quarters.

Fade to black.

Credits.

33. Shot

A metallic crashing sound echoes through the living room, the noise of a hatch coming down.

Louve, who I was busy drawing, leaps to her feet: her posing session is done for the day.

I switch off my sketching tablet and look up at Kelly, who's storming like a bulldozer from the upper floors of the living quarters. It's instantly clear from the red flush on her cheeks that there's been a problem.

'It didn't go well?' asks Fangfang, without it being clear whether the answer 'yes' or 'no' would please her more.

'Don't ask!'

The Singaporean gives a whistle.

But Kelly doesn't hear her. She practically lunges for the dining table, sends a few leftovers from breakfast flying into the trash can, leaving only a glass at one end of the table. Then she takes the bar of soap that's sitting by the kitchen sink and puts it at the other end. She crouches down; she takes a deep breath; she gives the damp bar of soap a flick,

236

and it slides along the table towards the glass but stops short of touching it.

'Missed,' grumbles Kelly under her breath.

She takes the washing-up brush and starts frantically scouring the steel surface, before retrying the experiment of propelling the soap.

Given the way she rebuffed Fangfang, nobody dares to ask her what's going on.

'I'm the same. Whenever I get stressed I relax by doing the housework,' Kris finally says kindly, to relieve the tension.

'I'm not doing the housework!' barks Kelly. 'I'm curling! To me it's like praying, so thanks very much for distracting me!'

And she goes on scrubbing even more.

'She's *curling*?' Kris repeats quietly.

'I think it's a bit like bowls on ice,' I say. 'You've never seen it on TV? One guy throws a stone onto an ice rink, and all the others brush wildly in front of it so that it slides all the way to the target.'

'It's nothing to do with bowls!' roars an outraged Kelly.

Oops, I spoke a little too loudly.

'For your information, curling is an Olympic sport!' she says imperiously, brandishing the bar of soap under my nose as though she were going to force me to eat it. 'In Canada we take it *very* seriously. Oh, for God's sake, why do I bother trying to explain to girls who are only interested in one thing: finding themselves a guy whatever it takes, even if there are only assholes here with us to choose from! So *ciao*, I'm going off with Jimmy, and everyone else can damn well just leave me alone.'

With a shot of remarkable precision, she tosses the soap into the sink. Then she angrily grabs her music player from the charging table and tears right through the living room to seek refuge in the bedroom – just as I did myself four days earlier.

34. Reverse Shot

The Villa McBee, Long Island, New York State
Friday 7 July, 3:30pm

'You really scared me, Harmony,' says Serena McBee, her voice heavy with reproach.

Dressed in an elegant mauve suit, she's sitting beside a large metal bed with a raised back, the kind usually found in hospitals. But the large space full of stunning antique furniture has nothing of the hospital room about it, and the girl stretched out on the bed is nothing like a patient in a hospital gown: the material of her grey lace dress is spread among the white sheets like a delicate foam.

'You must take better care of yourself. You have to eat properly, and take your pills. Ever since you were little you've always had a weak constitution, to the point that I had your bedroom windows sealed up for fear a gust of wind might carry you off. But lately things have been getting worse. When you were taken ill last night . . . Promise me you'll make an effort?'

'I promise, Mom,' replies Harmony.

She's still very pale, and her cheeks are hollow. But the rays of sunlight pouring through the large steel-barred window make her water-green eyes – so like her mother's – shine.

239

'Can I believe you?' Serena asks.

'You can, Mom. I'm making that resolution to mark my adulthood. To grow up. To become an accomplished woman, like you.'

Serena takes her daughter's hands in her own.

'Nothing could make me happier, my darling. Indeed, you do look more like me with every passing year! One day you'll take over from me, you'll proudly fly the McBee flag, with that noble crest that comes to us from our Scottish ancestors.'

Serena shows the gold signet ring she wears on her little finger, imprinted with its honeycomb and its bee.

'Yes, Mom,' replies Harmony.

The girl's transparent gaze is lost in the room. It passes over the row of porcelain dolls sitting obediently at the edge of the fireplace decorated with stucco foliage; over the silk mobile in the shape of a butterfly that floats from the ceiling; over all the memories that are scattered across this childish room. The only sign that the child has grown up: the novels on the bedside table, whose titles in gold letters glow weakly from the leather bindings. *Pride and Prejudice*. *Sense and Sensibility*. *Persuasion*.

'I know I haven't been around much these past months,' Serena continues. 'Organising the Genesis programme, the training in California, it's all taken up a lot of my time. But things are going to change, I promise. From today on, I'm going to be doing the job remotely. I'll only be leaving Long Island once or twice, to meet the Atlas people in New York – a matter of just a few hours. The rest of the time we'll be together, the two of us, Harmony, here in the Villa McBee. Heavens, that reminds me, with all this commotion I forgot to give you your birthday present!'

Serena bends down to remove an object from beneath her chair: a black case, which she puts into her daughter's slender hands.

'Oh!' whispers the girl as she lifts the lid.

A stunning diamond necklace is lying inside.

'There are eighteen stones, one to mark each of your years on Earth,' explains Serena, hanging the jewels around Harmony's neck. 'Do you like it?'

The girl sits back straighter against her satin pillow in order to see her reflection in the big cheval-glass opposite the window.

'Very much!' she exclaims. 'Thank you!'

Serena gets up and plants a kiss on Harmony's forehead.

'I've left some brioche and tea on your dressing table. I'll have you brought up a decoction of royal jelly from our hives a little later: it's an excellent restorative, and your blood pressure is still very low. For now you should rest, my dear. Take deep breaths, the way I taught you. I'll put the TV on to help you relax.'

Serena walks over to the large flat-screen embedded in the wall, between two pastel-coloured Impressionist canvases. She brushes her finger against the smooth surface; it switches on immediately to the Genesis channel. The cramped and windowless living room where the girls are gathered looks like an extension of this vast sun-filled bedroom.

'You remember when the six boys and later the six girls came by the house soon after being selected, before they left for Death Valley?' Serena asks.

'Yes, Mom. It was nice of you to invite them, and I was glad to have the chance to meet them at least once.'

'It's because they don't have families of their own, or not any more, you understand? I wanted to let them see a close-knit family before they left, something that might inspire them during their time on Mars. There's so much unhappiness in this world . . . We're lucky to get along with each other so well, Harmony.'

Serena heads for the door to the room, then stops just before walking out and takes a set of keys from her suit pocket.

'Harmony . . .'

'Yes, Mom?'

'You do understand why I keep you closeted away, don't you? I mean, you understand why I've kept you sheltered in the Villa McBee ever since you were little?'

'Because you love me, Mom.'

Serena smiles.

She closes the door behind her, double-locking it.

The sound of her heels recedes, giving way to silence, barely disturbed by the babbling of the Genesis participants who are arguing about something on the screen, whose volume is set to the minimum.

Only now does Harmony get out of bed – slowly, testing out each movement, as though she were afraid of shattering her thin limbs by doing something too abrupt.

She walks over to the window, puts all her weight against the glass to slide it up. A gentle breeze engulfs her through the bars – it's the breeze of summer in the Hamptons, the most fashionable part of Long Island and doubtless the whole

242

country, where the cream of New York's elite have their second homes. Despite the heat, Harmony shivers under the lace covering her shoulders and arms. She takes hold of a bar with each hand, and brings her face closer: stretching into the distance are the English gardens of the Villa McBee. Luxuriant flowerbeds brimming with rosebushes, the stems mixed with clematis, clusters of buttercups as dazzling as gold in the sunlight, lavender plants swaying in the breeze like the waves of a violet sea: it's an explosion of colours and scents. Down beyond the hedgerows, the roofs of the property's dozens of hives are sticking up. And further still, behind the trees, it's possible to make out the hundreds of fans who are laying siege to the fence of the Villa McBee in the hope of catching sight of the high priestess of the Genesis programme.

Harmony turns away from all that, to examine the cloudless sky.

She clinks her nail against the metal of the bar: *tink! tink! tink!*

. . . and look, there's something approaching, across the vaulted blue . . .

tink! tink! tink!

. . . a grey shape . . .

tink! tink! tink!

. . . a pigeon.

It comes to rest on the window-sill, with a great beating of wings that makes Harmony's hair billow up. A smile of relief appears on the girl's face when she notices the red tube attached to the pigeon's leg.

'Thank you,' she murmurs under her breath. 'Thank you.'

She hastily unties the tube, under the round, indifferent eye of the unmoving bird.

She takes a small golden powder compact out of the pocket of her dress, and opens the round case with a loud click. Inside, under the puff, there's nothing at all, not a single grain of powder. Harmony pops out the stopper of the red tube and tips its contents into the hidden compartment inside the compact: a very fine white sand, with iridescent reflections, glimmering like snow.

Only then does she look up again and remember the presence of the pigeon, which is still staring at her through the bars on the window.

'Yes, I know,' she says softly. 'I've got to pay.'

She opens the big jewellery case on her dressing table, revealing layers of purple velvet each covered in rings, earrings, necklaces like the one her mother has just given her. She chooses a gold earring inlaid with rubies: it just fits inside the little red tube, which she closes back up with care and reattaches to the pigeon's leg.

The bird flies back up into the sky, without a sound.

Harmony returns to her bed.

She sits down on the edge of the mattress, her lace dress barely rustling under the weight of her too-light body.

She takes one of the Jane Austen novels – *Pride and Prejudice* – and opens it to a page that she removes without making the slightest noise. With the corner of this torn-out page she lifts a few grams of white sand out of her powder compact. She deposits it on her bedside table, nudging the edges of the little heap till it forms a nice straight line. Finally, she replaces the powder-puff to disguise its treasure, closes the case and puts it away in her pocket, before leaning over the thin, shimmering line.

'Time to take a little trip, Jane,' she murmurs, rolling the page between her thin fingers, making a tube of paper and words.

She positions one end in the corner of her delicate nostril, the other at the start of the line of powder. Then she draws the furrow up, inhaling as hard as her lungs will allow.

She falls back onto the bed, letting go of the sheet of paper, which drops to the floor.

Her whole body clenches.

Her pupils contract.

Her arms, her legs, all lift from the mattress, and her nearly white hair swells up, rising as though weightless.

35. Genesis Channel

Friday 7 July, 11:00am

Fade in from black.

Shot of the empty Visiting Room.

Title: *Sixth session in the Visiting Room. Hostess: Safia, 17, India, Communications Officer (communication latency: 14 seconds)*

Drum-roll.

Safia appears on the left-hand side of the screen. She's put on her saffron-coloured sari, whose expertly folded fabric floats around her like the petals of a gigantic silky flower. Her long black hair, tied carefully back, shines like onyx. In addition to the red dot adorning her forehead, today she's wearing a gold ring in her right nostril.

Serena (off): '*Oh, Safia! So sophisticated! So exotic! Thanks to you, the billions of viewers watching are going to get a real feast for their eyes! But only one of the six boys will get the chance to enjoy the view. Which is it to be, Safia?*'

Safia: 'I'm torn between Samson and Kenji.'

The seconds tick by in the glass bubble, for the time it takes for Safia's doubts to reach Earth.

At last Serena's voice replies, repeating the names of the two boys like a distant echo: '*Samson and Kenji? Interesting . . . And why them?*'

Safia: 'Because neither of them has been invited yet. I imagine they must be a bit sad about that . . . I'd like to get both of them to come, but unfortunately that isn't possible.'

Serena's silvery laugh resonates around the glass bubble, with a fourteen-second delay: '*Oh, Safia! Such selflessness, like a proper Mother Teresa! It's all very well thinking about other people's feelings, but what is it that you want? Is there one of these two contestants who appeals to you more than the other? Who's it to be, Samson or Kenji? Kenji or Samson? You do have to choose!*'

The Indian girl hesitates a moment, before making her decision: 'Samson really is very, very handsome, but I think for today I'm going to go with Kenji, because he's the youngest of the boys. He's seventeen, like me: that gives us something in common.'

Drum-roll.

The voice off disappears, and Safia is left alone in the silence. She waits patiently, breathing calmly, the way Serena taught her. Just occasionally she brushes the fabric of her sari slightly aside with a graceful movement of her hand to bring it back into place.

The moments pass.

They become minutes.

Finally, Serena speaks again: '*I'm so sorry, Safia, we have a little problem . . . Kenji is refusing to come.*'

Close-up on the hitherto serene face of the youngest girl,

who is now making no effort to hide her distress. 'He . . . he doesn't want to see me?' she stammers.

The fourteen seconds of time delay are a real torment for the Indian girl. The most violent emotions are visible in her kohl-ringed eyes, while she awaits the answer to her question.

But Serena dodges the question: '*I don't know what to say, except that it means you need to choose another boy. The lovely Alexei, perhaps? Like the other girls, I bet you're dying to meet him.*'

Safia recovers her calm expression. Decisive. 'No. Not Alexei. Samson. I want to invite Samson.'

This time, she doesn't have to wait long. Samson's shaven head soon appears on the right side of the screen. The first thing that strikes you are his emerald-green eyes, which stand out against his obsidian-black skin. He is simply dressed, beige cloth trousers and a short-sleeved shirt that emphasises his slim body. A delicate bow tie gives him an undeniable touch of elegance.

Samson: 'Thank you for inviting me, Safia . . . even if I wasn't your first choice.'

Safia is a little embarrassed and gets tangled up in her explanations: 'I couldn't make up my mind . . . I thought about making the most of a sense of solidarity what with him and me both being the youngest . . . I should have asked you first . . .'

Samson bursts out laughing – a pure, sunny laugh, that reveals his dazzlingly white teeth. 'I'm just teasing! There's no need for you to apologise. I'm happy enough that I'm even your second choice, you know what I mean? And as for Kenji, well . . . he doesn't know what he's missing.'

Safia looks somewhat reassured.

248

She gives a smile. 'Do you know why he didn't come?' Then she quickly adds, 'Not that I regret it, far from it, but it's a little upsetting. He thought I was ugly when he saw me in the title sequence, is that it?'

Samson: 'There's no point trying to understand. Kenji's a bit weird . . . No, it's not quite that – to tell the truth he's totally cut off. He doesn't talk to anyone.'

Safia: 'He's mute?'

Samson: 'No, I'd say he was antisocial. Terrified by the least human contact, you know the type? Just imagine, six minutes tête-à-tête with a girl he doesn't know . . . and such a stunning one at that!'

Safia blushes slightly at the compliment. 'I don't understand. Why would the production team have chosen someone so antisocial for a mission like this?'

Samson shrugs: 'How should I know? Kenji does have other qualities. He's a genius at electronics. His brain is like a proper living computer. He knows the radio frequencies used in space by heart, he can calculate transmission times with his eyes closed; at any given moment he can tell you our position relative to Mars, to Phobos, to the Earth and everything in the whole spinning solar system. All that is worth having in a Communications Officer! And anyway, I don't know what it's like on the girls' side, but over on our side nobody's perfect – with the possible exception of Alexei. That guy seems superhuman.'

Safia: '*Nobody's perfect*. What do you mean?'

Samson shakes his head. 'I'm sorry, on the boys' side we've made a pact not to criticise one another. And in any case, I wouldn't want to grass on my pals. We have a saying in my country: *camels don't laugh at their humps*. It's for the others to say whatever they have to, here in the Visiting Room, to any girls who ask them questions. I can only speak for myself.'

Safia: 'Well, then I'll ask this question of you, Samson: what's *your* imperfection? Look at those magical eyes!'

Samson's wide smile quickly vanishes.

He lowers his voice. '*These magical eyes*, as you put it, are my most terrible curse. In the village where I was born, it's said that children are sorcerers if their skin is too white or their eyes too light-coloured, like mine. We reject those children, nobody wants them, because they bring bad luck: their parents abandon them, the elders expel them, and whenever there's a shortage of food, or illness strikes, people take revenge by killing them.'

Safia cries: 'But that's so unfair!'

Samson replies: 'That's the way it is. Nigeria is a magnificent country, full of amazing people. But there's nothing harder to uproot than tradition.'

At these words, Safia's face flushes. '*Tradition!* What good has *tradition* ever done us, apart from a few nice bits of cloth?' She flings the fabric of her sari violently over her shoulder. '. . . Wars, murders and orphans . . . ! Pain, and blood, and tears . . . ! That's what *tradition* has brought us. Because of *tradition*, my parents wanted to make me marry a man I didn't love, and all my people rejected me! If this programme has any purpose, if there's one thing all twelve of us ought to do, it's to stop *tradition* taking root on Mars!' She fixes her eyes on Samson's. 'I'm going to put you at number one on my Heart

List, Samson. And if I marry you in five months, I will be very happy. Our children will have your amazing green eyes. They will look over to Earth from a planet where human cruelty will never be able to reach them; and all those on Earth who suffer from intolerance can look to Mars as a symbol of hope that nothing will ever be able to erase.'

Samson's got his smile back. 'Not bad for a first interview! I was only your second choice, and now you're wanting to marry me. Maybe I'm not as unlucky as all that after all?'

The bell goes, bringing the interview to a close.

Serena (off): *'Who would have believed it! A speed-dating session transforms into a resounding plea for human rights . . . and a possible proposal of marriage! That's what I call a show! It's giving me chills; I've still got goose bumps! And I have no doubt it's the same for you, my dear viewers, ladies and gentlemen. If Safia and Samson have convinced you, don't hesitate to let them know by furnishing their Dowry, so that their green-eyed children can grow up in the most beautiful Love Nest in New Eden!'*

Fade to black.

Credits.

36. Out of Frame

Calvary Cemetery, Los Angeles County
Sunday 9 July, 3:30pm

'Sherman Fisher was a model husband and a model father. He was likewise an exemplary citizen of the city of Beverly Hills, in whose life he was an active participant. Finally, he was a well-respected member of the scientific community, as evidenced by his positions at the heart of NASA before the Atlas purchase and more recently with the Genesis programme, his last employer.'

The priest temporarily lifts his nose from the microphone attached to the pulpit to remove a handkerchief from beneath the folds of his white alb and wipe his forehead. This July afternoon, the sun is dazzling. Its scorching light stretches out the shadows of the gravestones that punctuate the yellowing grass of the Calvary cemetery, in the east of Los Angeles County.

About a hundred people dressed in black are gathered around a trench dug in the dry earth. The men undo their shirt collars; the women raise the veils on their hats to let in a bit of air, some of them even fanning themselves with the orders of service; somewhere at the back, a baby is crying.

'It was Sherman's dedication to his job that ultimately got the better of him,' continues the priest, putting away his handkerchief. 'Sending man to Mars had become his raison d'être. Having talked to him about it myself, as I was his parish priest in Beverly Hills, I know he saw this mission as a way of honouring God, of contemplating the beauty of creation closer up. Lately, then, Sherman had been one of a group of people to whom the responsibility fell to train the candidates for the colonisation of Mars, at the training camp in Death Valley. He devoted day and night to it, never stinting in his efforts, to the point where he was only able to return to the bosom of his family one weekend a month. Sherman, the man of space, didn't like taking planes, and so he would do the journey to Beverly Hills by car. It would seem that the asphalt, burning hot at this time of year, made the tyres of his Chevrolet explode. The Lord called his son to him just days before the departure of the mission for which he had toiled so hard. Some might see a cruel irony in this. For me, I believe Sherman was able to watch the take-off of the rocket from the best possible place, which is heaven, sitting beside the Lord. And I'm sure he will continue to watch over his protégés in the days, months and years to come. I will stop now and allow those who knew Sherman better than I did to speak. I would first like to call on the widow of the deceased, Vivian Fisher.'

The priest takes a few steps back to make way at the pulpit, at the foot of which stands a framed photographic portrait of the man to whom he has just paid tribute: a man with a hard expression, wearing a jacket and tie, his forehead creased with worry-lines. The coffin that has pride of place in front of the gaping grave has been thoughtfully left closed.

A tall, slim woman, elegant in spite of her mourning state, emerges from the crowd, leaving behind her two magnificent greyhounds sitting as tamely as though they were earthenware dogs – one completely black, the other completely white. While the widow makes her dignified way towards the pulpit, arranging her veil, a child's voice whispers between sobs, 'Drew, aren't we going to see Father again before they . . . they bury him?'

The little twelve-year-old girl who is speaking looks up with reddened eyes at her big brother, who is standing beside her in the front row. Standing very straight in his black suit, his hair slicked down with wax, the young man looks like a statue, as still as the greyhounds whose leash he is holding. His eyes are not red behind his black-framed glasses, but the tension gripping his face reveals as much as any tears.

'No, Lucy,' he murmurs in a strangled voice. 'We can't see Father again. When they found him in Death Valley, the accident had already happened several days earlier. We wouldn't . . . have been able to recognise him. Best to keep a memory of him as he is in that photo, there next to Father Daniel.'

'But he looks so severe in that photo . . .'

'Father *was* severe, Lucy. Specially since he'd been working for Genesis. He must have had so many worries, so many responsibilities . . . That photo is one of the last ever taken of him.'

Lucy swallows another sob, then falls silent.

Over at the pulpit, their mother is getting ready to speak.

'The first time I met Sherman, it was at the country club in

Berkeley,' she begins. 'He was a physics student, I was studying classical languages. Even then, space was already his passion. I commented to him that our specialities weren't as far apart as all that, since every planet had a Latin name. That was our first conversation, the first laugh we shared . . .'

Andrew closes his eyes.

He takes a deep breath.

His shirt rises and falls to the rhythm of his breathing, swallowing up his mother's tremulous speech, his sister's muffled crying, and the rustle of the burning wind in the branches of the ancient sequoias.

'I now call on Andrew Fisher, the son of the deceased.'

Andrew opens his eyes again abruptly.

He breaks away from the group and heads towards the pulpit, like a robot.

The sea of heads turning towards him looks blurred, like a mirage.

Andrew slips his hand into his jacket pocket to take out the scrap of paper on which he's scribbled his speech. But the words too are blurred, as though his glasses have stopped working, as though the entire world were disappearing.

No big deal.

Andrew lets go of the piece of paper, which is carried off by the wind.

In any case, he knows what he has to say.

'In a month, I will be going back to Berkeley,' he murmurs into the mic. 'The place is a symbol for me. You probably think you know why, after what you've just heard: that's where my father met my mother. So without Berkeley, I wouldn't exist: QED. But that's not really it, that's not what's important. What matters is that Berkeley has given meaning to my life. Because it's the path that Father showed me: of perseverance, of hard work, of dedication. I've always admired him hugely. He's always been my role model. Yes, it's true he was severe, but he was fair. Ever since I was very small, my greatest fear has been that I would disappoint him. My greatest satisfaction, hearing a compliment come out of his mouth.'

Andrew pauses briefly.

He grips the sides of the pulpit with both hands.

'Lately Father had been very absent. The Genesis programme was monopolising him, as Father Daniel recalled. I admit I felt jealous of those other teenagers who were getting so much of his time while he had so little for me, his own son. But the important thing is that before he died Father was in the process of realising his dream – the dream he had begun to nurture when he was my age, on the benches at Berkeley, and doubtless even before that – of reaching out and touching the stars. He was too old to be an astronaut himself. But he was doing everything he could to send other humans there in his place.'

Andrew takes one last deep breath.

His eyes rise up beyond the rows of people, up to the blinding sky, towards the man to whom he's addressing the final part of this speech.

'So today, Father, I make you a promise. I swear I will prove myself worthy of you. That I will also touch the stars, one day. That I will go to Mars. And that you will go too, through me.'

Andrew steps away quickly, leaving only just enough time

for the priest to put a sympathetic hand on his shoulder. 'Well said, Andrew.'

The remaining speakers follow on from one another as though in a dream, under a blanket of leaden heat. Until the priest calls the final one.

'I now invite Odette Stuart-Smith, who was both Sherman's neighbour in Beverly Hills and his esteemed colleague at the heart of the Genesis programme. Despite her current workload, which we can all easily imagine, she has made this trip over from Cape Canaveral especially to pay this final tribute.'

A slight woman emerges from the crowd, sagging beneath the weight of an enormous garland of flowers that she carries in both hands. Despite the scorching heat, she's wearing a turtleneck that goes all the way up to her chin.

She glances at the congregation over the top of the pulpit, though it's impossible to tell whether she can really see anything, since her pupils are entirely invisible behind her Coke-bottle glasses.

'One . . . two . . .' she says into the mic. 'One . . . two . . .'

'Um, no need to test it, my child,' offers the priest, a little put out. 'The microphone is working fine, we've been using it for the whole service.'

'Just a simple check,' replies Odette Stuart-Smith. 'In the aerospace world, we do always like to check our equipment twice; it's just a matter of professionalism.'

'Oh? Well, very well, if you say so . . .'

The small woman turns towards the congregation with a disconsolate expression.

'Ladies, gentlemen – and you, dear Fisher family . . . Sherman was more than a colleague to me: he was a close friend, whom I will miss for ever. Today my heart is ballasted with an immense pain as heavy as . . . as . . .' she searches for the right words for a few moments, then seems suddenly touched by inspiration, '. . . as this magnificent floral arrangement generously sent by the Genesis programme!'

She drops the garland against the coffin, very evidently glad to be rid of it. All the flowers in it are red, like the ribbon that runs across it with an emphatic dedication: *To Sherman Fisher, with the gratitude of the future Martian civilisation.*

'I would have liked to say more,' claims Odette Stuart-Smith, 'but I need to be back at Cape Canaveral this evening and my flight leaves in less than two hours.'

A murmuring in the congregation.

But Odette Stuart-Smith has already rushed off. She races towards the exit from the cemetery, while the priest returns to the microphone to make a start on one final prayer before the coffin is laid in the earth.

'*To everything there is a season, and a time to every purpose under the heaven;*

'*a time to be born, and a time to die;*

'*a time to plant, and a time to pluck up that which is planted; . . .*'

Andrew leans in to Lucy's ear, handing her the leash to the two greyhounds.

'Keep hold of Yin and Yang, I'll be right back.'

He detaches himself discreetly from the group and runs after Odette Stuart-Smith, the ancestral words from Ecclesiastes lost beneath the sound of his shoes hammering on the lawn.

'*A time to rend, and a time to sew . . .*'

'. . . a time to keep silence . . . and a time . . . to . . . speak . . .'

Andrew catches up with the small woman just before the cemetery gates, beyond which hundreds of people have gathered to watch the rites from a distance, held back by a police cordon.

'Ms Stuart-Smith!'

Odette turns sharply, a startled look behind her glasses.

'It's me – Andrew.'

'Ah, Andrew,' she says stiffly. 'Very touching, your little speech. I wish you all the best at Berkeley. But I've got a plane to catch now and I have to brave the crowds to get to my taxi.'

She gestures with her chin towards the strangers who have gathered beyond the fence. Some of them are holding up portraits of the deceased who has been made famous by the Genesis programme, others placards bearing brightly coloured inscriptions: *Sherman Fisher, space hero without whom nothing would have been possible; We'll never forget you, Sherman; Let's hope the first Mars baby is called Sherman!*

'Wait!' cries Andrew. 'I want to ask you some questions, since you were at my father's side in his final days. Did he talk to you about me? Do you . . . do you know why I wasn't chosen for the programme?'

'I've told you I haven't got the time,' retorts Odette drily, visibly in a hurry to get away as quickly as possible.

But Andrew's hand closes over her thin arm.

'I'm begging you, answer me, I need to know. When I learned the identity of the astronauts signed up, those fairground freaks who'd been chosen just to entertain the masses, it drove me totally nuts. I blamed my father so much! But in retrospect,

I'm so ashamed, as I'm sure he fought like a dog for me. He must have been under terrible pressure from Atlas if he wasn't able to secure my candidacy. Isn't that right?'

A grimace crosses Odette Stuart-Smith's face.

'Let go of me at once, you understand?' she commands. 'If you really want to know, Sherman didn't lift his little finger to support your candidacy. On the contrary: he formally declared himself to be against it.'

Andrew lets go of the old woman's arm as quickly as if he's been electrocuted.

'W-what?' he stammers, pale as a ghost. 'I don't understand. My father always encouraged me in my passion for space. We shared it. He instilled it in me from a young age. He always promised me that when the occasion presented itself he'd let me go to Mars, even if it was a one-way trip. He always said he'd be proud to see me making history, even if it meant leaving my family. That was why I so admired him: because he had the courage to say these things to me. To my mind that's the greatest proof of love a father can show his son.'

'Well, those were just words,' says Odette with a nasty smile. 'Your father wasn't a superman. He just gave in. If it had been up to me and the other organisers, we certainly would have given you a chance; we'd have sent you up there in a flash. But Sherman selfishly preferred to keep you here on Earth, rather than letting you take flight.'

Andrew staggers slightly.

He starts to tremble.

'Everything I thought I knew about my father was – was false . . .' he stammers. 'Everything he said to me was no more than a tissue of lies . . . I thought I knew him, but he was a total stranger to me!'

'My condolences, Andrew,' says Odette Stuart-Smith, turning on her heel.

37. Shot

D +6 days 21 h 30 mins.
[1st week]

'. . . and so we shall never forget Sherman Fisher.'

On the wide-screen, Serena lowers her eyes with an expression of profound contemplation. Behind her, a window overlooks the gardens of the Villa McBee, from where she now does all her voiceovers. The tranquil, sunny landscape is in sharp contrast with the mourning dress in black lace worn by our patroness. Tactfully, using just the right words as only she knows how to do, she has just informed us about the death of Sherman Fisher, who sadly died in a car accident, and who is being buried today. That explains his absence from the launch ceremony.

In the living room of the *Cupido*, there is only silence and dismay. With the exception of Safia, who was his pupil, none of us really knew the Communications instructor all that well. Seen from a distance he always seemed quite removed and cold. I'd even go so far as to say sullen, his face closed like a prison door, as if he were afraid of giving too much away. But that changes nothing: we're all in shock. The organisers of

Genesis have done so much for us! To lose one of them is like losing a member of our family.

'Life goes on,' continues Serena, full of bravery, looking back up. 'The Genesis programme goes on. The time to announce the first Heart Lists has arrived.'

The words spring from my mouth before I have a chance to hold them back, because that's the way I am, always saying whatever comes into my head.

'You don't think we could delay the announcement of the list just a little, Serena? Have a day of silence in tribute to Sherman Fisher?'

On the wide-screen, Serena's face is impassive at first; then a sad but gracious smile appears, when my request reaches her.

'It's a very sensitive thing for you to suggest, my dear Léonor,' she says. 'But Sherman wouldn't have wanted a day like that. Silence wasn't really his thing, you know. Don't forget, he was an expert in Communications! The best way to pay tribute to our dear departed is to keep on moving ahead. The show must go on!'

The artist in me can't help noticing how well mourning suits Serena, as do all her outfits. The black onyx earrings, the matching eyeshadow, the whole thing: this woman can pull off dressing the height of fashion even when afflicted.

A pre-recorded drum-roll sounds, unleashing a feverish hubbub across the living room. The girls are electrified – the announcement of Sherman Fisher's accident has just added to the tension preceding the announcement of the first Heart Lists.

And talking about hearts, I can feel mine beating practically out of my chest just now. Why? I've told myself so often that this first ranking meant nothing to me. That's the rule I set myself: to keep a cool head and not let myself get carried away by the weekly rankings.

'Each boy – and each girl – has carefully filled out their grid this morning,' Serena reminds viewers on the screen. 'It's a difficult exercise, this ranking, especially being the first one. I'm sure there were some hesitations . . .'

Hesitations? Not for me. Just method. I simply classified the boys in alphabetical order, from A to Z (well, A to T, to be more precise). No favouritism. In any case, this whole thing is just designed to get everyone going, to stir up the game of seduction, to feed the speculation on the part of the viewers and the passengers.

As though she's read my thoughts from three million kilometres away in her cosy villa, the black-clad Serena offers a reminder of the rules of the programme.

'After the announcement of this first ranking, and those that will follow each week, twenty-two times over, nothing will yet be finally decided. The intermediate Heart Lists serve principally as a way of testing the waters, allowing all the contestants to position themselves in relation to one another. The only Heart List that really counts, that will bind the couples together definitively, will be the last, the twenty-third: the one that will be announced immediately upon alignment with the orbit of Phobos. All those that come before may be considered preparatory sketches for the production of a masterpiece of love and harmony.'

I feel Kris's hand close around mine.

Just like on the launch platform, when I hesitated about accepting the mission.

That was only a week ago, seven little days, and yet it feels like a whole other lifetime.

'As usual, it's ladies first,' says Serena.

Her face disappears, giving way to a table with six columns.

Fangfang (SGP)	Kelly (CAN)	Elizabeth (GBR)	Safia (IND)	Kirsten (DEU)	Léonor (FRA)
1. Tao	1. Alexei	1. Alexei	1. Samson	1. Alexei	1. Alexei
2. Kenji	2. Samson	2. Tao	2. Alexei	2. Tao	2. Kenji
3. Marcus	3. Marcus	3. Samson	3. Marcus	3. Mozart	3. Marcus
4. Alexei	4. Tao	4. Marcus	4. Tao	4. Samson	4. Mozart
5. Mozart	5. Kenji	5. Mozart	5. Mozart	5. Kenji	5. Samson
6. Samson	6. Mozart	6. Kenji	6. Kenji	6. Marcus	6. Tao

'*This is the girls' classification of the boys,*' Serena's voiceover continues. '*As you would expect logically, those who have had the chance to demonstrate their powers of seduction in a one-on-one session in the Visiting Room with their respective beauties find themselves at the top of the ranking. The only exception to prove this rule is Mozart, to whom Kelly has been pitiless.*'

Kelly stops chewing her gum for just a moment to comment.

'And if it had been up to me, I'd rather not say where I would have ranked him!'

'No, you really mustn't say,' Fangfang warns her. 'It's prime time and the Genesis channel does try to avoid swearing.'

Kris nudges me and whispers some anguished words in my ear.

'Have you noticed, there are four of us who've put Alexei first! Including you, Léo!'

'I've already explained to you that I ranked the boys in alphabetical order. Next week I'll be using the reverse order and your beloved will find himself last on my list.'

'Yes, but still . . . I put Marcus at the bottom of my list, just so as not to tread on your toes, because I thought you really liked him after your speed-dating with him . . .'

Serena doesn't give Kris the chance to say any more.

'Without further delay, we now move on to the boys' ranking of the girls!'

A new table appears on the screen.

Tao (CHN)	Alexei (RUS)	Mozart (BRA)	Kenji (JPN)	Samson (NGA)	Marcus (USA)
1. Fangfang	1. Kirsten	1. Kelly	1. Kirsten	1. Safia	1. Elizabeth
2. Kirsten	2. Elizabeth	2. Léonor	2. Elizabeth	2. Kirsten	2. Kelly
3. Elizabeth	3. Kelly	3. Kirsten	3. Léonor	3. Elizabeth	3. Safia
4. Safia	4. Léonor	4. Safia	4. Fangfang	4. Kelly	4. Kirsten
5. Kelly	5. Fangfang	5. Elizabeth	5. Safia	5. Fangfang	5. Fangfang
6. Léonor	6. Safia	6. Fangfang	6. Kelly	6. Léonor	6. Léonor

Last in three out of the six rankings. I'd be lying if I claimed not to be affected by that. But honestly, what did I expect? I'm quite clearly the least appealing match. My Dowry is still down at ground level compared to the others, which is totally normal given how I've been behaving in front of the viewers, with my explosive changes of mood. And yet . . . I didn't think Marcus would rank me last too. I thought something had happened between us – something that was worth more than money.

'*Following the same logic, the girls tend to be very highly ranked by the boys they've met – with one notable exception here, too: Léonor, who seems not to have convinced Marcus.*'

Serena is just turning the knife in the wound now.

And it's a wound that really hurts me.

(*Of course something happened between you! That's precisely why he'll never forgive you. Remember how angry he was at the end of your interview. You've burned yourself for ever, with that stupid rule of inviting each boy once every twelve weeks. He's struck you off his list of potential partners once and for all, Léonor, and now it's too late!*)

I swallow to dislodge the lump that's formed in my throat, and to swallow up the horrible voice of the Salamander deep inside me.

If Marcus is too narrow-minded to accept my rule, too bad. It isn't him excluding me from his selection; I'm the one automatically excluding him. I could never marry a guy who was so impatient. *Seize the day*, you say! What I need is somebody poised, reflective . . . mature. If this is how Marcus reacts now, so impulsively, how will he react the day he sees the Salamander? The answer is that he's never going to see it.

Him and me are like poor Sherman: dead and buried.

38. Reverse Shot

The Villa McBee, Long Island, New York State
Wednesday 12 July, 3:30pm

'Arthur, my dear friend, thank you for coming so quickly!'
Serena gets up from the hive where she's been crouching.
Her apiary suit, made to measure, makes her look like a white
fairy among the bees. Her wide-brimmed hat adorned with
a protective veil looks like something a lady might wear on a
Sunday to a highly exclusive garden party. She even manages
to make the latex gloves protecting her hands against stings
look stylish.

'I came as quickly as I could, Serena,' says Dr Montgomery.
Standing ramrod straight in his elegant tweed suit, he keeps
a respectful distance from the cloud buzzing around the lady
of the house.

'It took me almost as long to beat a path through the hordes
of fans and journalists surrounding your villa as it did to fly
from Miami to New York! Is it about Ruben Rodriguez; is that
why you summoned me? His body's just been found in the
sea by a trawler, around the place where we left him to sink.'

'I'm fully up to speed with that. It would obviously have

been more practical if that pain in the neck had gotten eaten by the fish, great animal-lover that he was, but still, it's not too serious. We'll send one of the allies of silence to lay a wreath, the way we did with Sherman. And at the same time, they can check that Ruben didn't leave any compromising trails behind. But let's talk about the reason I've called you here: Harmony. She isn't very well. I'd like you to check her out, since I trust you completely.'

'She had another fainting spell?'

'She passed out during our birthday dinner. Such a disaster, such a fragile constitution! My cast-iron health is the one thing she hasn't inherited from me.'

'She really is more like you than any daughter has ever resembled her mother . . .' begins Dr Montgomery.

His forehead creases slightly.

'. . . but tell me, she isn't in the know – about the allies of silence, I mean?'

'Of course not! What do you take me for? Harmony isn't yet able to protect herself, so I'm hardly going to ask her to protect a secret like that! But enough talk about my daughter for now. You'll see her shortly, she won't be leaving her cage. So come and look at this wonderful thing, seeing as you're here.'

Serena takes a frame out of the hive. Inside the wooden rectangle is a network of golden honeycomb, to which clusters of black insects in their dozens are clinging.

'Come closer!' order Serena.

'It's just, I'm not protected . . .'

'Come now, Arthur, you aren't going to tell me you're afraid of a couple of little stings, a fine doctor like you? You've nothing to fear, I smoked the hive just a few minutes ago. It's the best possible bee-keeping technique: the bees get panicked by the smoke, they think there's a fire and gather round the queen . . .'

Dr Montgomery smooths his moustache nervously, but doesn't reply. He treads gingerly towards the bee-keeper.

'Just look at all those workers, toiling away for me,' she says, holding up the frame. 'All different and yet all identical. Each of them knowing exactly what she has to do, knowing her place, what task she must accomplish in her brief life.'

Serena gives a sigh that makes the net of her hat flutter.

'What you have before you, Arthur, is the ideal model for any society. No moods, no egotism. None of those psychological frictions that in so-called evolved species degenerate into arguments, into conflict, into internal warfare. A hive is a perfect union: the energy of a whole population aimed at a single goal!'

Serena carefully replaces the frame in the hive and lowers the lid that serves as its roof.

She takes off her gloves and hat – underneath it, her silver bob is perfectly intact, not a hair out of place.

'Thanks to you and the Genesis programme, the Earth is more united now than it's ever been before,' ventures Arthur Montgomery. 'Those billions of viewers trembling to the rhythm of the speed-dating sessions . . . It's unprecedented. Not even those rock star tours against hunger, not even the Olympic Games, have managed to create such unanimity. And to think it's all going to come tumbling down in five months' time. Aren't you scared the public will hold you responsible, as you were the person who selected all the participants, one of whom is going to eliminate all the others . . . ?'

Serena grabs hold of the doctor's arm, and he stiffens imperceptibly.

She rests her water-green eyes on him, shining with cold excitement.

'The public won't hold me responsible for a thing, Arthur. People will get too attached to the twelve astronauts over the twenty-three weeks of their journey to criticise the selection. The murder crisis will unleash horror and pity, not anger. As for me, I'll just need to say the appropriate words, shed some appropriate tears. It won't come tumbling down; on the contrary, it will be our very apotheosis. Just imagine! International funerals! A minute of silence observed the world over! A minute, yes, maybe it's just one minute, but for that one minute all humanity will be as united as the bees you've just seen. The *tragic event* will be like a great smoking-out: the entire human hive gathering around their queen – which happens in this case to be the executive director of the Genesis programme – me. You can understand that, my friend, not like the other allies of silence who are only motivated by the lure of profit. Not you, you're like me . . .'

Serena grabs Arthur Montgomery by his tie, pulls him towards her and places a latex-gloved hand on his cheek.

'You're a visionary, Arthur. A philanthropist. A poet.'

'S-Serena . . .' stammers the doctor.

All at once the glacier of his self-confidence has melted, the armour of his composure is cracked.

He trembles like a young man during his first flirtation.

'. . . y-you already know you've gone to my head. I fell for your charm the first moment we met, two years ago, at the start

271

of the Genesis programme. Since then, every night you grant me inflames my heart and my senses, every day I spend far from you tears me apart – but still I remain at Cape Canaveral to keep an eye on the other allies of silence, just as you asked me to. I will do anything you want, you know that. I think your beautiful eyes have hypnotised me too, like they've hypnotised the participant who will be responsible for the *tragic event*!'

Serena McBee bursts out laughing – that silvery laugh that she alone has, which streams like metal rain.

'No, no, my dear Arthur! You are a man of very distinguished character, not a disorientated teenager – in other words, you're too robust to be hypnotised. It is, moreover, precisely your manly self-assurance that seduced me. You've got guts, not like that total drip Gordon Lock and the old neurotics he's got surrounding him. They mustn't suspect our lovely story, they would only sully it – and in any case, you can watch them better like this, incognito, on the lookout for the slightest sign of weakness. But before you go back to Florida, since you're here, let me invite you to spend the night with me at the Villa McBee!'

39. Shot

D +10 days 21 h 15 mins.
[2nd week]

'Today, fortune has chosen Marcus!' Serena announces from the wide-screen in the living room. 'In a few minutes, we'll discover which girl he's selecting to join him in the Visiting Room.'

It's our second week on board the *Cupido*, the boys' week. On the three first days, Samson, Tao and Alexei were drawn by lot in turn; the first invited Liz, and the other two invited Kris – they would appear to be popular girls, those two . . .

'If Marcus invites me, I won't go, like Kenji did with Safia!' Kris whispers in my ear. 'I can't believe he ranked you last, after having seen you. You needn't have any regrets: he clearly has no taste at all!'

I struggle to give Kris a smile. She's standing in front of me, protective, adorable as ever in one of the little blue dresses that make up her wardrobe.

'You needn't worry,' I tell her. 'Marcus means nothing to me. As far as I'm concerned, he's free to invite whoever he likes.'

He's free to invite whoever he likes . . . Does that mean I'm including myself on the list of possibilities? Does one part of me still believe that Marcus is going to respect my rule, which says we can only see each other one time out of six? No, of course not. He made it clear that he didn't want to play the game. Well, it's his tough luck.

A flood of loud violins suddenly erupts from the wide-screen: the title sequence has begun.

'*Six girls on one side . . .*

'*Six boys on the other . . .*'

I throw a furtive glance at the other girls. They're all there, pretty as a picture, and as still as statues, hypnotised by the faces that are bursting onto the screen. Each day the title sequence seems to be over more quickly than the day before. I have the dizzying feeling that everything is accelerating towards the final outcome. Towards the Mars couples, who just have to be perfect? Towards conjugal happiness, as the programme promises? For those of us on board the *Cupido*, there's nothing at the end of the titles but a blackout, as the screen goes dark during the speed-dating session in the Visiting Room.

'*Marcus has just informed us of his choice!*' Serena's voice announces suddenly.

She seems to come from every direction in the living room at once – from the walls stuffed with speakers, microphones, cameras, and probably a hundred other sensors we don't even know about.

'*Confirming the wild popularity of our two leading girls, he's decided to invite Elizabeth!*'

Liz turns towards us, batting her long eyelashes, which aren't even fake.

'*Me?*' she asks with a roll of her incredulous eyes as though she's just been told she's won the lottery. 'I can't believe it!'

I struggle with a violent desire to make her eat her ballerina's bun.

Why?

Like I told Kris, Marcus means nothing to me.

And as for me, I mean nothing to him, as he's just proved to me for the second time.

'And wham, another kick in the teeth!' grumbles Kelly, opening a new packet of gum. 'Yet again, we've got ourselves ready for nothing!'

She's been on edge since her interview with Mozart last week. Despite everybody's questions, she hasn't wanted to reveal what happened in the bubble.

'Two hours of hair, make-up and preening, all up in a puff of smoke,' she adds. 'Would it be too much to ask for them to tell us in the morning when we wake up what's going to happen, rather than letting us stew?'

'You're right,' adds Fangfang, for once in agreement with her preferred enemy. 'So much time wasted that we could have spent revising!'

The Singaporean clearly hasn't come to terms with Tao not inviting her to the Visiting Room . . . She must have far more reasons than me to expect to be invited back.

'But that's the whole point of the game,' Kris tries to explain. 'The suspense . . .'

'*The suspense? What suspense?*' roars the Canadian, rocketing instantly to level eight on the Richter Scale. 'The whole thing's just between Liz and you, and you call that suspense!'

'No, it isn't just between us.' Kris tries to defend herself. 'Can I remind you that Mozart ranked you in first place, even if you don't happen to fancy him ...'

It's as though I can see lightning bolts shooting from Kelly's eyes.

'Give me a break with Mozart, or I swear you'll be the one hearing your own requiem!'

Kris buries her face in Louve's white fur, the way she does whenever she's hurt. As for me, as usual my heart skips a beat.

'Hey, disco queen!' I call out to Kelly. 'Just listen to your idol Jimmy Giant, OK? That would really give us a break.'

The Canadian gives me the finger, before sticking her earphones in her ears.

Fangfang picks up her revision tablet.

Safia keeps quiet, doggedly staring at the tips of her shoes.

I turn on my sketching tablet, ready to get back to work on my pictures of Louve. But the lines I've already drawn seem to float before my eyes, and the stylus remains unmoving in my hand. In the total silence of the living room, there is nothing to distract me but my thoughts, nothing to drown out the treacherous little voice murmuring behind me:

(Right now there's another girl seizing the day in your place.)

40. Reverse Shot

The Atlas Capital Tower, New York City
Thursday 13 July, 4:00pm

The elevator door opens on the fiftieth floor of the tower – the very top. Serena McBee steps out, dressed in a black pants-suit that seems to lengthen her already slender form. Her twelve-centimetre gold-tipped heels sink into the thick carpet covering the whole floor, muffling any sound. Opposite her, instead of a wall, a vast circular picture window offers a staggering view of the New York City skyline. In the middle of this astonishing room stands a huge bronze statue: a half-naked titan, holding up a terrestrial globe. This is Atlas, the mythological giant who lends his name to the investment fund.

A shape detaches itself behind the sculpture, silhouetted against the skyscraper backdrop. One might mistake it for a man in a dark suit, but there's something strange about its movements, something jerky . . . Its hands are covered in black gloves and on its head it's wearing what looks like a motorcycle helmet with a dark visor obscuring its face.

'*Ms McBee, welcome to Atlas.*' A voice emerges from the helmet.

A voice? A recording, rather.

This creature, without an inch of visible skin, has nothing human about it.

It's a robot.

'*May I please scan you according to the security protocol?*' crackles the synthetic voice.

'Go ahead, my good –' Serena leans over to read the badge pinned onto the thing's jacket – 'my good android Oraculon.'

Two red dots appear behind the black visor of the helmet.

The android tilts its neck slightly, in a perfectly regular movement that makes it possible to guess at the set of gears hiding behind its suit, a Swiss watch far more precise than any muscle and bone. Its laser 'eyes' sweep the visitor from head to toe, then from toe to head.

'*Nothing to report, no microphones or cameras – only fifty-nine kilos of living organic matter, a kilo of fabrics, five hundred grams of leather and a few grams of gold,*' announces the synthetic voice.

'Well then, that's a bit of good news, I've lost a kilo,' exclaims Serena. 'Could you also calculate my body fat and devise a personalised fitness programme for me, android Oraculon?'

The robot freezes.

'*Body fat eighteen per cent. As regards the fitness programme, I regret that is not available on my menu . . .*'

'These gadgets have no sense of humour . . .' sighs Serena. 'Forget it, android Oraculon.'

'*Information received: request cancelled. The meeting with the board of Atlas Capital can now begin. Please take your place, Ms McBee.*'

The android gestures to one of the seats arranged around

the sculpture of the giant Atlas. It allows its guest to sit down, then positions itself in front of her.

A few moments later, the black visor of the helmet is transformed into a screen – a round screen representing a three-dimensional white face, belonging to an androgynous being of no particular age, features or gender: the face of anonymity.

But this anonymous face expresses itself, becoming animated as the words come out of the helmet.

'*Good afternoon, Ms McBee.*'

'You've said hello to me already.'

'*A slight difference: that was the programme written into the robot's memory speaking to you before. Now it is the Atlas board in full that welcomes you, via the mouth of our cybernetic oracle – it's a wonder of technology, the android Oraculon.*'

Serena crosses her legs elegantly, and her water-green eyes stare deep into the helmet facing her.

'How many of you are there, behind that helmet? Why not come see me in person?'

'*You know very well why not. In general, the Atlas group does not court publicity, nor interpersonal contact. We do not aspire to be known to the general public, nor to our suppliers. We are an investment structure that buys up firms when they are very ripe, to squeeze them out completely and remove all the juice. Then we throw away the peel. We have invested a considerable amount of money to acquire NASA and we have entrusted you with responsibility for the Genesis programme. Nothing more needs be said . . .*'

'. . . and especially not that you've decided to launch the

programme despite the Noah Report and the death of the resident of the seventh Love Nest, isn't that right?'

The 3D face in the visor betrays no emotion.

'Come now, Ms McBee, as you are well aware, we have never heard of the Noah Report. You are well aware that we have not been informed about the non-viability of the Martian habitats. We do not know of the existence of the system that allows you to depressurise the habitats at a distance by remote control; nor indeed your plan to manipulate one of the astronauts to do the job in your place, before the defects of the equipment are discovered.'

Serena uncrosses her legs, then re-crosses them the other way. Her own face, likewise, reveals no emotion.

'Of course you don't know about any of that – what was I thinking? But why have you summoned me here today? It's not about that ridiculous hacker site, which we haven't heard from in weeks, is it? Or to reprimand me for having let a favela hoodlum on board the *Cupido*, to add a little spice?'

'No. We trust you to manage the operational details and put on the show as you think best. It's true that at the beginning we did receive a complaint from Mozart's platinum sponsor, the Brazimo construction company, unhappy that their name was being associated with that of a delinquent. But the public reacted sympathetically to the poor ranking the Canadian girl gave him, as the copious gifts that flooded in for him can testify – and all of a sudden, Brazimo withdrew their complaint. Nearly two weeks after the launch, the cash inflows associated with advertising and donations are twice our most ambitious predictions. At this rate, we will have recouped our initial investment before the journey

is even half done – and all the rest will be pure profit. You are leading it all masterfully, Ms McBee, and the Atlas company congratulates itself for having entrusted the reins of the Genesis programme to you.'

The psychiatrist tilts her head slightly to indicate that she appreciates the compliment.

'. . . but the US government, however, regrets daily its decision to sell NASA,' continues the android Oraculon – or, more precisely, the mysterious interlocutors hidden behind it. 'As you know, President Green's Ultra-liberal Party got itself elected nearly four years ago on a promise of liquidating the institutions belonging to the American state, in order to pay off the public debt . . .'

'Everybody remembers that campaign,' Serena interrupts. '"Take America out of the red with President Green!" – hats off to whichever publicists came up with that memorable pun.'

'Just so. But today, with the success of the Genesis channel, the same electors who swept Green to power are blaming him for selling off NASA at so far below its true value. The opposition accuse him of having sold the Mars programme on the cheap. NASA has proved extremely profitable since we bought it, and the advertising revenue would really have helped the government . . . Consequently, Green's popularity is at an all-time low and all polls indicate that he will not be returning with a second mandate after the presidential elections in November.'

'That's a shame for him, but I don't see what that has to do with me, nor with you for that matter,' says Serena. 'Atlas is a private investment fund and not answerable to the bureaucrats of the state. We don't do politics – we do business.'

The 3D face is silent for a second before responding. Its

281

white, pupil-less eyes resemble those of a marble statue – an oracle, like those at whose feet ancient people used to place their offerings in the hope of receiving a glimpse of their fate.

'*According to our sources, President Green's office is about to contact you to offer you the vice-presidential nomination going into the next election, now that you have become the most popular personality in the United States. It's an opportunity not to be missed, and we are even prepared to contribute a small percentage of the Genesis revenues to finance your campaign. If you are elected alongside Green, you will become his closest ally. You will be able to encourage him to speed up the sales, keeping the choicest titbits for Atlas Capital. There are still so many things we could buy, and make profitable in our usual way: schools, public hospitals . . . Imagine the range of compulsory advertising during classes, all the way from pre-school! Reality TV shows about the terminally ill, with that final breath getting broadcast live! There are vast sums of money to be made, roping in everyone from toddlers all the way up to the old. And of course, we would be sure to demonstrate our gratitude for the sacrifice you would be making for our great nation.*'

41. Shot

'Say aaah.'

'*Aaaaaah,*' says Liz, unhooking her jaw.

I turn on the little torch from my beginner's medical kit, and I sweep the beam of light around the gaping mouth.

'I don't see anything . . . It doesn't look red . . . I don't think it's a throat infection, Liz.'

'But are you *sure* . . . ?'

Sure? How could I be sure, never having diagnosed a throat infection in my life? The only tonsils I've seen this close are the ones on my revision tablet.

'I do feel like I caught a cold though, when I got out the shower yesterday,' Liz insists. 'My throat hurts a bit when I swallow, you know, and also my head feels really heavy. I should have dried my hair right away instead of hanging around like an idiot. I catch cold so easily! And I'm not sure about this whole system for recycling the urine, I bet there are still some germs it doesn't get rid of . . .'

'I can always prescribe you a course of antibiotics,' I say, just in case. 'But most throat infections are viral, so antibiotics don't do any good.'

'Oh! You see? So it is a throat infection!'

How am I to answer her? She's come to see me, as the Medical Officer, knowing in advance what she wanted: antibiotics to soothe her little hypochondriac nerves. As for my apprentice doctor's diagnosis, she doesn't care either way; and for what it's worth, I can understand.

'Here you go,' I say, handing her a small packet of capsules. 'Morning and evening for seven days, taken with meals. And take the whole course, even if you stop feeling the symptoms. We'll check in on things again next week.'

'OK, doc!'

She takes the capsules and is about to leave the bathroom where we've isolated ourselves for the consultation: it's already late morning, and in a few moments today's boy will be announced on the wide-screen in the living room.

'Liz?' I say as she opens the hatch.

She turns.

'Yes?'

'How was he yesterday, how was Marcus?'

I'm immediately angry with myself for asking the question. What's it to do with me, how he was? I can't stand this weak Léo, so unsure of herself, that Marcus has conjured up. I hate Marcus, simple as that!

Liz looks at me from under her long black lashes.

Beneath our feet, through the half-open hatch, we can hear the start of the credits being broadcast onto the screens in the living room. As the sound of the violins builds, I have the sense

284

that Liz is appraising me from some place very, very high up, as though she were at the top of a mountain I would never be able to climb. But I know it's me and me alone who projects this expression of disdain onto our utterly decent Liz, who is modesty incarnate.

'Marcus was just as you'd described him the other day,' she says at last. '*Weird*. I mean, in a good way. He did a magic trick for me . . .'

'The thing with the roses . . . ?'

There's more bitterness in my voice than I'd like, I'm well aware of that.

'*Roses*?' says Liz, raising her eyebrows. 'No . . . he just used a pack of cards. He'd ask me to think of a card secretly, and each time that was the one he took out of the pack! I've honestly no idea how he did it. There's something really seductive about his hoarse voice, don't you think? And those eyes . . . so intense! Would you say they're really grey-blue or blue-grey?'

'I wouldn't say anything. I don't remember them any more. Maybe the colour of goose droppings?'

'You're so ruthless!' laughs Liz. 'You're just getting your revenge because of the Heart List, isn't that it?'

'Not at all!'

'If you ask me, that's the weirdest bit about Marcus's behaviour, much more than his magic tricks: that he could have ranked a girl like you in last place. He really must be blind not to see how beautiful you are . . . Even though you go a long way to hide it. I don't have anything special to show off, but you, it's such a shame the way you disguise everything under your grungy jeans with those worn knees, and your turtleneck tops! And your hair – I don't know why you insist on tying it back; you're even more beautiful with it loose.'

I don't have time to thank Liz for her kindness, nor reassure her about her own lack of self-confidence, still less tell her that there no question of my baring myself a single centimetre more; at that moment Kris pops her head through the hatch – carefully (once bitten, twice shy!) . . .

'What are you still doing in the bathroom, girls?' she says. 'Especially you, Léo – it's Mozart's turn in the Visiting Room and he's just invited you for the session of the day!'

That last word – *day!* – resounds in my head like a bell.

The day!

Seize the day!

My heart skips a beat; my body goes onto automatic pilot. 'Just a minute!' I hear myself shout as I hurtle down the ladder.

I pass through the living room, down to the bedroom, and open the door of my wardrobe.

I extricate myself from my jeans and put on the first skirt I can lay my hands on – it's black, fortunately, the emblematic colour of Rosier elegance, but brilliant, and shorter than anything I'd ever imagined wearing. Then I slip my feet that are so used to sneakers into a pair of polished pumps – they're still a bit stiff, but they're a perfect fit, exactly my size.

'OK, I'm ready!' I say, undoing the satin ribbon and letting my hair flow onto my shoulders.

42. Genesis Channel

Friday 14 July, 11:05am

Léonor: 'Hello, Mozart from Brazil . . .'

The girl appears from the left side of the Visiting Room, floating up towards the glass behind which the day's host is waiting for her. Her skirt with an asymmetric hang in black taffeta wonderfully complements her grey jersey top. With each movement, the twinkling pleats of the rich, dark fabric come alive, catching the beams from the spotlights. High-arched in their polished pumps, her feet seem effortlessly to climb the steps of an invisible staircase. The luxuriant hair, let loose, finishes off the silhouette that is both classic and furiously modern: a Rosier model in all her glory.

Close-up on Mozart, mouth agape. 'Hello, Léonor. You're . . . very beautiful. Very different to what I'd imagined.'

He pushes back the black hair that is falling into his eyes with an awkward, almost shy movement. Even though he's wearing the same V-neck T-shirt as on his first day in the Visiting Room, he's changed. He seems embarrassed at his body, which only last week was so agile, at play in the zero gravity. What Léonor has gained in gracefulness, he's lost in confidence. His black sparkling eyes are wavering slightly; they're ringed with shadow, like the eyes of someone who's stayed up many nights in a row.

Léonor: 'Different?'

Mozart, hesitantly: 'Kelly told me you'd been abandoned as a kid, like me. I thought that would give us something in common. I didn't expect a girl as classy as you.'

He looks down, as though for him the game were already over.

As though he were already giving up.

But Léonor continues to come closer to the reinforced glass, her long hair undulating gently, like the waves of a sea turned red by the setting sun: 'Yes, I was abandoned as a child,' she says, without any fuss. 'Thrown in a trash can, to be more exact.'

'You, thrown in a trash can?' Mozart says. 'No way! You just invented that to wind me up. Kelly must have told you I'd grown up in a dump and you're messing me around just to make me feel what a loser I am. A piece of trash, a scumbag.'

Mozart's jaw clenches.

His eyes are shining a bit more – he seems to be holding back tears.

His voice is just a strangled thread, as though an invisible hand were gripping his throat: 'Kelly told you everything, didn't she? She told you she discovered who I really am? But why am I asking you this stupid question: of course she told you who I was, you and the viewers all over the world! Not just a jolly little pickpocket . . . Not a friendly Robin Hood of the favelas . . . But a member of one of Latin America's most

288

murderous gangs, the Aranha – it means *spider* in Portuguese, by the way. And there was me thinking I could go on normally, after what happened last week. What an idiot!'

Léonor opens her mouth to reply, but Mozart doesn't give her a chance. Now that the boil has been lanced, nothing will stop it all pouring out. 'I was convinced I'd be able to draw a line under my past by signing up to the Genesis programme, but it's impossible! Because you *can't* forget, when you've screwed up dozens of lives! Because my past is something I carry on my goddamn carcass like a goddamn tumour, for ever!'

He holds up his brown locks to reveal his tanned neck, on which gleams the small silvery marble that unleashed Kelly's fury: 'A *death's egg*,' he says bitterly. 'All the members of the Aranha have one, me included. They implanted it when I was nine years old, when little Mozart's reputation for thieving caught their attention – they're in the habit of doing their shopping in the poorest favelas to recruit their new members. If you say *yes*, they put an egg in your neck; if you say *no*, it's a bullet in your brain. I thought that here on the spacecraft it could just pass for a piercing, but Kelly somehow knew it wasn't a piercing at all: it's a capsule of venom from the *armadeira*, the most venomous spider in Brazil and the world, and it's directly connected to the spinal cord. So you see why members of the Aranha are so famously loyal. Anyone who tries to escape never gets far: all it takes is for the Boss to press a button to open up their egg remotely, wherever they are on the planet, and unleash immediate death by paralysis of the respiratory and cardiac systems.'

Mozart's face is nothing but a mask of pain. There are two

thick veins standing out in the middle of his forehead now, throbbing as though they're about to explode. His pupils are dilating.

Léonor throws herself against the glass and begins to drum on it with her closed fists, with the tip of her polished shoes. 'Mozart! What's going on! Is it that thing, that . . . egg, has it opened?'

She looks sharply up towards the top of the starry dome, throwing a shockwave through the floating red mass of her hair, and yells in search of the invisible cameras: 'Serena! Stop the interview! Do something! Mozart's been poisoned!'

But nobody answers. Her screams are lost in the void, beneath the indifferent gaze of the stars. At the bottom of the screen, the small stopwatch continues to turn inexorably. Still a minute of interview left, and nothing and no one will interrupt it.

Léonor turns quickly back towards her host; she fights to master her own panic, so as to let the Medical Officer do the talking. 'Slow breaths. Stop moving. You must at all costs avoid activating your circulatory system, to slow the spread of the venom. The moment this damn interview is over, your Medicine guy, Alexei, will inject you with a dose of serum and give you a cardiac massage to . . .'

Mozart cuts her medical advice short. 'I'm not poisoned. You can be sure that with everything I've just revealed, the Boss would have pressed the button by now, but I'm too far from the Earth for the egg to be activated. That was my plan to escape from the Aranha: outer space! But I wasn't able to escape my memories. I've brought them with me onto this craft, and they stink of death, so strongly that they stop me sleeping. *An asshole dealer in zero-G, the most repulsive drug in the world*: that's what I was before I came on board the *Cupido*!'

Tears are now running down Mozart's face – tears that seem to be made of acid, inflaming his corneas and tracking bright furrows down his cheeks. His misted-up eyes don't catch Léonor's – a mixture of shame and guilt.

But Léonor doesn't look away. 'The past no longer means anything,' she says.

Mozart looks up – slowly, as though afraid of being blinded by meeting his guest's bronze eyes.

His full lips, dampened by his tears, let an incredulous question slip out. 'What did you say . . . ?'

Léonor: 'I said the past no longer means anything. What we've done, who we were before, we've left all that behind. That's why they chose young people like us, don't forget: so we focus only on the future, on Mars. What matters, Mozart, is not what you've done with your life up to now, it's what you're going to do from now on. If you want to invite me back, you can count on me to accept – one time in six.'

A shrill bell rings.

Communication between the two halves of the Visiting Room ceases instantly.

Serena (off): '*Such sensational revelations, my dear viewers! The first time you saw Mozart, you thought you were dealing with a small-time hoodlum, but now he's admitted he's a real criminal! Or to be more precise, he used to be a criminal before boarding the* Cupido *. . . The production team were naturally fully aware of Mozart's past. We decided to select him in spite of everything, for two reasons. First, for his excellent piloting skills,*

291

and second, to give him another chance. Mozart really did move us to tears when he begged for the opportunity to redeem himself, just as he's moved Léonor today. Now you will be the judges, dear viewers! By leaving for Mars, Mozart has escaped the vendetta of his gang and the courtrooms of his country, but he will never escape your judgement. Do you, like Léonor, think he deserves a second chance? Or are you going to stop putting money into his Dowry and send him to the bottom of the rankings, and the most cramped little Love Nest in New Eden? It's for you to decide, through your donations.'

Behind the reinforced glass bubble, the unmoving stars shine with a brightness as cold as ice.

But the last look that Mozart gives Léonor, after he has wiped away his tears with the back of his hand, burns like embers.

Jingle.

Fade to black.

43. Out of Frame

California State Highway, Route 190, Death Valley
Saturday 15 July, 07:25am

A small motel stands by the side of a brightly lit highway, the only building for miles around. Rusty metal letters attached to the façade announce the name of the place: Hotel alifornia (the C has fallen off).

Behind the one-storey building, covered in reddish dust, stretches a dry landscape, already crushed by the sun even at this early hour. In front, in the small car park whose asphalt coating has turned liquid from the rising heat, three vehicles are parked: two cars and a black campervan with tinted windows and chrome rims.

In one of the bedrooms, a piece of symphonic music sounds all of a sudden.

It's 'The Imperial March' from *The Empire Strikes Back*.

A hand emerges from under the bed-sheets, onto which the blazing sun is pouring, barely blocked by the threadbare curtains. The fingers feel around for the phone that's playing this martial ringtone, to find it resting on the bedside table amid half a dozen empty beer bottles. But the arm is too short: it only manages to knock the telephone to the floor. It lies there out of reach, while continuing to emit its strings, drums and trumpets at full volume.

A young man sits up in bed, bare-chested. His torso is well developed from all the rowing practice. His preppy haircut is completely tousled, the glasses he fell asleep with against the pillow have printed the shape of their frame against his forehead and his cheeks: it's Andrew Fisher. With a horrendous hangover.

He's wearing a pair of plain boxers. He gets up with a grumble, dragging the bed-sheet behind him – which knocks over the bedside table and the empty bottles – to grab the phone.

'Mother?' he says, his tongue furred.

'No, Drew: it's me, your beloved little sis. I borrowed Mother's phone on the quiet to call you.'

Andrew Fisher rubs his eyes.

'Lucy,' he says softly. 'It's good to hear from you.'

'And I think it would be good to see you,' replies the little girl, her voice heavy with reproach. 'You left in such a rush, after the funeral! The house is so empty without you. Yin and Yang really miss you.'

'I'm sorry, little sis. I promise I'll be back soon. In the meantime, you can call me as often as you want. But for now, I need to be where I am.'

'Where's that?'

'Promise you won't tell Mother? She'd think I'm being morbid.'

'Mor-*what*?' asks Lucy.

'Depressing.'

294

'I promise.'

'I'm in Death Valley.'

'And is that *morbid*?'

'No, it's beautiful. It looks like Mars.'

'Mars: the planet where you want to go live someday.'

'That's right, Lucy. You remember: it's what I wanted most in the world. But now I realise that's hardly important. What really matters to me isn't going there, it's understanding why Father didn't send me. It's *understanding Father*, simply. Here, in Death Valley, the place where he disappeared, I might find some sign, some answer . . . Does that make any sense to you at all?'

The voice in the receiver is quiet for a few moments, pensive.

'I think so,' she says at last.

'Just to warn you, we ain't got no boiled eggs left, or bacon. All we got left is toast and beans in tomato sauce.'

An imposing-looking waitress, squeezed into a little apron whose seams look ready to burst, eyes Andrew up and down from her great height. Having found the strength to pull on his rowing-club T-shirt (back to front), he's now slumped on the table of the motel's on-site diner, behind a window that's so dirty he can barely make out the car park beyond it. A tune is playing in the background, coming from an old jukebox stuck on the same record: it's 'Hotel California', the old eighties hit by the Eagles, which seems to be the anthem of this place that has fallen into a time-warp.

Andrew massages his head, as if to drive his migraine away.

'How are the beans?'

'Real heavy and real starchy,' replies the waitress irritably.

295

'Perfect. I'll take a double helping. Maybe that'll absorb the rest of the alcohol I've got in my blood.'

The waitress sighs – without irritation this time, only sympathy.

'I'd better give you an aspirin too, then,' she says, shaking her head in commiseration. 'And you can keep the room for a late check-out. No way you can get back onto the road in that state – it's not like we're fully booked anyhow . . . Mind if I ask what it is brought you here?'

'It's my summer break before going back to college.'

'And you couldn't think of anyplace better to go than Death Valley? I dunno, the beach, the mountains, even Vegas? I've always dreamed of going to Vegas . . . What have you come looking for in this godforsaken hole?'

'Memories,' murmurs Andrew. 'Ghosts. One in particular, of a man I thought was the best of us. But he lied his whole life, dangling something he couldn't offer in front of my eyes. I can't decide whether he betrayed me out of love or out of cowardice, and the question is driving me mad.'

'You're wasting your time. Ghosts can't hear the questions of the living, still less answer them. All you can hear in this place is the whistling of the wind, and the rattlesnakes.'

But Andrew's mind is elsewhere.

He gazes unseeing through the barely transparent window and the stench of alcohol.

Understanding that she won't be able to get any more out of him, the waitress turns on her heel and heads towards the bar. There's an old man in shirtsleeves leaning on it, his gloomy eyes following the TV news that's playing, muted, on a large set with faded colours.

'Poor kid,' she murmurs. 'Drunk as a skunk this early in the morning. I'm sure he's not even legal, he's not yet twenty-one. Say, Mr Bill, did you ask him for his ID before serving him booze last night?'

'Oh, Cindy, we can't let ourselves be too fussy about our customers nowadays, what with the crisis,' the owner answers distractedly. 'Death Valley has never deserved its name more than it does right now. There were still a few people up until last month, inquisitive types who wanted to try to get a look at the Genesis training facility. But since the lift-off, it's been deadly quiet. We haven't even got the right to the tax breaks they promised, which sure would've helped us out, small businesses like us: those suckers in the government won't see a cent of the income from the commercials on the show, and nor will we. Oh, hang on, darlin' – look, it's that clown Green going to do his thing!'

The TV is showing a man in a black jacket and green tie gesticulating behind a podium – behind him, the famous blue backdrop of the White House press room. Bill picks up the remote and turns up the volume.

'. . . and I will continue to do what I've promised, the things for which I was elected.' On the screen, President Green is hammering away. 'By selling off our institutions, not only am I erasing the astronomical national debt left by my predecessor, but I am also ridding the American people of the old bureaucratic mammoths that weigh so heavily on our tax returns.'

Reverse shot on the press room crammed with journalists. A woman in the first row takes the microphone that's held out to her.

'Mr President, since the launch of the Genesis programme, nobody now thinks of the former NASA as a bureaucratic mammoth . . .' she says.

She glances at her notes, then pours her figures into the mic quick as machine-gun fire: 'Seventy-five per cent of humanity connected live . . . A hundred million in advertising revenue per day . . . Fifteen billion dollars minimum earnings estimated by the end of the journey . . . Not to mention the donations from the viewers . . . Or the future receipts to be generated by the broadcast of the lives of the astronauts once they are on Mars . . . And all that going into the coffers of a private investment fund, instead of benefiting the American people!'

Clinging to the podium, President Green takes the burst of figures that sound like accusations.

'I shall continue to do what I've promised,' he repeats like a scratched record. 'Minimise the state, minimise expenses, minimise taxes. History will be my judge.'

At that moment, an alarm goes off in the diner. It comes from the mechanical clock attached to the wall, between a glazed poster of Jimmy Giant and a yellowing photo of James Dean, the two icons from two periods separated by decades, but strangely similar with their ash-blond hair, their rebellious smiles, the dark look in their eyes.

It's 8 a.m.

Cindy's face lights up.

'It's time, Bill! Eleven o'clock Eastern!' she cries. 'Make that loser Green shut up, change the channel. Quick, quick!'

The old man leaps at the remote as nimble as if he'd suddenly got twenty years younger. President Green disappears from the screen to be replaced by the title sequence of the Genesis programme at full volume.

At the back of the diner, Andrew sits up and shudders. But neither Cindy nor her boss notice, their eyes glued to the show.

'*Six girls on one side . . .*

'*Six boys on the other . . .*

'*Six minutes to meet . . .*

'*An eternity to love!*'

The womb-planet Genesis logo bursts through the screen, and is replaced by a shot of the Visiting Room filled with stars.

A title appears: Twelfth session in the Visiting Room. Host: Kenji, 17, Japan, Communications Officer.

'The mysterious Japanese kid!' cries Cindy, more excited than ever. 'He's finally decided to come out of his den . . . He's kinda stylish, in his way! Kinda like a cartoon character!'

A young man with mid-length hair has appeared on the screen. The spiky locks are going off in every direction, according to some kind of physics that seems to defy both the laws of terrestrial gravity and those of space weightlessness. He's wearing a matt grey outfit that looks as futuristic as his hairstyle, somewhere between a hoodie, a biker outfit and a ninja kimono.

A voiceover comes from the TV set – it's Serena McBee.

'*I'm thrilled to see you at last, my dear Kenji, and I'm sure our viewers are too! You're the final boy to take his turn this week. Whom are you going to call? Safia, whose invitation you mysteriously refused last week?*'

299

Close-up on the young man's face. The stiff locks of hair look like the visor on a knight's helmet – a kind of protection, behind which his dark eyes can take refuge.

Kenji: 'I want to invite Léonor.'

Drum-roll.

In the practically deserted diner of the Hotel California, three million kilometres from the craft that has been launched through space, Cindy claps her hands.

'Léonor! She's one of my favourites! I even put a few bucks in her Dowry last week – what little I could afford. I hope her rankings will go back up, that she'll find the man of her life and wind up in one of the most beautiful Love Nests. Her hair is just so . . . awesome! If I could just get mine to go that colour . . .'

She pulls one of her own carrot-coloured locks and stares at it in dismay, but not for long – her attention is quickly drawn back to the screen.

Léonor's red mane appears, dancing like a naked flame in the zero-gravity setting. She's wearing her jersey top and her asymmetrical black taffeta skirt.

Léonor: 'I thought you didn't want to take part in the game, Kenji. Did you change your mind? Or was it just Safia you didn't want to see? You're wrong – she's a really cool girl.'

Kenji's eyes studiously avoid those of his interlocutor. 'It wasn't Safia. It was the flare.'

Léonor: 'The flare?'

Kenji starts talking nineteen to the dozen, swallowing up the

*ends of his phrases like somebody who isn't used to being allowed
to say what he wants to say.*

'Yeah, the solar flare. The probability that the sun would emit
a jet of ionised matter into space was at its highest point last week,
when Safia invited me. Predicting that is part of my remit as
Communications Officer. Because of the possible interference to
radio transmissions that solar flares can cause. Not to mention the
risks of irradiation by cosmic rays. I preferred to stay in the shelter of
our quarters rather than coming up to the Visiting Room. I'm sorry.'

Cindy puts her hands on her hips.

'What's all this gibberish? I don't understand a word this
guy is saying! What about you, Bill?'

The manager shrugs doubtfully.

At the far end of the diner, resting on his elbows on the
table, Andrew looks like he's completely sobered up. Behind
his black-framed glasses, his eyes are glued to the screen and
to Léonor, who says: 'You've nothing to fear for your health
in the Visiting Room, Kenji, I can assure you as the Medical
Officer. Even though the bubble is transparent, we're protected
here from carcinogenic rays . . .'

' . . . because the magnetic shield generated by the nuclear
jet covers the entire craft.' Andrew completes the phrase
simultaneously with Léonor, as though he's telepathically
linked to her. He knows the workings of the *Cupido* better
than any of the participants.

On the screen, Kenji nods.

He still doesn't dare meet Léonor's eye, and murmurs quietly:

'I do know that the magnetic shield is supposed to protect us. But what do you expect? I guess I'm just a bit paranoid.'

He hesitates, then starts talking again. 'Actually, the truth is I'm really kind of phobic, if you believe the shrink who's been looking after me since I signed up for the Genesis programme. Phobic – that comes from phobos, like the name of Mars's moon – you know it means fear in Greek? Astronomers named it after mythology: Phobos, the god of fear, was the son of Mars, the god of war. War engenders fear – makes sense, right? Apparently I'm afraid of everything. Apparently I worry for no reason over invisible things that don't exist. But what does my shrink know about what does or doesn't exist anyway? We can't see cosmic rays, but they're there, all around us!'

Kenji's eyes sweep nervously across the room, as though the cosmic rays are about to pierce him at any moment.

'Hey, would you mind if I put on my hood?' he says finally, a bit embarrassed.

Léonor smiles: 'Not at all. I know what being shy is like. But you needn't worry: I'm not going to eat you.'

Kenji: 'It's not shyness, it's just that my tracksuit is lined with a wave-shielding layer of aluminium, a simple precaution in the event of a magnetic storm. Serena said I should accept my paranoia. After all, she's a shrink too, and super highly qualified: she thinks it's good to have one member of the team who's particularly vigilant on board the Cupido and later on Mars, to watch out for the tiniest details that might start playing up. And she also said that brushing right past Phobos, for someone phobic, that's treating the illness with the very thing that makes me ill; it'll cure me! – I hope she's right.'

Léonor: 'Serena's always right. We're all here because she believes in us, because she's convinced that each of us has a role to play in the success of the Genesis programme.'

Kenji's expression relaxes.

Now it's his turn to smile. 'Thanks for the reassurance. Actually, I love your idea of seeing each of the boys just once every six turns, it limits the amount of time we're exposed in the Visiting Room. That's why I invited you here today, on that basis.'

He pulls his deep hood over his head, all the way down to his eye-level. All you can see now are his lips, which are still murmuring a few words. 'There you go, that'll protect me from one of the two suns at least.'

Léonor: 'One of the two suns?'

Kenji: 'The one outside the spacecraft – the yellow one, the less dazzling of the two. The other one, the red one, is right in front of me at this moment. Marcus was right: this sun is radiant!'

The camera zooms in on Léonor's head, with its long hair spread around all 360 degrees like a red star.

'Such gorgeous hair!' whispers Cindy, torn between wonder and envy. 'She really does look like a sun!'

On the screen, the bronze eyes of the sun-girl are wide open, rimmed with lashes that the Rosier mascara has made infinitely longer. 'A sun . . . ? Marcus said that about me . . . ?'

Kenji: 'Yes, and he's the Planetology Officer so he knows what he's talking about. He said you were like a red giant – you know, those stars at the end of their lives that burst into flame, turn red, and burn up their entire solar system around them as they die.'

ACT IV

44. Shot

D +73 days 01 h 15 mins.
[11th week]

'I've turned into a monster!'

'Don't be silly, Fangfang,' I say. 'It'll all be fine.'

Sitting on a stool that's screwed to the bathroom floor, the Singaporean girl bursts into sobs.

Tears flow down her oversized cheeks, which are swollen like toy balloons.

'But seriously, have you seen what I look like?' she hiccups. 'You'd think I was a marmot, with grain stuffed into my cheeks!'

'It's not grain, Fangfang. It's your blood leaving your legs and rising to your face. With the near-weightlessness, the gravity that directs the circulation to your feet works less well.'

'But I spend my days revising in the bedroom, where there's forty per cent of the Earth's gravity!' Fangfang protests.

'After three months' travelling across space, that's no longer enough. You need to switch off your revision tablet a bit and move around. Do more sport. Not just for your circulation, but to avoid muscle wasting too.'

Fangfang gives a heartrending cry.

'A marmot with frogs' legs, and on top of that as soft as an overcooked old noodle! I get uglier and uglier every day. Meanwhile, you started right at the bottom of the pile, when nobody would have bet a nickel on you, and you're getting more and more beautiful! It's not surprising Tao doesn't invite me to the Visiting Room any more!'

I decide to let the 'nobody would have bet a nickel on you' line pass, because deep down even I wouldn't have put money on my own candidacy. But contrary to all expectations, over the weeks, I've been rising progressively up the Dowry funding ladder, and up most of the boys' Heart Lists too. Léonor, the speed-dating diesel engine: slow to get started, but with the stamina to keep going.

'You're exaggerating,' I say. 'Tao's invited you three times already.'

'Three times is nothing for a couple who are destined for each other!'

It's better than *not at all*, I suddenly want to reply.

But I restrain myself.

That might suggest I'm upset that I'm the only one of the girls Marcus has never invited in eleven weeks of travelling, which is of course totally not true. It might imply I'm the kind of girl who lets herself get turned upside down by a guy in just six minutes, which is of course not the case. On the contrary: good riddance! Marcus is the only boy not to have accepted my rule. The only one for whom I'm a hundred per cent sure that we have no kind of future together. The other five boys, as far as I'm concerned, are all still in with a chance. Well, some more than others, obviously . . . And one of them most of all . . .

From today on, you spend at least two hours a day in the gym,' I say to Fangfang, cutting my own thoughts short. 'I'm also prescribing you one hour a day in the hyperbaric chamber, to activate your heart pump and get the blood back into those legs of yours. We'll check on your progress regularly at your weekly consultation: you'll see, three weeks from now you'll have recovered your beautiful shape very nicely!'

'Yes, but what if Tao decides to invite me before that?' says Fangfang.

'No need to panic. I don't just have capsules and syringes in my pharmacy kit, I've also got *this*.'

Out of my medical bag I take a little compact of bronzing powder, which I apply copiously onto Fangfang's cheeks to hollow them out, with the help of a large paintbrush. In three months, I've learned to use the products supplied by my platinum sponsor, which so intimidated me at first, just as I've started daring to take some pieces of clothing out of my Rosier wardrobe (always avoiding that slit dress in red silk chiffon). Ultimately, make-up is no different from drawing: it's about lines and colours and how to combine them harmoniously. It's even more fun than on my drawing tablet, to be touching the palette of assorted eyeshadows, putting my fingers in the colours, using real pencils and real brushes rather than always the same stylus. I never imagined it would give me so much pleasure. I've practised often on the page of my face, standing alone at the bathroom mirror, inventing a thousand appearances and a thousand characters for myself, before washing it all off and going back down to the girls in the living room. When I've been with the boys in the Visiting Room, I've only ever allowed myself a little mascara. Most of my various looks are like most of my drawings: I keep them to myself.

'There!' I say, putting down the brush. 'A bit of optical illusion never did anybody any harm.'

The smile is back on the Singaporean girl's face.

'Thank you, Léo! You're a true artist!'

Fangfang heads for the hatch that leads up to the gym; but Kelly is coming down the ladder at just the same moment. Covered in sweat in her pink leotard, a sweatband on her head, she's the exact opposite of Fangfang: for three months, she's been spending her days running on the treadmill, and I haven't seen her turn on her revision tablet once.

'Have you got a raging toothache?' she asks Fangfang, taking out her earphones. 'Or are you in the process of transforming into a hamster?'

'Hamster yourself! I'm not the one who's been running in a wheel like a maniac since the start of the journey!'

'It wouldn't be such a bad thing if you did.'

'I'm not going to take advice from a total sport junkie!'

Kelly freezes.

'Hey, what did you just say?'

'I said a *sport junkie*. Are you stupid? Or has making all the blood rush to your legs left none for your brain?'

Fangfang shrugs and climbs up the ladder, leaving me alone with Kelly.

The Canadian girl immediately takes me aside.

'Did you hear the way she just insulted me?'

310

'*Sport junkie* isn't really an insult,' I say. 'And anyway, she's partly right. You shouldn't overdo it. You really do spend a lot of time in the gym, and over-training isn't good; there's a risk of nervous exhaustion. While we're on the subject, you're the last up for today's consultation. Shall we start by taking your blood pressure?'

'I'm not a *junkie*,' says Kelly, unable to get the idea out of her head.

The way she says the word *junkie*, I immediately understand that that's the problem.

'Of course not,' I say gently. 'It's just a metaphor, just a manner of speaking.'

'Junkies are weak. Pathetic victims. People who fall prey to bastards like Mozart.'

As she speaks the Brazilian's name, Kelly's expression hardens. It's no longer the usual grumpy-but-sexy look, seeming a bit shallow but lovable beneath the surface – it's the look of a killer.

'Mozart didn't choose to be a dealer,' I say. 'He was forced to do it, and that's why he signed up for the programme, to escape that fate. He was a victim of Zero-G too.'

'*A victim of Zero-G?*' barks Kelly. 'Are you kidding me? Victims of Zero-G don't go around flirting and batting their eyelids: their eyes are just empty marbles with contracted pupils, that can see nothing but hallucinations. Victims of Zero-G don't play at being hot-blooded Latin lovers: their blood is as cold as the blood of an astronaut left floating in the void without a spacesuit. Victims of Zero-G don't fly off on a space cruise: after a certain number of trips they end up six feet underground, nicely wedged between four wooden boards.'

Kelly's rage takes me by surprise. I remember the state she was in when she came out of her first – and only – interview with Mozart: wild with fury. But not only fury, I can see that now – she was wild with pain too.

I put my hand on her arm – it's shaking.

'What's up, Kelly?'

She glances around her, nervous. It's become a habit with all of us over the weeks, whenever we're tired or anxious: looking for the cameras. But Kelly's eyes find only her own reflection in the large round mirror above the sink.

'Here in the bathroom we're on our own, you know that,' I say gently. 'If you want to talk to me, you can. If you want to keep quiet, you can do that too. In any case, I'm not going to say anything. Doctor–patient confidentiality.'

Kelly nods.

She sits down on the stool, her eyes fixed on the sink. Seen from above, there are darker roots beginning to break out at the base of her platinum-blonde hair – it's been a little while since she's dyed it. It's the kind of detail that never escapes my artist's eye.

'I lied when I said I'd left my caravan because I felt too cramped,' Kelly murmurs. 'Honestly, if I'd wanted more space, would I have moved into a tiny four-room cabin with five roommates who are all at their most hormonal?'

She gives a little bitter laugh.

'What made me leave was not being able to bear my own family any longer. It's just that if I'd stayed, I would have ended up diving in too. I was within an inch of doing it. My mother, my brothers: all four of them were drugged up to the eyeballs, unable to think or breathe or live without Zero-G. Well, if you can call that living, that zombie state they stayed in for hours, sometimes days . . .'

Kelly's voice cracks.

I don't dare say a word. But I keep my hand on her arm, just to show her I'm there.

'Mum hasn't left her bunk at the back of the caravan since my twelfth birthday – that was the last one when she had the strength to make me a cake. As for my brothers, they only found the energy to get up when they were jonesing – to go off and do a bit of moonlighting, or gross missions for the Aranha – the gang have got a near-monopoly on Zero-G in Canada. I worked eight hours a day as a cashier at the supermarket, and eight hours as a cleaner; all that to see my salary disappear into Zero-G powder at the end of each month. I nearly did try it myself, that damn powder, just to see what it did, to understand what was going on behind my brothers' contracted pupils each time they did a line, a launch-pad without having to lift off from the caravan . . . You know what they say: it makes you feel weightless, like you're tearing yourself away from all the problems of the world, like in zero gravity? That it makes all the muscles in your body contract, even those that stand your hair up, that it's like making love with the stars? Yes, I nearly did try it . . . But finally I chose to go touch the stars in reality instead.'

Kelly looks up at me now for the first time since she's started talking. Her eyes are shining.

'I recognised Mozart's piercing the moment I saw it – our dealer in Toronto had one just the same. But I said nothing in front of the cameras. I don't want the whole thing to come down on my family's head, with the cops showing up at the campsite to lock my brothers up. I feel bad enough for having abandoned them, even if I didn't have a choice. You must think I'm a dirty quitter, right?'

'No, Kelly, I don't think that at all! Your story . . . I never would have imagined . . .'

A sad smile passes across Kelly's face.

'Right, like you say,' she says. 'Who'd imagine a backstory like that for the airhead in love with a singer for little schoolgirls? It's a really dumb thing to say, but since I was twelve, Jimmy Giant's kept me going. OK, his music is really commercial, his lyrics are silly and his pretty-boy smile is surgically enhanced – you think I don't know all that? But when that horrible sticky silence took hold of the caravan, and it was just me and the clenched-up bodies of my brothers and my mother, hair sticking up all over the place, I'd put Jimmy on full volume in my ears and I'd go curling on my own on the frozen lake. It did me a world of good. Like being on the treadmill, upstairs in the gym. And like talking to you, now.'

Kelly gets up and hugs me, in her slightly surly, slightly clumsy, but completely sincere way.

'Thanks, Léo,' she says, taking a step back to look at me. 'You have a gift for listening – maybe that's why they made you Medical Officer. But you never confide in people yourself. Well, maybe to Kris, but not to us. You know, I don't even know which of the boys you like. Are you wild about Alexei's smile, like the others?'

314

'It's true he has a nice smile, you can't deny that.'

'Go on, don't mess me around, which is your favourite?'

'It's too early to say.'

I can guess which name Kelly suspects of me. My interview with Mozart the other day really had an effect on me. On him too, because ever since then he's put me at the top of his Heart List every week.

'This eleventh week is the sixth for the girls to take their turn, and Mozart is the only boy you haven't yet invited,' says Kelly, confirming exactly what I'd been thinking. 'So on Saturday, tomorrow, he's the one you're going to call into the Visiting Room, isn't he?'

'That's my rule,' I say, trying not to betray any emotion. 'I won't go against that.'

'I'd have been amazed if you did. The Determinator never goes off the rails. Totally pig-headed! Just one thing: if you like the guy . . . don't let yourself get taken in.'

'Don't worry. I'm not the type to let herself get fooled.'

45. Out of Frame

University of California, Berkeley
Friday 15 September, 07:53am

'. . . and that's how relativistic quantum electrodynamics attempts to reconcile electromagnetism with quantum mechanics, via relativistic Lagrangian formalism. We'll get a chance to go over this again later: we've only been back a couple of weeks since the break and we've got a whole semester ahead of us to explore the wonders of the subatomic world together, in my famous "Electromagnetism 101" class . . .'

The jacketed professor draws a line at the bottom of the large touchscreen that serves as a blackboard, and in doing so concludes the list of equations he's been writing up over the past two hours. He puts down his stylus and looks up at the clock on the wall.

'Five to eight!' he exclaims, rubbing his hands. 'It's nearly time for the speed-dating! As you know, the only reason the university's been scheduling our classes so much earlier this semester is so we can be done by eight and all you students can enjoy the show – nobody pays attention to classes once it's started . . . and nor does anyone want to teach them!'

He presses a button on the control panel set into the desk. The equations disappear one by one as though an invisible sponge were being drawn across the touchscreen.

A feverish murmuring runs through the desks arranged in a semicircle around the rostrum. Seated there are dozens of young people who seem even more excited by the show that's now starting than by *the wonders of the subatomic world*. A good quarter of the female contingent have curled their hair into crowns of braids, some of them very skilfully, others somewhat more approximately. Some of the female students have even bought '*Kirsten Special*' hairpieces, attached to their heads with a lot of help from hairclips, whose effect is more or less successful depending on how blonde they are underneath.

Among the male students, it's possible to make out several white jackets with grey seams in Alexei's style, and several manga haircuts directly copied from Kenji, sharpened with scissors and sculpted with hair gel. If they haven't all opted to copy the look of one of the astronauts on the Genesis programme, most of them are at least wearing T-shirts and badges making their preferences clear: *Team Marcus* can be read on the chests of several of the girls, closely followed by those who declare themselves proudly *Team Alexei* or *Team Mozart*. Girls supporting the other contestants are fewer and further between, though there's a group of Asian girls who are all wearing Tao's smiling face printed on their backs.

'Yes!' shouts a boy who's checking out the news on his phone. 'Léonor's been chosen today. We're in for a treat, guys!'

His announcement unleashes a flood of commentary, the girls in raptures over the gorgeous outfits the French candidate has been wearing these past weeks, the boys speculating daringly about the dream physique hidden behind those same outfits.

Only one student does not seem to be sharing in the general enthusiasm. In his red polo shirt, with neither badge nor slogan, Andrew Fisher is sitting alone on the back row, at the very top of the semicircle. He looks very different to how he was at the start of the summer: his thick brown hair is dishevelled, as though he's just got out of bed, and discoloured by the Death Valley sun; his skin has taken on a coppery tint; behind his black-framed glasses, his eyes are staring into space. He is sitting there in the lecture hall, but in reality he feels as though he's on a different planet.

At the very bottom of the semicircle, on the big black screen, the final equation disappears.

The lights of the hall go out.

The image of the starry cosmos replaces the mathematical formulae and is welcomed by a satisfied 'Aaaaah!'

The music to 'Cosmic Love' fills the amphitheatre, with the familiar silhouette of the Cupido sketched out against a background of space.

The voiceover starts reeling off the programme's slogan:
'Six girls on one side . . .
'Six boys on the other . . .
'Six minutes to meet . . .'
The assembled crowd takes up the final phrase in chorus:
'An eternity to love!'
Shouts.
Applause.
General mayhem.

The womb-planet fills the enormous touchscreen, containing its foetus, while the voiceover concludes:

'*The Genesis programme. When the most ambitious scientific programme meets the most thrilling speed-dating game, you get to be the live witnesses to the most beautiful love story of all time!*'

Fade in from black.

Title: Sixty-fifth session in the Visiting Room. Hostess: Léonor, 18, France, Medical Officer (communication latency: 2 minutes, 51 seconds)

Drum-roll.

Léonor appears. Today she's wearing fitted combat trousers in black satin and a matching safari jacket; cinched at her narrow waist, the jacket covers her shoulders and arms, but opens wide at her chest. The girl has dared to wear a piece of jewellery for the first time: a thin chain of white gold whose three loops float over her alabaster skin, like rings protecting access to some mysterious planet.

Serena (off): 'Léonor! So elegant! So flawless! And most of all, so sensual! Your transformation has truly been one of this programme's greatest surprises. You started from such a low base. And now look at you!'

'... it's an atomic bomb!' yells one of the guys in the Berkeley auditorium. 'Léonor ought to be in the Electromagnetism 101 class! She's electrifying me and magnetising me at the same time!'

The other male students nod vigorously.

The girls roll their eyes, sighing exasperatedly.

'Shhhh!' says one of them, a member of Team Mozart, according to her T-shirt. 'Be quiet, you're going to ruin it!'

A kind of calm settles back over the semicircle.

Serena (off): 'But enough chitchat. The spacecraft is currently eighty-five light-seconds from Earth. Doubling this for the communication latency, this means that my voice has already travelled to the Cupido and come all the way back to be broadcast internationally with a two-minute fifty-one-second time lapse . . . Now, I'm sure viewers are just as impatient as I am to watch the rest of the programme! So, Léonor: whom will you be seeing today? Your fans are used to your rule, they're expecting to see Mozart, who like you has seen some remarkable progress made in the donations to his Dowry.'

Léonor: 'The viewers will get what they're expecting. I've always respected my rule, and I will continue to do so until 10 December.'

A silence, time enough for Earth to send the pre-recorded drum-roll to the Cupido's speakers.

A few moments later, Mozart appears on the right of the screen, at the same time as the small superimposed stopwatch. He has abandoned the tight-fitting T-shirt and the low-slung jeans that revealed his boxers, for a white shirt and black trousers. He isn't any less seductive, quite the contrary.

Léonor: 'Hello, Mozart do Brasil.'

Mozart: 'Hello, Léonor de Paris.'

He smiles.

So does she.

The silence between them is highly charged, the expectation almost palpable.

It's him who breaks it, with his warm voice. 'You really are amazing.'

Léonor: 'I could say the same about you.'

Mozart shoots her his most ardent look. 'As a Brazilian, I have blood from all over the world. Why choose one of the other boys, when you can get the best of all six combined in one person?'

Léonor, laughing: 'And modest with it!'

A few more seconds of silence, while their bodies drift slowly towards each other, supple and graceful.

Mozart: 'I've been waiting for this moment a long time, you know? The moment when I'd get to see you again. What you said to me in our first interview, that the past didn't matter any more . . . it moved me. It touched me. Will you think I'm totally lame if I say I've dreamed about you every night since then?'

Léonor: 'Lame? No. A smooth talker, perhaps. But aren't words what the Visiting Room is for, after all? For us to use our six minutes to speak about everything we want, to show what it is we hope for?'

Close-up on Mozart's tanned face. His long eyelashes open a little wider over his dark eyes, suddenly very serious.

He's not joking. 'I'm not telling you what I want,' he says. 'I'm telling you what I feel. I'm not showing you what I hope for. I'm showing you who I am.'

A concert of sighs fills the Berkeley auditorium. Leaning on their desks, the girls' eyes devour the Brazilian's handsome, serious face.

'He's the bomb, that guy,' says the girl who called for silence a few moments earlier. 'I love that bad-boy thing he's got going

321

on, so badly hurt by life, it really gets you. You just want to take him in your arms and console him, and never let him go.'

'Yeah, but deep down he's still a filthy Zero-G dealer,' remarks a boy sitting nearby.

'He *was*,' the girl corrects him. 'Have you been watching all the episodes, or what? Forgiveness, second chances and all that, did it all go over your head, or are you just jealous of Mozzie?'

The cocky boy hurries to bury his nose behind his tablet, to escape from *Mozzie*'s fans, who are staring daggers at him.

On the screen, Léonor too seems moved.

Her big bronze eyes are trembling slightly, her lips are half open. 'But what about me?' she says, her voice just a murmur. 'How can you be sure I'm showing you who I am? How can you know I'm really showing you everything?'

Mozart: 'I don't need to see everything. Not all at once. Even if I'm dying to. Choosing the rhythm is up to you.'

His movements become cat-like, as though he is almost brushing against the reinforced glass.

'We have this dance in Brazil, which the favela girls taught me – samba requires perfect harmony between the two partners, body against body, breath against breath. There's a famous tune that reminds me of you, "The Girl from Ipanema". It's about a beautiful girl, tall and tanned, who walks on the beach so gracefully that she seems to be dancing, not noticing that all eyes are on her . . .'

Mozart starts singing softly in Portuguese, in his deep, sensual voice.

Léonor tries to defend herself. 'I'm not really that tall, even if my spine has grown a centimetre or two in this reduced gravity, and my complexion isn't tanned at all.'

But Mozart keeps singing, as though he were murmuring in Léonor's ear, as though nobody could see them or hear them, as if they were all alone in the world.

Léonor can't help but laugh. 'If you'd ever seen me walking, especially in my astronaut boots, there's nothing like a samba dancer about me!'

It's Mozart's turn to laugh, giving her a smile filled with gratitude and hopefulness: 'I could teach you, if you like. Only if you like. It's like I said: the rhythm is up to you, for our private dance à deux. You lead me. I will follow you. Wherever you want to go.'

Drum-roll.

The interview is over.

Serena (off): 'I don't know about you, my dear viewers, but I'm having hot flushes! It's so intense! You see how the Genesis programme makes us dream, and journey, from Earth to Mars, from the darkness of space to the sunlight of Ipanema! Will Léonor and Mozart dance together for real? Find out the answer to that question soon, on the Genesis channel!'

Fade to black.

Credits.

The channel switches to the on-board cameras that are capturing life on the Cupido twenty-four hours a day. The first sequence comes from the living room on the boys' side, where the boys are welcoming Mozart back from the Visiting Room.

'Well?' asks Tao, whose large athlete's body is squeezed into a small folding wheelchair.

'Well, that was definitely worth waiting for,' replies Mozart. 'But you guys shouldn't expect me to write you a whole novel about it; what happens in the Visiting Room is private . . .'

Then he adds, with some emotion in his voice:

'. . . especially when it concerns Léonor.'

Alexei claps Mozart on the back. 'Oh, man, you're hooked!'

'It's true that Léonor is hard to resist,' admits Samson. 'Seriously, that girl has not one thing wrong with her . . . apart from her warped rule.'

'I actually like that rule,' says Kenji. 'It's clear, tidy and precise.'

Marcus keeps quiet. Playing cards are spread across the brushed-steel dining table, and his thick eyebrows are frowning over his grey eyes – he seems to be absorbed in a round of solitaire.

Mozart seems to notice his silence.

'You were right when you said that girl's a red star,' he calls across the room. 'Every time I see her she sets me on fire.'

Marcus slams the last card from his deck down onto the table.

The ace of spades, as sharp as a dagger.

For just a moment, the grey eyes of the American and the dark eyes of the Brazilian meet.

A moment later, the former resumes his game, the latter his conversation.

'Well, in a word, it was awesome, and I'd be the happiest guy ever if Léonor was to choose me in three months.'

'And you didn't say anything about . . . about my disability?' asks Tao.

'Of course not. Why do you have to ask that each time one of us goes up to the Visiting Room? I take my word seriously, and

I respect our agreement. We don't talk one another down, that's what we decided, and I've always stuck to that . . .'

He puts his hand on Tao's shoulder.

'. . . but you know, man, you really should tell the girls you're paralysed, at some point or other. I swear, for me, revealing my horrible past to Léonor was really liberating. At the time, I felt like I was tearing out my own guts, live on TV in front of the viewers, but right now . . . I'm not saying I've forgotten all about it, but I feel a whole lot lighter.'

Tao clenches his powerful jaw. Doubt shows in his face.

'But you landed on your feet,' he says. 'Léonor accepted you as you are. Who's to say the other girls will be as understanding? I really like Fangfang, but she sets the bar so high with all that statistical compatibility stuff, her eight babies and her doctorate in pure mathematics. She's besotted with me, an acrobat who's never studied – imagine if she discovers that to top it all I'm actually in a wheelchair?'

Mozart shrugs.

'I don't know what to tell you about the pure mathematics, but as for the eight babies, you should be able to reassure her about that,' he says. 'After all, it's only your legs that are paralysed, not the rest of you!'

Tao's face breaks into a smile, the other boys laugh good-naturedly and the tension is defused.

Warden, the dog, suddenly starts barking.

'And what's up with you?' Kenji asks, stroking the head of the mongrel, a powerful Doberman-like animal. 'Let's hope at least that you're not getting sick? Animals are often more sensitive to radiation than humans.'

'Stop it with your radiation, Ken!' says Samson, the Biology

Officer in charge of Warden. 'I think the poor boy's just fed up of having to stay locked up in these quarters without being able to see Louve. After all, the dogs are the only ones not to get a session in the bubble.'

'The Visiting Room is made for talking though, not for barking,' Kenji points out, very seriously.

'Doesn't matter.'

Samson turns toward the camera.

'Hey, Serena – are you listening? Wouldn't it be possible to arrange a little interview between Warden and Louve?'

After two minutes and fifty-one seconds of silence, the wide-screen opposite the fireplace lights up to reveal the face of the executive producer, as though she'd been summoned in a spiritualist séance.

'It'd be pointless, Samson,' she says, smiling. 'Louve and Warden have no choice to make; they don't have a Heart List to rank.'

'Yes, but all the same, it would allow each of them to tell the other about their bitch of a life . . . I've been wondering about what their names mean. I've looked them up in my tablet and apparently louve is the French word for a she-wolf. The girls' dog must be a magnificent wolfhound from the French forests, with as high a pedigree as Léonor. And our Warden, where might his name come from? The dictionary says it means "guard".'

'Oh, so like he could be protecting a flock of sheep?' asks Kenji.

'More like "prison guard".'

Alexei bursts out laughing.

'Maybe Warden had a job in a prison before joining the programme. After all, we all have a past, so why not him? I can easily picture him swaggering around on sentry duty, given the way he looks. Maybe he's eaten dozens of prisoners who were trying to escape, the beast.'

'What have you been smoking?' asks Samson. 'The things you come out with! You know Warden wouldn't hurt a fly.'

'Chill! I was just saying.'

'It's stupid to judge anyone based on what they look like – I nearly got burned because of my eyes.'

'Stupid to judge based on what people look like? So you think the girls are judging us based on what exactly, then?'

'Given that you're way ahead at the top of the rankings, it certainly isn't for our IQ.'

Before the tone escalates further, Serena intervenes at a lag, responding to the suggestion made by Alexei nearly three minutes earlier.

'Your four-legged friend comes from the pound, not the prison,' she says. 'He was behind bars before being taken into our animal store, not in front of them. But you must be right, Alexei, I suppose he must owe his name to his impressive appearance. It was the much-missed Sherman Fisher who took on the task of christening the animals himself, seeing as he loved dogs so much – may he rest in peace.'

In the back row of the Berkeley auditorium, Andrew Fisher sits up abruptly.

He blinks his eyes behind his glasses as though waking from a dream.

He hasn't taken a single note in the past two hours, but now he picks up his stylus and starts to scribble on his tablet: LOUVE and WARDEN.

'Right, guys, that's enough for today,' says the professor from the rostrum. 'You'll be late for your next class, and so will I.'

The large touchscreen goes black.

The lights in the hall come back on.

The students stand up.

It's not that they've had their fill of Genesis for the day, on the contrary: the moment the big screen goes off, they take out their phones and tablets to keep following the show without missing a second.

Andrew gathers up his things, throws them in his backpack and heads down the stairs towards the exit.

'*Louve and Warden . . . Louve and Warden . . .*' he mutters over and over, as if it were a magical incantation. 'Father got to baptise Louve and Warden . . . Now, he never left anything to chance. So what if there was a message, an answer of some kind? Why *Louve*, that French name? And why *Warden*?'

He's too caught up in his thoughts to notice the two pretty girls watching him with interest, a couple of rows down.

'That one's really cute,' says one of them. 'But he never talks to anybody. And I've never seen him at the speed-dating sessions organised every evening at the campus bar. And it's so *in* right now, six minutes head-to-head sipping a Cupido cocktail!'

'He's a loner,' replies her friend. 'Apparently, he spent the whole summer on his own in Death Valley. That's where he got the tan, chasing after a ghost.'

'A ghost?'

'His dad's: Sherman Fisher – you know, the manager from the Genesis programme who died at the wheel of his car just before the lift-off.'

'Oh, poor guy! That's so awful! And it must have been so cool having a dad like that!'

'I don't think they parted on the best terms, something to do with Andrew not having been chosen for the programme. Anyway, let's go, we're going to be late for linear algebra!'

46. Shot

'*Happy birthday to you,*
 '*Happy birthday to you,*
 '*Happy birthday, dear Kri-is,*
 '*Happy birthday to yoooooou!*'

I put the 'cake' down on the table, in front of Kris who flushes with pleasure while the other girls applaud loud enough to bring the house down.

'We're just sorry we haven't got any candles. It's a safety issue,' explains Fangfang. 'But you can blow on it as if there were.'

Kris complies, blowing out imaginary candles.

'It's gorgeous!' she says.

'Gorgeous?' I say, looking at the sort of flattened pancake that Safia and I managed to put together. 'You're too kind. It's really just the sad evidence that without you in the kitchen we haven't got a clue. But I've got something else for you which I hope you might like a bit.'

I take my big drawing tablet out from under the table, and turn it on to reveal my latest creation. I've been working on it in secret for the last two weeks, taking advantage of the moments when Kris was busy slaving over the stove.

A whirlwind of blues and whites, iridescent reflections, explodes onto the surface of the tablet. It's a digital painting, a portrait of Kris in large format, in the same pose as the Botticelli Madonna decorating her wardrobe. She's in her most beautiful dress. Except that instead of fibres of sky-blue silk, I've woven the material line by line in threads of frost. I've sprinkled her natural crown with sparkling flakes; I've decorated her forehead, her neck and ears with chiselled stalactites, which gleam like diamonds.

'The Ice Princess,' I say, 'who makes every Ice Prince in the world melt. I wish you all the best for your twentieth year, Kris!'

Overcome by emotion, Kris collapses into my arms.

'It's . . . it's *really* gorgeous,' she stammers. 'Thank you, thank you, thank you, my darling Léo! We're going to hook this picture up to the screen above our bunk and I'm sure it'll bring me luck.'

'Happy birthday, Kris!' Serena's voice comes all of a sudden, as clearly as if she were sitting right here in the circle with us.

'We turn towards the screen above the fireplace, where our protector's face has appeared against a background of glowing red foliage – it's mid-September in America, and the gardens of the Villa McBee have their autumn colours on display.

'My gift to you is in the form of an announcement: Alexei has just been selected for today's speed-dating, and a little birdie has told me that you're the one he means to invite . . . for a very special session.'

* * *

331

Several long minutes later, Kris is back in the living room, and so radiant that all our eyes are dazzled. Unlike the excitement that usually greets each girl's return from the Visiting Room, there's silence. Nobody dares ask the smallest question. Because this time is different, we can feel it. Something *very special* has clearly happened up there, as predicted by Serena, who's never wrong.

'That's it,' murmurs Kris. 'Alexei's done it.'

'What, what's he done?' asks Kelly, who can't bear to wait any longer. 'Did Serena finally decide to open the glass partition and he threw himself onto you like a condemned man in the visiting room of a prison?'

'Alexei isn't an animal – he's a gentleman. He . . . he proposed to me.'

Everybody falls silent, even Louve.

But the most eloquent expressions pass across each of our faces – astonishment, joy, jealousy, sometimes all three at once.

'He proposed?' repeats Liz as though she might have misunderstood. 'But we haven't yet aligned the craft with the orbit of Phobos . . . The final Heart Lists haven't been announced . . . We still have three months of travelling ahead of us.'

'Alexei told me he'd seen enough to make his choice now. For him, the engagement is just as important as the marriage itself. He showed me an exquisite ring, saying that if there weren't a wall between us he'd put it onto my finger. He's going to wear it on a chain around his neck until he can give it to me on Mars.'

* * *

The rest of the day passes in a strange atmosphere.

Each of us attends to whatever she's doing in silence. Fangfang revises; Kelly curls; Liz checks the on-board instruments; Safia organises our weekly laundry in the UV-ray textile steriliser, which cleans, deodorises and disinfects our clothes without needing to use any of the precious water we have on board.

Kris, meanwhile, is floating on a little cloud. She spends her afternoon grooming Louve, humming. It's as if she were in another world, in a different space and time, separated from us by a barrier as unbreachable as the one that splits the Visiting Room.

She has been chosen.

She has chosen.

For her and Alexei, the game is done.

It isn't till the following morning, when we find ourselves in the bathroom getting ready, that her tongue finally loosens.

'I wanted to say it one more time, Léo, from the bottom of my heart: thank you.'

'It's nothing,' I say, rearranging the pins and elastics that are needed to construct the crown on Kris's head. 'I enjoyed doing the digital painting.'

'Not just for the artwork. For all the rest of it too. For your encouragement, which has always kept me going, for your good humour which has always brought me such relief, for your example which has always inspired me. Without you I wouldn't be here, living a romance that's crazier than anything I've read in a book, and about to marry the man of my dreams. How can I ever thank you enough?'

I smile.

'I like seeing you so happy – that's the greatest thanks I can get. Because you really are happy, aren't you?'

'More than I've ever been in my life. Things between Alexei and me, they're so intense, so . . . connected. You know what he promised me, when he made his declaration? That he wouldn't invite any other girl but me between now and the end of the journey. And he's asked me not to invite any other boy but him.'

'So it turns out I'm not the only control freak making my own rules then!'

We burst out laughing, like in the good old days, as though our forthcoming marriages aren't about to change everything between us.

Then we become serious again, more quickly this time.

Kris gets up from the stool screwed to the bathroom floor.

'Now you sit down,' she says, with a gentle authority. 'There's no point bothering to braid my hair today, since I won't be going up to the Visiting Room even if I'm invited. It's my turn to do yours.'

'Oh, you know my hair has never experienced anything more than a basic bun, or just freedom.'

'I'd like to try something.'

Kris takes the elastics and the pins I had prepared for her, and starts to twist my thick red locks. While her nimble fingers move, she talks to me, examining my reflection in the round mirror.

'And how about you, darling Léo: are you happy?'

'Yes, I think so . . .'

Pictures from the last three months run through my mind. The excitement of the departure, the slow appropriation of the Rosier wardrobe and make-up, the anxiety about the first interviews with the boys . . . the ardent look in Mozart's eyes, twice, coming to rest on me.

This memory makes me shiver.

It was a pleasant experience.

More than pleasant, really.

Yes, I can admit it, I can allow myself to feel it, I have the right: I liked that look in his eyes, and everything it promised, and everything I'd like to promise him in return.

'No, actually I'm absolutely sure!' I correct myself. 'I'm happy! Really.'

'Mozart?' Kris guesses.

'Yes. That boy . . . does something to me. He's like me, a dustbin baby, a cast-off who rebelled against his destiny, an escapee from life. Things really could work out between us. At least, I think so.'

'He's completely in love with you. He told me so, you know, last time he invited me to the Visiting Room. I could tell I wasn't the one he really wanted to see: he spent the whole six minutes just talking about you, how your rule is making him suffer so terribly, but he's following it because it's what you decided. Are you sure you don't want to see him more often?'

'Like you said: my rule . . . and the Salamander . . .'

'The Salamander won't change anything about the way Mozart feels, I'm sure of that, him being the guy with the spider's egg on the back of his neck. Why wait till the final week to tell him about your scar . . . to show him? Maybe it'll bring you even closer. He's confided everything to you, Léo; he's at your feet. It's your turn now.'

335

I don't answer.

Kris has put doubts into my mind.

She's undermined the rule.

Reveal the existence of the Salamander to Mozart right away, at the risk of ruining everything?

It's true I haven't heard it hissing in my ear for weeks now. But I know it's always there, hidden away in my back.

'I just want a bit more time,' I say. 'To get to know him better, to be sure he's the right one. That's all I ask: a bit more time.'

Kris nods.

Her fingers are still working away in silence.

'There!' she exclaims, finally.

I look at myself in the mirror. The bun Kris has fashioned for me has nothing in common with the barbaric knots I used to force my hair into back when I was working at the factory, nor even with the improved version with the black satin ribbon. It's a symphony, an arpeggio of curls, a wonder of elegance and geometry: a hairstyle worthy of a Rosier fashion show.

'A proper bridal bun,' I say.

'So you'll do me the favour of putting on something other than black today, for a change!'

Clearly today it's Kris who's in charge, so why argue?

A few minutes later, we're standing beside my cupboard and its treasures.

'This thing is amazing,' says Kris, her fingertips brushing over the slit dress in red chiffon, which is resting on its hanger like an exotic, dangerous animal.

'Don't even think about it!'

'But it would suit you so well! That dress is a weapon of mass seduction – absolutely any boy would pass out at the very sight of it. Look how fine this fabric is . . . The precision of the cut . . . And this neckline . . . It's also the exact same colour as your hair.'

'If you don't stop talking about it I'm putting on my jersey top pronto and we won't discuss it any further, I'm warning you.'

'OK, OK, I get the message: the red dress will be for another time. So what to choose? All the rest of your wardrobe is black –' she runs her hands over the precious outfits – 'apart from this!'

From the back of the wardrobe, Kris extracts a white silk ensemble, in an oriental style, made up of trousers and a long tunic worn over the top.

'A Vietnamese dress!' she says. 'The height of style and modesty: and long sleeves, so you have no excuse!'

After a lot of contortions to change clothes with my back to the wardrobe, shielded from the cameras, I find myself in the dress that has been made to measure for me by the people at Rosier. The broad, silky trousers caress my skin; the tunic with the mandarin collar, shaped to my chest, my shoulders and my arms as intimately as the undersuit, before moving down into two flaps separated by slits that come all the way up to my waist. Almost my entire body is covered by this fluid silk. I may know that it's opaque enough to hide the Salamander, but still I can't help wondering.

'I don't know if this is such a good idea . . .' I start.

'Are you kidding? You look amazing!'

'Yes, but –'

I don't have the time to say any more: the screens in the bedroom come on, to show the Genesis programme's opening titles.

Kris leads me to the ladder that goes up to the living room.

'We were doing some fittings and we missed the announcement about which boy has been chosen for today,' she says. 'So who's it to be, girls?'

'It's Marcus,' replies Fangfang as the titles come to an end, leaving a black screen in its place.

Serena's voice appears in the living room with us.

'Calling Léonor to the Visiting Room!'

47. Genesis Channel

Léonor's silhouette rises into the left side of the screen.

The long flaps of her tunic undulate on each side of her statuesque body, like vast wings. The glowing white of her dress, revealing her perfect curves, blends with the matt white of her hands and face. The only colour in her dazzling appearance: the red splash of the virtuosic bun, the purple dots that sprinkle her high cheekbones and her lips coated in the deepest Rosier crimson.

Opposite her, on the right side of the Visiting Room, Marcus is all in black – trousers, shirt and jacket. His determined expression is sculpted by the spotlights, and the shadow of his thick eyebrows emphasises the contrast with the metallic grey of his eyes.

Marcus: 'Hello, Léonor.'

His voice is rough, a bit hoarser than the first time – as though the effort of restraining himself were breaking it even more.

Close-up on Léonor's face, as smooth and seemingly expressionless as her host's. But to anybody who knows what to look for, there's a trembling in the iris that doesn't lie. It looks like liquid gold.

'Hello, Marcus,' she says.

Reverse shot on Marcus, in very close-up.

The substance of his eyes has melted too, like molten silver.

Léonor: 'I thought you weren't going to invite me again.'

Marcus: 'I thought you wanted me to respect your rule. One time every six weeks. Well, this is the sixth week. Now is the time.'

Léonor: 'You've always placed me last in your Heart Lists.'

Marcus: 'You've always claimed that the final ranking is the only one that counts.'

The two young people are perfectly still on either side of the Visiting Room, just suspended there.

Léonor: 'What game are you playing?'

Marcus: 'The same game as you.'

Léonor: 'No, I don't think so. It's not the same game. Mine is clear and logical. Yours is vague and unpredictable. You talk to other people about me as a red giant who burns everything around it, leaving total devastation, Kenji told me . . . I didn't think I'd see you again on this trip. I'd have preferred it that way. It would have been simpler.'

Marcus: 'Death is the only thing that's simple, and eternal. Because life, you see, is complicated, and it's terribly short. We think we have all the time in the world ahead of us, but the reality is that it's like a speed-dating session – the moment you're in the bubble, it's already time to let go.'

Léonor: 'You sound like an old man!'

Marcus: 'Old people are just young people for whom everything has passed too quickly.'

Léonor blinks.

She freezes, suddenly, like an animal.

Her whole face turns leopard-like. 'What is it you want, Marcus, with your riddles and your charades? Why me and not one of the others?'

Marcus holds the big cat's eyes with his eagle gaze. 'You know very well why. What's happening between us, you feel it too, I know it.'

Léonor: 'You don't even know me.'

Marcus: 'And that frightens you?'

Léonor: 'Shut up! You're totally unfathomable! It's impossible to tell what you really think!'

Léonor's nostrils flare.

Her chest rises under her white silk tunic.

She looks down at her own body. 'I don't know why I'm wearing all this, why I've made all this effort, *for you*. I should have come in my crappy old jeans. Wrapped in a bin-bag. Because you don't deserve any better. Because that's who I really am!'

She grabs the loose ends of her tunic and knots them angrily at her waist, bringing their floating to an abrupt end. She kicks off her pumps, sending them flying to the back of the Visiting Room. She wipes her mouth with the back of her arm, drawing a gash across her cheek. Finally, she yanks out the pins that were holding her bun in place, destroying its fragile architecture and leaving her hair in a glowing red nebula surrounding her head. 'This is what *Léonor* is, without any packaging, or almost none!'

Close-up on Marcus's face, marked with emotion, his eyes wide.

A murmur escapes his lips, and all of a sudden his voice is no longer rough nor hard, but gentle as a breath of warm wind. 'The red giant . . .'

Léonor's pupils sparkle behind her wild hair. 'What did you say?'

Marcus, who has so far not moved at all, begins to spin around, using his body as a counterweight. The flaps of his jacket fly out to his sides, the flaps of his shirt come untucked from his trousers, in a whirlwind of black fabric that the panic-stricken camera is no longer able to keep up with.

A sharp pan out.

Stabilising on the image in a wide shot.

Marcus has abruptly stopped spinning. He's frozen in the air, panting, his eyes fixed on Léonor's. He's naked from the waist up, his chest and upper arms covered in a fantastic foliage of tattoos, branches of lines that finely trace words, whole sentences, mysterious plant-like calligrams on the parchment of his skin. Two dark shapes float above him, thrown up by the centrifugal force: the black jacket to his right, the black shirt to his left.

Marcus: 'This is what *Marcus* is, without any packaging, or almost none! You see, it's not so hard to tell what I really think: everything I am, everything I believe, is in my skin.'

The camera focuses on the calligram on his right pectoral muscle, the black rose that opens and closes again to the rhythm of Marcus's breathing. *Seize the day*; it goes all the way down the indented muscles that define his flanks, where a flourishing of verbs that stretch out like laurel leaves quivers: *Run . . . Believe . . . Change . . . Give . . . Desire . . . Dance . . . Love . . .* It goes all the way along his biceps, around which a quotation scrolls like a bracelet of brambles: *Dream as if you'll live forever, Live as if you'll die today*. Each letter that covers Marcus's torso seems alive, as if it isn't ink printed in his skin but his own blood: rising up from the depths of his being, it has flowered on the surface of his skin to tell his story.

Marcus: 'The page of my life is already quite well filled, and one day it will be totally blackened. But for now, there's one virgin spot, where I've never known what to write.'

He points at the left side of his chest, the place where his heart is. The skin is completely white and smooth, free of any inky plants, of any inscription.

The bell rings.

The interview is over.

48. Shot

'The moment for publishing the twelfth Heart Lists has arrived! Now, my dear viewers – and you, dear participants – we are at the exact halfway mark, at the midpoint between the Earth and Mars, and so this announcement carries a very particular symbolic significance. As of tomorrow, I predict everything is going to speed up. The last three months of the journey will pass much faster than the first three. Because the final outcome is approaching. Because the travellers have already used up half the time they have for getting to know one another. The time for them to make some big decisions is at hand!'

On the wide-screen, sitting in front of the window that overlooks her gardens, Serena is doing her thing as usual. With a perfectly smooth professionalism, and a very precisely measured enthusiasm – not too much, not too little. Her utter control is in violent contrast with the storm I have raging inside me. Everything I've been able to construct in the last three months, the barricades I've set up in my head, the ramparts I raised to protect me from the madness of the game, it all flew to pieces last Tuesday, during the second interview with Marcus, in a whirlwind of fabric and frustration.

And I gave way . . .

'Without further ado, let us look at the girls' lists,' says Serena.

The six-column table appears on the screen.

Fangfang (SGP)	Kelly (CAN)	Elizabeth (GBR)	Safia (IND)	Kirsten (DEU)	Léonor (FRA)
1. Tao	1. Marcus	1. Marcus	1. Samson	1. Alexei	1. Mozart
2. Mozart	2. Samson	2. Mozart	2. Mozart	2. Tao	2. Kenji
3. Marcus	3. Kenji	3. Alexei	3. Marcus	3. Samson	3. Tao
4. Alexei	4. Tao	4. Samson	4. Alexei	4. Kenji	4. Samson
5. Samson	5. Alexei	5. Tao	5. Tao	5. Marcus	5. Alexei
6. Kenji	6. Mozart	6. Kenji	6. Kenji	6. Mozart	6. Marcus

'Léo!' cries Kris, throwing herself into my arms. 'You've finally decided to stop ranking the boys in alphabetical order!'

She smiles at me, her face lit up with happiness, while Serena's voiceover comments on the rankings. '*The most impressive progress these past weeks has undoubtedly been that of Mozart and Marcus, who are well on their way to becoming the most eligible contestants on the boys' side, since the early announcement of Alexei and Kirsten's engagement. Tao and Samson have their admirers, too, while Kenji is trailing slightly . . . but there's still time for everything to change!*'

'You've broken your rule!' Kris whispers in my ear, as though I'd just won a great victory over myself. 'You've finally dared to show your real feelings: I'm so happy for Mozart and you!'

But I feel as though I've experienced a bitter defeat. And yet it was stronger than me, when I filled in my list this morning: I needed to send some kind of signal to Marcus. To tell him he doesn't have the right to play with me the way he's been doing. To show him that I too can rank him last. To put an end to his delusion. And, as this was the moment when I abandoned the security of alphabetical rankings, I had to go all the way, and show Mozart how he'd touched me. By putting him in first place.

'No, I haven't broken my rule,' I answer. 'Only the way I've done the rankings has changed. As for the rest – what matters most – it's still the same thing: the same boy every six weeks. And revealing the Salamander at the end of the journey. I won't be going against that.'

But the boys' table has already appeared on the screen.

Tao (CHN)	Alexei (RUS)	Mozart (BRA)	Kenji (JPN)	Samson (NGA)	Marcus (USA)
1. Fangfang	1. Kirsten	1. Léonor	1. Léonor	1. Safia	1. Léonor
2. Elizabeth	2. Elizabeth	2. Elizabeth	2. Elizabeth	2. Elizabeth	2. Elizabeth
3. Safia	3. Léonor	3. Safia	3. Kirsten	3. Kirsten	3. Kelly
4. Léonor	4. Kelly	4. Kirsten	4. Kelly	4. Léonor	4. Safia
5. Kirsten	5. Safia	5. Fangfang	5. Fangfang	5. Fangfang	5. Kirsten
6. Kelly	6. Fangfang	6. Kelly	6. Safia	6. Kelly	6. Fangfang

'*So many surprises!*' exclaims Serena, in voiceover. '*So many emotions! Here, too, Kirsten's engagement has changed the situation. I don't know what's more amazing: our little leopard now in first place for three out of six, or our high-powered English girl who is second in every single ranking!*'

346

The other girls are giving me strange looks, as if I'd done something stupid, as if there were a bug in the system and they were waiting for me to say, 'No, wait, me in first place? It's not possible!'

Up above, I force myself to smile – I suspect it's what the viewers expect of me.

But down below, against my body, I clench my fists tight.

If Marcus were here, he would get them in his face.

Because the girls are right, there really is a bug in the system, and it's *him* . . .

– *him*, who sent me into a terrible rage, and I can't even work out why;

– *him*, who stirs things deep inside of me that I don't understand;

– *him*, who opened himself up like a book whose pages I'm afraid to turn;

– *him*, who suddenly ranks me in first place, after twelve weeks at number six;

– *him*;

– *him*;

– *him*!

(*No, he's not the bug*, whispers the little voice I haven't heard in weeks, but which wasn't dead, just sleeping. *The bug is your warped rule, which even you aren't able to respect. The bug is the illusion that you're a girl like all the rest, a girl who deserves to experience a normal love story. You are the bug, Léonor!*)

The table disappears, bringing me some semblance of relief.

I take a deep breath to recover my composure, to silence the Salamander, while Serena, back on screen now, announces the next part of the programme.

'And now, what better time than the halfway point in the journey to introduce the base at New Eden, which awaits our brave pioneers in their new world, whose components they will be able to buy at auction with your generous donations, my dear viewers? Ladies and gentlemen, young men and women, welcome to the planet Mars, in the company of the Genesis programme instructors!'

The autumnal gardens of the Villa McBee fade into a different backdrop, which is redder still.

Scarlet.

The screen is filled with computer-generated pictures of a landscape, flown over by an imaginary camera: a desert of glowing red sand, dotted with craters that plunge abruptly into a vast chasm.

'*Mars, the Valles Marineris, one of the largest canyons in the solar system,*' comes the high-pitched voiceover of the Planetology instructor, Odette Stuart-Smith, a voice we'd recognise anywhere. '*The positioning of the Martian base of New Eden was carefully selected. Deep enough for it to be possible to reach the frozen water contained in the ground: the Valles Marineris is as deep as Mount Everest is high. Far enough south for optimal use of solar panels: it stretches right across Mars's equatorial line, from east to west. Vast enough to drop the equipment in without any difficulty: it's twenty times larger than Colorado's Grand Canyon.*'

The camera plunges into the fault, which is studded with

enormous outcrops with whirlwinds of red dust spiralling around them. It races across the rocky bottom, along the foot of a huge, imposing cliff. There are eight domes that look lost in the middle of this outsized setting, like those pebbles left by Hop-o'-my-Thumb in the fairy-tale to find his way home in the enormous forest.

The central dome, all made of plates of glass, is the largest. The other seven, covered in a kind of gleaming black cladding, stick out all around it, linked to the centre by tubular passageways. A ninth shape, rectangular and flat, completes the circle.

'*The modules are dome-shaped to help withstand Martian storms, with the exception of the support station which is buried three-quarters underground,*' comes the rasping voice of Geronimo Blackbull, the Engineering instructor. '*The central structure, the Garden, is a large greenhouse in reinforced glass, which will make it possible to cultivate the settlers' food. The Love Nests themselves are opaque to protect their inhabitants from radiation, and covered in solar panels to generate the electricity necessary for the smooth running of the base. As you can see on the screen, two of them are significantly more spacious than the others – those are, if you like, the Royal Suites of the base. They will go to whoever offers most: couples can bid for them. You thought real-estate costs were astronomical in New York? Just wait till you see the square-metre rates in New Eden!*'

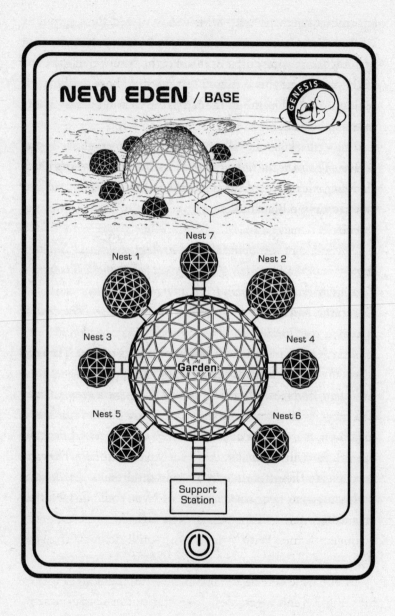

Kris nudges me with her elbow.

'You and Mozart have plenty in your Dowries, like me and Alexei!' she says enthusiastically. 'Maybe we'll be neighbours: us in Nest 1 and you in Nest 2! That would be great!'

But it isn't only the habitats that are on sale. The list of equipment available to buy continues to scroll up the screen, starting with a kind of two-seater car, like a granddad's golf-cart.

'We will also be auctioning four all-terrain mini-rovers, to allow the young married couples to freely explore this dream location . . .' says Geronimo Blackbull.

The next image: a kind of robot on wheels, with arms as long as a gibbon's, pincers in place of hands and a single Cyclops eye instead of a face.

'. . . two programmable robots, able to do the housework and the cooking, and look after the children when Dad and Mom want to have a good time . . .'

Next image: a large cube covered in buttons, with a little glass window opening in the middle.

'. . . a 3D printer capable of recycling the Martian sand and transforming it into virtually anything – a rattle, a doll, a rocking-horse, in detachable parts: the couple who purchase the printer will be able to play Father Christmas whenever they like, to the utter delight of their children.'

'Just imagine, Léo, what someone like you could do with that magical printer!' whispers Kris, as though the printer already belonged to me. 'With your talent, you'll do such amazing things!'

On the wide-screen, the technical equipment gives way to tubs of fruits and vegetables grown in a soil-less environment.

351

It's my own instructor, Dr Montgomery, who stands beside them to talk about the nicely lined-up vegetable display.

'Now, as for food,' he says in his posh accent, 'the basic minimum nutritional level recommended for the Genesis programme will be supplied for each individual. For any extras, however, they will have to pay – that is, for anything that goes beyond starches and vitamin pills. Each tray of cultivated goods will have a price on it. And the same goes for the hot water tanks and all utilities that are associated with comfort rather than survival.'

The market gardener's basket disappears from the screen, to be replaced with Serena's face.

'So there you have it, my young friends, now you have a better idea of what the money in your Dowries is for. And as for you, my dear viewers, you understand why your gifts are so important. Raising a family in a home without hot water, where you eat mash for every meal, where Father Christmas never comes along, it's hardly ideal. I can assure you that the Genesis programme really would have liked to offer the very best to every single couple, but regrettably the equipment that NASA left on Mars is in limited supply: we've just set out the complete list for you . . . Resources in New Eden are hard to come by – it's up to you, dear viewers, to decide who will live a five-star lifestyle, and who will have to settle for the budget option!'

49. Reverse Shot

The Grand Park Hotel, Long Island, New York State
Tuesday 26 September, 10:30am

'Do please follow me, Ms McBee. I'll take you over to President Green.'

Serena McBee follows the butler across the lawn. She's wearing a stunning ruffled dress in grey satin, which turns every head – unless they're turning because of her tanned legs, or is it her incredible fame? The dozens of ladies in designer dresses and the gentlemen in designer blazers murmur admiringly as she passes: 'That's Serena McBee, the executive producer of the Genesis programme!'; 'She's the most high-profile woman in the United States!'; 'She's the most influential personality in the country!'; 'So the rumour was true – she is really here in the Grand Park Hotel for President Green's garden party!'

Serena seems to pay no attention to any of this, nor to the brass band playing the American national anthem on a stage at the end of the lawn, nor to the hundreds of star-spangled flags hanging from the trees in the garden. She just smiles calmly under the brim of her huge hat whose pale green organza bow is the only touch of colour in her ultra-stylish outfit.

She joins two people who are deep in conversation, flanked by bodyguards. The first is none other than President Green himself, in shirtsleeves and green tie, his tan carefully tended under the UV lights, all the wrinkles exhaustively botoxed out, teeth impeccably laser-whitened. The second is a casual-looking young blond man, the spitting image of James Dean right up to his pompadour haircut, the black shadows under his eyes and his leather biker-jacket.

'Serena McBee!' says President Green, shooting the new arrival a smile worthy of an electoral poster. 'So delighted to meet you in person, after all those video conference calls my campaign team organised! It didn't take you too long to get here, I hope?'

'Not at all, Mr President. The helicopter you sent for me was perfect. And as you know, my villa is only a few miles from here. So thoughtful of you to have chosen a hotel so close to my place for your garden party!'

'Well, today's your day, my dear Serena,' replies the president obsequiously.

He seems suddenly to remember the presence of the young blond man standing beside him.

'. . . no offence to our young Canadian guest, of course!'

'No worries; you're paying me and Stella well enough to be here, I don't mind giving up star billing. And in any case, seriously, who could really rival Serena McBee? Nobody, not even you, Mr President, isn't that right?'

President Green gives an uncomfortable little laugh, then hurries on to the introductions.

'Serena McBee: Jimmy Giant, the new James Dean; Jimmy Giant: Serena McBee, the queen of outer space. I'm so glad to have the two of you by my side for this battle. Republicans *and* Democrats have joined forces to bring down the Ultra-liberal Party at the presidential election on 7 November. Have you heard their latest brainwave? *Show Green the Red Light!* It's so low!'

President Green pulls an outraged face before continuing. 'This fundraising lunch is barely more than a month before the election, and the polls have me losing. But that's not counting on my secret weapon: *you*, Serena!'

He looks at his watch restlessly.

'A quarter to eleven . . . Just a few minutes now till the big announcement, which will be broadcast live on all the national TV stations. Serena, my dear, it's nearly time for you to make your leisurely way towards the rostrum.'

He gestures towards the huge screen that takes pride of place at the foot of the Grand Park Hotel.

'I'm on my way, Mr President,' says Serena with a smile.

She takes her leave and heads towards the podium that's been set up beside the screen, decked in the Ultra-liberal party colours.

But she only gets halfway before being stopped by a bearded old man.

'Ms McBee!' he cries. 'Do you recognise me?'

Serena looks the man up and down: his slightly over-long beard, his slightly over-large suit, his big old-fashioned bow tie just a bit askew.

'Professor Barry Mirwood!' he says. 'Formerly of NASA! I was involved in the construction of the *Vasco da Gama* – uh, I mean, the *Cupido*. But that was, well, it was before Atlas Capital made me redundant, like so many others.'

'Oh?' says Serena evenly. 'I'm sorry to hear that.'

'Don't be. I had a few months without work, but now that the cosmos has become the latest big thing, President Green has taken me on as his special scientific advisor on space issues.'

'Perfect, so your career is back in orbit. Now if you'd just excuse me, there are people waiting for my speech.'

But the bearded old man is too excited to get the message.

'I'm really so delighted to meet you at last!' he says. 'The phenomenal success of the Genesis programme, nobody could have imagined it. All it took was a bit of marketing packaging, changing the name of the craft and the base, choosing some appealing young nobodies . . . Bravo! But what are those Atlas people planning to do with that colossal revenue? We have no way of seeing their plans, since they're a private firm. Say, do you think they'll be re-investing it in space exploration, in the conquest of Mars?'

The old man's eyes are sparkling, like a child who's been given the spaceship model he wanted for Christmas.

Beneath the brim of her big grey hat, Serena's face remains impassive.

'Ms McBee, that much money would make technologies possible that weren't even conceivable in the NASA days. I *ab-so-lu-te-ly* have to talk to you about the space elevator project I've been working on for thirty years: a revolutionary way of dispatching people and equipment through space, without the use of massive rockets, and –'

But Serena has already turned on her heel, and moments later she steps onto the stage.

No sooner is she in position behind the green podium than

she's greeted by the sound of a pre-recorded drum-roll, based on the one that punctuates the programmes on the Genesis channel. As one, the hundreds of guests and the dozens of cameramen with their equipment on their shoulders turn to face her.

'Ladies and gentlemen,' she says into the microphone, 'young and old, voters from every state – in short, all of you, the American people, I am speaking to you live from this garden party being held in support of the Ultra-liberal Party, not as the executive producer of Genesis but as a citizen who is convinced by the programme of the one man who can save our country. I speak as vice-presidential nominee on the ticket of Edmond Green!'

A huge round of applause bursts out from the end of the gardens, camera flashes crackling furiously. Serena smiles throughout.

'There are many people today who criticise President Green for his decision to sell NASA – but those who are allowing themselves to criticise are the exact same people who have failed for decades to make it profitable! I have three things to say to those people today:

'*Yes*, President Green was absolutely right to sell the American space agency at the moment when he did.

'*Yes*, the decision was absolutely necessary to rebalance the nation's finances . . .

'. . . and *yes*, President Green and I have persuaded Atlas Capital to pour five per cent of the revenues back into this great nation of ours, the United States of America!'

This time, the applause is so overwhelming that Serena

has to gesture for the cheering to stop – reluctantly, it would appear, as she seems to be enjoying it.

'This morning, for symbolic reasons and with the agreement of Atlas Capital, I have decided to make an exception and present the day's speed-dating from this garden party. Music!'

The Genesis title sequence begins to roll on the giant screen.

But instead of the pre-recorded soundtrack, what comes from the speakers is a live version of '*Cosmic Love*'. On the stage opposite the screen, Jimmy Giant and Stella Magnifica have replaced the brass band – him with his cowboy-of-the-road look, her in a holographic dress that projects iridescent rays thirty metres around her.

'*You sky-rocketed my life,*' he purrs into his microphone.

'*You taught me how to fly,*' she replies, batting her fluorescent fake eyelashes, which must be at least ten centimetres long.

'*Higher than the clouds,*' he sings.

'*Higher than the stars,*' she agrees.

They cross microphones, each holding theirs out to their partner, for the final surge of the melody:

'*Nothing can stop our cosmic love*

'*Our cosmic love*

'*Our co-o-osmic lo-o-o-ove!*'

The speakers fall abruptly silent, and the credits stop, to reveal a wide shot of the Visiting Room, with the digital titles:

Title: *Seventy-fourth session in the Visiting Room. Hostess: Léonor, 18, France, Medical Officer (communication latency: 3 minutes, 16 seconds)*

Drum-roll.

Léonor's red hair appears, free and wild, on the left side of the screen. The French girl is wearing her ripped jeans and her faded T-shirt, the way she used to at the start of the journey three months earlier, before her transformation into a Rosier model.

Standing at her green podium, Serena leans in to the microphone. 'Hello, Léonor . . . So, today it's loose hair and casual attire! Whom have you decided to invite for your thirteenth interview – this being the seventh time you have the choice in the Visiting Room?'

For three long minutes, the time it takes for Serena's question to get up to the *Cupido* and Léonor's answer to get back down to Earth, the French girl floats in space.

Suddenly she turns to face the audience, full-on and glowing. The guests give a murmur when confronted with this red giant – who has never deserved her nickname more – broadcast eight metres by six on the huge screen. But it's not them she's staring at – from where she is, thirty million kilometres from Earth, she can't admire the sophisticated grooming of the ladies, or the handsome suits of the gentlemen in their Sunday best; she can't see the waiters that keep the champagne flowing freely, or the buffet laden with petits-fours, with glasses, with canapés arranged on silver platters; the only thing she can see is the black eye of the camera watching her, at the back of the Visiting Room bubble – in the depths of space.

Léonor's voice echoes through the speakers, as powerful and determined as the look in her eye.

'It's not me who decides,' she says. 'It's my rule. It requires that I call back the boy I met first, three months ago.'

'Marcus?' Serena whispers into her microphone.

Three minutes and sixteen seconds later, Léonor replies: 'Marcus.'

Drum-roll.

The small stopwatch appears at the bottom of the screen, as Marcus enters the Visiting Room. He too has dropped his high-fashion outfits, his black jacket and shirt. He's now wearing a white T-shirt and jeans. He looks like Léonor's reflection in the reinforced glass; the air between them is charged with tension.

Léonor takes a deep breath. 'So that's your magic trick for today? After the roses and the striptease, you've gone psychic on me, like you guessed what I was going to be wearing this morning?'

Marcus: 'You don't need to be psychic for that. You said it yourself last week, you may remember: that I wasn't worth anything better than a pair of crappy old jeans or a bin-bag. I hesitated over the bin-bag, then finally decided it was best not to waste kitchen supplies, so I went for the old jeans.'

Léonor: 'And what's next on today's programme then, Houdini? Pulling a rabbit out of a hat?'

Marcus: 'What would you say to a live escape act, like those guys who get trapped in a tank of water and only have a few minutes to get out before they drown?'

Léonor looks around her, at the transparent glass bubble behind which space stretches out to infinity. 'As the Medical Officer I would not advise you to leave this particular tank,' *she says.*

Marcus: 'You're forgetting I know space like the back of my hand, and not just because I'm Planetology Officer. I had time to learn my way around, during all those nights I spent sleeping under the stars, when I was begging in the cities of America.'

He points to the back of the bubble, towards a body that's bigger and brighter than the stars around it, shining with a reddish splendour. 'That one's Mars,' he says.

Then he starts pointing out the other directions in turn.

'Over that way, that's Jupiter! This one here, Saturn! And right there in front of me, I can see Venus . . . um, no – it's actually you, Léonor.'

The girl receives Marcus's compliment impassively, and holds his gaze without blinking. 'I wasn't talking about the risk you might get lost in space. You'd never get the chance. Because out there you wouldn't be able to catch your breath: you'd puff up like a toy balloon, your tongue would start boiling and your skin would burn. That forest of tattoos you seem so proud of would catch fire in a second.'

Marcus bursts out laughing, glancing at the black lines flourishing on his biceps, just below the hem of the sleeves of his T-shirt. On his right, the words whose thorny letters appeared last time: Dream as if you'll live forever, Live as if you'll die today; *on his left, perfectly symmetrical, another bracelet of brambles answers them:* Life is short, break the rules, forgive quickly, kiss slowly, love truly.

Léonor: 'That's quite a plan! Did you make those up?'

Marcus: 'No, they're from two friends of mine. Mark Twain on my left and James Dean on my right – the real one, not the Genesis version. A writer from the days when cowboys roamed the plains, and an actor from the time in the movies when a star really was a star. They're two of the people who taught me that words can help you escape. Like, for example, all the words I'd like to say to you . . . all the ones I'd like to hear from you.

But six minutes is too short a time!'

Léonor smiles at last. She really is very beautiful, when she lets her face blossom like this. 'You really never give up, Marcus, do you?' she says. 'But you do know that if I invited you today it's only because that's how my rules work. My next invitation to you will be the last, in twelve weeks' time, just before we align with the orbit of Phobos.'

For the first time since she originally took refuge behind her rules, a hint of regret is clearly noticeable in Léonor's voice. She does nothing to resist the way her body is drifting slowly towards the partition – towards Marcus.

He tenses his left arm, making the Mark Twain quotation stand out. 'Listen to Mark. Break the rules.'

Léonor: 'If you really cared about me, you'd respect my rule instead of asking me to break it. Like the other boys have been doing. Like . . . Mozart.'

At the mention of Mozart's name, Marcus's thick eyebrows frown: 'Loving someone doesn't mean just accepting everything about them, without any question or challenge.'

The camera zooms in on his face, on his grey eyes with their metallic, magnetic reflections: 'Loving someone means fighting for what you think is best for the other person . . . even if they don't know it themselves. The love I offer you, Léonor, is a battle. Mozart's is a capitulation.'

Millions of kilometres away, in the gardens of the Grand Park Hotel, five hundred people hold their breath. There is absolute silence. Even the birds seem to have stopped singing, to listen to Marcus.

On the huge screen, the camera cuts to a reverse shot of Léonor's face.

Something has changed.

A dam has given way.

The one that had kept Léonor's eyes dry, stopped them from shining.

'Love . . .' she murmurs. 'Already . . . So soon . . .'

'It's just that we haven't got much time, Léonor. I'm not asking you to abandon your rule completely, just to adjust it. If the final really is to be played between Mozart and me, then stop wasting the time that's so precious inviting those other boys, to focus only on the two of us: each of us in turn, every other week. Do you think you could do that?'

Léonor nods slowly, her red locks spreading in curls around her sparkling eyes.

The bell goes.

Under the screen, Serena takes up the microphone again.

'A *yes*! It's a *yes*!' she exclaims. 'And you are all witnesses, my dear viewers: Léonor has just confirmed that as far as she's concerned the whole game is now between two contestants. Which one is going to win her? Mozart or Marcus? The dark Brazilian or the mysterious American? Latin sensuality or hypersensitive romanticism? I invite you to join us on 10 December on the Genesis channel to discover the answer to that . . . and before that, of course, I invite you on 7 November to join us at the ballot box to re-elect President Green!'

50. Out of Frame

University of California, Berkeley
Monday 6 November, 6:00pm

'The library closes in fifteen minutes, young man. It's been requisitioned as a polling station for tomorrow's presidential elections, and we need to set everything up.'

Andrew, the only student still in the vast university library, looks up from the atlas he's been reading. The book is open to the United Kingdom page, the county of Kent. Andrew has his finger on a little village called Warden. His laptop screen shows a map on which he's marked all the Wardens in the world: one in South Africa; two in Canada, in Ontario and Quebec; two in the United States, in the states of Washington and West Virginia; three in England alone, in Northumberland and in Bedfordshire as well as the one in Kent. Over the map a list of definitions appears, every possible meaning of the common noun *warden* – yes, prison guard, but also university rector; gamekeeper; parish clerk; officer rank among the freemasons.

'I'm just leaving,' Andrew says to the librarian.

He closes the *WARDEN* file on his computer, as well as the *LOUVE* file in which he's compiled a huge mass of information

364

about wolves and France, from the Beast of Gévaudan to Little Red Riding Hood.

'You can borrow the book if you like,' says the librarian, pointing to the atlas.

'Thanks, but there's no point. The more I look the more muddled up I get . . .'

He glances vaguely towards the windows that overlook the campus, where young activists are handing out leaflets for the following day's election – most of them in green T-shirts bearing the Ultra-liberal party's latest slogan: *Green is the color of hope!*

'. . . it's as though there's really nothing to find,' murmurs Andrew. 'As though there just isn't a message at all. Just two dogs' names chosen in five minutes by a guy in a hurry.'

'You're looking for names for little dogs?' asks the librarian kindly, thinking she might be able to help. 'It's a real head-scratcher, I know; how can you be sure you're getting it right! My advice is to get to know the little doggie's personality properly before you decide.'

'Personality?' says Andrew, taken aback.

'Yes, you just need to ask at the pet store. They're the best place to help you find names that suit puppies. That's what happened with my gorgeous little Chihuahua, Stradivarius: the saleswoman mentioned that he yapped with pleasure whenever she put classical music on in the background at the store. Anyway, I'll leave you in peace to gather up your things.'

'The store,' murmurs Andrew. 'I hadn't thought of that.'

He opens the web browser on his computer and types into the search engine: '*Louve + Warden + Animal store*'.

The search results appear instantly on the screen.

The first corresponds to an article published on a Florida local news site:

Louve & Warden Orphaned!
Genesis animal store keeper drowns in the sea

Three days later, Andrew is pressing the button on an intercom with a cracked glass screen, next to a little label that reads *RODRIGUEZ*.

He looks up at the building: it's an old six-storey walk-up, its façade decrepit-looking. Traces of rust are running down the walls; in many places there are even small holes – could they be bullet-holes?

Night is falling, and far away in the town he can hear police sirens and broadcasts playing '*Cosmic Love*', the unavoidable hit of the moment.

Beep!

A woman with a Hispanic accent answers the intercom.

'Hello, what is it you want?'

'I'm sorry to trouble you, Mrs Rodriguez. I just want to talk to you.'

'Who are you? Are you a door-to-door salesman? I can tell you now, I don't need anything.'

'I haven't got anything to sell. I just want to ask you a few questions about your husband, Ruben Rodriguez.'

The voice on the intercom doesn't answer; but listening carefully Andrew can make out a muffled sob.

'You're a journalist, is that it? Get out of here.'

'I'm not a journalist, and I'm not selling anything, and I'm not a cop. I'm just someone like you, I've lost somebody close to me . . .'

Andrew swallows, a lump in his throat.

'. . . someone who knew your husband well.'

Bzzz! – the door is unlocked and Andrew is in the building.

A pretty blonde woman of about thirty, with olive skin, is standing in the doorway of a door held back by a metal chain. Her troubled eyes stare at Andrew, his tangled mop of hair, his polo shirt with the rumpled collar, his black-framed glasses.

'Cecilia Rodriguez,' she says, without removing the chain.

'Andrew Fisher.'

The young woman's eyes open wide.

'Fisher?' she repeats. 'As in Sherman Fisher, Ruben's colleague, who died in the car accident just before him?'

'He was my father.'

Andrew's eyes are shining behind his glasses, in the gloom of the stairwell. He's at his wits' end after all these months of searching, of getting increasingly frantic, of wanting so badly to re-establish some kind of contact with his vanished father.

'Oh! I'm sorry,' says Cecilia Rodriguez, visibly moved.

'And I'm sorry about what happened to your husband,' says Andrew, visibly struggling to hold back his tears.

The young man and the young woman look at each other in silence for a moment, but it is a silence filled with emotions.

Suddenly Cecilia Rodriguez seems to remember the security chain.

'Do come in, please,' she says, taking it off.

Andrew steps into a small well-kept apartment, that smells pleasantly of lavender and cleaning products. Its cleanness is in contrast with the dilapidation of the building.

In the living room, the TV is turned on to the news, at low volume.

'It's a historic moment! A real green wave – what am I saying? – a tsunami!' enthuses the on-screen presenter, as she stands in front of a map of the United States – three-quarters of the states are coloured in green, and only a handful in red and blue, the traditional colours of the Republican and Democratic parties.

'The Ultra-liberal Party, which only a month ago looked to be losing, received more than seventy per cent of votes on election day at the start of the week! As you know, according to our polling system here in America, this popular vote determines the electoral college who will in turn vote in mid-December to confirm the president and vice-president. But with seventy per cent of the electoral college pledged to Edmond Green and Serena McBee, it should be no more than a formality. Over at the White House, at least, they are certain of their victory . . .'

Cecilia Rodriguez picks up the remote control.

'Sorry, I'll turn it off,' she says. 'I'm not sure this re-election is such good news anyway, at least not for areas like this, where there hasn't been any infrastructure for years, and not a dime of public investment. It's the gangs who make the law here, dealing their Zero-G right outside my window. Didn't you see them, those shadows prowling like zombies with their hair sticking up? It's not easy to live round these parts, especially for a woman alone with a young kid. Ever since Ruben died, four months ago . . .'

Her voice wavers.

She takes a deep breath, collects herself, gestures towards the sofa with a delicate hand.

'Please, have a seat – Andrew, right? And tell me why you've come to see me.'

Andrew sits down on the sofa, smiling shyly. The cocky, self-confident young man he was not long ago has disappeared, replaced by someone sensitive, filled with doubt and grief.

'I . . . I don't know where to start,' he says. 'I've driven like an idiot all the way from California, and now that I'm here everything in my head is confused. I'm sorry to be bothering you.'

Cecilia Rodriguez puts her hand on his.

'Stop apologising. You aren't bothering me. I know what it's like to lose somebody, the way every point of reference is wiped out all at once. I feel just as disoriented as you. It'll do me good to talk. Though we must keep our voices down so as not to wake the little one – she's asleep next door.'

A grateful smile appears on Andrew's face.

'Thank you. I need to talk too. Maybe because my father didn't talk all that much himself. Specially not since he started working on the Genesis programme.'

'I know what you mean. It was the same with Ruben. The programme took up all his time; I hardly saw him at all. He was so stressed out, ever since Atlas bought NASA! The only time he relaxed was when he allowed himself an occasional dive in the bay at Cape Canaveral. He loved all animals, but sea creatures especially. He always told me that his dream was to swim with a great white shark, but I think he just said that to freak me out, as there haven't been great whites seen off the Florida coast in a long time: he just wanted me to hold him tight and tell him how much he meant to me.'

A faint smile passes across Cecilia Rodriguez's face, as she recalls those happy moments now lost for ever.

'It was his passion that ended up killing him,' she says. 'He dived once too often, when he was too exhausted to do the necessary checks. The medical examiner thinks there was a decompression incident when he surfaced too quickly – but it's just a hypothesis, they weren't able to do an autopsy. When the police found Ruben's body . . . he'd been dead for quite a long time . . .'

Cecilia's voice cracks.

Now it's Andrew's turn to place his hand supportively on hers.

'Like my father,' he says. 'During the training phase of the programme, he was driving back to Beverly Hills on the highway, across Death Valley. He crashed into a rock. I guess he must have been on his last legs too. It was days before they found his body. It had been left to the coyotes. Unrecognisable.'

He falls silent for a moment, replaying his memories.

'Mars killed them both,' says Cecilia bitterly.

'No, not Mars. Mars is just a planet, a dot in the sky which little kids look at and dream of adventure, and which grown adults look at and dream of posterity. It's the goddamn Genesis programme that chewed them up. After it changed them first.'

'Changed them? Yes, I think so too. My Ruben was never the same again.'

'Nor was my father. The man I knew wasn't a coward, scared to answer questions from his own son, running away from the smallest attempt to make contact. If he'd just had the courage to tell me to my face that he'd refused to send me to Mars so as to keep me close to him! But we weren't even able to have that conversation. And now all I have left are some little crumbs to cling to. Like the dogs your husband raised. It was up to my father to name them. He didn't have any particular reason to do it. So why did he? Why did he choose *Louve* and *Warden*? I was convinced there was something for me hidden behind those names, some kind of message. I'm sure I should drop it, turn the page, but I can't seem to do it.'

Andrew looks up at his hostess with trembling eyes, torn between reluctance to continue on a ridiculous quest and a last hope of hearing his father's voice once more.

'Cecilia, I'm not strong enough to give it up. I need to ask you: did Ruben ever say anything to you about the names of the dogs? It's the mark my father imprinted on the Genesis programme – his signature, if you like – and even if there's only one chance in a hundred that it means something, I've got to go for it. Maybe he said something about it to your husband?'

The young woman thinks for a moment.

'No, I'm sorry, I can't think of anything. Ruben talked about the programme so little . . . But wait, there's always his laptop! I know he used it for work. Maybe there's something in there that might interest you? I haven't touched it since he left us.'

'Would you let me have a quick look?' Andrew blushes slightly as he says these words, seized by doubt. 'But of course you don't have to. I'm sure there's nothing to find, and I know how awkward this is, a total stranger asking to look through your husband's things . . .'

Cecilia cuts him off before he can say any more.

'Not at all. On the contrary, it would make me happy, if it could give you some peace. I'll go fetch it.'

A few moments later, Cecilia returns with the laptop.

'I've just realised I don't know the password,' she says apologetically.

'I should be able to get it started without the password. I know a thing or two about computer science,' Andrew says modestly, pressing the powering-up button. 'May I? You can watch while I do everything, and I won't open any files you'd rather stayed closed.'

'Please, go ahead. Ruben and I had no secrets from each other.'

The computer comes on.

But the screen is empty, as black as space.

'What's going on?' asks Cecilia. 'Is it a virus?'

Andrew taps a few keys at great speed, sending requests to which the computer replies with lines of white text.

'No, it's not a virus. The hard disk has been formatted.'

'Formatted?'

'Erased. Wiped. Deleted.'

The two of them exchange a tense look.

'Why would Ruben have done that?' Cecilia murmurs at last. 'Now we'll never know what he had on this computer.'

'Not necessarily. On a hard disk, the data never completely

disappear; they're just overwritten by other data. Sometimes they're buried so deeply that it's impossible to ever recover them – but it can't hurt to try.'

Andrew takes a USB stick out of his backpack. He puts it into one of the ports, and types a few lines of code on the keyboard. A humming comes up from the depths of the machine. After several minutes, the black screen gives way to a desktop full of files, with a background photo of Ruben with his wife and daughter in his arms. But that's not all. A large inscription in capital letters cuts across this happy family:

SILENCE IS GOLDEN

Andrew and Cecilia are taken aback for a moment by this phrase, this command which seems to be asking them to be quiet, to switch off the laptop and never switch it back on again.

Somewhere far away in the dark depths of the city, there's a shout.

'*Silence is golden?*' mutters Andrew. 'Do you know what that means?'

'No . . . Well, maybe . . . I'm not sure . . .'

Cecilia frowns.

'For several months, Ruben wore a gold tag around his neck with that word, *silence*, on it. I remember asking him where it had come from, as we really couldn't afford that kind of thing. He said he'd had the trinket engraved to remind him of the silence of the deep sea, which brought him such peace. So that it'd be the first thing he'd see in the morning when he shaved, before his hard day at work. So that he'd always have a little

373

bit of silence with him, and be able to hold out despite the stress of the programme. As for the cost of the gold tag, he told me not to trouble myself about our finances, that everything would get better when the mission touched down on Mars, when he'd get his bonus for having contributed to the success of the first phase of Genesis. He even promised me that we'd go off round the world on a boat with the little one, that we'd be together again at last, the three of us, to enjoy the silence of the sea together, far from Miami, from Genesis, from all of it.'

The trembling in Cecilia's voice reveals that she's not entirely convinced by the explanation her husband gave her about the gold tag. Now especially, with those words on the screen.

Andrew opens the first of the folders on the desktop, named 'Animal store accounts'. Inside there are several spreadsheets. But when Andrew clicks on the first of these, nothing happens. The same for the second, the third, and all the rest. The folders 'Veterinary balance', 'Feeding supplies' and 'Reproduction plans' likewise contain only zero-byte files.

'Empty shells,' says Andrew, discouraged. 'My retrieval software only managed to get back the names of the files, no more than that. Your husband did things properly. He didn't just carry out a quick formatting of his computer, or I would have been able to retrieve a lot more: he ran a deep formatting, as good as the ones the government use to wipe military secrets.'

Suddenly Cecilia points at the screen, down in the bottom right-hand corner.

'Look!' she says. 'The name of the last folder!'

The word *Silence* is displayed under the small glowing icon. Andrew clicks on it.

374

The folder opens, to show the list of the file names the *Silence* folder once contained.

Noah01.karma
Noah02.karma
Noah03.karma

. . . and so on, all the way down to *Noah56.karma*.

'They were picture files,' murmurs Andrew. 'With that extension they must have been photos taken on a Karmaphone . . . I'll try one last scan, just in case.'

'N-Noah?' stammers Cecilia, while he runs the software. 'Could it be the name of an animal?'

'Maybe . . . or maybe not. Cecilia, try and remember: has anybody else besides you had access to this computer since Ruben's death?'

'No. Well, I don't think so. Why do you ask?'

Andrew's eyes are sparkling behind his black-framed glasses.

He points at a window that's just appeared on the screen, announcing the results of the scan. No more data recovered. But a date. The date when the hard disk was formatted.

Cecilia's pupils widen.

In surprise.

In terror.

'*Twenty-third July*,' she reads in a voice without expression. 'More than two weeks after the day the police think Ruben died.'

Night has fallen by now. Long shadows are pushing the walls of the small apartment infinitely far back. Sitting at one end of the sofa, Andrew and Cecilia look like they are trapped on a tiny dinghy lost in an ocean of darkness.

'I think we've stumbled on something huge,' murmurs

Andrew. 'Something monstrous. Try to remember, Cecilia, I beg of you: what happened on 23 July?'

The young woman's chest rises haltingly, with difficulty. She suddenly seems to be having trouble breathing.

'It was the day of the ceremony,' she says. 'I opted for a cremation, given . . . given the state of Ruben's body. After the crematorium, I organised a small memorial reception at home, for the family and close friends . . .'

'Only family and close friends?' asks Andrew, hanging on her every word.

'Somebody from Genesis came too, to bring flowers. Mr Blackbull, one of Ruben's former colleagues. At the time, I was surprised he'd come all the way here; this isn't a neighbourhood people venture into very often . . . Yes, I was really touched actually.'

Andrew looks Cecilia straight in the eye.

'And what if Blackbull had some other reason for coming? What if the flowers were only a pretext . . .'

'. . . to get access to Ruben's computer while I was looking after the guests, you mean? He'd only have had a few minutes.'

'That's long enough to launch a formatting procedure if you know what you're doing. Just disposing of the lot is the best way to be sure of wiping anything potentially compromising when you don't have time to look through all the files in detail.'

Cecilia puts her hand over her mouth to muffle a cry, so as not to wake the sleeping child.

'Wh-what have we got ourselves caught up in, Andrew?' she stammers. 'Why would Genesis have sent somebody to format the hard disk? What are these Noah photos in the *Silence* folder? And Ruben's disappearance – was it really just an accident? We've got to contact the police!'

Cecilia is already reaching for her phone.

But Andrew stops her before she gets the chance to start dialling.

'Don't do that, I'm begging you. The police have closed the case on your husband's death, just like my father's. They'll dismiss what we've discovered too, after telling the Genesis people about it and putting them on their guard. A formatted hard disk, some file names erased: that's nothing against the colossal economic and now also political stakes of the Genesis programme. We need more proof before notifying the authorities.'

'Proof? But how are we to get that? Where do we go to find it?'

'To the source. To the heart of Genesis. I can tell you – and only you – I've hacked into their headquarters in Cape Canaveral. I got a miniature spy drone into the building last July, thinking it would get my father really angry, to get back in contact with him. I was such a spoiled kid back then . . . It never even occurred to me that if Father was keeping quiet, perhaps it was because he had no choice!'

With these words, Andrew takes his own laptop out of his backpack, along with a joystick. Cecilia moves closer to him on the sofa, their two pale faces illuminated by the light from the screen. A video interface appears in a window. It shows the control room as seen from the ceiling, plunged in near-darkness. It's possible to see the tops of the heads of dozens of engineers in grey jackets leaning over their screens, busily monitoring every set of parameters for the *Cupido* in real time.

'My little bug has been sleeping up in the slats of the ceiling for four months, where nobody has been able to dislodge it,' murmurs Andrew. 'It's time for him to wake up. To resume contact with my satellite phone. And go find the truth.'

Andrew presses a key on the laptop and takes hold of the joystick. The image in the window starts to tremble: the mini-drone is taking flight. It circles slowly down towards the banks of computers, picking up the clacking of the keyboards and the engineers' hushed conversations.

'The base is huge,' Andrew whispers to Cecilia, 'but my bug is free to go wherever it pleases, and we have all the time in the world ahead of –'

Before Andrew can finish his sentence, a black triangular object whizzes down from the ceiling where it was hidden. *Bam!* – a ray comes out of the corner of the triangle, flooding the window with a white light.

Andrew's computer gives a *beep!* of protest.

In the next-door room, the baby wakes up and starts to cry.

The window turns black, with a highlighted message, like an epitaph engraved on a tombstone:

SATELLITE CONNECTION LOST // MINI-DRONE DESTROYED

51. Shot

D +147 days 21 h 05 mins.
[22nd week]

'Listen to this, girls: the electoral college date has just been confirmed for Monday 11 December, the day after we touch down on Mars!' says Safia, rushing into the living room in her saffron-coloured sari, tablet in hand.

As our Communications Officer, she receives the messages issued from Cape Canaveral. On the whole, they tend to be technical information regarding the *Cupido*'s trajectory, tests to be carried out order to confirm that the antenna and laser transmitter are in perfect working order, and lists of oxygen and CO_2 levels that the ground team ask us to produce regularly for our living quarters. Ever since Serena has been in contention for vice-president of the United States, we've also been allowed to follow the electoral news as it happens. At first we were astonished, but now it seems quite natural for us to imagine her at the head of the country that made NASA and the Genesis programme possible – so the presidential campaign is getting us almost as excited as the speed-dating itself.

'It's so cool!' cries Kris, adorable as ever in one of her sky-blue dresses. 'Our Serena's a real superwoman: TV host, world-class psychiatrist and soon vice-president of the United States! But there's one thing I don't quite understand – I thought Serena and Mr Green had *already* won the election, in mid-November.'

'You weren't listening to my explanation the other day, then, were you?' grumbles Fangfang, who has perked back up ever since her cheeks stopped swelling and Tao started inviting her back into the Visiting Room. 'The American elections happen in two stages: first of all, voters vote for the members of the electoral college belonging to different parties; then these electors in turn have to confirm the presidential ticket in a second stage. That's happening in mid-December, and the official presidential and vice-presidential inauguration takes place in January.'

Kelly, in her tiny wrap top made of pink angora wool, shrugs.

'Thank you to our walking encyclopaedia, but it's not like those details matter in the least. Serena is super-popular – there's no chance she won't be confirmed by the electoral college. Didn't you hear the news from Safia? Seventy per cent of people are with the Ultra-liberal party. I don't care about politics at all, but I'm really happy for Serena. And anyway, I think it's awesome that the final vote will take place just exactly as we're arriving on Mars, in two weeks' time!'

In two weeks' time . . .

Kelly's right.

There are only two weeks left before the end of the speed-dating game, just two little weeks. I've spent the last ten inviting Marcus and Mozart, alternating, and they've invited only me. I'm not proud of having broken my rule; but at the same time, I know it's the best decision I've ever made. Because it's allowed me to get to know two amazing boys better . . . Mozart has taught me my first samba moves through the glass partition; in his warm voice, he sang tunes that spoke of elsewhere, that made my heart tremble, that made the bubble disappear, along with the spacecraft and everything else. And Marcus told me the name of every constellation in the sky, as he knows them all from having fallen asleep so many nights under the stars, and the significance of each tattoo on his body – after the interview was over I hurried to copy down the blossoming words on my sketching tablet so I would never forget them.

'Yeah, I get it,' says Kris, yanking me from my thoughts. 'Serena will be chosen by the electoral college at the same moment as we reveal who've been chosen by our hearts.'

'You've already revealed your choice,' says Liz suddenly.

She's curled up in the corner of the sofa, bundled in one of her famous turtleneck jumpers. While some of the girls like Kris have blossomed over these past weeks, Liz has languished. She's currently pale as an aspirin, dark shadows under her eyes – still beautiful, but with a beauty that is ailing, anguished.

'Everybody knows you're going to live out a beautiful long fairy-tale with your ice prince, Alexei; he hasn't seen anybody but you since you got engaged. It's the same with Fangfang – we all know she's going to end up with Tao – and Safia with Samson: and you talk about it like there's any suspense. And it's no wonder Marcus and Mozart are at Léo's feet: look at her, she's glorious!'

I glance down nervously at the day's outfit. For the final week when it's the boys' turn to choose, I've finally surrendered to Kris's entreaties and dared to put on the masterpiece of my Rosier wardrobe: the slit dress in red chiffon. If you'd told me when I was at the Eden Food France factory that one day I'd be wearing something like this, the very height of sexiness and style! And yet here I am: I've changed since my time in the factory. When I boarded this ship, I thought Mars was the only thing that mattered. But I no longer want glory. I also want love. Yes, me – the Determinator – I want people to like me!

So I'm wearing this dress that delicately hugs my shoulders, that sculpts the curve of my chest, that holds in my waist with made-to-measure pleats, that has a long split that reveals my leg. It's cut so close to my body I should feel it squeezing me all over, but in fact I don't at all: the silk chiffon is so fine that I feel quite naked. It's such an unsettling feeling that I keep running my hand over my back every couple of minutes just to reassure myself that the Salamander is well hidden beneath the material.

'Isn't it maybe a bit too glamorous?' I ask.

'You can never be too glamorous,' Liz answers with a sad smile. 'Anyway, you could dress in dishcloths and you'd still be a knockout. But who knows who I'm going to end up with? I was born under an unlucky star. I'm fated to be a loser, an eternal failure, just like when I was competing to join the Royal Ballet company, who didn't want me.'

'Stop feeling sorry for yourself,' Kelly butts in. 'I haven't snagged a guy either, and you don't see me making a meal of it. I do like Marcus a lot: he's just so rock 'n' roll, the way he looks like doesn't care about anything, the whole *Live Fast, Die*

Young thing he's got going on. Not to mention the awesome tattoos decorating his godlike body! But we can only guess at them, eh? Since he only shows them to Léo, the lucky thing! I could get excited about Samson too . . . So long as I don't end up with Mozart, that's all I ask.'

Kelly glances over to me. I'm the only person she's confided in, the only one to whom she's revealed the reason for her dislike of the Brazilian, which remains an inexplicable mystery to the other girls.

'Oh, Mozart would do me very nicely,' sighs Liz. 'But knowing my luck, I'm going to end up with Kenji, the weirdest of the bunch.'

'Stop that – he's really cute, and so stylish!' says Kelly. 'I do like him too, actually, and that "lost soul" thing he has going doesn't scare me. Don't forget, Liz, at the beginning of the show you thought he looked "wild" and "mysterious".'

'Well, it turns out he's just too wild for me.'

'You should look on the bright side: two hypochondriacs together, you can grow chamomile in the greenhouse and brew teas like the kind Serena makes.'

This time, Kelly's slightly heavy-handed sense of humour doesn't work: Liz scowls, tears in her eyes.

I'm sorry to see her like that, especially as she's always been the upbeat cheerleader of the group, ready to tie herself in knots to keep things harmonious and good-tempered in our quarters. If only I could choose between Marcus and Mozart, right now, that would free up one of the boys, giving poor Liz some reason to hope.

Mozart, the trashcan prince I feel I know like an alter ego . . .

383

Marcus, the beggar of the stars, who is a living enigma to me . . .

(You're going to have to decide, either now or in two weeks, hisses the Salamander, which the red dress might have managed to hide, but not to gag. *And you'll have to take off all these dresses, each more fantastic than the next, to show the poor boy the horrors that will be his until the last day of his life!)*

The wide-screen opposite the fireplace comes on all of a sudden, cutting off my thoughts.

Serena appears, dressed in an elegant suit in a Scottish wool tartan. She is sitting in front of a window that looks out on gardens with bare trees, onto which a cotton-wool snow is falling. The light of a wood fire from an invisible fireplace seems to turn everything golden. It's a very gentle, very tender image, a tableau of the kind of Christmases I've never known.

All of a sudden I want to share all my doubts with Serena, the best-known marriage counsellor in America, and also the person most like a mother to me. But that's impossible, of course, that's not part of the show.

'Girls, Mozart has been selected for this Monday session!' she says. 'And I think we all know whom he's chosen to call to the Visiting Room . . .'

52. Genesis Channel

Monday 27 November, 11:05am

Léonor appears at the left side of the screen, stunning in her chiffon dress, whose long skirt moves weightlessly about her in glowing red scrolls.

The only make-up she's chosen to wear is a lipstick the same shade of red as her dress and her magnificent gleaming curls. Behind her, beyond the glass bubble, the planet Mars is no longer just one more celestial body among many others: it's now the largest object in the sky, the size of a tennis ball, and the same red as the chiffon, and Léonor's hair, and her lips.

A smile appears on the girl's flaming mouth, a charming mixture of teasing and shyness. 'Hello, Mozart. I'm ready for today's samba lesson.'

But the Brazilian floating opposite her in his white shirt is not smiling.

At all.

Mozart: 'There isn't going to be a samba lesson today. Or tomorrow. Or ever.'

Mozart's voice is ice-cold. Hoarse with emotion. His features drawn, dark shadows under his eyes, he looks in just as bad a state as he did the day after his interview with Kelly, five months earlier.

Reverse shot on Léonor's face, where her smile in turn disappears; she looks nervously down at her own body, then back up again. 'Is it the dress? Do you not like it? Have you . . . have you changed your mind? You don't want me any more?'

Mozart's mouth widens into a bitter crease. '*Me? I don't want you?*' he says. 'Just drop your act for a couple of seconds, OK? It's not funny. It's actually a really ugly thing to do. And in that dress that could lead a saint astray, you're asking me if I don't like it! Asking me if I don't want you any more, you, more beautiful than any carnival queen in Rio! You're cruel, Léonor. Much crueller than I could have imagined.'

Léonor throws herself towards the reinforced glass, trailing a wake of vaporous chiffon behind her. 'I don't understand, Mozart. What's going on?'

The young man remains unmoving, his arms straight down at his sides with his fists clenched. 'You're not done? You still haven't had enough? What have I got to do now – should I start sobbing? Do you want to take a photo, to show Marcus? *Look, I'm a magician too, I can bewitch guys and make their hearts disappear with a click of my fingers – abracadabra!*'

Léonor: 'Marcus? Why are you talking to me about Marcus? My rules are clear, the journey isn't over yet; we visit every other time, right up till the end.'

Mozart's voice starts to tremble. 'Give me a break, with your goddamn rules that even you don't respect! It was OK as long as you were actually playing the game – if you ever were. But from the moment when you've *already chosen* . . . To then keep seeing me, making me stew, exciting me, it's torture! It's deceitful! It's . . . it's disgusting! I'm really such an idiot. A girl like you isn't made for a guy like me, a filthy little dealer, a piece of favela scum. Deep down, you're just like Phobos. You know why its orbit is considered ideal? Because it's close enough to Mars that we'll be able to see its surface in detail before the casting-off, and far enough away for Mars's gravity to prevent the *Cupido* from leaving again once we've ejected. That's just what you're like: close enough to make me crazy, too far for me to keep you. I should have suspected. Jesus, it serves me right!'

At the bottom of the screen, the small stopwatch is only halfway round its cycle, but already Mozart turns back towards the access tube that leads to the boys' quarters.

Léonor presses up against the glass. 'Wait!' she yells. 'I don't know what gave you that idea, or what Marcus has told you, but it's not true: I haven't chosen yet!'

At the entrance to the tube, Mozart turns around, his black curls tumbling over his temples, two damp furrows shining on his cheeks. 'Don't wear yourself out, Léonor,' he says in a strangled voice. 'I've got proof. And you've got my tears. You've won. Goodbye.'

53. Shot

D +147 days 21 h 41 mins.
[22nd week]

'Léo, you must have driven him mad with that red dress!'

The girls are all waiting for me in the living room, every bit as excited twenty-one weeks into the journey as they were on the first day.

But I'm just doing my best to put one foot down after the other and not slip off the ladder that's burning my hands.

Mad.

That's the word.

I made him mad, and I don't know why.

(You do know why, whispers the Salamander. *Mozart told you. It's because you're playing with him . . .)*

Playing with him? All I wanted was to give Mozart and Marcus a fair chance . . . to give myself a fair chance. I like them both. A lot. I really do. Whatever Mozart says, I haven't lied to him.

(It's because you're playing with your own feelings . . .)

'I'm a bit dizzy,' I murmur.

Kris immediately rushes to my rescue.

'What? What's the matter, Léo? Is it the weightlessness in

the Visiting Room? But you're fine with it normally. You're the Medical Officer: tell us what we ought to do.'

'Nothing, really, I'm just going to lie down a bit, on my own in the peace and quiet. It'll pass.'

I go down the ladder that leads to the bedroom, avoiding the eyes of all the other girls.

(It's because you're playing with fire . . .)

(It's burned you before, don't you forget!)

I just want to disappear ten feet underground.

But in the middle of space there is no ground, no means of escape other than my thin cashmere blanket. I throw myself under it, sheltering from the cameras. I bite the sheets so as not to cry out, and shove my hands under the mattress to stop them from tearing at my back until they've ripped the Salamander out of me.

Suddenly my nails find something.

Something I'd stuffed under here five months earlier.

Something I'd completely forgotten about.

Shark's-Tooth's phone.

My anger disappears instantly, while I extract the little device from under the mattress. In the gloom of my lair, there's just enough light to make it out, and the protective case decorated with the *Jaws* sticker.

I feel like an archaeologist exhuming a relic of a different age, of a different life: my life before the speed-dating, when everything was still possible, when I didn't yet know Mozart and Marcus, when I was making a mental film for myself about some guy I'd bumped into by chance.

So how did we leave Léo the Red and Shark's-Tooth then?

My fingers brush across the keys, instinctively recalling the password I discovered twenty-one weeks ago: *SILENCE*.

The screen comes on to show the last photo viewed, the one that had depressed me, of Shark's-Tooth and a pretty blonde woman, with a baby in his arms. But now, at the ending of the trip, the feelings this picture unleashes in me are not the same at all. That girl isn't an imaginary rival: she's me. That baby, it's mine, the one I'll be giving birth to only months from now. The only unknown is the identity of the father. In Shark's-Tooth's place, it will be Marcus or Mozart.

But which?

I slide my finger frantically across the screen to move on to the next photo, as though a stranger's telephone could provide the answer to my own question.

The new photo doesn't show a paradise beach, or a sunset, or a romantic dinner with a happy family. It's a selfie showing Shark's-Tooth kneeling in a room whose walls are covered in cages housing rats, lizards, and all kinds of similarly cuddly little animals. Wearing a new Hawaiian shirt, his tooth mascot around his neck, he's grinning widely. His muscly arms are hugging a dog of uncertain breed, whose hanging tongue seems ready to lick the telephone the man is holding at arm's length. I'd recognise those floppy ears, that curly coat, those white pompoms and those big affectionate black eyes anywhere: they could only belong to Louve, our on-board dog.

I don't understand.

The guy whose phone I took was supposed to be a journalist who wanted to get a statement out of me just before lift-off – right? So what's with this selfie with Louve, then?

The possible scenarios start to spin around my head, turning around and around like the sides of a Rubik's Cube that need to be lined up to restore some logic.

An animal journalist.

Yes, that must be it, Shark's-Tooth is an animal journalist!

I move on to the next picture, which helps to strengthen my hunch, as it shows the Latino guy now with Louve *and* Warden.

He must work for *Thirty Million Friends* magazine, or *National Geographic*, or maybe he's even a correspondent with the Animal Protection Society, producing a campaign on the most famous doggies of our time, in the hope of boosting the adoptions of animals abandoned in shelters. The things I'd been imagining!

Next photo: another selfie, this time without Hawaiian shirt or animals. Shark's-Tooth took the photo at arm's length, vertical, the way you do when you want to check your clothes look right. Except he's got an expression like somebody off to a funeral, and he isn't wearing a particularly nice outfit. It's just an old grey Genesis jacket, with its easily recognisable badge on the pocket.

My photographic memory is triggered immediately. Once again, I see the setting for the lift-off in my mind's eye. I hear Shark's-Tooth's hoarse voice again, yelling in my ear: 'Wait . . . !'

No, hang on, he said something else, it's coming back to me now. 'You mustn't . . .' At the time I ignored this; I turned on my heel and left him without looking back. In my mind, the end of his sentence was all set – something like 'Wait . . . ! You mustn't leave without answering one crucial question: do you like blond guys or dark ones?' or some other feeble thing of that kind. But what if he actually meant to say something else?

The more I think back, the more clearly I can see Shark's-Tooth's tousled hair, his cheeks shaded by the beginnings of a beard, his dark-ringed eyes: the look of a real insomniac, a mere shadow of the carefree guy he'd been so recently, if I was to believe the gallery of photos stored away in his phone. And what if he'd been trying to keep me back for some other reason than to ask a stupid question? What if he wanted to pass a message on to me? What if he wasn't really a journalist? 'You mustn't . . .' Mustn't *what* exactly?

The thought makes my head spin, my heart race.

Bzzz! – the telephone vibrates sharply.

The screen turns red, lighting up the walls of my cave with its glow, as though the sea of propellant from lift-off has been reignited all of a sudden and I'm caught in the middle of it.

A message in digital letters appears on the screen:

LOW BATTERY. RECHARGE IMMEDIATELY.

In a mad rush, I zoom in on the tag pinned beneath the Genesis badge. A name appears: *Ruben Rodriguez*.

Bzzz!

The phone's imminent shutdown is stressing me out.

I continue scrolling through the photos as fast as I can – more dogs, rats, unpleasant little things with fur and unpleasant little things with scales, cut in with self-portraits of Ruben Rodriguez who is deteriorating before my very eyes, getting more and more worried and tired, as though he wanted to keep a record of his own decline.

Bzzz!

The third vibration hits me like an electric shock. I'm reminded that the battery is about to die. I can't let the phone go off, not now! I stick it nervously in the pocket of my jeans and throw back the blanket.

The lights dazzle me as I leave my woollen cave.

It's as though I'm seeing the spacecraft for the first time. The bunks lit by spotlights, the varnished panelled walls, the new carpet on the floor: the whole thing looks like a stage set.

And the silence . . .

Bzzz!

I hurry over to the ladder at the back of the room.

I climb the rungs three at a time.

I push up the hatch that opens into the living room.

The five girls are there.

Ten eyes are trained on me.

'Feeling better, Léo?' Kris asks kindly.

I open my mouth to answer that I've got to recharge the phone, and fast.

But no words pass my lips.

Bzzz!

I realise I can't say a thing.

Not here, not in front of the cameras that are still rolling, all the time, in front of viewers the whole world over.

So far, I've been able to hide the phone's presence on board, so as not to be thought a thief. I've got a hunch it should remain a secret.

'Well?' asks Kelly now, fiddling with her golden hoop earrings. 'How long do you mean to pose on the ladder in your ball-gown? We were getting ready for lunch: Kris has done wonders again, she's managed to make cubes of freeze-dried tofu into a delicious beef bourguignon. Seriously, Alexei's the one who's really lucked out in this game.'

I climb the last few rungs of the ladder, struggling to keep my impatience in check.

Bzzz!

'Has any of you got a battery?' I ask expressionlessly.

'*A battery*?' Kelly repeats the question, articulating it clearly as though she might not have understood.

'Yes, a universal battery. I was reading a thriller, downstairs in the bedroom, when my e-reader went off. Completely dead.'

The girls, taken aback, exchange looks.

Liz smiles indulgently at me.

'Even if your book is really thrilling, Léonor, you can pick it up again later.'

'You can save some food for me – I trust you. I do just need to finish my chapter.'

Bzzz!

'I don't understand, Léonor,' says Fangfang in her most unbearable teacherly voice. 'You can just put your reader on the charging table, like the rest of us.'

She gestures with her chin towards the black table beneath the wall clock, on which all our various gadgets are lying, along with the revision tablets, in full view of the cameras. No way can I leave the phone there.

'I'd never have the patience to wait for it to charge. I need power for it immediately. It's crazily suspenseful, this book.'

'But it's a super-fast charging table,' insists Fangfang. 'It should only take a few minutes.'

'But I need to know what happens next *right now*.'

'We're supposed to be displaying self-control and cool heads throughout this process. Just because we're near the end of the journey doesn't mean you should start acting on every little whim. I really don't see why you're getting yourself in such a state for a simple book which –'

'Look, do you have a goddamn battery or what?'

And there it is, I've lost control, yet again.

All because of a stupid obsession over a crappy cellphone.

And the winner in the *Writing-yourself-off-in-the-eyes-of-your-teammates-and-two-billion-spectators* category is . . . Léo!

At the same moment, I feel three consecutive vibrations in my jeans pocket, like three mocking sniggers – *bzzz! bzzz! bzzz!* – and then nothing.

I don't need to take the phone out of my pocket to know it's turned itself off.

ACT V

54. Shot

D +148 days 20 h 30 mins.
[22nd week]

'Safia, can I talk to you a minute . . . ?'

The Indian girl looks up from her revision tablet with her big doe eyes. Judging by her expression, I suspect I'm not a very pretty sight. No, I'm not just imagining it, I know it for sure: I saw myself very clearly in the mirror this morning, with the black bags under my eyes from a sleepless night spent worrying myself sick trying to guess what Ruben Rodriguez, aka Shark's-Tooth, wanted to tell me. I didn't even take the trouble to get myself ready this morning; I just went for the easy option, jeans and a T-shirt. And now I only have one idea in my head: talk to Safia, our Communications Officer.

'My poor Léo, I have to be honest, you've looked a bit unwell ever since your speed-dating session yesterday,' says Safia. 'Is it really just space sickness that's come over you so suddenly? I can't quite believe that. Did Mozart give you a hard time? Kelly always said we shouldn't trust him.'

'No, it has nothing to do with Mozart,' I say.

But it does, of course. Mozart, Marcus, Ruben, the phone:

the whole thing was turning around and around in my head like a whirlwind all night until I had a terrible headache.

'It's just little bad patch I'm going through, now that we're approaching the end of the trip.'

'I understand,' says Safia. 'I'm nervous too. The final Heart Lists . . . The marriages . . . The wedding nights! That's some serious pressure. But I'm sure it's all going to go well, and once we're on Mars, we'll all be as tightly knit as before. Maybe even more than before, free of the feeling of competition, each of us with our husband and our babies!'

Safia smiles wholeheartedly, her face radiant with optimism.

'So what was it you wanted to tell me?' she asks.

'Umm . . . not here, if you don't mind. Under my blanket, like at the beginning of the journey.'

Safia nods and follows me down to the bedroom without a word. This time she doesn't worry about what the viewers are going to think when they see us hiding like this: the game's nearly over, the Dowries have been gathered in, and in a few days we'll all be married.

The moment my thin cashmere blanket has been pulled over our heads, just as it was five months earlier, she whispers, 'It's about your tiny insignificant little birthmark, isn't it? That's why you're so anxious? Because we're coming close to the time you have to strip naked? You really don't need to worry!'

I force a smile; and once again I make myself lie, even if it breaks my heart to do it. Of course the so-called 'tiny insignificant little birthmark' is poisoning my thoughts. But it's not only that.

'Safia, the real reason I wanted to talk to you in private is going to seem really lame. It's this.'

I take the phone out of my jeans pocket and hold it up to the ray of light that's filtering through the opening to our den.

'*Jaws?*' murmurs Safia, confused, as she notices the case and the movie sticker on it.

'More particularly the telephone. And to be more precise, a telephone that's out of battery.'

'Like your e-reader?'

'I haven't got an e-reader. But yesterday I didn't want to admit in front of everyone and the cameras that I was after a phone battery, since we're not allowed to have them. And all the more so because I stole it.'

Safia's eyes open wide. Their opal white shines in the gloom, in contrast with the black of the kohl, which makes her expression troubling.

'You stole this phone?' she asks. 'Who from? Why?'

'Yes – well, I didn't do it on purpose. Let's just say I borrowed it accidentally, from a guy who grabbed hold of me on the launch platform – the one who inspired Captain Shark's-Tooth; you remember him from my pictures? At the time I thought he was a journalist, but now I'm sure he works for Genesis. Judging by the photos I saw in his gallery, he seems to have been involved in getting Louve and Warden ready for the mission. And I saw him wearing one of the programme's official jackets! With his real name pinned onto it: Ruben Rodriguez!'

'Ruben Rodriguez? I've never heard of him. And even if he is on the programme staff, I don't see what the problem is?'

'The problem is that he was trying to tell me something before we left, but I couldn't hear him. I've been thinking about

401

it all night. I didn't want to believe it myself, but listen to me: he was holding me back as if he didn't want me to leave . . . didn't want any of us to leave. Listen, Safia, I know I've got an over-active imagination, but I really get the feeling something in this mission isn't quite right.'

The little Indian girl stares at me in silence, in the half-light. It's as if I can see her thoughts spooling along behind her forehead – adorned with its blue dot – like a mirror of my own thoughts since the spacecraft set off: the doubt, the fear, the common sense that says there's no basis to any of these vague worries.

'The best thing would definitely be to talk to Serena, don't you think?' Safia suggests at last. 'I mean, there's got to be a logical explanation for all this and I'm sure we'd have a laugh about it if we knew what it was. Even if there was a slight concern about the mission at one point, Serena must have just sorted it out without telling us, not wanting to worry us unnecessarily. I'm sure she'll be able to reassure you. And that she'll forgive you for the phone you *borrowed*.'

I take a deep breath. It's hard to get air into my lungs.

'You're right,' I say, breathing out. 'If there's one person I can trust, it's Serena. Without her I'd still be packing dog-food at the factory. But otherwise you're the expert in this stuff: is there any way of charging this thing without revealing it to everyone at the charging table?'

Safia takes the phone in her hands to examine it more closely.

'A Solaris 3,' she murmurs like a real connoisseur – Karmaphone is her platinum sponsor, after all. 'You're lucky, they're a range of all-terrain models, whose screens are equipped with photovoltaic cells: they can use light as an electric source. The little flashlight you use to examine our throats every week should do the trick – it won't take too long.'

'Safia, you're a genius!'

I'm so excited I want to shout, but naturally I restrain myself. It's not surprising I haven't noticed the solar panel integrated into the screen: since lift-off I've only kept the phone in the darkness, under my mattress or in my pocket!

'I'm so glad to see you smiling again,' says Safia. 'And if you need to talk about anything more important, such as the boys, for example, don't hesitate.'

'Agreed. In the meantime, please don't mention all this to the other girls. No point making them worry for no reason.'

No sooner has Safia left the room than I open my wardrobe door wide and climb halfway inside – my medical bag is there, way in the back. I take out the little flashlight, which I switch on and wedge into a pile of old T-shirts. Then I come back out of the wardrobe with the red chiffon dress; I throw it onto my bed and extricate myself from my jeans.

The viewers must think it's really strange for me to wait till the very end of the morning before transforming myself into a *femme fatale*, but I've got no choice. The only thing that matters is getting the phone into the wardrobe as discreetly as possible.

I fold up my jeans, trying as best I can to disguise the bulge in the pocket, before diving back into the wardrobe and placing them on a shelf. It's only there, in the gloom, that I take the phone out of its denim hiding place and position it on the pile of T-shirts, so it receives the beam of the already lit flashlight full in the screen.

'On you go then,' I murmur.

After a few moments, a small message in digital letters appears at the top of the black screen:

Light source detected: 200 lumens

Estimated time for complete charge: 110 hours

Turning on in: 30 minutes

Satisfied with the arrangements I've made, I hide the phone behind the long white silk Vietnamese tunic that's hanging over it. Finally, my head re-emerges from the wardrobe and I shut the door carefully, intending to go up and change in the bathroom, shielded from the cameras.

At that moment, the screen over the bed comes on to reveal Serena's face.

'Léonor? What are you doing half-naked at ten to eleven? Marcus's name has just been drawn, and we all know you're the one he's going to invite!

55. Genesis Channel

Tuesday 28 November, 11:05am

As on the previous day, Léonor appears in the Visiting Room in her red chiffon dress.

But the resemblance stops there. She's not wearing a speck of make-up, she hasn't had time to put her polished flats on her feet. Her hair is hanging loose and neglected. The chiffon itself seems to have changed, to reflect the mood of the girl wearing it: instead of spreading about her in calm curls, it swells up like waves turned red by the setting sun.

Marcus is wearing his black trousers and shirt.

Marcus: 'Hello, Léonor. How are you?'

Léonor gives a helpless gesture towards her face. 'I'm sorry . . . I didn't get the time . . .'

Marcus: 'You look amazing, my red giant.'

The two young people float there silently in space for a few moments, consuming each other with their eyes.

Léonor is the first to break the silence. 'There's something bothering me, Marcus –' she begins.

She breaks off abruptly, to look at the glass bubble all around her – looking for the stars? No, her eyes find the camera, and stare straight into it, full of defiance.

Marcus decides to finish the sentence for her. 'You want to talk about Mozart, is that it? It's him who's bothering you? You told him you've chosen me and he took it badly.'

Léonor's bronze eyes flash.

'No! I didn't say anything to him. I haven't made my choice. And nor have you, by the way. You can both still accept invitations from other girls, as well as our interviews. You have until the very last minute to draw up your final Heart Lists. That's our rule. The one we agreed, between the three of us.'

Marcus approaches the glass partition slowly, his grey eyes fixed on Léonor.

'The last minute is very soon, Léonor. Only ten days before we align with the orbit of Phobos. Today has been my last chance to invite you. And next week, when it's your turn to invite a boy, you'll only be able to see one of us again. You're the only person who can make this choice, and it's time. All I can do is help you. If you tell me what's troubling you.'

Close-up on Léonor.

She bites her lip.

A whirlwind of emotions passes across her freckled face. 'There are two things . . .' she begins.

Then she stops again, hesitates, then resumes. '. . . two things I can't really discuss with you here.'

Her body too has drifted closer to the fortified glass as though a magnetic force were drawing her towards Marcus. 'The first thing I don't even really understand myself,' she goes on, 'and I'm not even sure it's a problem. I'm probably imagining things. I'll be all set with that very soon. I just need a little more time.'

Marcus's face is only a few centimetres from the glass, a breath away from Léonor's. His black shirt absorbs and dissolves the too-harsh spotlights, creating an aura of intimacy.

'And the second thing?' he murmurs softly.

Léonor's eyelids flutter slightly.

But she doesn't look away.

'The second thing, on the other hand, I do understand perfectly,' she says, 'and I know it's a problem. A huge problem, which I've always had, and which I've hidden from you since the start of the journey, and which could change everything between us.'

Marcus puts his hands up against the glass, at the exact places where Léonor has hers. 'The only thing that's going to change between us is this damn glass wall which soon won't exist any more.'

Léonor: 'You don't know what I'm talking about.'

Marcus: 'I know what *I'm* talking about.'

Léonor: 'You have no idea.'

Marcus: 'I do. When I look at you, I have ideas. Thousands of ideas. Millions of ideas. As many as there are stars in the sky. Some of them, as pure as comets of ice. Others burning like balls of fire. There's something that draws us together and overwhelms us, you and me. I know it, you know it. We've both known it since the very beginning.'

Léonor starts to tremble.

She is so close to Marcus – so close to confessing, at last!

'My skin . . .' she begins.

'. . . I dream of touching it. I can feel it through the glass. I can feel the heat from the palms of your hands. Do you feel mine? The things that separate us are already too much: this barrier, this ship and the whole universe; my clothes, my magic tricks and my clumsy attempts to provoke you; your dress, beautiful as it is, because the treasure it hides within it is a thousand times more beautiful still. We are two little drops of life in the middle of the vast cold of the cosmos, which will all end up being extinguished eventually – the stars as well as the galaxies. But for now we're burning, Léonor. For now, we exist! This moment belongs only to us, and we can make it last longer by holding each other tight. You only need to say the word. Say the name.'

The bell rings before Léonor has the chance to add anything further.

All audio communication between the two hemispheres is instantly cut off.

Slowly the two bodies drift apart from the glass, away from each other, but they remain for several minutes in the bubble, no longer able to communicate with each other but not yet ready to part.

Serena McBee (off): '*So Léonor has decided to draw the suspense out until the last minute, even if it means torturing her two lovers, as well as the viewers who, in their hundreds of millions, are awaiting her decision.*'

Léonor turns sharply towards the camera. 'No, I don't want to torture anybody! That was never what I wanted! I just wanted to set a rule! One simple rule . . .'

Her voice cracks.

She looks towards the other half of the Visiting Room, distraught. Marcus seems so small, as though he were very far away, off in the darkness of space. He nods, a slight bow, before disappearing down the tube.

'Serena,' Léonor manages to get the name out. 'I need to talk to you. To you and nobody else. It's really important.'

The girl's words ring out in the silence – the long, terrible silence that now lasts five and a half minutes, the time it takes for the laser signal to travel fifty million kilometres to Earth, and back again.

'*Understood, Léonor,*' replies Serena at last. '*You and I can have a private communication in the gym when you leave the Visiting Room.*'

It's now Léonor's turn to disappear down the tube towards her living quarters.

56. Shot

I'm trembling as I make my way down the ladder.

I was *this close* to revealing the existence of the Salamander to Marcus.

But I didn't do it.

I couldn't do it.

I only managed to get out two pathetic words: 'My skin . . .'

Because at the moment I spoke those words, my stomach clenched like a fist.

Because at the moment I was articulating those two syllables, the fear that comes from a whole life in hiding collapsed on top of me.

Then came the tolling of the bell, before I was able to recover my breath.

'Well, Léonor, what is it you want to tell me?'

Serena's voice makes me jump.

Her face is reproduced a dozen times on the dozen screens that look down over the exercise bikes, the treadmills, the fitness machines: each piece of equipment in the gym. The image of the executive producer of Genesis is already becoming mixed up with that of the future vice-president of the United States; today Serena is wearing a green suit, in the Ultra-liberal party colours.

I swallow down my pain so as to concentrate on the reason I asked for this private exchange: Ruben Rodriguez's cellphone.

'Thank you, Serena,' I say first. 'Thank you for agreeing. We aren't being broadcast on the Genesis channel now, right?'

Five and a half minutes go by. I feel my hair rise each time I breathe in – in the gym, with ten per cent gravity, it weighs almost nothing.

'No, you needn't worry,' Serena replies at last. 'Right now, the channel is focusing on the living room, where your friends are impatiently awaiting your return. You can speak freely, no need to be afraid. That's what I'm here for. To listen to you. To protect you. You can tell me everything, you know that. We just ought to be as clear as we can when we talk, so as to manage the communication latency. So, to begin: why did you ask for this private conversation?'

I'm about to tell her about the phone, which is waiting for me in the lower level of the ship, safe at the back of the wardrobe where I left it recharging.

'It's about your scar, isn't it? That's what made you change your mind in front of the handsome Marcus? You're dreading the moment when the viewers and the boys learn of its existence, particularly after your argument with Kirsten at the beginning of the journey?'

The words stick in my throat.

Serena has taken me by surprise.

In trying to anticipate my questions so as to make our conversation as efficient as possible, she's gone down the wrong track: it wasn't the Salamander I wanted to talk to her about.

'You shouldn't worry about it,' she adds. 'It's like I explained to you during the selection interviews: the viewers will never see your scar if you don't want them to. And nor will the boys either. It'll be our secret, just between you and me . . . and the boy you choose for your husband.'

'That's kind of you, Serena. But how do you know my scar was the reason for the argument with Kris five months ago? There are no cameras in the bathroom, as far as I know. And Kris swore to me that she didn't tell anyone.'

More silence.

Cold, impenetrable, endless, like the void of space.

Until Serena's little crystalline laugh breaks through it.

Her smile, multiplied a dozen-fold, widens imperceptibly.

'Oh, Léonor, Léonor! You don't miss a thing, with your legendary powers of observation, do you? I guessed it was something to do with your scar, from the way Kris reacted, and the way you went off to hide under your blankets. I'm a very good psychologist, don't forget, and I know the six of you as though you were my own creations! She was scared, you were ashamed, but finally the two of you were reconciled. I'm sure it'll go just as smoothly with whomever your heart chooses. And again, there's no reason you have to reveal your little *peculiarity* before your wedding night: once you are married, anyway, the man you've chosen won't be in any position to go back. It will be too late for any regrets!'

Serena's words chill my blood.

Too late for any regrets.

412

'So anyway, it's fine for you not to say anything; just worry about choosing between Mozart and Marcus,' advises the twelve-headed green hydra opposite me. 'Now, you should rush back down to the others. Unless there was something else you wanted to talk to me about?'

Lie to Mozart and Marcus, who have revealed everything about their lives to me?

I never imagined Serena could be so manipulative.

And at no point did I intend to behave like that.

My plan, my rule, has always been to show the Salamander to my favourite contestant at the last moment, so he would have all the facts before he had to make his choice – if the interview had lasted a few seconds longer, I'm sure I would have found the strength to talk to Marcus about it.

'No, I don't have anything else to say,' I murmur – and then immediately correct myself – 'Actually, *yes*. I'm worried about Louve.'

My instinct tells me I need to improvise.

To try to learn a little more.

'I know dogs pretty well,' I say, 'after my years at the Eden Food France factory. Their gastronomic formulas are tested and approved by the most demanding of dogs, did you know that? Anyway, Louve has been refusing food for a few days. Even *Granny's Blanquette de Veau*, our flagship product, which she liked so much at the start of the journey. As the Medical Officer, I'm really worried. Serena, I do think Louve is sick. That she has some hidden flaw, a bit like me, but maybe something even more serious – how are we to know? I mean, we don't even know where this dog came from!'

413

After five and a half minutes, on the twelve screens, Serena frowns her perfectly plucked eyebrows exactly forty-five degrees, with a geometry as perfect as her silver bob.

'I'm sure you're worrying over nothing,' she says. 'It's just a passing thing. Louve is in perfect health, as confirmed by the file from the NASA animal store, which is where she received her training after having been selected from a shelter.'

'You mean Louve was selected just like me, like us, and trained for this mission?' I ask innocently. 'But then who was *her* instructor?'

The minutes pass again.

I try to break through into the thoughts hidden behind those water-green eyes, reproduced in a dozen copies.

I can't do it.

'Several people were responsible for Louve and Warden,' Serena replies at last, 'as the various teams took it in turns at the animal store. But I will look into Louve's medical history with Archibald Dragovic, who as the Biology instructor supervised the selection of the dogs. But I'll say it again: I'm sure there's no problem with them. I will, however, keep you informed if there's any need to give that fine little dog some treatment or other. I hope you're reassured, Léonor.'

I no longer have any idea what to think.

Memories of Ruben Rodriguez burn my tongue. A part of me wants to hurl everything in Serena's face, describe the photos with Louve and Warden, demand that she explain who he is, this guy who is clearly a member of the staff, who has the word *SILENCE* engraved on a tag under his shirt, who

414

wanted to stop me boarding the rocket. Because the more I think about it, the more certain I am that what he wanted to say to me was: 'You mustn't get on board!'

But another part of me clenches my jaw to stop myself speaking.

The woman on the screen looks expectant too. As though she's waiting for me to say something, as though she suspects what I have on the tip of my tongue. This interview should be over, and yet she doesn't bring our conversation to an end.

It's unbearable.

'If there's anything else at all you'd like to talk to me about, you know you can always count on me, anytime; anytime up to the end of the journey, right? Now, I'll let you get back to your friends. Give Louve a big hug from me.'

The screens in the gym go off at last, leaving nothing but silence.

I had so many questions to ask, and that was the only answer I received: silence.

I go back down through the hatch.

My hair weighs more heavily on my shoulders, now that I'm back in the bathroom with its twenty per cent gravity. My reflection appears in the round mirror, reassuring me. I'm sure Serena was hiding something from me. She started talking about my scar without a moment's hesitation. There aren't too many possible explanations for that: either she really is a mind-reader, or there are cameras behind the bathroom mirror.

The thirty per cent gravity in the living room seems to bear down on me like a lead weight, even if it's still only a third of the gravity on Earth. The tension is palpable. The girls don't dare to say a word to ask me how it went; I suspect I must have an expression like grim death. Yesterday with Mozart, and yet again today with Marcus: they must think I'm in the process of screwing everything up.

'Lunch will be ready in half an hour,' says Kris very quietly. 'I've made a vanilla tart.'

'OK.'

I walk over to the hatch that leads down to the bedroom, moving as casually I can, forcing myself not to look up at the ceiling in search of the cameras.

I make my way down the rungs of the ladder, focusing on my breathing. By this time, Ruben Rodriguez's phone ought to be turned on; it's been more than half an hour since I left the light pointing at it.

Once I'm in the bedroom, I force myself not to dash straight to the wardrobe. Strange: the door is half-open, and I'm sure I closed it properly when I rushed up to the Visiting Room.

I stick my head and shoulders into the dark recess.

I move aside the white silk Vietnamese tunic.

The flashlight is still there, its thin beam cutting through the gloom.

But it's alone.

The phone has disappeared.

57. Reverse Shot

The Villa McBee, Long Island, New York State
Tuesday 28 November, 2:00pm

'Goodbye, my dear. I won't be long, you'll see. I just need to get back to the base at Cape Canaveral for the final week of the voyage, for the ship's alignment with the orbit of Phobos and the landing on Mars. People won't understand if I'm not there with the Genesis team for the grand arrival. By the time I get back, the electoral college vote will already have taken place: your mother will be vice-president of the United States of America! Are you proud of me?'

'Yes, Mom,' answers Harmony.

Wearing her green suit in the Ultra-liberal party colours, Serena McBee leans over to kiss her daughter's forehead. The girl, paler and sicklier-looking than ever, is nestled in a big Chesterfield armchair at the edge of the stucco fireplace that warms her room. She has a book on her knees, which are covered in several alpaca rugs: *Sense and Sensibility*.

'Now, be good,' says Serena. 'Balthazar will bring your meals to you in your room, the way we usually do it when I'm away.'

Serena leaves the room, shutting the door behind her.

She takes a key out of her crocodile-skin handbag – which matches her suit and her shoes – and turns it twice in the lock.

Then she goes down the stairs, pressing the micro-brooch that's pinned to her collar.

'*Serena to Brandon and Dawson.* I'm ready to go.'

The two servants in waistcoats and silver earpieces appear in the entrance hall. The first helps Serena put on a lavish mink coat, while the other takes care of the luggage.

A butler in a dress coat – also equipped with an earpiece, like everybody in the service of the lady of the house – is waiting at the large front door.

'Ms McBee,' he says with a nod. Then he adds, 'Just one thing before you leave: there's that young man at the villa gates; he's been waiting to see you for several days.'

Serena shrugs.

'Come now, my dear Balthazar. There are *thousands* of men, young and old, who have been waiting for several *months* to see me, even to catch a glimpse at a distance,' she says haughtily.

'Yes, but this particular young man is the son of your late colleague, Sherman Fisher.'

Serena raises an eyebrow.

'The Fisher boy?' she says. 'He thinks because his father contributed to the programme, this gives him free access to the most prominent woman in the world? I'd bet he's here to snivel and beg me to include him in the next batch of astronauts headed to Mars. He'll wait till I get back, like the others.'

With this, she turns on her heel and walks into the gardens of the Villa McBee, which are covered in a shroud of snow. There's a helicopter waiting, beside a frozen pond.

Serena holds her hand out to the man carrying the luggage so that he can help her take her place in the cabin, beside an anoracked pilot.

'Apologies, Ms McBee,' the pilot says, 'but with the hordes of admirers laying siege to the villa, it's impossible to get out with the limo. We'll get to the Long Island airport much faster by helicopter.'

Serena puts on a mink hat, and a pair of sunglasses that swallow up her entire face.

'Do what you can, my good fellow,' she says. 'But fly quite low. My fans will be so thrilled to catch a glimpse of their idol!'

58. Out of Frame

'Look, that's Serena McBee flying off!'

Thousands of faces turn as one towards the snowy November clouds. Most of the noses are wrapped in thick scarves, as it's freezing hard, but the woollen mufflers aren't enough to stifle the clamour that rises up towards the heavens.

'Se-re-na! Se-re-na! Se-re-na!'

The hats covering all the heads are either red like the Genesis programme logo, or green like the posters of the Ultra-liberal Party.

All the heads?

No: one young man standing at the front of the crowd is wearing neither red nor green, just a dark anorak hood.

It's Andrew Fisher, his face white with tiredness, his skin covered in dry sores from having been on the lookout outside the Villa McBee in the winter cold. Behind his black-framed glasses, his eyes follow the trajectory of the helicopter as it cuts through the air, flying over the enraptured crowd and the hundreds of cars parked higgledy-piggledy around the villa.

Some of them have been there for weeks, as evidenced by the layer of hardened snow that has formed on their roofs, and the translucent icicles under their chassis.

Only Andrew fails to cheer the heroine of the moment, whose gloved hand waves from the helicopter window like the Queen of England on her coronation day.

A groan escapes from a man's chapped lips.

'No . . . she can't just leave like that . . . She has no right . . .'

His hands grip the frozen bars as though he wanted to pull them apart with his brute strength.

'Hey! Get your hands down!' barks a guard, one of the dozens who are posted on the other side of the huge barriers, charged with keeping the fans in check. 'You don't touch the property of the vice-president of the United States! Anyway, you can all beat it, now the boss has gone. Then we can stop freezing our asses off out here too. Go on, move it, there's nothing to see here.'

The human tide is already beginning to ebb.

Engines that haven't run for ages are sputtering into motion.

Many of these are people returning home for the holidays, who will be following the final part of the *Cupido*'s journey from somewhere nice and warm.

Andrew also returns to the cabin of his campervan, cluttered with disembowelled crisp packets, black cardboard coffee cups and all the other traces of his long wait. But he doesn't turn on the ignition. He just watches through the windscreen as the improvised car park empties out, the vehicles leaving behind furrows of frozen earth all around the Villa McBee.

The tinted glass is being slowly covered with ice crystals.

Up there, in the sky, it's starting to snow again.

All of a sudden, the phone on the dashboard starts to ring. The ringtone associated with this incoming call is not 'The Imperial March', it's another tune from *Star Wars*: 'A New Hope'.

'Cecilia?' says Andrew, answering the phone.

'Andrew. How're you doing? I've been thinking about you a lot. Are you still up on Long Island? You haven't gone back to class? And most important: aren't you freezing?'

'Ever since we started to suspect Genesis of being behind my father's death and your husband's, I've been burning on the inside. As for my classes, Berkeley can wait.'

'I've just seen on TV that Serena McBee has left her villa. Were you able to talk to her? Confront her with what we've discovered?'

'No, but I can tell that our time is coming soon. People are starting to leave the surroundings of the villa. The security's going to be relaxed, now that the lady of the house isn't here any more. I'm going to try and get myself inside, as soon as I can.'

'Take care of yourself.'

'Don't worry. They may have brought down my drone in Cape Canaveral, but they won't get me!'

59. Shot

'Safia, I need to talk to you.'

From her place on the living-room sofa, the little Indian girl lifts her nose out of her revision tablet, where she's watching a lecture about electromagnetic waves.

'Sorry?' she says, taking out her earphones. 'Did you say something to me?'

'I've got something to tell you,' I say again, struggling to control the trembling in my voice.

Safia seems to notice at once that there's something wrong.

'What is it, Léo?' she asks, concerned.

'It's about those drawings I showed you, at the start of the journey.'

'About the drawings?' she says, taken aback.

I don't give her time to say any more. I lean in to her ear, wedging my hand in tight so nobody else can hear me.

'It's nothing to do with the drawings, but I needed an excuse to whisper in front of the cameras. The truth is that Ruben Rodriguez's phone has disappeared. Don't ask me if I'm sure, or if I've checked carefully, or other pointless things like that, since we don't have much chance to talk without arousing suspicion, and anyway I'm sure their microphones are ultra-sensitive. I'd put the phone to charge with the flashlight at the back of my wardrobe this morning, like you suggested, and it was still there when I went up to the Visiting Room. That was when somebody took it. The question is, *who*? You're the only person on board I told about the existence of the phone. So I'm begging you, if you've told any of the other girls, I need to know now!'

I pull my face away from Safia's and conclude my speech at full volume, with some phoney thing for the cameras.

'. . . so, yeah, it's true, the drawings in my sketching tablet, they're like my secret world – Léo the Red, Marcus's tattoos, the whole thing. Even if I did show them to you, I wanted you do keep them to yourself. So tell me, have you told any of the other girls about them?'

I fix my eyes on Safia's.

My heart is racing, nineteen to the dozen.

I guess I must look like a total nut to the viewers, a kid who lives in a dream-world and wants to protect her little private diary nobody gives a damn about anyway – but I don't care. What I'm waiting for from Safia is a name, and fast!

'I haven't talked to anyone,' she says, in a voice that sounds too hesitant, horribly fake.

No. That isn't the answer I am expecting. She *must* have told somebody, because the phone disappeared despite all the precautions I'd taken to hide it from the cameras.

'Are you absolutely sure?' I insist. 'You haven't mentioned it even *just a little bit*?'

Safia puts her revision tablet down and gets slowly up from the sofa.

Across the living room, one by one the other girls are stopping what they're doing to see what's happening on our side.

'I swear I-I haven't . . .' stammers Safia, glancing furtively around her, like an animal caught helplessly in a trap.

Liar! Everything about her behaviour suggests that she's lying!

'What's going on?' asks Liz, walking over from the fireplace in front of which she'd been sitting.

'Something about secret pictures, from what I heard,' explains Fangfang.

Sitting at the other end of the sofa, Fangfang is the closest to us, and she heard the last bit of our conversation – badly enough to distort it. 'Apparently, Marcus showed her some private tattoos, which she's copied onto her sketching tablet!'

Now Kris looks up from the kitchen table, where she and Kelly are busy swotting up. Kelly herself is the only girl who seems not to have noticed what's brewing, with earphones blasting Jimmy Giant into her ears at full volume. A few days ago, she finally turned her revision tablet on and she now spends her days on the flight simulator to practice for our capsule's landing on Mars, which she will be piloting via a link-up with Cape Canaveral – while Mozart will be doing the same with the boys' capsule.

'Everything OK, Léo?' Kris asks in her gentle voice.

'Yes, it's fine,' I reply, forcing a smile.

But it isn't fine at all.

One of the five girls, who're all behaving as though they've got nothing at all to hide, has taken the phone from my wardrobe. There is no other possible explanation. Somebody can't just have wandered in here off the street!

'I was just asking Safia a simple question,' I say.

Ideas scroll quickly through my mind. The possible scenarios race past one another like the pages of a book that never ends, making me crazy:

Option 1: Safia's lying.
a) *She's told one of the girls and is too ashamed to admit it.*
b) *She's told the organisers, who convinced one of the girls (possibly Safia herself) to take my phone.*
c) *She hasn't told anybody, but she's stolen it herself for some reason I don't know about.*
Option 2: Safia isn't lying.
d) *The cameras caught my little trick, inexplicably, despite all my precautions; then, as with 1b, one of the girls was tasked with stealing it from me.*
e) *Somebody was rifling through my things by chance and said, 'Oh wow, look, a phone! Maybe I should take this and play a little trick on good old Léo?'*
Conclusion: Trust no one.

'You do look funny, Léo,' says Kris, taking my arm. 'You sure you feel OK? I hope it wasn't my tart from lunchtime; I did wonder if the Daisy Farm powdered milk might not be very fresh any more, after five months of travelling.'

'Shit, I've crashed again!' cries Kelly, sending her revision tablet flying.

She yanks out her earphones.

'What are you all standing there talking about? Is there some last-minute problem?'

Yeah, there's a last-minute problem.

I want to reveal it for everyone to see, to rid myself of the doubts that gnaw at me, and which are now no longer doubts but certainties.

But I can't.

Because there might be a traitor in our cabin. Or several.

Because if the organisers really are hiding something serious from us, and really aren't aware of the existence of the telephone, I absolutely mustn't reveal it to them.

Because that would mean I'm completely on my own.

'I was just talking to Safia about my drawings,' I say. 'Just some little doodles.'

'Oh, new drawings!' cries Kris, clapping her hands. 'Can I see them, Léo?'

Kris has always been my best audience, more than ever since that time I portrayed her as an ice princess. This enthusiasm is normal for her. And yet a small part of me can't help wondering whether she isn't playing it up. If maybe she's the one who's gone rifling through my wardrobe, which is right beside hers . . .

No!

I mustn't even imagine that possibility.

Kris would never lie to me like that!

'I've still got to polish the drawings up a little,' I say at last. 'I'll show them to you as soon as they're ready to be shown.'

'I thought they were *your secret world*?' says Fangfang, not that anybody has asked her. 'Which you didn't want to share with anybody.'

And what if it's her, what if she's the traitor, with that butter-wouldn't-melt way she has about her?

I shoot her an icy glare.

'You must have misunderstood, Fangfang. I said I'd share them when they were ready for people to see them.'

The rest of the afternoon seems to go by as slowly as molasses, that black sugar syrup we used to add to the dog desserts in the factory, and which made the ladles as sticky as fuel oil.

The hardest thing is to keep pretending – pretending to smile, to be relaxed, to kid around. Safia makes various attempts to approach me. I force myself to respond as naturally as I can, as casually as I can. Because if she's telling the truth, she doesn't deserve to have me sulking at her; because if she's betrayed me, she absolutely shouldn't know how much the loss of the phone has traumatised me.

'I swear I didn't tell anybody,' she whispers to me, having volunteered to do the washing-up with me after dinner.

'You said. I believe you.'

Claiming the opposite wouldn't get me anywhere anyway.

'And anyway, it's not serious,' I add ambiguously. 'I'll reveal everything soon, to everyone, as soon as I'm ready.'

A doubt flashes across Safia's face. I can see she's not sure she knows what I'm talking about – is it the famous drawings, which were after all only a pretext, or some actual revelations that I claim to possess?

She looks nervously up at the camera that's filming us from just above the work surface. Because she's afraid of being spied on? Or because she looks instinctively towards the people who are giving her orders? She says nothing and keeps wiping the dishes in silence with the electrostatic cloth.

The reduced lighting that we have at night makes things even harder than in the daytime. Stretched out in my bunk there's nothing to distract me from my thoughts.

Who took the phone?

Why?

Who? – Why? – Who? – Why? – Who?

I don't get a moment's sleep. Several times I'm taken with a sudden desire to tear off my blanket, get up and go rummaging in the other girls' wardrobes. But I restrain myself: in such a cramped room, where each girl's sleep hangs by a thread, I'd be asking to get myself caught.

I try to think about something else.

But the only thing that comes to me is Marcus's face, with his grey eyes that look at me the way nobody has ever looked at me before.

I didn't lie to Mozart two days ago, when I told him I hadn't yet made my choice. Because then it was true. I was filled with doubts and conflicting feelings. But since then, Mozart has closed himself off to me. And Marcus has opened his heart.

I am not a Determinator made of cold cogs and wheels: I'm a being of flesh and blood, who shivers whenever I think of him.

I'm not a wild leopard who rejects all men: I'm a cat who wants to curl up in the arms of just one of them.

I'm not Léo the Red, willing to die rather than admit that she has feelings: I'm just Léonor, and I'm in love with Marcus.

60. Genesis Channel

Monday 4 December, 11:00am

Fade in from black.

Static shot of the empty Visiting Room. On the top of the glass bubble, the halo of the transmission dish sends out its silent laser beam, a thread of light that maintains the constant link with an Earth which is now much too far away to be visible. At the back, behind the Visiting Room, a bloody sphere stands out, the size of a basketball: the planet Mars.

Title: *133rd session in the Visiting Room. Hostess: Elizabeth, 18, United Kingdom, Engineering Officer (communication latency: 5 minutes, 53 seconds)*

The English girl appears on the left of the screen and hurriedly shuts the hatch behind her.

Just as she does each time she goes up to the Visiting Room, she skilfully removes her jumpers and shawls, to reveal the daring ballerina who's been hidden in this cocoon of knitwear and false modesty, to which the other girls have been completely oblivious. Today she's all in white, wearing a pearl-coloured leotard and legwarmers.

Serena (off): '*My dear Elizabeth, I think it's fair to say that for this, your last invitation to the Visiting Room, you have saved up something extra-special, a grand finale!'*

Elizabeth: 'What do you expect, Serena? I'm a performer at heart, I've always been aware of putting on a show.'

She takes out her red lipstick and applies it carefully to her mouth; she's in no hurry, as it will be almost six minutes before the executive producer answers her.

Serena (off): *'As an entertainment professional, I can only applaud you wholeheartedly. Thanks to you, our viewers have enjoyed plenty of narrative twists. Like last week's, with Mozart.'*

Elizabeth's hand trembles slightly as she's applying the last stroke of red; the vermillion goes slightly outside the line of her lips.

'I did it for his own good. Y-you know that, the-the viewers know that . . .' she stammers.

With the tip of her finger, she delicately wipes the red that went over the line to redraw a perfect mouth.

'I'm fond of Léonor,' she continues quietly, and it's not clear whether she's addressing Serena, or the viewers, or just herself. 'I find that girl impressive, and fascinating, and . . . inspiring. But the way she behaves with Mozart just isn't fair. Not to him, who's being encouraged to nurture false hope. And not to me, who's stuck on the sidelines. I did what I had to do. Isn't that right?'

Serena's voice emerges from the depths of space, cutting short the English girl's qualms, which have not yet had time to reach the Earth. *'I shall call in Mozart, so you can reap what you've sown.'*

Drum-roll.

431

A few moments later, Mozart appears on the right of the screen. He's back in his smarter outfit, the white shirt and black trousers. His tanned face, visible between his brown curls, is touched by melancholy. Under his long silky lashes, his eyes are shining slightly.

Mozart: 'You're very seductive, Elizabeth. You'd be any man's dream.'

Elizabeth: 'Call me Liz, please. And I don't want to be any man's dream; I want to be yours, Mozart.'

She continues immediately. 'No, actually I don't want to be your dream: I want to be your reality. Léonor was a dream – her and everything she made you believe.'

Mozart clenches his jaw and relaxes it again.

Doubt is visible on his face.

He's unable to move on from Léonor, he's still clinging on to her. '*A dream?*' he repeats. 'Last time I invited her, she seemed real enough. She denied absolutely everything. She said no, that she hadn't yet chosen. She really did seem to be telling the truth.'

Elizabeth smiles sadly: 'You're still in love with her, I see that. But didn't you see for yourself, in her sketching tablet I secretly borrowed to show you last time we met? Léonor has only drawn Marcus! Pages and pages of drawings, reproductions of every tiny tattoo, every part of his body. It gives me no pleasure telling you all this behind the back of a girl I really do like very much, believe me. Open your eyes, Mozart. Wake up. The dream is well and truly over: Léonor decided months ago who she was going to make a life with. She's just been toying with you!'

Mozart's face hardens. 'It's true. You're right. She *has* just been toying with me. The whole thing's been a game to her. Her damn rule was just there for her own amusement.'

Elizabeth glides towards the glass partition like a sylph.

'You've got to forget. She's made you suffer enough already. I'm here now. I'm here for you.'

Mozart's eyes open a little wider. 'You aren't afraid of ending up with a hoodlum?'

Elizabeth lowers her gazes. 'I'm very far from irreproachable myself, believe me.'

Her voice trembles a little, but this time it isn't the quavering of a great actress, it comes from genuine emotion.

'Borrowing the tablet, my costume changes on the quiet in the Visiting Room . . . All the things I've said, the things I've done behind the backs of the other girls . . . I'm someone who's only ever lived to compete, ever since I took my first dance steps, and I've had enough. I can't wait for this to be over. I just want to be happy, with a man I love, surrounded by friends who are important to me. That's all.'

Mozart nods slowly. 'So you really think we could be happy, the two of us?'

Elizabeth looks back up. 'Yes, Mozart, I promise you: we will be happy together. As happy as Léonor and Marcus.'

The bell goes.

The interview is over.

Mozart has recovered something like a smile.

61. Shot

Our wake-up music bursts into the bedroom.

It's never sounded so discordant.

And the light from the halogen spotlights, simulating daylight, has never seemed so harsh.

It pitilessly illuminates the other girls' faces as they sit up in their beds, revealing the bags under their eyes, the creased cheeks, the furrowed foreheads. I'm quite sure that, like me, not one of them got a wink of sleep last night. If they're feeling stressed it's understandable – it's the day before we publish the final Heart Lists and land on Mars – but their stress is nothing compared to mine.

Which one of these girls, my companions for a year of my life in Death Valley and five months journeying across space, stole Ruben Rodriguez's phone from me five days ago?

Which of them, behind her frown, is not only a girl anxious to know which boy she's finally going to marry, but also a double agent?

Is it Fangfang, who in spite of her satin sleeping-mask hasn't

434

managed to avoid insomnia? She so likes lecturing other people, and she's well aware we're not allowed to have phones on board, so she could easily have confiscated it from me to teach me a lesson . . .

Is it Safia, whose drawn features suddenly seem a whole lot less young and innocent? She's the only one who knew of the phone's existence, before it disappeared . . .

Is it Kelly, who's already pushed the earphones into her ears, blasting out Jimmy Giant at full volume? Her confession about her family was touching, but honestly, she couldn't have invented a better story if she'd really just been trying to soften me up . . .

Is it Liz, whose well-sculpted face seems suddenly so hollow with remorse? I know she's been avoiding catching my eye these past few days, as if she had something to be guilty about . . .

Or is it Kris after all, whom I considered my lifelong friend, though in truth I've only known her a handful of months? Even if I can't conceive of any motive for her to have stolen the phone, that doesn't make her innocent . . . She's presumed guilty, just like the others, until proved otherwise.

As I'm brooding over these thoughts, all three screens above the beds come on at once to show the most ambiguous, impenetrable face of all: that of Serena McBee. She's in Cape Canaveral again, just as she was at the start of the show, leaning back in her padded leather armchair.

'Good morning, girls!' she says in her sugary voice.

Yes, *sugary*.

Not *gentle*, or *maternal*, or *compassionate*, or any other adjective I've always so readily attached to her in the past. I only now realise just how fake her voice sounds.

'I hope you've all managed to get a bit of sleep despite the excitement, my dears, for your penultimate night on board the *Cupido* . . .'

That dripping voice, like a thick syrup sticking in my ears, like the honey Serena used to put in my chamomile tea in Death Valley to help me sleep; her eyes never managed to hypnotise me, but her voice, yes, that did get me to drop my guard for the five months of our interplanetary journey.

'. . . in a few hours, the nuclear engines will stop automatically and the retrorockets will brake until the *Cupido* is in perfect alignment with the orbit of Phobos, only six thousand kilometres above the surface of Mars. That will be the moment for us to publish the last Heart Lists and to establish the final couples, before the great leap into the unknown! But for now we have one speed-dating session left, the last one of all. Our own favourite little leopard has the honour of bringing the game to a close.'

If only you knew, Serena, just how much this leopard would like to pounce at your throat and tear that beautiful, smooth face of yours!

I know you've been spying on me from behind the two-way mirror in the bathroom, for all these weeks when I've thought I was alone . . .

I can tell there's no compassion in the way you talk about my scar, just an unhealthy voyeurism . . .

I'm guessing there's something huge you're hiding . . .

But what?

What?

Oh, if only I had the phone!

Kris comes over to me, in her little cream-coloured silk nightie.

'This morning I'm all yours, my dear Léo,' she says. 'To help you get ready for your final session.'

I smile as best I can.

'Thanks, that's really nice of you, but I think I'd rather be alone today. I need to be by myself before my last interview.'

Kris nods sadly.

'Whatever you prefer,' she says.

Does she look put out because she really did want to help me prepare? Or because she's been tasked with keeping an eye on me?

She comes closer and murmurs a few words in my ear.

'You still can't choose between Mozart and Marcus, is that it? You should talk to me about it. Love triangles are awful, I know all about them, they're always happening in romantic novels.'

My scathing answer bursts from my lips. 'It's not a triangle, or a square, or any other stupid geometric shape! Or rather, yeah, it is, it's a twelve-faced polygon, because we are twelve, condemned to live together. Open your eyes, Kris: we aren't in a romantic novel. We're in reality. And I really need to be here *on my own*.'

Kris gives me a look of astonishment, then finally moves away.

I don't try to stop her.

Now isn't the time to feel bad; in the week since the phone disappeared, I've used every possible excuse to find myself alone on each floor of our quarters and to search it from top to bottom. So far I've found nothing, but that's only because I haven't unearthed the right hideaway! I grab the red chiffon dress and the Rosier make-up case from my wardrobe, pass through the living room without so much as a glance at the dining table – I've got too much of a knot in my stomach to eat anything at all – and retreat into the bathroom.

'I'd appreciate it if no one bothered me!' I shout to no one in particular as I close the hatch.

I drop the dress and the case onto the stool, and hurry upstairs to the gym. It's at least the fifth time I've searched it. I turn the yoga mat upside down, I raise myself onto my tiptoes to look on top of the exercise machines, one by one I open the dozens of drawers built into the walls, which contain equipment and machinery whose function I don't know – the *Cupido*'s entrails. Wires, diodes, buttons galore; but no phone.

All around the room, the black domes of the cameras observe me like the eyes of a spider watching its prey struggling uselessly in its web.

'Where could I have left that black satin ribbon? I've been looking for it for weeks,' I think out loud, as though to myself. 'I wonder if I lost it up here when I was exercising? . . .' It's actually the viewers I'm addressing, to try and pull the wool over their eyes, to supply them with some explanation for my behaviour. Otherwise they're going to think I'm a housekeeping maniac hunting down every speck of dust. Or that I'm just nuts, plain and simple.

Eventually I come back down to the bathroom, dripping with sweat.

There are no obvious cameras here, but that's even worse.

I continue my search, the fabric of my pyjamas clinging to

the Salamander. I empty each drawer of the unit under the sink, where the girls have arranged their toiletries: brushes, combs, elastics, but still no phone.

Then I attack the biggest bit: the large storage cupboards at the back of the room, which are also covered in mirrors. This is where all the edible goods for the trip are kept. The shelves of preserves and dried produce are almost empty, as we're starting to run short of provisions; but there's still a whole jumble of tools, for carrying out any minor repairs on board the ship, attached magnetically to large metallic panels – electrical screwdrivers, pliers, adjustable spanners, hammers, scissors, screws of every possible size, and all manner of other things that only Liz, our Engineering Officer, knows how to use. But amid all the accessories that have been supplied for dealing with every tiny problem, the only thing that's missing is the one thing that would be useful to me.

Quivering with frustration, I shut myself away in the shower cubicle with the dress, which I slip on just about well enough – there's no way I'm going to strip naked in front of that mirror one more time.

'Léo, we've still got some tart left from yesterday – are you sure you don't want to eat anything?' asks Kris, making one more attempt while I hurtle through the living room.

'I'm sure,' I say, glancing at the digital clock. 'No time. Only half an hour till my session. I'm going down to do my make-up in the bedroom.'

The bedroom.

Of all the rooms, this is the one with the greatest number of possible hiding places.

It's the most dangerous too, since if I'm caught rummaging around in other people's belongings . . .

I'd rather not think about it.

I hurl myself at Kris's wardrobe, still decorated with its 'Virgin with Child', who watches me reproachfully. Everything inside is blue, or practically blue, as if I'd opened a window to a piece of sky – not the black empty sky of space, no, the blue sky of Earth, filled with birds and clouds. I close the door again, sheepishly – there's no way she could have betrayed me, not her, not my Kris.

Without letting shame hold me back any further, I open Fangfang's wardrobe. Everything there is ordered with obsessive precision. I slide my hand between the dresses, all of which look like they're just back from the dry cleaner. I feel around amid the piles of clothes without a crease out of place, in search of the phone. My hand trembles, hesitates. I know Fangfang would notice right away if I were to accidentally displace the tiniest part of her geometric universe. My heart is beating in my temples, nineteen to the dozen. I find nothing.

I turn to Kelly's wardrobe. This is the exact opposite of the world I've just left: an indescribable chaos, a jumble of clothes in all colours and all fabrics. I stick my two hands in and start kneading the whole thing in the hope my fingers will feel a solid, rectangular object. But no, there's nothing, no more than there was all the other times I looked . . .

I race frantically round the bed to reach Safia's wardrobe. On my way, my eyes catch the black dome of the camera, next to the screen showing the moonlit sea with dolphins. Once again, shame pierces through me. There are billions of viewers watching me rummaging like a thief through other people's belongings: might they still believe my story about a lost ribbon? I shouldn't think about it. And I should hurry. Because right now Serena McBee is watching me too, and she might suspect what I'm really looking for, and she might intervene at any moment to order me to stop.

62. Reverse Shot

Fallout Bunker, Cape Canaveral Air Base
Saturday 9 December, 9:15am

'All that for a ribbon?' asks Gordon Lock.

The allies of silence have once again gathered around the circular table, in their armoured concrete lair, buried at the deepest point beneath Cape Canaveral air base. All seven of them are there, turned to face the digital wall that shows the streamed images from each floor of the *Cupido*, with a three-minute delay – the time it takes for the laser signal to reach Earth.

The light emanating from the gigantic screen makes Director Lock's bald scalp and Geronimo Blackbull's long, greasy hair shine; the changing colours are reflected in the thick lenses of Odette Stuart-Smith's glasses and on Archibald Dragovic's white shirt; the dancing shadows accentuate Roberto Salvatore's double chin and Arthur Montgomery's manly wrinkles. From her padded throne, Serena McBee presides in silence, wearing her green suit on which a silver bee-shaped brooch is gleaming.

'There, on screen G1L,' says Gordon Lock. 'The French girl. There she goes again! Has she gone nuts or what? She's been rummaging around all over that place for a week now, as if her precious satin ribbon were the eighth wonder of the world.'

'It's nothing to do with the ribbon,' says Serena McBee. 'What she's lost is much more serious. It's her unwavering self-confidence.'

A smile forms on the executive producer's lips.

'It'll be the highlight of the show, I've predicted it all along: the mid-flight explosion of the Determinator! All through the journey, Léonor has thought she could control everything. I've done all I could to encourage her to persist in this mistake, submitting to her deluded, ludicrous rule. But now that the end is in sight, she's realising that she can't live with her deformity. Because in the meantime she's fallen in love, poor little thing! She can tell she's going to have to be naked in front of Marcus and the whole world. She knows there's nothing she can do to avoid it. And so she's cracking up. It started on Tuesday, when she asked to talk to me in private about Louve, claiming that the dog was sick.'

'Louve?' frowns Gordon Lock. 'Sick? You wouldn't think so. She eats like a horse.'

'Oh, Louve is behaving impeccably,' replies the psychiatrist. 'Léonor is projecting, quite simply. She felt ill, she felt ugly, and without realising she's projected it all onto that ridiculous animal. For days it's been getting worse: her permanent state of nerves, her frantic mood, her compulsive searching . . . She thinks she's looking for the lost ribbon, but it's only a feeble pretext constructed by her superego to prevent her from going crazy: what she's looking for, unconsciously, is an escape route. A way out. Some means of escaping the trap in which she is caught. But there is no possible way out. She can't escape the *Cupido*. All she can do is lose face in the eyes of the viewers, who won't understand her obsession and who've stopped making donations to her anyway. In the next few hours there will be drama, and tears, I predict it! I'll be letting them have really graphic close-ups of the monstrosity that's living like a parasite on Léonor's back. Then they really will get an eyeful! And then we'll witness the rebound effect; the viewers will end up sending even more money to Léonor's Dowry, just to ease their consciences . . . a large portion of which, I must remind you, will be handed over by Atlas Capital and end up in our pockets.'

A sigh of satisfaction and relief rises around the table.

For the allies of silence, it will soon be the end of a painful period of waiting, marked by impatience to get their hands on their bonus, and by anxiety about being discovered.

Turning away from the digital wall, Gordon Lock clears his throat.

'My dear Serena,' he says, 'today, on the eve of the landing, I must thank you on behalf of all of us seated around this table. We may have had our doubts at certain moments in this adventure, I'll be the first to admit. Good God, you've really put me in a few cold sweats!'

The little gathering laugh heartily, as though this were one of those farewell party speeches at which employees make good-natured jokes about their boss who is leaving them.

'But you've always kept us on track,' Gordon Lock continues, serious again. 'You've known how to make the right decisions, at the right time. When Sherman Fisher and Ruben Rodriguez threatened our security, you had the courage to say *Enough!*, firmly and humanely: two perfectly dosed lethal injections, and we know they didn't suffer. When the site that was hacking Genesis first came online in July, you took the necessary measures without any panic: it was closed down within hours. And a month ago, when the mini-drone came back into action, it took five seconds for it to be brought down by one of the Rapax drone-chasers you wisely positioned to lie in wait in the control room. The examples of your professionalism just go on and on. And finally you've led us all safely into harbour. We are all grateful. And we'd also like to tell you that we all voted for you on November 7th.'

'Ah, that's so sweet!'

'We admire your energy, the fact you're throwing yourself into this new challenge when you could easily be retiring thanks to the superb bonus Atlas is about to pay us: half of it in a few hours, when the participants arrive on Mars, the other half in a few days, after the *tragic event* that you have been so kind as to arrange on our behalf.'

'Oh, you know, Gordon, I can't take any credit: I'm just one of those hyperactive people,' Serena explains. 'I always need to be busy, taking things in hand, making myself useful. I'm a little bee buzzing right and left, never able to stop. But do look over at G2Z, the bird's-eye view of the second floor on the girls' side: there's something interesting happening.'

The instructors look back at the digital screen.

In the living room, the girls have abandoned their breakfast and are gathered around the half-open hatch in the floor. They are crouching in silence, all five of them, watching what's happening in the bedroom.

445

The executive producer presses her brooch-mic.

'*Serena to the editing suite.* Switch the Genesis channel immediately to the girls' bedroom. I sense something exciting is about to happen – it may already have started, given the picture delay, and I don't want the viewers to miss the tiniest bit of it!'

63. Shot

'Léonor, what are you doing in our things?'

I spin around, my heart racing.

I was so absorbed in my search that I didn't hear the hatch in the ceiling open. Five suspicious faces are watching me, and they may have been watching for some time.

I hurriedly shut Safia's wardrobe.

The words rush out of my mouth, words I'd prepared to say in case I was discovered.

'I've lost my ribbon! I think it must have accidentally fallen into the fabric steriliser and got mixed up with someone else's clothes during the last round of UV laundry. I just wanted to check, not to bother anybody.'

Safia shoots me an accusatory glare, full of disappointment – or is it defiance?

'What are you talking about, your ribbon?' she says. 'I already said it wasn't me who took that.'

What bursts out of my mouth isn't a shout, it's a bark.

'Shut up!'

Safia mustn't mention the telephone, not in front of the girls, not in front of the cameras, at any cost!

'Shut up, or you're going to regret it!' I snarl a warning, as the girls stare at me like I'm totally off my head.

'What's going on, Léonor?' asks Kris, her face contorted by fear, just like when I slammed the bathroom hatch down on her head five months earlier. She turns to Safia. 'What's happened to her?'

The Indian girl shakes her head.

'She's having an attack of paranoia. Totally crazy. I really think I have to talk to you about it, girls, for her own good.'

I don't let her say another word.

I throw myself onto the ladder and grab hold of her saffron-coloured sari's loose end, which she is wearing like a scarf around her neck.

The knot tightens around Safia's throat like a noose, preventing her from saying another word.

At that same moment, the three screens in the bedroom come on, playing the title sequence of the Genesis programme – for the final time.

The voices of Jimmy Giant and Stella Magnifica fill the room, deafeningly loud, while the girls all start yelling, adding to my confusion and panic.

'Stop!'

'You sky-rocketed my life'

'She can't breathe!'

'You taught me how to fly'

'You're going to kill her!'

'Higher than the clouds, higher than the stars'

Before my reflexes let go of the scarf, Kelly pushes Safia through the hatch to loosen the knot that's clamped around her. Safia crashes all the way down to the floor beside me, while Kelly jumps down onto me with all her weight. I feel her nails dig into my flesh, while she bombards my eardrums.

'Let go of her! Let go of her! Let go of her!'

I feel hands pulling my hair.

Others tearing at my chiffon dress.

I hear the sinister noise of the fabric ripping.

I feel the air of the room on my naked skin, on my naked shoulders.

The title sequence stops, and the girls fall suddenly silent.

They look at me, horrified.

Safia lies unmoving on the floor, exactly where she fell.

I throw myself at the ladder, while the grim voice of the Salamander hisses in my ear:

(It was a long time to wait, but it was worth it.)

I cross the living room, my eyes filled with tears, with just one idea in my head: to get as far away as possible. But it's no use, because I can't escape the *Cupido*, because I can't escape the Salamander.

(At long last, I've won.)

I rush across the bathroom, climb the ladder that leads to the gym, cracking my nails on the rungs . . .

(And you've lost everything.)

. . . my shoes catch on the yoga mat, the straps on my ankles rip, I collapse onto the floor.

(This time you won't ever get up again!)

64. Out of Frame

'Oh! Did you see that?'

A horrified clamour rises from the impromptu campsite set up outside the gates of the Villa McBee. There are now only a quarter of the besiegers who were there two weeks earlier, when the lady of the house was still living here. Those who have remained are the die-hards, the real fans, who want to be the first to see their star return home to the bosom of her family after all the contestants have landed on Mars.

But right now there's nobody striking up a hymn to the glory of the great Serena – the campers emerge one after another from their vehicles, clutching their telephones and tablets.

'It's so awful!'

'Léonor's gone nuts!'

'Safia's not moving at all!'

The Genesis channel is also playing on Andrew Fisher's laptop, which is resting on the dashboard of his campervan.

But the young man isn't watching it. He's staring at the gates of the Villa McBee through his tinted windscreen.

450

There are only two guards positioned here to monitor access to the property. Both of them are glued to their phones, hypnotised by the tragedy unfolding fifty-five million kilometres away, at a three-minute lag.

'Now's the time,' murmurs Andrew.

He pulls on his anorak, puts his laptop into his backpack and gets out of the campervan.

The people all around him don't even register his presence.

He might as well be invisible.

At that moment, five billion human beings have their eyes fixed on space, without so much as one of them looking upwards to the sky. Everything happens through screens. And Andrew doesn't appear on any of them. No one can see him.

He climbs the fence silently, behind a fir tree he spotted weeks ago.

Then he drops down lightly onto the freshly fallen snow that carpets the gardens of the Villa McBee.

65. Shot

D +159 days 21 h 40 mins.
[23rd week]

There's a noise, like a door creaking, or an untuned violin.

My eyes wander across the gym, at ground level where I've just fallen, the floor surface sticky with my warm blood – the skin above my eye was cut open during my fall.

Two shining black eyes are looking at me, from under the base of the treadmill.

Is it a ghost, sounding its grim lament?

No, it's Louve, whimpering as she watches me.

She crawls out from her hiding-place. She's holding a piece of cardboard in her white mouth, which she drops in front of my face like an offering. It's a playing card. It's the king of hearts that disappeared during the tarot game at the beginning of the journey – Fangfang had accused Kelly of having it in her kitty, but it was the doggie who'd taken it.

'Louve,' I murmur between sobs.

Now it's my turn to start crawling towards the running machine. From a standing position, it's impossible to see the recess under the base of the machine, or even to tell it exists.

But now that I'm on the floor, I can clearly see all the objects Louve has spirited away over the five months' travelling, and hidden in her secret den.

odd socks;

a spare cashmere blanket;

a chewed-up old sponge;

and Ruben Rodriguez's phone.

'Léonor?' I hear Serena McBee's voice coming from the twelve screens in the gym. 'What's happened to you, Léonor? What kind of madness has taken hold of you? And above all: do you really intend to miss your final session in the Visiting Room? The countdown has already begun.'

Distraught, I slip my arm under the belt of the treadmill.

My fingers close around an object that has been haunting my every thought for a week.

I drag it back along the floor towards me, holding it face down beneath my hand, blocked from the cameras.

'Here I am, Serena,' I say, straightening up, the phone hidden in my palm against the folds of my torn dress. 'I'm ready.'

With the back of my hand, I wipe away the blood that's trickling down from the cut above my eye – it doesn't even hurt any more. Then I climb the final ladder, barefoot, and enter the access tube to the Visiting Room: a cylinder barely a metre long, with smooth walls, the only place on board where I'm certain there can't be a camera. Crouched inside, I turn on the phone.

It shows the final image I was looking at a week ago: Ruben Rodriguez in his Genesis jacket. At the top of the screen, the battery gauge is blinking dangerously, all the way down into the red. It must have scarcely had time to recharge before Louve stole it from my wardrobe, presumably recognising her master's smell.

Bzzz! – first warning; if I counted correctly last time, the eighth buzz will be the one that turns it off.

I slide my bloody finger across the telephone, to move to the next image.

It's a screenshot.

Or to be more precise, it's a photograph taken from a computer screen, of what looks like a slideshow. The title appears in capital letters:

NOAH REPORT

Beneath this, two words in red:

STRICTLY CONFIDENTIAL

Bzzz!

Breathless, I move on to the next photo, and zoom in to read what is written there:

Report summary: The sensors indicate that the six pairs of rats, lizards and cockroaches that were sent secretly to the seventh habitat of the Martian base survived for eight months, and reproduced at a pace comparable to terrestrial conditions. But at the end of the ninth month, every one of the organisms died suddenly, for reasons unknown.

Bzzz!

Conclusion: As things stand, and until there is greater understanding of what caused the inexplicable loss of the trial animals, the habitats are considered not capable of sustaining life in the long term.

Bzzz!

My heart freezes in my chest.

My finger is suspended above the screen, unable to move on to the next slide. In any case, everything has already been said, it's all been written there in black and white: 'died suddenly'; 'not capable of sustaining life in the long term'.

Bzzz!

For the thousandth time, I see Ruben Rodriguez rushing towards me. *'You mustn't . . . !'*

For the first time, I finally understand fully what his warning meant, and it is more horrific than anything I could have imagined.

Ruben Rodriguez was aware of this report. His name appears at the bottom of the page, alongside those of the technical director and the Biology instructor.

Report authors: G. Lock; A. Dragovic; R. Rodriguez

Bzzz!

'Well, Léonor, what are you waiting for?' I hear Serena's voice from the gym beneath me. 'Are you still stuck in the access tube or have you finally made it into the Visiting Room? Here in the editing suite we're watching the pictures of what's happening with a three-minute delay, it's maddening. We do also have a schedule to respect, and the speed-dating is supposed to be over by now. If you don't show yourself in the Visiting Room straight away, I will regretfully have to cancel your final session.'

Bzzz!

I swallow down the nausea that rises in my throat when I hear the sound of Serena's voice, and I croak: 'I'm coming!'

I hide the telephone in my hand, clutching it tight like a talisman to give me strength.

Each movement requires a superhuman effort.

But I keep going, just the same.

I push open the hatch.

And I enter the glass bubble of the Visiting Room, where the planet Mars is now so large that it's blocking a quarter of the view of space: a gigantic sphere of red earth, with the dreadful gash of the Valles Marineris canyon across it, at the bottom of which our tombs are waiting for us.

Nestled in the palm of my hand, the phone gives up the ghost for a second time – *bzzz! bzzz! bzzz!*

66. Genesis Channel

Saturday 9 December, 11:16am

Léonor appears on the screen, dishevelled, a wide trail of dried blood running from her eyebrow down to her mouth. She shuts the hatch behind her, then fiercely covers her chest with her arm: her dress is torn from her neck down to her hip, revealing the whole of her left shoulder. As she rises in silence, during the long minutes it takes for her image to reach earth, the muslin skirt roils furiously: the gentle waves have become unbridled rollers.

While she waits for Serena to respond to her appearance, a title comes on the screen: *138th session in the Visiting Room. Hostess: Léonor, 18, France, Medical Officer (communication latency: 6 minutes, 04 seconds)*

Serena (off): '*Oh, my poor beautiful Léonor! What's happened to you? What is it? That brawl . . . Tell me, are you hurt?*'

Léonor peers through her wild curls into the camera; her eyes are shining with defiance, with questions. 'It's nothing, don't worry about it. A little scratch, nothing at all. We had an argument . . . about the boys.'

Six minutes, as heavy as droplets of lead, fall through the

hourglass of time, while Léonor's lie forces its way through space and the answer from Earth returns.

'*About the boys, of course!*' cries Serena at last, her voice quite tender now. '*It's quite normal to let yourselves get a bit carried away at the end of a journey like this, a competition like this. It's perfectly understandable! But once you're all married off, you six girls will once again be the best friends in the world, I can assure you! For now, don't worry, Léonor, you look stunning just the same. That streak of blood, which matches your hair and dress so perfectly . . . you're like a Valkyrie out of a Wagner opera. Tell us, because we're short of time: can we call in Marcus, who's waiting in the access tube?*'

The girl's lips only barely open. 'No. Not Marcus. It's Mozart I want to invite today.'

After the six minutes of communication latency, Serena's voice rises to a frantic pitch.

'*Oh, we have a completely unexpected turnaround! My dear viewers, you can forget about Wagner, what we've got instead is Mozart, for a finale worthy of a great opera!*'

Léonor doesn't move during the pre-recorded drum-roll, her right arm bent across her chest, her left held flat against the foaming folds of her dress, until her guest appears on the far side of the screen.

He's wearing a simple sleeveless T-shirt and a pair of sports shorts that show off his athletic legs.

The camera zooms in on his face, which is trembling with emotion.

'Léonor . . . I didn't dress up. I didn't think you were going to invite me for your final session. I – I was sure you were going to call Marcus.'

He's stammering.

And then suddenly he notices the state Léonor's in.

His long-lashed eyes open wide. 'But . . . who did this to you?'

Léonor: 'I did it all by myself.'

Without moving her hands, she kicks her bare legs against the red chiffon to propel herself towards the glass barrier. 'Come here.'

In answer to her request, Mozart immediately propels himself towards her; supple and strong, he joins her at the glass.

'Forgive me, Léonor,' he murmurs. 'Forgive me for not believing you. I . . . I misunderstood what was happening. I was sure you'd chosen Marcus. I was wrong, wasn't I?'

Léonor's expression is resolute as a statue's; her voice is unwavering.

'Mozart, you're the boys' Navigation Officer. You have to tell me: is there any way for us to get back to Earth?'

The Brazilian's face freezes in a mask of incomprehension: 'What?'

67. Reverse Shot

Fallout Bunker, Cape Canaveral Air Base
Saturday 9 December, 11:35am

Gordon Lock jumps up from his chair, his whole six-foot-five frame trembling.

'What the hell is she saying?' he thunders. 'Get back to Earth? It's total madness! Serena: cut the images, make her shut up!'

'Make her shut up?' gasps the executive producer, sitting up in her leather armchair, her eyes shining with excitement. 'Never! On the contrary, we need her to speak! Don't you see, Gordon? This is the final aria of the opera, the loveliest scene in the last act, the most heart-breaking part of all. It's Léonor cracking up, refusing to face up to what she is, regretting everything: her candidacy for the programme, her dreams of glory, her hope of finding love. Good God, just look at the ratings – we've never had an audience like it!

But in the central window in the digital wall, does Léonor really look like she's cracking up? Is it not Serena McBee who, for the first time in her life, has lost her grip on reality?

Léonor says again: 'Is there any way for us to get back to Earth, Mozart? Answer me. Quickly.'

Mozart hesitates, before answering reluctantly: 'Yes, in theory we could. When the ship is aligned with the orbit of Phobos, we're supposed to get back into our capsules for the final push towards Mars. Meanwhile the Cupido will be returning to Earth, travelling back in the opposite direction on automatic pilot: it will fire up the gas towards Earth as soon as it has dropped us off, to welcome new astronauts on board in two years' time. There's nothing stopping us staying on board. But it would be suicide. We don't have enough food left, or water, or oxygen, even with the recycling: there was only just enough to get here. If we just turn right around, we'll die of hunger, thirst and asphyxiation within weeks. It'd just be our dead bodies that would make it back to Earth. Not to mention the scandal of all those billions of dollars frittered away just to let us have a merry-go-round ride in space. It'd be ludicrous!'

For the first time since the start of the interview, Léonor lifts her left hand, which has been down beside her body, and holds it up to the glass. 'There is a real scandal, but it's not what you think,' she says. 'In a few moments, you'll be able to understand for yourself.'

'Is she asking him to read her palm now?' asks Odette Stuart-Smith, blinking her little mole eyes behind her thick glasses. 'We're watching divination now? That's hardly what the Genesis programme needs! Redheads are always part-witch; our ancestors knew it and that's why they sent those people to the stake.'

'No, no,' replies Geronimo Blackbull. 'Her hand isn't empty.

She's holding something.' He turns to the executive producer, who's supposed to possess the answer to every question. 'Do you know what it is, Serena?'

In her padded armchair, Serena McBee is no longer smiling.

Frantically she presses the bee-shaped brooch-mic and giver her orders: '*Serena to the editing suite*. Stop transmitting the pictures from the Visiting Room at once. I repeat: stop transmitting the Visiting Room pictures *at once*, and cut to B2R.'

At these words, the glass bubble disappears from the central window in the digital wall, to be replaced with a view of the boys' living room. The boys are waiting for the interview to end, not suspecting what's going on above their heads. Alexei, Tao and Samson are absorbed in a game of cards; Kenji is playing a video game on his tablet, while Warden snores at his feet; Marcus is pacing up and down, frowning, visibly eaten away by his distress at not having been invited.

A new window opens on the digital wall beneath the Genesis channel feed, showing Samantha, Serena's personal assistant.

'We've carried out your orders, Ms McBee,' she says. 'But I wanted to point out that the speed-dating stopwatch hasn't yet completed its six minutes.'

'I'm perfectly well aware of that, I'm not blind!' Serena retorts.

Then she adds, her voice softening, trying not to let her nerves show: 'You've been doing so much work these past months, you and the rest of the editing team. I'm giving you a little well-deserved break. Not least because I'd also like to treat myself to a go at editing, for the final speed-dating session. I'm going to complete the production of this morning's broadcast myself.'

Samantha opens her mouth to answer, but Serena doesn't give her a chance. She presses the red button in the middle of the control panel set into the table in front of her.

The assistant's window immediately vanishes and a message in glowing red letters appears at the top of the digital wall:

CRISIS PROTOCOL ACTIVATED

'What are you doing, Serena?' asks Gordon Lock, his forehead covered in sweat.

'I'm doing what has to be done. I'm redirecting all the data streaming from the *Cupido* to this bunker.'

'But why?'

'Because of that!'

Serena springs out of her chair and rushes to the digital wall.

She puts her finger on one of the upper windows, the G5Z, which corresponds to the ceiling camera of the Visiting Room, on the girls' side, and then taps furiously on the picture until the zoom is close enough to see what Léonor is holding in her hand. It's a cellphone.

On the phone screen, it is possible to see three lines:
  Light source detected: 10,000 lumens
  Estimated time for complete charge: 1 hour
  Turning on in: 10 minutes
  Mozart looks totally disconcerted. 'That's what you want to show me? A phone? I don't see where the scandal is in that, except that we aren't normally allowed to have them.'

463

The young man's voice is uncertain.

He understands that he hasn't been called into the Visiting Room for the reason he'd hoped.

He's been wounded before.

Now he's suspicious.

But Léonor continues to hold up the phone, with the screen pointing towards the dazzling spotlights that pierce the Visiting Room, and beyond them, towards the twinkling stars. 'It's what's inside this phone that I want to show you. It's what the organisers of Genesis want to hide from us. It's what a guy called Ruben Rodriguez wanted to reveal to me. It's the Noah Report, which says that we will all be dead in nine months.'

'No!' cries Geronimo Blackbull.

'It's impossible!' bellows Archibald Dragovic.

'I destroyed the Noah Report files myself,' objects Gordon Lock, 'after we decided that Atlas was never to see it.'

'We must assume that little traitor Ruben photographed it before it was destroyed, to keep as a souvenir,' says Serena McBee icily. 'You were at his cremation, Geronimo. Were there any copies of these photos at his place?'

The old rocker stammers a few words, his long hair trembling pitifully on either side of his appalled face.

'I don't know . . . I don't think so . . . I ran some formatting on Ruben's hard drive to wipe everything, without checking what it had on it . . . I didn't have time . . .'

A panic-stricken Roberto Salvatore drags his huge body out of his chair and hurries over to the retinal identification box that controls the bunker door.

Serena stamps her foot.

'Calm down!' she orders. 'There's no point running away!'

Roberto is too wild with terror to hear her. The door slides open. He takes off at a desperate run, down the neon-lit corridor, towards the elevator that goes up to the surface.

Odette Stuart-Smith is already on her feet, ready to follow suit; but with a single word Serena stops her dead.

'Stay!'

The psychiatrist's chest rises and falls regularly, as she practises her own breathing relaxation technique.

'Everything is under control,' she says, her voice perfectly smooth, perfectly authoritative, which instantly restores total silence to the bunker and returns little Odette, trembling, to her chair.

Serena points at the central window, the one that corresponds to the Genesis channel broadcast.

'At this moment, our viewers are only able to see the boys' living room. Just like the staff in the control room and the editing suite, upstairs, over our heads. Nobody on Earth but us has heard Léonor mention the Noah Report. Nobody else can see what's going on in the Visiting Room. And that's how it will stay until we have solved this little problem.'

With a firm gesture she shrinks the central window, which continues to broadcast the Genesis channel to the whole world, to expand that of the Visiting Room, which only those in the bunker can see.

Then she brings her microphone to her lips.

'Léonor? This is Serena. Can you hear me?'

68. Shot

'Why have you made me come today?' Mozart asks, his eyes trained on me like bullets.

'I've already told you! The telephone! The Noah Report!'

But that isn't the answer Mozart wants to hear.

'I thought it was to tell me I still stood a chance with you,' he mutters bitterly. 'Now I understand you just wanted to play your little seduction games on me one more time.'

'No, Mozart! This isn't a game!'

I don't get the chance to say any more: a voice sounds above our heads, like a thunderclap.

'*Léonor? This is Serena. Can you hear me?*'

I look up, glancing at the glass bubble all around me. Serena's voice, sent three minutes earlier from Earth, seems to be coming from every direction at once.

'*I don't know where you found that telephone – an object, let me remind you, that is strictly forbidden under Genesis programme regulations.*'

She seems to be speaking to us from the blackness of space,

from the stars that are sending their precious lumens towards the photovoltaic phone screen, from the planet Mars with its canyon that grimaces at us like a bloody mouth.

'I don't know what you think you've seen there, but I can assure you it's just a misunderstanding. Do you hear me, Léonor? You're imagining things for no reason.'

'I hear you perfectly, Serena. Better than ever before. Unclouded by my naïveté, you come through much more clearly. As for the phone, never mind where I got it. It's no longer up to you to ask the questions. Just wait a few minutes till it turns on and then you'll see if it's really nothing.'

But Serena has no intention of waiting, not this time.

While my words travel towards her at the speed of light, which takes three full minutes to get from the surroundings of Mars to Earth, she keeps talking without a break.

'It would be better for you to worry for a proper reason,' she says, her voice suddenly filled with reproach. *'These are serious times. Our poor Safia hasn't got up since she fell. Imagine if she's dead, because of you!'*

The guilt is crucifying me, as I think of Safia's body lying immobile on the bedroom floor, her scarf tight around her neck. Dead? Is that possible, or is Serena just saying it to make me crack? If Safia really was dead or seriously wounded, Serena would surely have had to tell me the moment I'd arrived in the Visiting Room and not leave it until now . . . She's got to be bluffing, right?

On the other side of the reinforced glass, I can sense Mozart's questioning look as he searches my face for a confession. My whole being wants to race back down to the bedroom to administer first aid to Safia.

But if I do that, I lose control of the game. There are four floors from the Visiting Room to the bedroom, where anything could happen. Where Serena could have devised who knows what kind of stratagem for shutting me up. Whereas here, floating opposite Mozart, I can speak. I must. It might be my only chance to try to save all twelve passengers, rather than just one.

'What happened to her is *your* fault,' I shout, 'not mine!'

My denials disappear into space, and won't be heard for another three minutes. But in the meantime, Serena continues her diatribe.

'*The viewers are judging you right now, Léonor. Is this really the spectacle you want them to see, a maniac demanding to turn the ship around? A crazy girl experiencing a full-blown paranoid delirium, exposing herself to the entire world? So go back down into the girls' quarters without making a scene. Your six minutes are over. The interview is finished. I'm cutting your sound.*'

Serena's voice stinks to high heaven.

She's playing for time, I can tell.

'Don't try and make me believe our conversation is currently being broadcast on the Genesis channel. Don't claim you know nothing about the Noah Report and the guy this phone belongs to, Ruben Rodriguez. I'm sure you do know them. Enough lies! I don't believe you! I don't believe you any more!'

On the other side of the glass partition, Mozart seems unreachable, as though there were a distance even greater separating us than that between Mars and Earth. Serena's venomous words have poisoned his mind, and now there's nothing between us but silence.

I beat my fist against the glass, yelling. 'Stay! The phone will turn on in five minutes!'

His whole body is shuddering with doubt and rage.

His lips move, but I can't hear what he's saying, as communication between the two halves of the Visiting Room has been cut off.

At that moment, the woman who just a week ago I thought was like a mother to me drives another blade into my heart.

She does it with such gentle fake-sympathy, like a velvet glove holding a dagger.

'Don't be too angry with her, Mozart. Her "little games", as you call them, are only a pitiful strategy for protecting herself. You see, Léonor has a painful problem. I thought, in choosing her, I could give her a second chance, as we did you, as we did all the passengers. I wasn't able to detect just how psychologically fragile she was. Mea culpa. I think it's time now to reveal Léonor's secret. The reason she's refusing to go down to Mars, why she wants to stay on the ship to return to where you started. She'd rather travel to certain death than face up to what she really is. She should turn around and show you her back, the side she's kept hidden, rather than trying to distract you with that telephone, which is of course a mere diversion. Come on now, Léonor: turn around.'

Serena's dreadful voice keeps echoing in the bubble. *'Turn around now, my dear. Turn around.'*

It echoes even louder in my head, and mingles with the voice of the Salamander:

(Turn around!)

(Turn around!)

(Turn around!)

But it's Mozart who turns his back on me first.

'Wait!' I yell at the top of my lungs. 'Just one minute till the phone comes on! Just one minute and you'll understand!'

He can't hear me.

Powerless to stop him, I watch as he glides silently towards the back of the bubble, where the vast reddish globe is floating in space. He opens the hatch and enters the access tube, never looking behind him. He's chosen not to turn around: to head on towards his destination.

That's when it appears, for the first time: Mars's moon.

It rises from behind the red planet, on the orbital path that we're approaching ourselves, getting nearer every second. It's a black, gleaming rock, irregular and battered all over, pitted by the impact of meteorites. The shallow rays of sunlight hollow out the shadows of its two main craters, and I can't help being reminded of the eye sockets of a decapitated head.

Phobos.

Fear.

It's the most hideous thing I've ever seen in my entire life – more dreadful even than the Salamander itself.

69. Reverse Shot

Serena rushes to the other end of the digital wall and presses on the window that corresponds to the boys' gym. Since leaving the Visiting Room, Mozart has been taking his anger out on a punch-bag, channelling all his rage into his fists.

He looks like a little wax model in a dolls' house, which a capricious child can manipulate however she pleases. A child with an ageless face, with a silvery bob and big water-green eyes, who whispers into her mic.

'Mozart: this is Serena. Listen carefully, as we don't have much time. I know that Léonor's decline is very painful for you, in spite of everything she's made you suffer, because you're a fundamentally good person. But she's not well, you're a witness to that. She's attacked her companions, first Kirsten at the start of the journey and now Safia. She's tried to manipulate you so that you refuse to pilot the boys' capsule down to Mars. Who knows what she's going to try next? To do away with herself? I'll do everything I can to calm her down and reason with her, using all the professional skills I have at my disposal. But I must

471

not be disturbed during this session. You do understand, don't you? There's no point answering. By the time you receive this message in three minutes' time, I will already have resumed communications with the Visiting Room. I'm counting on your discretion. Don't tell anybody just how much Léonor has cracked up. If you really do care for her, you'll allow her to explain herself once she's snapped out of it, rather than showing herself up even more than she's already done in front of the other boys and the whole world. Allow me just fifteen minutes with her, one on one, that's all I ask.'

With a wave of her arm, Serena brushes aside the video feed of the gym where Mozart is, then with her hand she pulls the video feed of the boys' living room out of the central window.

The Genesis channel frame in the middle of the digital wall is left empty, showing nothing at all.

70. Out of Frame

A screen, someplace on Earth
Saturday 9 December, 11:47am

'*What a bolt from the blue! Right now, for the first time since the Genesis programme began, we find ourselves with no news from the Cupido! The screen's gone blank! Blackout! What's going on? Why was the speed-dating session between Léonor and Mozart ended so abruptly? Is this connected to the attack of madness that seemed to grip the French girl just before she went up into the Visiting Room?*'

The TV news anchor who's firing out all these questions is being eaten away by anxiety. The last images broadcast on the Genesis channel before the blackout are scrolling across the screen behind him: Léonor grabbing hold of Safia's scarf; Léonor fighting with Kelly; Léonor making a bloody entrance into the Visiting Room; the violent cut in the broadcast to the boys' living room, abandoning the speed-dating session before it was over.

Zap!

Another channel.

Live images from each country appear one after another on the screen. Title: New York, USA

The famous Times Square is filled with a huge crowd, who've gathered to watch the final interview between Léonor and Marcus, or so they thought. There are still American and French pennants in every hand, but nobody has the heart to wave them now. And nobody has the heart to hold up the photo-collages showing the French-American couple in each other's arms either. No, instead many of the fans have taken their marker pens out of their pockets to angrily scrawl out Léonor's face.

Title: Rio de Janeiro, Brazil

Hundreds and hundreds of people have moved into the esplanade around the Christ the Redeemer statue, which dominates the city from the top of the Corcovado hill. A huge temporary structure has been set up behind him: the shape of the Cupido, whose two wings exactly match the iconic statue's outstretched arms. Most of the pilgrims are kneeling in prayer. The samba band who've been playing 'The Girl from Ipanema' stop and put down their instruments.

Title: Mumbai, India

It's night-time, but there's even more activity than during the day. The streets, thronged with pedestrians, rickshaws and sacred cows, lead to a huge square plastered with pictures of Safia. There is dismay on every face. Women raise their arms to the dark skies weeping, twisted by grief as though they have lost their own daughter. Some of the men react differently: they are slashing French flags, crying out for revenge.

Zap!

Another channel.

A panel of experts, all of them wearing worried frowns, have been assembled for an emergency session around a journalist who is frantically consulting her notes.

'. . . it might be a magnetic storm that's caused some interference,' suggests one of the experts tentatively. 'Solar flares can sometimes cause telecommunications problems of this kind . . .'

The journalist interrupts him.

'Professor, what do you make of those views that have been expressed on social media suggesting that Serena McBee might have cut off the transmission herself, in order to spare viewers a scene of carnage unleashed by the fury of the French candidate?'

'It's possible . . .'

'And those who claim that Léonor has blown up the Cupido?'

'I think we can rule out that hypothesis, since according to the technical information we've received from Genesis at this point, the ship is about to go into orbit around Mars, in the wake of the moon Phobos.'

Zap!

Another channel.

A reporter who looks utterly out of her depth is standing in the Place de l'Étoile, which has been so overwhelmed by crowds that it's no longer possible even to move. Behind her stands the Arc de Triomphe, over which still floats the enormous banner showing Léonor in an astronaut suit, her face lit up by a radiant smile, eyes turned towards space.

'Here in Paris, there's a feeling of utter shock!' shouts the reporter into her microphone, trying to be heard above the din. 'The French people can't understand why their candidate has behaved the way she has.'

She turns to a young woman standing beside her.

'Can you tell us, mademoiselle, why you've come down into the streets today?'

'To show our support for Léonor! She's under so much pressure, poor thing. It's the last speed-dating session and they're just about to arrive on Mars. That's a lot for one day! It isn't hard to understand why she's going off the rails! Everyone with Léo! No one will be able to say we abandoned our national leopard!'

An older woman, very prim and proper, doesn't hesitate to butt in.

'That girl Léonor brings shame on our country. A terrorist!'

'You're right!' A man squeezed into a raincoat joins in the conversation, a furious look on his face. 'What will our neighbours think of us? That's not what France is like.'

'Shut it, granddad!' shout a gang of young people, all of whom have their hair dyed red, the boys as well as the girls. 'Long live Léo! Long live the red giant!'

A rumbling rises up from the crowd, who seem about ready to come to blows.

'Oh! Look!'

The camera cuts abruptly away from the reporter to focus on the Arc de Triomphe, where instead of the usual flame commemorating the unknown soldier, another flame is burning, much brighter.

Some men have splashed the enormous banner of Léonor with petrol, before setting light to it. Watched by the dumbstruck crowds, the flames climb up the banner, their fiery tongues tangling with the red giant's long flame-coloured locks.

Harmony stops zapping between channels to remain on this one.

The flames that light up the large flat-screen embedded in

476

her bedroom wall are reflected in the sheets of the bed where she's sitting, on her porcelain face, in her eyes with the fine, white, almost transparent lashes.

Suddenly there is a noise at the window – *tink!*

Harmony looks away from the screen and walks over to open it.

But it's not the beak of a carrier pigeon.

It's hailstones falling from the sky and drumming on the bars – *tink! tink! tink!*

Disappointed and shivering, Harmony is about to close the window and return to her bed, when she notices a dark shape in the middle of the snow-covered gardens.

The intruder looks up at just the same moment, revealing a hooded face behind a pair of black-framed glasses. He's a young man about Harmony's age, with pale skin that resembles her own.

He freezes.

He has no right to be there.

Harmony should report him.

But she doesn't sound the alert.

Slowly, as though trying not to scare off a doe surprised in the depths of a snowy field, the young man raises his index finger and brings it to his cold blue lips.

'Silence?'

Behind the bars of her window, Harmony makes the same gesture, bringing her index finger to her diaphanous lips.

'Very well: silence.'

71. Shot

D +159 days 22 h 15 mins.
[23rd week]

'Léonor – wait!'

In any other circumstances, the very fact that Serena still dares to give me orders would make me burst out laughing.

I propel myself furiously towards the hatch that opens to the access tube, trailing a length of red fabric behind me.

'Don't do something that can't be undone!'

But Serena already has. The moment she selected us for the programme that's so appealing on the outside but deadly on the inside. The round red Genesis logo is Snow White's apple, and Serena is the witch holding it out to tempt us.

'Stay in the Visiting Room!'

I grab the lever of the hatch. I can feel vibrations passing into my fist, making the chiffon that floats around me tremble: beyond the steel panel that muffles any sound there are fists hammering down like a heavy shower. The fists of the other girls who are trying to gain access to the Visiting Room. The only things that matter now, now that Mozart has turned his back on me, is to warn them and to take care of Safia as best I can.

And after that? After that, I don't want to think about it.

'I can save your life!'

At the last moment I freeze, hand on the lever, gobsmacked by Serena's sheer nerve.

Her words, spoken three minutes earlier, are still reaching me in waves that begin in Cape Canaveral before travelling across fifty-five million kilometres of emptiness.

'Safia's regained consciousness. She's told your companions to go up and fetch you, to protect you from yourself and stop you doing anything stupid. They're behind the Visiting Room hatch, crazy with worry about you. But they can wait, it's not going to kill them. The deal I've got to offer you, however, cannot wait.'

A deal?

From Serena, who is nothing but lies and deceit?

'How can you imagine I could possibly believe a single word coming out of your venomous mouth, Serena?' I whisper hoarsely. 'You've betrayed us all, and why? Probably to make yourself richer – you, who have everything already!'

I have nothing else to say to that woman, and I don't want to hear any more from her.

So why do I stay where I am?

Why do I wait for six minutes, while my voice travels down to her ears and her reply returns to mine?

Because deep down, I know there's a new order now, and Serena knows it too.

'The terms of our relationship are no longer the same,' she says. *'Yes, I sent you to your deaths, and I did it for the money; but now I'm gambling with you for my life. The cards have been*

479

re-dealt. Like in a game of tarot, when you have a hand full of trump cards, it changes everything.

'Trump card number one: you have the irrefutable proof of the Noah Report in that phone;

'trump card number two: I'd find it hard to claim that I didn't know about the existence of that report, seeing as the phone belonged to Ruben Rodriguez, who worked directly under me, just like your six instructors – I don't need to tell you they're all just as implicated as Gordon Lock and myself;

'trump card number three: as you've observed quite correctly, we're off-line at the moment, but I can't keep you off the radar for ever; a ship like the Cupido can't simply disappear from everyone's screens just like that.

'But I don't need to explain any of this to you, do I? You're very well aware that you've gained the upper hand. You and I are so alike, deep down. I've been betrayed by weaklings like Sherman, Roberto or Ruben, who refused to trust me – taking photos of pages from the Noah Report! So very foolish. And you've been rejected by your shipmates who didn't understand you were just trying to open their eyes. You're a solitary wildcat who struggles to find partners of your calibre. A superior being, born to be in command. To the point of creating your own rules of the game.'

'I'm nothing like you!' I spit, exasperated by this last provocation. 'But you're right in one respect at least: I am holding all the cards, and I will beat you with them once and for all. I'm going to warn all the passengers on the Cupido. The viewers you've kept in suspense for months will demand to see us, to hear us. And then they'll learn the truth direct from our mouths. You will never be vice-president.'

But Serena keeps talking, unaware of my threat, which won't reach her for another three minutes.

'*You're a clever girl, Léonor. Too clever for this mission, certainly. It was the biggest professional mistake of my career, choosing you. Look, I'm not going to try lying to you, claiming that the report in the telephone isn't true, I know it's a lost cause, and we haven't much time. I'm even going to admit to you that I have a mechanism that allows me to depressurise the Love Nests remotely rather than wait for them to reveal their failings over time. I just need to press a button. Aha! Truth or bluff? Well, it seems I might still have one or two trump cards up my sleeve myself.*'

The blood boils in my veins.

I crush the trapdoor lever in my hand, as though it were Serena's neck.

But there's no Serena here to strangle, not even a face on a screen to smash.

There's just the voice, impossible to grasp, among the stars.

'*Allow me to tot up the current scores, at the halfway point in our game,*' she says. '*If you decide to denounce me on air and remain on board the* Cupido *only to turn right around again and head back to Earth, you will die along the way. If you agree to keep your mouth shut and travel down to Mars, you will have nine months to identify the reason for the dysfunction of the habitats, and to try and fix them; perhaps all that's needed is a simple bit of repair, who knows? It would be up to you to discover that. This, naturally, would have to be with absolute discretion and never allowing the public to find out about the existence of the guinea pigs that went before you to Mars. In short, the Noah Report gives you a chance to put up a fight for your survival.*'

Serena's self-assurance takes my breath away.

Acting as though the Noah Report is a stroke of luck for us! I want to scream, but I know I mustn't let my emotions show.

Because it really is a game that we're engaged in now, Serena and me, just as she said with that horrifying cynicism of hers: a poker game. I need to raise myself up to her level, an international media expert with years of experience, though I'm just an eighteen-year-old orphan. I need to imitate her icy calm, to keep my cool, even if all I want to do right now is spew my rage and contempt into her face like a torrent of lava.

'If we go down to Mars and don't say anything, what's to stop you depressurising the habitats anyway?' I ask.

Six minutes pass, as I wait opposite the most impenetrable poker player in the universe, whose face is nothing more than a black emptiness filled with stars, expressionless.

'*It wouldn't be in my interest,*' Serena replies at last. '*In that case, you'd still be able to survive a few hours in your suits, long enough to reveal what you know to the world.*'

'And if we don't manage to repair the habitats?'

Six minutes, again.

Above the hatch, behind the glass bubble, the vastness of the universe is sucking me in like a bottomless gullet.

'*At least you'd have nine months to try,* knowing *there's a problem, which is immeasurably better than knowing nothing and dying like ignorant animals, unable to do a thing.*'

I'm beginning to understand the hateful choice Serena is trying to force me to make, more dizzying even than the interplanetary void.

'So you're basically asking me to choose between the

certainty of bringing you down if I talk, and the uncertain possibility of pulling through if I keep quiet,' I say. 'You're asking me to choose between justice and hope. It's an impossible choice.'

The silence of the communication latency has never seemed so deafening.

The cosmic darkness has never seemed so blinding.

The infinity of space is just a delusion, I see now, an optical illusion that conceals an impasse. What an irony: I'm floating amid billions of kilometres of sky, higher and further than any human being has ever travelled before me, and yet I can't see any way out, suffocating as though I was buried alive in the narrowest of coffins.

'*It's the only choice you have,*' says Serena, once the six minutes are up. '*And you alone can make it.*'

The way she says the word *alone* makes me realise suddenly that I'm not. I sense a presence behind me, at the back of the silent Visiting Room.

I let go of the hatch and turn around, my long hair floating in front of me like sheets of Martian cloud. Above the glass vault, the black skull of Phobos, god of fear, continues its orbit around its father Mars, the god of war. From behind the reinforced glass, Marcus is watching me.

His hands are purple with bruises from having pummelled the perfectly impenetrable glass.

While I've been absorbed in my life-and-death negotiations with Serena, he's had plenty of time to look at my bare back, that Salamander I've struggled so hard to hide since the start of our journey . . . since the start of my life.

'Marcus . . .' I say, knowing that as I speak his name, no one can hear me – not the boy a few metres away from me in the soundproofed hemisphere, not Serena, who will only pick up my voice at a delay.

Marcus's serious eyes watch me in silence. They aren't filled with horror, or disgust, or any of the terrible things my nightmares had projected into him.

His lips speak soundless words, perhaps for the thousandth time.

'I can't understand, Marcus . . .'

He pulls aside the collar of his shirt to reveal his inked chest – his torso that can be read like a book, that invites you to lose yourself in it as in a forest. He opens his hand: it's holding a penknife, sparkling beneath the stars. With the tip of the blade, he begins to trace fine letters on the only place that still lies fallow, where the brambles of words have not yet grown, which the tattooist's needle has never touched: his heart.

L . . .

É . . .

The start of an O . . .

'Stop!'

I rush to the glass, feeling my eyes fill with tears.

I put my fingers to the unbreakable partition, level with Marcus's heart, as if to wipe away the blood that's beading on the first letters of my name, like drops of dew.

His hand freezes.

He smiles at me.

The Salamander at my back is no longer hissing.

It no longer itches.

It no longer exists.

Marcus lets go of his penknife. Behind him, five shadows, as silent as ghosts, are outlined at the back of the soundless bubble. Worried at his failure to come back down, the other boys have come up in turn to the Visiting Room. Mozart . . . Alexei . . . Tao . . . Samson . . . Kenji – all the boys I've lived alongside all these weeks, without ever having seen them for more than a few minutes. But those brief moments were enough for me to know that none of them deserves to die, that they are all worthy of a life filled with happiness and love, for many long years.

'*Marcus has been there practically since the start of our conversation, which he hasn't been able to hear at all,*' says Serena suddenly – it's taken her three minutes to realise that I've turned around, and another three to let me know it. '*Despite my instructions not to come to the Visiting Room, he has, because Mozart wouldn't answer his questions about the last speed-dating. He can't understand what's happened. None of them can – not the boys, who I'm sure by now must have joined Marcus in the Visiting Room, nor the girls who are waiting for you in the access tube. You alone have the keys. My advice is to give them to the others once you've landed on Mars, not before. If you talk to them about the Noah Report now, you run the risk of their having an unfortunate reaction, wanting to turn right around with the* Cupido, *just as your own first reflex was to do – it's reflex governed by panic, not a maturely thought-through decision. But once you're on Mars, they'll be forced to play the game you've chosen for them. The decision is yours, and yours alone. Come now, admit it, isn't it an exhilarating sense of power, having twelve lives in the palm of your hand? You have a leader's soul, Léonor, and leaders have to*' *choose for others. Now: an answer. Our suspension of the Genesis channel has already gone on for far too long. We'll tell the viewers that there was a technical problem, but now the show must go on. Give me an answer. Tell me we can resume the live feed, that you will leave the Cupido to return to Earth without you, you'll go down to Mars in your capsules, and for nine months try everything you can to survive.'*

'No.'

This time I don't close my eyes during the communication latency. I keep them wide open, deep in Marcus's.

'What do you mean, no?'

There's irritation in Serena's voice.

Anger too.

But most of all, surprise.

'I've already said it's no longer up to you to ask the questions, have you forgotten so soon? I don't accept the terms of your so-called agreement.'

I turn to look into the starry vault, towards that woman who thinks she's a god, free to discard us at a whim, like simple playing cards.

'Don't expect me to keep the truth from my brothers and sisters, and present them with it on Mars when it's too late to change. This power doesn't exhilarate me: it sickens me. You've said I was the biggest mistake of your professional life. You're the biggest mistake in my personal life, the way I considered you and the other instructors like my substitute family. Today I know for certain that my real family are the people making this journey with me. I'm going to reveal everything to them, right away, as I've meant to since the very beginning. And it's

486

us, all of us together, who will give you our answer. Turn right around, and immediately hand you in: justice. Or travel down to Mars and try to survive: hope.'

I fly towards the access tube and turn the lever all the way.

'You were wrong, Serena, I'm not like you. Because you really are alone.'

The hatch opens, and the girls fly up into the bubble like birds into the open sky.

'. . . but not me: I am one of twelve!'

72. Genesis Channel

Saturday 9 December, 12:13pm

WE APOLOGISE FOR THE INTERRUPTION TO THIS SERVICE.
WE ARE WORKING TO RE-ESTABLISH CONNECTION WITH THE
CUPIDO AS QUICKLY AS POSSIBLE.
THANK YOU FOR YOUR PATIENCE, AND FOR YOUR LOYALTY TO YOUR
FAVORITE CHANNEL: THE GENESIS CHANNEL!

To be continued . . .

Acknowledgements

I would like to thank all those who, by my side aboard the spaceship or in the control room, made the *Phobos* take-off happen.

At the French launch base: my editors Glenn, Fabien and Constance, who confidently signed up to take the one-way trip to Mars with me.

At the British launch base: my translator Daniel, who did a fantastic job rendering my world and words so smoothly that you don't even feel the communication latency; my editors Jane, Georgia and Talya, the Engineering Officers, who expertly designed the book you currently hold in your hands; Tina, the Communications Officer, who continuously ensures the contact between the spaceship and planet earth.

Last but not least, a big thank you to my family for always encouraging me, and to our two on-board cats, Billie and Rasco, who gaze at the stars from the glass bubble where I write every night.

The first phase of the mission could never have been achieved without the support of this wonderful crew!

Explore the world of Phobos on Victor Dixen's site:
www.victordixen.com